W9-AON-167

THE STORIES

Jane Gardam

THE STORIES

Europa
editions

Europa Editions
214 West 29th Street
New York, N.Y. 10001
www.europaeditions.com
info@europaeditions.com

Library of Congress Cataloging in Publication Data is available
ISBN 978-1-60945-199-8

Gardam, Jane
The Stories

Book design by Emanuele Ragnisco
www.mekkanografici.com

Prepress by Grafica Punto Print – Rome

Printed in the USA

For Richard Beswick

C O N T E N T S

THE STORIES

INTRODUCTION

I have always preferred writing short stories to writing novels. Not that there is much similarity and not that a writer can usually get away with writing only one or the other (Katherine Mansfield almost did). Stories of all lengths and depths come from mysterious parts of the cave. The difference in writing them is that, for a novel, you must lay in mental, physical and spiritual provision as for a siege or for a time of hectic explosions, while a short story is, or can be, a steady, timed flame like the lighting of a blow lamp on a building site full of dry tinder. For me it was James Joyce's *Dubliners*, written in 1921, seven years before I was born, that showed me how (or at any rate that) short stories can have the power to burn up the chaff, harden the steel without comment or embellishment or explanation. I like Irish, French, Russian and American short stories best. They are the strongest.

Human beings, it seems to me, are dependent on story—stories—painted on cave walls, sung on jangling instruments, chanted or spoken in lullaby from their beginnings. Children deprived of stories grow up bewildered by their own boredom.

My own first awareness of stories was when I was four years old, listening to my mother as we sat at my bedroom window and I writhed and wriggled on her knee as children do when they listen without looking. I had just lately realised that the marks in the middle of the small, shiny pages of Beatrix Potter's *The Tale of Peter Rabbit* were words. They had sounds invisibly attached. Attaching the sounds to the marks was called 'Reading'. Pictures were great, but they were extras. It was a moment of joy.

At the same time, it was a moment of disquiet for above my head, at the window behind the curtain, there was something terrible. I couldn't see it but I knew that it was there ('Will you please SIT STILL!') 'But there's something there behind the curtain.' 'Don't be silly.'

I jumped up and tweaked the curtain, and behind it sat a disgusting freckled blackish parrot with loose-skinned leathery claws. I knew that the parrot was death.

I wriggled on. Out of the window the huge sky, the weedy railway line, the space between two empty shabby mansions, the distant Cleveland Hills. Eight years later (1940) I was sitting doing my homework and still I didn't care to look up at that curtain when a little aeroplane flew past, very low. It had a swastika on its side and I could see the dark round bullet of the pilot's helmet. I shrieked out: 'There's an enemy plane.' Up from the kitchen came the command not to be silly when from somewhere near the steelworks to the north of us came the most almighty explosion. The dangerous presence was still there.

Five years ago, at eighty, I went to look at my old home again and it looked exactly the same as in the '30s—beautifully kept, polished door-knocker and letter-box, rows of perfect antirrhinums straight as pink soldiers—except that I found I could still only manage a quick glance at my bedroom window, now covered in net. I found myself shaking. 'Jane has always had her *ecstatic* side,' my mother used to say, 'and ecstasy is all very well, but—'

It wasn't ecstasy that got me away from the burden of home. It was English literature and an award to London University that set my ecstatic side aflame. Then it went out. The work was dreary, heavy with Anglo Saxon, and there was no money for theatres or extra food. Though I didn't admit it,

I was bored except for when I was in the wonderful but ice-cold Bedford College Library (no coal or heating in the '40s). At school the domestic science mistress who was vague about geography had asked me when I reached London to go and visit her niece—newly arrived from 'the Colonies' and very shy. Her school was near Reading (which she pronounced as in reading) and that sounded promisingly like a suburb of London. I nearly turned back when I found the train fare was ten shillings. I used my last faded bank note.

And then I was greatly humbled by the school-girl niece herself who looked all of twenty-one, wore wonderful clothes, was bronzed by African sun and was clearly not home-sick at all. She didn't know what to do with me. Desperately, she said there was a lecture that afternoon by L. A. G. Strong, a well-known critic then, on 'The Short Story'. Would I like to come to it?

I had read his book, *The Short Story* at school and what he thought, I thought too. In it he says, 'Think of the reader not yourself. Make everything interesting. Write about every-thing—even linoleum.'

On the way back to the London train I followed L. A. G. Strong. I climbed into the same carriage. I sat down beside him. He looked dejected and tired with deep lines between his nose and his sweet mouth. I fell in love. I began to talk. This may sound like nothing, but for me, almost pathologically self-conscious, it was like removing all my clothes and belly-dancing. In time he said, 'I believe you *write*' and I said yes. 'Send me something.' Looking weary, he courteously passed me a card.

I went back to college (ecstasy in the ascendant) and sent him a short story (called *The Woman Who Lost a Thought*—and I have it yet) and waited.

Silence. Silence for two weeks. Then a letter typed in royal blue ink, 'Jane—you are a writer beyond all possible doubt.'

And for a while I stayed with short stories. The first volume of them was about children on a white beach, and I called it *A Few Fair Days*. I posted it in a letter box on the corner of Murray Road in Wimbledon. After three weeks I telephoned the publisher and asked if she was going to accept them as there were other publishers who might like them. Astounded silence. The publisher, at Hamish Hamilton, said afterwards that she had told her secretary there was a mad woman on the phone and would she find her manuscript and send it back. The secretary found it in the three-foot high pile of unsolicited manuscripts and said 'D'you know—I think these might just do.'

I have written and published eight or nine collections of short stories and ten novels since then. One won the Katherine Mansfield award, two won the Whitbread and another was a collection about Jamaica, where I had only spent sixteen days, and it won nothing. I was getting rather above myself. These early stories are somewhat wild. Then a new publisher asked for a collection with 'more stories, if you think you can' and I airily said, 'of course'. I don't think this was true. I turned for some years to novels and harder work and was shortlisted for the Booker Prize.

Writing fiction has been my life for the past forty years. I finished what I thought should be my last book a year ago, the final novel of a trilogy called *Old Filth*. *Last Friends* is a novel, but I like to think it has short stories embedded. When I finished, 'Farewell,' I said. 'Amen.' I must learn when to stop. That is what short stories teach you.

Yet perhaps the most gratifying thing since writing this book and its two companion volumes before, which have taken eight years, was the phone call this year from my most faithful and enduring publisher, Richard Beswick of Little, Brown. He asked for 'a big, chunky anthology of all your favourite short stories.' I said that I understood that nobody wanted to read short stories now but he said, 'You are wrong. Look around. Choose your favourites. Times are changing once again.'

The deathly parrot recedes. Maybe he was never there. How much more and how much better I might have written had I not been so timid.

Reading Claire Tomalin's *Thomas Hardy: The Time-Torn Man* the other day I came upon the ballad of *The Outlandish Knight* where the heroine escapes death and returns home to safety. There is nobody there but a parrot in the window (I swear I had not read this poem at four years old).

The parrot being up in the window so high
And hearing the lady did say
'I'm afraid some ruffian has led you astray
That you've tarried so long away.'

Well, the parrot is vanquished and the ecstasy is now fitful. The luck in the writer's life always is to have been able to use the sweets of fiction to get near the truth.

JANE GARDAM
May 2014

THE STORIES

HETTY SLEEPING

Seeing the tall man's long back she thought with a lurch, 'It's like Heneker's back.' Then as he turned round she saw that it was Heneker.

He was standing on a pale strip of sand near the sea, looking down into the cold water, quiet as he had always been, peaceful, unmistakable.

'How *could* it be?' she thought. 'What nonsense! Of course it can't be.'

She went on folding the tee-shirts and jeans, gathering flung sandals, then made two neat heaps with a towel on each, for when the children came out of the sea. She took off her cardigan, pushed her hands back through her hair, gave her face for a moment to the sun; looked again.

She watched her two children run with drumming feet over the hard white strand, splash past the man into the sea, fling themselves into it in fans of spray, shrieking. Then she looked at the man again.

Long brown legs, long brown back. He was watching with a painter's concentration the movement of the water and the shapes of the children playing in it. Twenty, thirty yards away, yet she could not mistake the slow smile, the acceptance as he narrowed his eyes and looked at lines and planes and shadows, that there are wonders on the earth.

It was Heneker all right. Ten years older but decidedly and only Heneker.

He turned, came up the beach, dropped down beside her

and said 'Hello.' He was wearing black swimming trunks and had a beard. 'Funny,' she thought, 'I always laugh at beards in the sea, but he looks all right. He always did look all right. Wherever he was.'

'Hello,' she said.

He hadn't said her name. Perhaps he'd forgotten it. He had never used people's names much. He had been cautious. Except in his work.

'Hello, Hetty,' he said. 'It's a long time.'

'It's a funny place,' she said. He smiled, not looking away from her face. 'To meet again,' she said. 'It's a long way from Earl's Court. Connemara.'

'A holiday,' he said gently and began to take the sand and sift it through his fingers. Her heart started to lurch again seeing his fingers. 'I know each nail,' she thought, 'I know each line on them. Every half moon. Oh God!'

There was a shriek from the sea and he looked over his brown shoulder at the children. 'Yours?' he said.

'Yes.' She began to babble. 'They're eight and four. Andy and Sophie. We're here for a fortnight. We've taken a house.'

'And their Papa?'

'He's following. He was to have come with us but at the last minute there was a crisis. We came ahead. We'd booked the house you see. The Pin.'

'The Pin? Lord Thing's house? Ballinhead?'

'Yes. It's a fishing lodge—'

'I know.' He swung round on to his stomach and got hold of her bare feet and held them tight. 'Hetty,' he said, looking closely at her toes. 'Wonderful feet,' he said. 'They always were. I once drew your feet. So you've married brass?'

'No,' she said. 'When we married there was no brass at all. He's clever. He's good. At his job. Marvellous if you want to know.'

'Top brass?'

'Not at all. Don't be silly. I was a painter. Would I have married top brass?'

'Very silly not to if you had the chance. Colonel and Lady Top-Brass, V.C., X.Y.Z. and Bar. Are you Lady Brass? You look it a bit, with your white, white skin.'

'Don't be silly—'

He held her feet tight and put his forehead against them. 'Lord and Lady Top-Brass and all the little alloys.'

'Shut up!' (This can't be happening! We arrived yesterday. We've hardly been here ten minutes! Heneker!) She tried to free her feet and giggled. 'You're tickling,' she said. 'Don't *breathe* over me.'

He let go of her feet and said, 'What is he then?'

'A banker.'

'Christ!'

'Do you know any bankers? Men with international work?'

'No, thank God. "Men with international work." Do you know any painters still?'

'No,' she said.

'Do you do any painting?'

After a long time she said no.

He lay flat on his back now on the sand and spread his arms far out and closed his eyes. His bearded, gentle face and fine nose and peaceful expression were like an icon. She thought, 'He ought to be picked out in jewels he's so beautiful. He's wicked as ever. Oh God, I love him,' and getting up she gathered the two heaps of clothes with a swoosh into the beach bag and the cardigan and her book and the towels in her arms, and was off down the beach to the sea's edge. 'I'm moving,' she called to the children. 'I'm going back up to the car. Don't be long, darlings. Ten minutes.'

'But we've just got *in*! We were staying in all morning.'

'There's a wind.'

'But it's *lovely*!'

'No, it's cold. I'm moving out of the wind.'

'There's not a breath of wind,' shouted Andy. 'Not a bit. You're crazy. It's a *boiling day*.'

'I'll be up in the car,' and resolutely, not looking back, she tramped up the beach alone and sat by the car in the sharp grass among old picnic papers, where red ants nipped her and noisy wild dogs from the fishermen's cabins came and barked endlessly for food as she pretended to read.

She was bathing Sophie at The Pin that evening in water that foamed like Guinness into the noble old Guinness-stained bath-tub when a noise of thundering hooves began to rock the bathroom ceiling and the water from the tap turned to a trickle and died.

'Now what!' Hetty sat back on her heels. 'Sixty pounds a week! Sixty pounds a week! The phone is dead, the electrics flicker and the beastly peat ... And now this.'

'Whatever is it?' Andy came flying in.

'I don't know. I think it's the boiler or something. I think it's dry.'

'The water's hot as hot.'

'Yes, but it's stopped coming. The tank must be empty. It comes from that bog thing in the grounds—we saw it yesterday. I thought it looked awfully shallow.'

'It looked awfully dirty,' said Andy, 'and so does the bath.'

'No. It's lovely brown water,' she said. 'But, oh!'

'I expect it'll all blow up soon,' said Andy. 'Shall I go and throw the main switch? It might be safer.'

'No. Shush. Let me think.'

'Above the kitchen door. That great heavy big one?'

'No. Oh do shut up. Let me *think*. There's the pub. We might go to the pub. There might be a man.'

'There is a man.'

'At the pub?'

'No, here.'

'Here?'

'Yes. In the hall place. He's that man on the beach. He's playing with our plasticine. Wait, I'll ask him.'

Hetty on a cane chair by the bathroom window, with Sophie wrapped in a towel on her knee, saw Andy and Heneker walking thoughtfully together, hand in hand through the wild garden towards the source of the bathwater.

The thunder in the roof, however, continued.

When she brought Sophie down the stairs Heneker was at the big trestle table in the hall making a plasticine dinosaur and without looking up said, 'There seemed nothing wrong down there. Must be a block in the pipe.'

She sat down with Sophie at the far end of the table and the booming grew less, then less still and finally stopped. A blessed trickle into the tank could be heard.

He said, 'Irish plumbing.' Sophie eating biscuits sidled round to him and watched his fingers and Andy who had been having his bath, which for safety's sake had been Sophie's not-run-out, came down again and leaned against Heneker watching the emergence from the plasticine of a fat porcupine on elephant's legs, armour plated on the stomach and with a rhino's spike. Sophie coming closer gazed at it with love.

'Could I have it?' said Andy.

'Someone can,' said Heneker. He put it in the middle of the table with its nose in a bowl of fuchsias.

'Thirsty,' said Sophie. 'Poor pig.'

'It's not a pig. It's a—what is it, Heneker?'

'It's a swamp wanderer.'

'What's that?'

'It wanders through swamps. It squelches through bogs. It thunders in roofs—' They squealed with joy.

'Now then,' said Hetty, 'bedtime.'

Heneker made a roaring and thundering noise. They clung to him. '*Bed*time,' Hetty said, hearing her Surrey voice. 'Now that will do. You're over-excited. Go to bed.'

'Oh please—'

'No. If Daddy were here—'

'He's not. Can't we stay?'

'Off,' said Heneker. 'Quick before the squelcher gets you.'

They fled, Sophie stopping on the bend in the stairs, minute, delectable in a flowery nightgown. 'You won't go away? You'll come back tomorrow?'

'Yes,' said Heneker.

She brought coffee to the sitting room where he was sitting in one of the two comfortable, shabby armchairs and watching the crumbling peat fire. Four long windows lit the chintz sofa, the shelves of Lord Thing's books about fishing and birds. Outside shone the Irish night, black and silver, with long bumpy spars of land running out towards America. Not a sound anywhere, never a light moving along the road. There was the sense that all about the holiday house lay miles of silence, darkness, the ancient mountains inland making a long barricade against the usual world.

Heneker's face as he sat far back in his chair was in shadow. She put the coffee between them on a stool and leaned back in her chair, too. They did not speak for a long time.

'It might have been like this,' he said at last. She felt her heart begin to thump and hung on to the chair. (This is *Heneker*. Heneker I have thought of every day.)

'No,' she said.

He said, 'Yes. Oh God!'

'You never asked me,' she said. 'Not once.'

'Well you know why.'

'I don't know why.'

'Oh Hetty—'

'I don't know why. I never knew why. I couldn't ask you. All that year. That room ... The bed made out of ropes. The roof like a greenhouse and the curtain over the corner.'

'Where our clothes were.'

'No. Our clothes were in heaps. Well your clothes were in heaps.'

'I loved your clothes.' he said. 'Always clean and neat. And small. All the buttons were real buttons with proper button-holes.'

'I used to gather up yours,' she said. 'Like gleaning. A sock here. A shirt there, a shoe on the light.'

'On the *light*?'

'Yes. To dim it down. Very dangerous.'

'And smelly.'

She laughed.

'Oh go on,' he said.

'What?'

'Laughing,' he said. 'I'd forgotten.'

'And now you're famous,' she said, looking up at him. He had stood up, all the long length of him, resting his forehead against his arm on the high chimney piece and looking down at the grey fire. 'Heneker Mann.'

'"What a piece of work is Mann." Have you—?'

'Yes. I've been to all of them.'

'Exhibitions,' he said. 'God knows what they amount to really. I was doing better stuff that year.'

'No,' she said. 'You are very much better now.' (He still says things in order to be contradicted. He knows I will contradict. He knows that I know that he needs to be contradicted. Our thoughts move completely together. They always did. We sit here. We are like Darby and Joan ... And it's ten years. He's wicked still of course. I suppose he's married, I wonder—)

'She's a painter,' he said to the fire.

Hetty said nothing.

'She's a painter, Lady Top-Brass, just a painter.'

'Well I suppose so. She would have had to be.'

'No. You know that. All that year you knew.'

'I didn't. Anyway, I was a painter.'

'No. You picked up my clothes. Took the shoe off the light.'

'Good painters are often tidy. Usually in fact. You must have been reading novels about painters, Heneker.'

'No,' he said. 'Not tidy like you. The tidiness was growing. It was getting dangerous. It got in the way.'

'Not often,' she said. 'As time went on you weren't there to see. I tidied round nothing and nobody. You were always out. Later and later. More and more.'

'You should have painted instead. If you'd painted then, instead of minding and tidying—' he flung away and looked out of a window at the gigantic sea. 'God, I missed you.'

One of the children called out upstairs and in a second she was out of her chair and the room and gone. Sophie lay like a seraph, her face lifted to the moonlight but Andy was flinging about in a heap, one arm flailing the air. 'A spike,' he cried. 'Kill it.'

'All right,' she said. 'Hush. Wake up a minute.'

'Beast,' he cried. 'Thump it.'

'It's just a dream,' she said. 'You're asleep. You're sleeping—remembering the water tank.'

'Huh!' he said and, turning into a hump, was asleep again. She stood looking at herself in the glass at the top of the stairs, put back a strand of hair. 'Thirty-one,' she thought. 'Honestly, you wouldn't think so.' She felt gloriously happy, drifted back to the sitting room. But Heneker was gone.

'After all, it was you left me,' he said.

'No.' She folded clothes. The children splashed, called, 'Heneker! Come and look. *Crabs*, Heneker!'

'Soon,' he said. He sat on a rock with a towel round his

neck. She sat a little below him on the sand, his bare brown leg from knee to ankle beside her shoulder as she pushed Andy's socks into sandals. It was next day, still boiling, still un-Irishly hot.

'Your parting,' he said, 'is very beautiful.'

'"Was", I suppose.'

'No. Is. Your parting now, I mean. In your hair. All the hairs are bending back and shining down each side.'

'Oh, Heneker.' (Why is it that when he decides not to touch you it's as good as other men touching you? Better.) 'I thought you never liked my hair.'

'I never said that. Just thought it was—too symmetrical in those days. Over-nice. Better now.'

'I wasn't over-nice in the end.'

'Indeed no,' said Heneker. 'It was you left me, as I remarked.'

He slid down off the rock and sat beside her. 'And got married,' he said, leaning the back of his head against the rock he had been sitting on, 'about ten minutes later. God knows all about it I suppose. I didn't. The boy next door. Number three in *The Times*. Wedding in Scautland among all the dowdy dowagers. To which I was not invited.'

'Hardly.'

'Incidentally, is dowager a derivative? Of dowdy? One should look it up. Will you be a dowager? I'll marry you.'

'You're being cruel.' She began to get up.

'STOP!'

The long brown hand, ten years older but as familiar as her own, at last fastened over hers. 'Stop. Don't go.'

'Why the hell shouldn't I?'

'Don't go. With your white, white skin.'

'If I'm dowdy—'

'Oh, Het. Shut up.'

They sat on the almost empty strand. Some Dubliners far

across were assembling a boat. There were one or two other people. Two fishermen trudged up from the day's work carrying a plastic bag with heavy fish in it staining the bag with blood. They were dressed in ageless clothes. They had very ancient faces. But for the plastic bag they might have been ghosts. They walked up past Sophie and Andy who were digging a fortress, Sophie patting the top of a Norman keep with a little pink spade. Her forearms were gold.

''Tis a beautiful day,' said the older fisherman as they passed by. 'You have beautiful children.' The younger fisherman looked at Hetty. They went on up the beach.

'I love you so,' said Heneker.

She pulled hard against his tightening hand.

'So what did you do?' she asked in the end.

He was leaning back still with eyes closed.

'Got married I suppose.'

'Suppose? You must know. To the one who—to the one you were—'

'No,' he said, sitting up. 'Not her.'

'Well, to a painter.'

'Yes. To a bloody good painter if it is of any interest to you.'

Andy came up and flung down crabs. Sophie fell on a squishy thing and cried. Comfort. Handkerchieves. Clothes. Home for lunch and the children's rest; Heneker back to the pub where he was staying.

'Will you come up after and do plasticine beasts, Heneker?'

'Yes, all right, Andy. Half past seven.'

'I was supposed to be a bloody good painter too.' She put down the coffee tray again between them, tried to brighten the fire, opened the curtains wider to the evening sea. 'Until I met you.'

'That's what I mean.'

'You destroyed it.' She poured the coffee into mugs. 'That's all. Anyway you were no good to me. You're no good to any woman.'

'Any brown sugar?' he said.

'No.'

'I'd have thought that Lord Thing kept brown sugar for his coffee, Lady Top-Brass. Lady Brass-Tops.'

'The groceries aren't in with the rent. They're provided by me. Well, by Charles. You can't get demerara in the village—' she had to stop.

'Darling,' he said, coming over and taking her hands. 'Darling, for God's sake, don't. Don't cry. Whatever—'

'You're so bloody cruel. You always were so bloody cruel.'

'But truthful,' he said squeezing her hands so that they hurt. 'Always that. And to no one else. Not truthful like this.'

'Thank you very much.'

'Oh, Het. Don't be cruel back. God, you were always crueller. You know you were, too. You could get in where it hurt. Because you knew— Where're you going?'

He caught up with her as she reached the hall, at the foot of the stairs beside the telephone which stood in the curl of the banisters—an old-fashioned telephone with a trumpet and a very old wire drooping out of it like a brown string chain. 'Het,' he said, grabbing her. The telephone tottered and he caught it and, 'Marvellous!' he said, looking at the telephone. 'God, it's nice. Like a black daffodil. Does it work?'

She flung off up the stairs leaving him with the telephone next to his heart. 'I'll go back to the pub then.' She answered by closing her bedroom door and heard him walk slowly down the weedy drive between the giant rhubarb, the wilderness of fuchsias, to the great, crumbling gate-posts. Once, twice she heard him stop. Savagely, delightedly, she imagined him looking back at the house all in darkness, her bedroom window dark as all the rest.

'Don't move.'

She put an arm across her forehead and looked out under it. He was drawing. 'Shut your eyes again. Put your arm down, Het.'

After a time she said, 'Can I open them now? I want to see if the children— I fell asleep.'

'They're all right,' he said. 'I can see them. They're shrimping in a pool. I've been drawing them, too.'

'However long have you been here?'

'About an hour. You were deep asleep. With the red ants walking all over you.'

'I don't believe that.'

'The fishermen had a good look, too.'

'I didn't sleep much last night.'

'You went to bed too soon, Hetty of the white, white skin. Here you are, you never were one to get sunburned.' He threw the drawing across to her. 'Hetty Sleeping.'

'It's—lovely.'

'And here's the children.' Sophie's round, firm cheek, a sweep of eye-lash, her wrist still with its foetal crease over the wrist top.

Andy's long head, clear eyes; another drawing of his head from behind, the heart-breaking tail of hair (left from babyhood) lying in the dent down the back of the neck.

'Have you any children, Heneker?'

'No.'

He got up and loped towards the sea and Sophie and Andy seeing him nearby sprang up to follow. She saw Andy show him something from a pool, Sophie lift her arms to be picked up. Heneker, examining in one hand the object from the pool, swung Sophie up with his other arm onto his shoulder and the three of them stood reflectively together, illuminated, at peace.

'Tomorrow,' said Heneker, eating her sandwiches at lunchtime—it was too beautiful a day to go back to the house, too good for the children to waste in resting—'tomorrow we'll go to the Clifden Show and see the ponies. We'll go on the bus.'

'Whyever the bus?' she said.

'To see some people.'

'Will you draw the people on the bus?' asked Andy.

'I might.'

But he didn't.

They sat in a row on either side of the gangway, Hetty with Andy, Heneker with Sophie who soon got on his knee, and listened to the talk around them and watched the sea and the bog and the procession of the Connemara mountains, purple and graceful behind the orange gorse and the great scattering of white stones. At Clifden they walked the fair and touched the ponies and brought things and ate things and drank things and lived in the lovely crowd. Heneker in washed-out blue denim, brown-faced, lanky as a cowboy with the two small children trotting behind him, turned heads. Hetty carrying the picnic in a big, round basket she had found among the fishing tackle in the house, in sandals and a handkerchief over her head and a faded red dress bought years ago in Florence, walked easily along feeling she might be taken for a tinker. Happy and weary at five o'clock they caught the bus home, Sophie falling deep asleep in Heneker's arms, Andy moving over beside him. Hetty set the basket on the seat left empty beside her, and, like a peasant, shielded her eyes from the levelling sun.

Back at Heneker's pub where the bus stopped he lifted Sophie carefully down and put her in the back seat of Hetty's car. Andy stumbled in beside her, then stuck out his head.

'You coming back too, Heneker?'

'No. It's supper-time at the pub.'

'Mummy could cook you some with us.'

'No, they'd be cross at the pub if I didn't turn up. It'll be ready.'

'Why would they? You could still pay. Why don't you come and stay with us? There's heaps of room. You could sleep next to Mummy.'

His clear voice carried across the pub yard and some people coming up from the beach looked amusedly at them, and a girl—the waitress or barmaid who had been leaning against the bar door—disappeared, slamming it behind her.

'I can't do that.' Heneker flicked Andy's nose. 'But you must go. It's been a long day.'

Hetty started the car. He came round to her side of it and said, 'I'll walk over later.'

It was a question made to sound like a statement. Not looking at him but busily at the gears she said, 'All right,' and swung through the gate and up the hill.

When the children were fed and in bed, drugged and rosy with sun, she bathed and changed, trying on first one thing and then another, ending up with a long cotton dressing-gown. She put up her hair on top of her head where it immediately began to fall down. Rather successfully. She took off her shoes and wandered to the kitchen to find something for supper, but nothing seemed to make her feel hungry. She ate a tomato by the fridge, staring through the kitchen window at the high, neglected grass and the tall Evening Primroses that slapped the pane. She laid the coffee tray.

Then she walked to the sitting room and struggled half-heartedly with the faint fire. The sun, now setting in a blaze beyond the point, turned the room to glory, lighting up a filmy silvery peaty dust on the old furniture, making a great vase of flowers and leaves she had gathered yesterday glow rose red. 'It's like a dream,' she thought. She walked all round the house and then into the garden, pacing its boundaries on her bare feet, discovering an overgrown fishpond, peering into long-empty stables with trees growing through the roofs, disturbing three lean sheep from under an old mounting-block. She walked the long way back to the front door and stood a while looking out to sea and determinedly not towards the road.

Then she went in and lit the kettle. Then she turned it off. She went up to look at the children and coming down again looked at last unashamedly down the long, empty drive. She went back to the sitting room and sat in the arm chair and looked at the black turf on the fire. The sun had quite gone and the room was cold. It was half past ten.

He was not coming.

As she fell asleep she saw a sudden image of Charles's alert and prudent face. She thought, 'Charles always saw me right home to the door.'

'Hetty sleeping.'

She jumped with such a jerk she felt quite sick, and sat bolt upright. Heneker was opposite her in the other chair. He was laughing. 'Hetty very deeply sleeping.'

'Where were you? Where am I?' she cried. 'Heneker—it's midnight. Where've you been?' It was ten years ago. But where was the glass roof, the smell of Earl's Court? 'Where've you been. I've been all alone.' She looked around. It was now. Ireland. The expensive, rented house. Children. Charles somewhere in the world. Charles—

'The children,' she said, 'I must see if the children are all right. The doors are all open. Anyone could have walked in.'

'It was I walked in.'

'But anyone could have. The I.R.A.—'

'Don't be silly, Het.'

'You had no *right* to walk in.'

'You said I was to come.'

'But it's the middle of the night.'

'I was held up. It's a long walk here.'

'You've never been as late as this.' She heard the voice,

high, accusing. Oh God! Like a wife. Like then. It's no different.

Wearily she got up. 'I must go and look at the children, Heneker,' and walked slowly away.

But on the stairs she stopped and after a while gave a sigh and turned and sat down, resting her head against the banisters. All the doors were open in the hall, and through the open front door on the right the moonlight flooded in, and the heavy, dementing scent of the night flowers in the garden. She shut her eyes.

'Het,' he was at the foot of the stairs beside the ancient telephone. 'Het,' he lifted his arm. 'Oh, my dear Het.'

She pulled herself up and helplessly walked down back to him until she was two steps above him, level with his eyes.

'Sleep with me, Hetty,' he said and she said, 'Of course.'

Between them on the banister the telephone began to ring.

'It can't! It doesn't!'

'Well, it is.'

'It can't. It never has. It's terrible.' She covered up her ears.

'You'd better answer it.'

'I can't. I can't,' she cried.

'Well I can't, can I? For God's sake, stop the bloody thing.' He walked over to the open front door.

Looking at him all the time she picked up the heavy earpiece and heard a tremendous crackling, then the voice of a sleepy post-mistress, more crackling and then from some ethereal wasteland, Charles.

'Hester? Hester? Where on earth? God-forsaken—'

'Here I am,' she said, 'Yes? Charles?'

'... coming at once.'

'You're coming when?'

'I'll be there ...' more huge crackling, '... over at last.'

'I didn't hear. When? Where are you? When are you coming?' The crackling grew and became a pain in the ears, then stopped. There was silence.

'He's— He's— Charles. He's on his way.'

'Where is he?'

'I don't know. Perhaps in Clifden.'

'At twelve o'clock at night? Well, he'd not get here till tomorrow if he's off a bus.'

'Perhaps he's even at Ballynish.'

'Don't be silly. Why bother to ring if he were already at Ballynish? He's probably still in Dublin. Or more likely still in London. Ringing from the Hilton. Carousing with the clients.'

'No. No. You don't understand Charles. I'm sure he's almost here.'

He grabbed the phone and threw it on the ground and took her wrists and said, 'Look. Sleep with me.'

'I can't. I can't.'

'All right.' He walked back to the door. She watched him turn back to her. Behind his head was the dazzle of the sea. 'There never was anyone but you, Het,' he said, and was gone.

'HESTER!' Charles's pleasant voice in the hall. Sounds of dropped luggage, Irish voices from the taxi. Half the village in attendance, much information being simultaneously imparted. 'What a journey! What a place to get to.' Shrieks from Sophie and Andy. 'Daddy! Oh—fishing rods! Did you remember to bring my orange bag? There are crabs, huge ones. Lobsters. We went to the fair.'

She watched them from the stairs, fickle, leaping like puppies, the taxi man, the taxi-man's assistant, the taxi-man's grandfather brooding by.

'Hester. Thank God. Damn thing over. Come and give us a kiss.' The attendants were paid off.

'How are you, love? Can't see you. Aren't there any lights?

What's that thundering noise? Good heavens, what a telephone. Did I manage to get through on that?'

'The lights come and go,' she said. 'The thundering does too.'

'I'll fix it,' he said. 'The electrics will be the generator. I'll get on with it in a minute. It's very cold here.'

'We can't light the peat.' said Andy.

'But peat's marvellous, you useless creatures. I'll make a blaze. Where's the sitting room? Better turn off the stopcock for the present. We're going out to supper.'

'We can't, there's only the pub. You have to book.' (What's the matter with my voice?)

'I've booked.'

'But the places round here don't— Hardly ever,' she said.

'I stopped at the pub on the way. Went in and booked. Come on. Get the children out of their night shirts, we're away to eat lobsters.'

'Charles—I can't go to the pub. I'm a mess. I'm tired. I waited all last night. We've waited around all today. It's after eight o'clock.'

'All last *night*? You didn't expect me last night? I didn't ring till midnight. I was still in London.'

'And by the way, something else,' he said as he drove them all fast down the hill. 'The Bartletts are at the pub.'

'The Bartletts? From home? From Denham Place? Oh no!'

'Yes—Have you got a sore throat? Said they saw you yesterday. With some splendid man.'

'I didn't see them.'

'I did,' said Andy. 'When we dropped Heneker at the pub.'

'Children are so odd,' she said to Cathie Bartlett in the pub. 'Andy saw you yesterday but he never said.'

'You seemed in a bit of a trance.' Cathie Bartlett's eyes were careful. Charles's great laugh rang out at something Bartlett had said. They were alone in the pub dining room. A Bartlett child had come in from the television room and been gathered onto its mother's knee. (But every knee is his knee. Every child is his child. Oh Heneker. Oh Heneker.)

'Famous chap,' said Bartlett. 'The great artist. Caused a stir.'

'Oh Heneker *Mann*,' said Charles. 'Oh, that's it. Old flame of Hester's, hey?'

'Yes,' said Hester. (I feel so far away.) 'I was a student of his at the Slade. Oh, donkey's years ago.' (Oh what can I do?)

'He's gone?' asked Charles.

'Gone all right. Disappeared this morning. Barmaid's gone too, I believe. There's a great to-do. Well—he'd been with her every blessed night.'

'Oh Noel!' said Cathie.

'Well he had. Be your age. These passages creak. We've not had a wink of sleep, Cathie and I, all week.'

'Don't blame her anyway,' said Cathie. 'Gorgeous. Don't mind telling you, Hester'—she lit a cigarette expertly above her child's head—'I was green with envy when I saw you with him on the beach. You ought to watch out, Charles.'

'Don't you worry,' said Charles.

They got up to go.

In Lord Thing's sitting room the peat fire shone hot and bright. Charles brought in the tray and put it on the stool, then drew the curtains. He said, 'I've settled the children. And I've had to make tea. I couldn't find any brown sugar.'

'I forgot it.'

'Never mind. Tea won't keep us awake. I say, what's this? "Hetty Sleeping".'

'Give me that.'

'No. Let me look. It's lovely. Wonderful.'

'It's mine. Charles—give it me. Give it me. *Give* it me.'

'No,' he said. He held the drawing at a distance under the

brilliant electric light. '"Hetty Sleeping".' He put on his glasses.

'Give me that. Give me that. Give me that!'

'"Hetty Sleeping",' he said. 'Very sadly.'

He put the drawing delicately down on Lord Thing's writing desk. Pouring tea for her he said, 'Sweet Hetty, wake up soon.'

LUNCH WITH RUTH SYKES

She was crying again last night and that made it easier for me this morning.

I said, 'I'm having lunch with Ruth Sykes today, dear.'

'Mmmm,' she said, black coffee one hand, toast the other, peering down at the morning paper laid all across the kitchen table—she never sits down at breakfast.

'So you'll be all right, dear?'

'Mmmm.'

'For lunch I mean—after surgery. I'll leave it ready in the oven. Just to take out.'

'What?'

'Your lunch, dear. After surgery. And your visits. It'll be in the oven.'

She looked at me through her big glasses—such a big, handsome daughter. How could such a great big woman have come out of me? I'm so small. Jack was small, too. And neither of us was anything much. Certainly nothing so clever as a doctor in either of the families, anywhere. It's funny—I look at her, my daughter, my Rosalind and I can't believe she's the same as the baby I had: the fat little round warm bright-eyed thing holding its wrists up in the pram against the light, carefully watching the leaves moving in the birch tree like a peaceful little fat cat. She's so bold and brave and strong now—fast car, doctor's bag slung in the back, stethoscope, white coat. So quick on the telephone. Oh it's wonderful to hear her on the telephone!—'Yes? When was this? All right—do nothing until

I'm there. I'll be with you in ten minutes.' Oh the lives she must save! She's a wonderful doctor.

But the crying is awful. It was really awful last night.

'Why can't you be here, mother?' (Flicks over page of *The Telegraph*. Peers closer.)

She never lets herself go even when she's happy. I think the last time I remember her being overwhelmed in any way by feeling happy was when she got into Oxford. And then she just opened the telegram and said, 'Oh my goodness!' and spilled a whole cup of coffee all down her school uniform—all over the clean floor.

'I'm having lunch with Ruth Sykes.'

She finished her coffee. ''Bye,' she says. 'Have a nice time. See you for supper—oh, no I won't. Forgot. I'll be at the hospital.'

'Till when, dear?'

'God—I don't know. Ten? Eleven?'

'All right, dear.'

The road outside as well as the front garden and the house is diminished without her. Energy has gone out of the morning.

I go back in the kitchen and start clearing up the breakfast.

Am I *really* going? Dare I?

I wash things up and stand for a time looking at the china cupboard door before putting them away. I go upstairs and change into my dark blue wool suit and good shoes and stockings and look at my face in the glass.

It is a very silly face. Like an unintelligent bird. Birds are supposed to have intelligent faces, but I don't know. Mine is like a bird's but not a very bright bird. A C-stream bird. It's a timid self-conscious face. Ready to be made an ass of. An ass to be made of a bird. Rosalind does make me feel such an ass. She didn't as a baby—she used to get hold of bits of me then—my ear or my chin—and hang on tight, and laugh and laugh. It does seem a pity—

Anyway I'm better looking than Ruth Sykes. I'm not an ass when I'm with Ruth Sykes either. I'm perfectly easy. We were at school together and she was nothing like so clever as I was though I was nothing special at all. I wish I were having lunch with Ruth Sykes.

I'm not though. I decided a fortnight ago and I'm not losing my nerve now. No I'm not.

Not with all the crying.

I'm going to London to see Michael.

The crying didn't start as soon as Michael stopped coming here. She was quite sane and calm and quiet at first, even rather nice to me. I remember she said would I like to go to the theatre with her once, and I got tickets for the two of us for *Rosenkavalier*—just locally. It's not my favourite at all and I expect she loathed it but we sat there together very friendly, side by side.

'Is Michael busy tonight?'—I hadn't realised then.

' 'Spect so,' she said.

She didn't stay in at home though, not at all. And she never mentioned him. She kept on being very nice to me for several weeks—sometimes she'd come and sit by me and watch the telly for a bit, and once I remember she said she liked my dress. Once she seemed to be looking at me as if she was going to say something and I just waited, I was so afraid of doing the wrong thing. I talk far too much you see. I'm a bit of a joke the way I talk once I get started.

She didn't say anything though and all I said after a day or two more was that Michael hadn't telephoned lately and were they going on holiday together again this summer. And she just got up and slammed out.

Then that night I heard her crying—awful, awful long sobs. They woke me up and I couldn't think whatever they were—like terrible sawing noises, seconds apart. I went out on the

landing and they seemed to be coming from the top floor
where she sleeps, and I went running up and stood outside her
door.

Awful sobs.

Well, I daren't of course go in.

I went down again to my floor and back to bed with the
door open and listened—just shaking, my eyes wide open, trying to imagine her face, all so smooth and assured, twisted up
in the dark with the mouth crooked and those awful noises
coming out of it.

Yet at breakfast she was just the same—coffee cup one
hand, toast the other, peering down at the newspaper. Perhaps
two lines had appeared above the nose, creased together, that
was all.

'Sit down, dear. You'll strain your eyes.'

She didn't answer. I got up in a sudden rush and went all
round the table and I put my arm round her waist—she's so
much taller than me—and I said, 'Darling, can't you sit down
a minute?'

She said, 'Oh for Godssake, Mother,' and pulled away.

I said, 'You'll hurt your eyes.'

'Is there any moment of the year,' she said, 'when you don't
say that?'

'Do you think,' she said, 'that just once you could express a
single original thought?'

I didn't hear her crying for a while and then three weeks
ago it began again. For a week she was crying every single
night. I got up each time. At first I walked round my room
bumping things about. Then I took to going out on the landing and clicking on and off the light. Once I pulled the lavatory
chain. The crying just went on. In the end—like last night—I
took to going and sitting on the stairs outside her bedroom. It
did no good of course, but it was all I could do and so I did it.

I took the eiderdown and put it round me and I just sat there praying she would stop. Sometimes I told myself stories that she would come out and trip over me and say, 'Oh Mother!' and then I would hug her and hug her and say, 'Oh Rosalind, what happened? Tell me what happened. What *happened* to him?'

She never did.

The crying always stopped in the end—longer pauses between the sobs and then when the idiot birds began to wake up she'd be quiet at last. So funny. When she was a baby that was the time she would always wake up. She got a real nuisance about one and a half and I had to be quite firm. I used to go in and she'd be standing in her cot with her nappies round her ankles and her nightie all frills and her face like a rose.

'Now, Rosalind. Back to sleep. Too *soon*, baby. It's only five o'clock. The day hasn't started yet.' 'But the birds has begun to tweet,' she said. Oh she was lovely! 'The birds has begun to tweet.' And she wasn't two—still in nappies! I still tell that story, I'm ashamed to say. I oughtn't to because I know she hates it. She glares and stamps out or, even worse, she *withers* me with an icy stare. 'I wonder how many times Ruth Sykes has heard *that* story,' she says.

Well, I know I'm a fool.

Our doctor thought I was a fool all right a couple of weeks ago when I went to see him and said I had a bad heart and wanted to see a heart specialist. 'Well, well, Mrs. Thessally,' he said. 'Shall I be the judge of that? What does your daughter say?'

'I haven't told her,' I said. 'I don't want her to know. But I am sure myself and I want to see a specialist. I want to see Dr Michael Kerr.'

'He's not the man I usually use. And anyway, let's have a look at you and see if we need to use anyone.'

He examined me and said he was glad to say that we need

not use anyone. 'Perfectly normal heart it seems to me. Very good for your age. What are you—fifty? Fifty-two? No signs of trouble at all.'

But I went on and on at him. I do rather go on and on when I am not with Rosalind and then I hardly speak.

'Look, my dear—I can't send you up to Harley Street with absolutely nothing wrong with you,' he said.

'My daughter says that three-quarters of the people she sees have absolutely nothing wrong with them. It's all in their minds. This is my mind,' I said. 'I can't get it out of my mind.'

'Not sleeping?' he said.

'No.' (That was true anyway.)

'Eating?'

'Not much.'

'Something worrying you?' he said, putting his fingertips together and looking over them like an advertisement for medical insurance. Whatever use in the world would it be to tell him.

'My heart,' I said at last. 'I know I'm being a fool.' I have big blue eyes. As a matter of fact I notice that if I look at people steadily with my eyes open wide and think very honestly of what I have just said they often smile at me as if I had given pleasure. The doctor did now.

'*All* right,' he said undoing his fingertips. 'We'll give you a letter for Doctor Michael Kerr and make an appointment.'

I had it in my handbag now and I carried my handbag with great care as I went to the tube station and took the train to Oxford Circus. I had a hat on and good gloves and pearl studs in my ears though only Woolworths. I walked to Michael's nursing home calm as calm and one or two people—one of them a tall black man with a lovely smile—noticed me and I smiled back, particularly at the black man who looked kind.

I didn't feel so good in the hospital though. There was a

dreadful woman behind the reception desk. 'For Dr Kerr?' she said and looked at me as if nobody as insignificant as me had a right to see Michael. 'Are you Private?'

'No. Not really,' I said. 'But I am today.'

'I'm sorry. I don't understand.'

'I'm National Health but I didn't think it was right to see Dr Kerr on the National Health because my doctor doesn't think there's anything wrong with me. So I insisted on paying.'

Up shot her neat, pencilled eyebrows. 'I *see*,' she said (another nutter). 'Will you sit over there and wait please?'

She took my letter and opened it and smoothed it out and pinned it on a board and read it. Had she the right to do that? I must ask Rosalind.

But this was something I couldn't ask Rosalind. This was very private. Rosalind would never know. I was Private today all right.

The receptionist looked closely at me now and then with gleaming eyes, and I tried to look at other things. I looked at two doors marked MALES and FEMALES. They had been newly painted over. You could still just see where LADIES and GENTLEMEN had been. 'Males' and 'females' looked dreadful somehow. Like a zoo.

I have always dreaded and hated hospitals though Rosalind of course doesn't know. I kept looking at the notices and thinking 'This is why', though I couldn't begin to tell you what I meant.

'Would you come this way please, Mrs. Thessally?'—a nice, frizzy nurse as fat as Rosalind was when she was a baby, took me along to a waiting room and then after a minute another pure, thin Chinese nurse came out of a door and held it open and said, 'Come in, Mrs. Thessally.'

I tried to get up but was unable to move.

'This way, Mrs. Thessally.'

Still I sat.

She came across and said, 'Come along, Mrs. Thessally. Dr Kerr doesn't bite,' and laughed showing little neat teeth.

And there I was sitting in front of a desk the size of a tennis court and there behind it sat Michael who used to be always having supper with us, making funny faces at me through the kitchen window as he came round by the back door, making me drop the teapot. Weeding the garden for me, looking at his watch and saying, 'Where is the woman? Why does your daughter work so hard? Why isn't she coming to play tennis?' Two years and more Michael had been in our lives.

He looked older, grimmer and even bigger in his white coat. He had glasses—that was new—and he was reading my notes with the same drawn-down expression Rosalind has now.

'Now then,' he said, 'Mrs.—er?'

I sat.

'Mrs. *Thessally*!' he said.

And I sat looking at my hands in the good gloves. I didn't look at him any more. All that I needed to know I knew. I knew it from the horrified, upward-rising inflection of his voice. 'Mrs. *Thessally*.'

And there on the table was the note from my own doctor saying that there was nothing wrong with me but that I had insisted on seeing him and only him.

I knew there and then how terribly I had blundered. And, as with Rosalind and as never before with dear Michael, I was quite unable to speak.

A nurse creature came in and said, 'So sorry, doctor—could you just sign these,' and he did. She went out. He moved the ashtray and things on the tennis court about and cleared his throat. I could hear the small tick of the little gold clock on the shelf behind him—one of Rosalind's birthday presents.

The door burst open behind and someone called, 'Oh sorry—could I have a quick word?' and a young, carefree-

looking houseman came in with coat and stethoscope flapping.
'I say, Mrs. Arnold's doing well.'

Michael said, 'Oh yes.'

'Marvellous. She could go out today, I'd think.'

'You wouldn't think if you'd seen her last night. She collapsed.'

'What!'

'Yes. We were with her two hours.'

'Oh God. Nobody told me.'

'Then it's just as well you saw me, isn't it? I hope you
haven't told her?'

'What?'

'That she can go home today.'

'No. No.'

'She needs a good bit of care.'

The houseman vanished and the door closed.

Michael got up and went and stood looking out of the window and I got up, too.

'I'd better go,' I said. He said nothing. I got to the door and
I just had to look round at him and there was his familiar shape
made so godlike and all-powerful by its setting, larger than life,
so different from when it used to be crawling in and out of my
delphiniums setting slug-pellets and calling down curses on my
absent, over-working, non-tennis-loving daughter. Oh, however had I dared!

'Mrs. T,' he said to the distant chimney pots of Bayswater,
'this is absolutely none of my doing. I want you to know.
Nothing at all can come from me. I think that since Rosalind
clearly hasn't told you then I should. It is very much all over.'

'Female,' I said.

'What?' he said turning round.

'Female.' I was thinking of the awful notices on the door
outside. I don't know that I really knew what I was talking
about but I went on. 'She couldn't come to you, you know. I

know all the equality and things, and she does seem to be so completely a doctor. But there are still very deep conventions.'

He frowned and swung away and looked out of the window again.

'There are things a woman can't do. It's so odd—but she can't. Unless she's a man-woman. It has nothing to do with status, Women's Lib and so on. It is an instinct. Rosalind would never, never write or ring you up—unless for a death or something. She would let all you have had together go before—'

And I was gone, out of the room, out of the waiting room, out of the hospital, back into Oxford Street and my heart was beating so loud it was probably making more noise than Mrs. Arnold's who'd collapsed. I seemed to be crying, too. I walked the whole length of Oxford Street looking in all the shop-windows and what was in them all I don't know. When I got to Tottenham Court Road there was a huge cinema and I bought a ticket and went in. It seemed to be a film made for giants. The screen was so big you had to turn your head to get it all in. Enormous people came bounding out of it at you, singing at the top of their voices—happy children—nuns who became governesses and married princes and escaped from the Germans and sang and sang and sang. What curious lives people lead.

There were very few people in the cinema—an old woman in my row was fast asleep and the only other person was a greasy young man with his feet up on the seat in front who kept on getting up and going back to buy ice-creams. At the end of the film when there seemed to be some sort of a royal wedding going on I got up and went out and found it was quite dark; and I thought I would look for a cup of tea.

But I walked all down Bloomsbury Way without finding one and at the end of it I found I was standing instead on the steps of an hotel.

It was a very busy, ugly-looking hotel with a lot of students sitting about in the foyer with haversacks and the carpets very threadbare and not clean, and without knowing what on earth I was about to do I pulled the glass doors open and went in and booked a room for the night. It was six pounds in advance and I paid out of my purse, and went upstairs. I lay on the bed which was narrow and hard and looked at the ceiling. 'What is the good of it? Suffering like this for her,' I thought, and I was so tired I hadn't even taken off my shoes—'After all,' I thought, 'it isn't me.'

I must have fallen asleep then because it was suddenly very still, and from something in the silence and the blackness of the window it was obviously the middle of the night. I sat up and felt frightened and dazed for a moment, until I remembered where I was. Then I found that my thoughts had not moved on though my watch said three A.M. I was still saying, 'Why suffer so? It's not me. It's not my affair.'

I began to think in a way I had never thought before in all Rosalind's twenty-seven years. I thought of the breakfasts when she never looked in my direction; the months and months and months when she was only a hurried figure appearing for meals, retiring to her study, rushing out to see to others; of all the years when—except for Ruth Sykes and Mrs. Somebody in the road or Uncle James at Hastings, because we've so few relatives and since Jack died I've not had much interest in friends and going about—all the years when every telephone call and letter and message and enquiry and invitation has always been for her. I thought of her great big handsome face that never smiles at mine, the way she winces whenever I open my mouth, the way she so clearly despises me. Of how the only times she had ever softened at all into the Rosalind of long ago and before Jack died was when Michael was there—and she had never actually *invited* Michael, now I came to think of it. He had found his own way to us, first just dropping her at the gate, or picking her up, usually too early for her. 'Oh Lord! Sorry,' she had always said, bursting in on us as we sat together talking or Michael weaving about, looking under saucepan lids in the kitchen. 'It's all right,' he'd say. 'Your Mama and I have been enjoying ourselves.' I remembered the slight surprise I had seen in her face sometimes at this remark—the frequent quick look at me to see what I was wearing and relief if it was something she didn't think ghastly.

As the dawn began to make the sky grow pale and dirty over Bloomsbury, I realised that after all I didn't like Rosalind very much.

And as I fell asleep and the local sparrows began to tweet I said clearly and out loud, 'I have had enough. Oh, I have had enough.'

When I woke about half past nine I washed in the nasty little basin, but only my face and hands and not with any real interest and, still just in the same wool suit I had slept in, I went downstairs and I sat for a time in the foyer. There were more students about than ever, getting hot drinks in paper cups out of a machine on the wall. I felt out of place in my hat and gloves and pearl studs and rather faint in all the bustle and heat. A gingerish little girl of about eighteen or nineteen flopped down on the seat beside me and began to read a map of London. She knocked my arm. 'Oh, I'm sorry,' she said. 'Oh! Are you all right?'

'If I gave you the money,' I said, 'could you get me a cup of tea out of the machine?'

She got it and came and stood over me while I drank it, with a serious, earnest face. '*Are* you all right?' she said. 'Shall I get someone?'

She asked like a child asking someone wiser. 'No, dear,' I said. 'Thanks so much though.' A funny, ordinary little thing. The sort I might have had. The sort really you'd expect Jack and me to have had. The sort I wish—

I went out into Bloomsbury Way and into Museum Street and thought I might go to the British Museum, but the street looked very long and I didn't seem to make any great progress down it. I felt really most odd. 'I shall buy a present for that poor Mrs. Arnold,' I said to someone passing, who looked alarmed. A bus passed very close to me at some lights. I felt the wind of it. It blew my skirt against me. A taxi driver yelled at me as I just made the kerb. I thought, 'I suppose I should really be more careful and perhaps I should move on now?'

What I meant by move on was left for my subconscious to decide and I was pleased that it did, relieving me of responsibility. It directed me to Russell Square tube station and suggested that I descend. I changed, or I supposed I changed, at a couple of stations because in an unspecified time—an hour or a day—I found that the train had stopped at Putney Bridge. I was home it seemed. I got out.

Now our house is in one of those streets to the right of Putney High Street and a long walk from either Putney Bridge or the High Street Station. Even a bus doesn't take you very near. You have to get across the High Street, too, at the outset, and that isn't nothing on a Saturday morning. 'Look alive,' someone shouted as I dithered on an island. I made the further shore and trudged on. I trudged down Lacey Road and Cawnpore Terrace. On I trudged past all the plum and purple houses, row upon row with names like Quantox and East Lynne. Jack was so fond of Putney, I've never liked it much.

Perhaps I'll move. I'll just go away. Well, really, it's very silly just waiting hand and foot on a great twenty-seven-year-old woman you don't like and who doesn't like you.

The elastic went in my locknits. I've always worn locknits—briefs and loose legs are not nice on anyone my age and I like a gusset. They have the old-fashioned elastic which you can still get at the Home and Colonial, very reliable and long-last-ing whatever Rosalind says. Never before in all the years has the elastic broken and the knicker leg begun to fall.

Then I turned into our road and I saw the police car.

And I ran.

I ran past Mrs. Fergusson at number 63 though she was waving her arms about and calling, and Mrs. Atkinson next door was calling too, standing in her front garden and looking over at our house. It didn't seem like our road at all somehow. Very lively it seemed. And myself at the centre of things—my knicker leg hanging.

Then a policeman came out of our house and Michael with him, talking together. And then I knew. There and then at once I knew.

She had killed herself.

She had cried last night and come out of her room to the bathroom and got all the aspirins and killed herself. The one night I had not been on the landing waiting, the one night in all her life I had abandoned her and ceased to care. A suicide note. Michael's name on the envelope. Michael summoned to the house by the police.

And then I was lying flat on my back on my own sitting room sofa with three faces looking down at me—one I had not seen before, a policeman's, very young and sensible. One was Michael's face and one—Oh God, oh God, oh God be thanked!—was Rosalind's!

And her face was all wet and streaming all round and under the glasses and she seemed to be shouting in a fierce and furious way—yelling, yelling, 'Where were you? Where were you? How could you?'

The policeman shook hands with Michael who saw him I suppose to the door while Rosalind's maniac yelling went on. 'We thought you were dead. We thought you were dead. Under a car—'

Michael came in and got her by the shoulders and shook

her. 'Shut up at once and go and get your mother some tea.' Sobbing like a great booby she went and I sat up and Michael and I looked at each other.

'Oh Michael, I'm so sorry. I shouldn't have. I shouldn't have interfered. It was nothing to do with me. I don't know what I was thinking—'

'Hush,' he said. He sat down on a stool and took my hand and we sat quiet.

'I rang Ruth Sykes. Don't pretend you were with Ruth Sykes,' Rosalind cried hurtling in with a milk jug. 'Out of our minds with— Oh! Good heavens! Knicker *leg!*' she shrieked. She disappeared and there was a great noise of crockery crashing in the kitchen.

'Oh dear,' I said. 'She's so hopeless. I'd better go—'

'Hush,' he said.

'She rang,' he said, 'she rang this morning.'

'So I was even wrong about that.'

'No,' he said, 'she left a message. She said, "It is my mother. It is a matter of life and death". You said, "Only if it were a death".'

'Well, it wasn't,' I said.

'From the look of you at the moment it might have been.'

'Oh Michael. I'm sorry. I didn't want to make you feel you had to come running—'

'I didn't. I decided yesterday I'd come back. After you'd gone. They caught me leaving for here after she'd rung off. I was leaving when she phoned but she doesn't know that. She said, "Oh how quick you've been," when she opened the door. I felt—not commendable.'

I closed my eyes, for it was all too difficult. Then in flew Rosalind again with a tray of oddments—the old brown teapot and three stray cups. She'd taken off her glasses and her hair was falling down and her cheeks were bright pink right up close under the eyes, all roses like a child again. She really is a lovely girl.

'How could you?' she was still crying out. 'Out of my mind—You've never, ever—Whenever did you—?' and so on. Michael stretched up his other hand and took hers and said 'Hush,' again, 'Let your poor mother rest.' He said, 'I've never met such an emotional pair. If you don't both stop I'll have to call a doctor.'

'Oh don't try to be funny, Michael.' But, 'Hush,' he said again. 'Your poor Mama is going to need all the strength she's got to organise this wedding.'

And Rosalind poured a whole cup of tea all down the front of her dress and onto the floor and dropped the cup and smashed it (the last of the Worcester) and she just gazed at him.

'It beats me,' he said—but gazing back at her with such joy—'It beats me. Medically,' he said, 'genetically' (and I shall tell Ruth Sykes) 'it beats me how such an intelligent woman could produce such a stupid great child.'

The Great, Grand, Soap-Water Kick

Now and then you get to get washed. Now and then you start needing bath.

Not often. Every second year maybe.

Comes over you. Sudden. You begin think, hello now. Sun hot. You see big toe lookin out of slit boot, yellowish grey. Like ivory. On elephant.

People start moving away.

I'm tramp, see. Hobo. Drop-out. Gentleman of road. Swagman. Tramp. May have seen me on road anyday fifteen years. Push pramalong. Full gear. Got long black coat. Rags other clothes under. These not see for many years at time. Not observed. Between these and skin lining newspapers. The news is old. Keep all about me, day night. Pushing pram.

Stop. Have good burrow. Rubbish bins. Sleep park, steps cinema, back church, back seat parked car. Places people gleaming faces nothing do hand soup bread. Grand what pick up too.

Name Horsa. Daft silly woman mother. Dead all I know. Hengist dead too. Julius Caesar dead. Napoleon, Churchill, Harry Pollitt, Hitler.

Dead. Horsa sixty. Maybe seventy. Give take year. Never count up.

Until start thinking wash. Comes on like said—slow, slow.

Hot day. Wash.

Water. Wash.

Wash. Bath.

Soak. Steam.

Grand.

When boy, town called Nevermind (Mugstown, Mutstown) one good thing. Bath. Oh boy! Someone scrubbing away ears, back, toe-nails pure pink-white, shiny. Not elephant slab-grey.

SO.

Go this day down road town maybe Mugstown, Mutstown all I know. Get there over hill, through wood, up village, out village and it was raining. My rain! Deepest Paper under-linings wet as sump and soggy.

Rain turn snow. Horsa shacks up barn. Farmer looks. 'Get out there, you or I'll getmegun.'

So pushoff. Pram sticks every tenyards icy mud. Sits down splat. 'Great goodfornowt,' yells farmer. 'Firing hay bloody fags.' 'No fags,' says Horsa. 'Don't smoke, farmer,' but comes out bad: 'burble-wurble-yah-blah-splot.'

Tramp, see. Loner. No practice mouth, tongue, vocal cordage of sarcophagus.

'Bad words, filth!' yells farmer. Horsa steps on. Staggers on.

That night hedge back, bath idea begins rise. Begins simmer. Dog comes up sniffs. Howls. Runs off.

Bit high, Horsa. On high-Horsa. Time go.

What do is this. Look for house good class, empty. Look see water pipes growing up walls. Pass nowagain maybe week and watch what goes.

He goes out.

Kids out.

She goes out.

Twelve clock she back.

Maybe Fridays or somedays she always later. Maybe teatime. Maybe keepfit, yoga, coffee Mugstown friends.

So after two Friday, on Friday three in nips Horsa, first hiding pram outhouse, garden shed, find way bathroom, start in. Oh boy!

So finds this house, oh verynice. Verygoodclassperson.

Green grass of Mugstown well-cut, metal-edges. Keep grass not feeling too fullofself. Keep place. Gravel paths of mustard yellow. Windows white nets, swags like innertent. Front door smart boxsweets. Good chain for pullbell.

He goes out.

Kids go out.

She goes out. Big bag so out all Mugstown day.

Up steps goes smelly Horsa pulls chainbell.

Now if one comes, one Gran, one serving-maid, one lodger one mad aunt kept close within, says Horsa, 'Besogood. Give poor tramp glasswater,' which sings out 'Wurble-burble-splash-woosh-splot-PAH,' and Horsa screamed upon, yelled upon, scourged upon, sentonway.

But if no answer then it's the great, grand, soap-water kick. Oh boy!

SO.

Up steps—pram hidden safe below. Nobodybout. Road dead nine-thirty clock o' the morning. Nice quiet houses, nice quiet burglar-alarm red boxes just stand. Inside each, all tables, chairs, clocks, pictures sit looking each other warm-clean out of wind, rain, weather, poor sods.

Up steps smelly Horsa.

Rings bell no answer.

Ringsgain no answer.

Ringsgain turns look updown. Not living soul. Not motor car. Not bike. Only cat gatepost watch through yellow slits. Cat stands, stretches on four fat sixpences, turns round, curls upgain, goes sleep. 'Carry on Horsa. Have bath.' Like cats. Clean, interesting.

Round back house kitchen window open. Thought silly woman. Right. Water taps inside window knobbly, window small. Horsa big. Yuge. Elephant Horsa. Horsa the elephant tramp. Horsa theyear. (Hobo. Drop-out, Gentleman road. Swagman. Scrappy. Tramp. Oh boy!)

Maybe left something else open like perhaps back door?

Don't bedaft Horsa. Not your luck and you are lucky. Kick three milk bottles and one little disc. Disc says three more please. SHATTER SHATTER SHATTER. Sounds Horsa killed street greenhouses. Stand still. All well—no alarm. Change disc twenty-seven more please. Very funny joke. Try back door and back door open!

HALLELUIA HORSA! In go. Up stairs. Right in bathroom. Big lump pink soap size breadloaf. Rosepink. Falseteethpink. One, two, three, four towels big, thick, hanging on fat hot coppery pipes. Oh boy!

Horsa works taps, drops in plug. Bath (pale rosepink babypink, Mugstownpink) fills up up. Three jars salts green, yellow, lilac. Lilac favourite colour. Lielack.

Pour whole jar lielack in very hot bath and steamrise smells gardens heaven.

Offcome Horsa-boots. Hard work but off come. In time.

Off come black coat, trousers, jacket, waist-coats and let linings now unroll, telling tales of timegoneby. Plop. Dropping noises. Things falling off Horsa into deep hairy carpet. Some move fast. At a run. On various numbers of legs. They dash—not pausing to pass timeday.

All extras gone farewell. Horsa peels last newsprint and good scratch. Hasgo peeling newsprint footbottoms, but these old intelligences must soak. How is it boot in water-closet? It floats. Horsa's great big black left boot floats tasteful toilet like lobster (uncooked).

Beholdnow mirror. Amber-tinted-rose! And there (how he glares) is Horsa.

AND NOW—

Horsa mustersgether—

soap

flannels

back brushes

front brushes

sponges
nail brushes
sit there you lot
now then—
HERE COMES HORSA
In we go. Oh boy!

Maybe half-hour, maybe hour, maybe four hours. Best bath ever. Friends, let me say, let me proclaim—

PROCLAMATION
oh friends
THIS IS A REAL GOOD
BATH

When water goes off lovely boil have to twiddle butterflies. Golden butterflies, fat kind golden taps twiddle great big slab-elephant toes. OUCH! Get lost! Oh dear! No sense being burnt throwing back—brush. Mirror cracked now. Maybe yes, maybe no?

Maybe yes.

Hot water unending here—picked my house friends—hot water neverends like drizzle and mizzle and deluge and flood of wet night field-end somewhere down old green track. But HOT water, SOAPY water, on-on-ever, constant water. Just the ask. Just the twiddle.

Horsa how you spread!

How you swell in bathtub, how you rise in mound as tide washes steep pink shores.

Lotwater seems over bathroom carpet, soppingpink carpet. Pink carpet not very pink at present. Pink carpet black now where lielack water sops. Oh boy!

Horsa peers out over bathside. Horsa rests big nose-end on smoothpink bath-edge. Pink carpet not pink and now not carpet. More water-meadow. Flooded bog. Little movements in it occur and take place. Hereanthere. Some of Horsa's creepies drowning. Sad world.

Then down in again Horsa—slap, splursh. Deep, deep down in it.

So out gets last and hangs all towels allover Horsa—one round fatbelly, one round old shoulders, old soldiers, one round fine black headofhair, one last over all as second cover like tent. Tent with pink legs moves off down passage.

His room.

Kids room.

Her room.

Upagain—did Horsa turn off golden twiddleflies?—and what's this? Dad's room. Old Dad by look room full old stuff, boxes, rubbish, mess, hats. Dusgusting. Two big wardrobes.

Big fellow grandad. Wheregone not-here?

Maybe dead.

Maybe can't quite bring selves get rid old clothes.

Think nothing of it Missus. Can help there.

Big fellow grandad, same size Horsa. Good black suit, shirt, tie. Good boots too Horsa, getemonfeet. Ow! Grandad's toes not spread like Horsa's. Not gentlemanroad. Better get slit cut grandad's boots. Waitabit—here's good coat now—maybe hat. Horsa hears rushing waters.

Horsa fancies hat.

Something for dark wet ditches.

Something for howling storm.

Bowler hat oh very nifty Horsa!

Pork-pie hat no not quite.

Whatsthisnow? Tall box!

TOP HAT!

Look-in-glass, lookinglass, Horsa. Good morning sir, and how do you do? Glory!

Oh boy!

*

Down again long landing and noise waters. Ah—new boots seem not let in landing waters. Landing stages landing waters and down kitchen get knife cut slit ease toe boot. (What's new noise?)

Here's knife. Now then—whataboutit! Food. A foodstore and we have

ham,

   cheese,

      bread,

         tomato sauce,

           Suzie's sauce,

             Uncle's sauce,

               and

sweetie bics,

           pork pie (not hat)

             pork pie juice sticky crust.

Bite pie, blow flakes, out of beard PUFF!

And here is cold dark stew on cold dark shelf.

Now then find bag. (What noise again? Bell?) Nowthen Horsa takecare. Goslow. Put stew in paperbags. Don't get stew down nice new coat. What's fallen then eggs? All slippery. Crunch-crunch (Yes door bell—getopram). Dear me, long shelf full jars whole silly little cupboard comes way from wall. Red jam, orange jam, lumpy black-purple jam. Very pretty. Mind glass. Down go porridge plates unwashed off draining board, very sticky. But such tidy little Mugstown lady shoulda washed up. Now then—

Stew in pocket, sauce bottle otherpocket. Sausages where—top hat TOP HAT! O.K. Horsa, bestgonow. Somebody out there front steps. Oh! Best crawlalong under housewall. Quiet now under steps. Grab pram.

Little cough, little twitter steps above. Lady ringing doorbell up above. Coming down steps.

'Excuse me? Hello? Good morning? Is anybody there? I believe there are some old clothes for charity to be collected from this address. Excuse me sir, I wonder if you have anything for The Homeless?'

'Nothing about me, Ma'am, nothing about me.'

(Wurbly-burbly-gloshy-woshy-WAH)

'Eeeeeeeeeek!' screams good woman, 'Helphelp. Mad man!'

Nobody notices. Goodbye friend.

Cat openseye. Smiles shuts it. 'Take your ease, Horsa.' What's Homeless?

Like cats.

And Horsa passes downstreet. Top hat (TOP HAT) full of sausages and pockets full of stew. Smell, smell the lielack as Horsa passes by. Shuffle, shuffle behind pram, shuffle under freezing trees. Grandad's leftboot bitight. Disremembered knife. Never mind find something soon. Maybe sell boots for real good used ones.

Now Horsa, get moveon. Openroad now boy. Loosen necktie, maybe chuckaway. In bin. Here's bin. Might find old sandwich. Good newspaper bin anyway—keep for later, Horsa. Back normal later. Horsa smells of lilac notforever. Paper padding needed soon as nights draw down. Monthortwo, yearortwo—Horsa no good telling time—but round beginningain. Thinking bath.

Hot day. Bath.

Water. Bath.

Bath. Etcetera.

Whileyetacourse—monthtwo, yeartwo, ('Evening officer, splendid day. Wurbly, burbly, gurgly—')

Yeartwoyet.

Smellsalielack.

Top hat full sausages. TOP HAT!

Great world.

Oh boy!

The Sidmouth Letters

L ookit, Annie, Lois died.'

'What!'

'Hello? Annie? Lookit, Lois died.'

'When? What?'

'She died. Can you come round here?'

'Of course. Of course. I'll be there at once. Shorty—did you say? You didn't say—?'

'Claridges. Take a cab. Oh, and Annie—'

'Oh Shorty, Shorty!'

'Annie, will you bring a night case? I'm goin' to get you to take a train journey for me.'

So that I was in the train to Axminster, a stifling July midday, with a cheque in my pocket for a thousand pounds and a bag by my side with nightdress and toothbrush in it and my feet on the seat opposite saying, 'No! Lois dead. Dead!'

Yesterday I'd talked all day to her. Drunk as she was we had talked all day. All the way down the Portsmouth Road nearly to Winchester and back, in the hired Mercedes, Shorty driving, oblivious of her with his high-pitched literary friend beside him.

Lois dead.

And I doing Shorty's dirty work.

Yesterday if anyone had told me that I would ever work for Shorty I'd not have believed it.

Nor was it for any love of Lois. Not *love* of Lois. Not even friendship for Lois. I'd hardly known her.

But Lois dead! I lit a cigarette and thought.

I first met Shorty Shenfold years and years ago when I was his student doing a year's course with him on the English Novel at a small university in the Middle West. It was he who had chosen me for the scholarship, gone in to my qualifications with the greatest thoroughness, almost asking—I believe he did ask—for my English birth certificate, my mother's maiden name and the name of even my kindergarten through to my Cambridge College before deciding on me.

He was impressive. He was not I think called Shorty because of his enormous size—no one got affectionate about Shorty—but because of his predilection for the short: short story, short polemic, short but searching criticism, short shrift. Even for an American his style of lecturing was monumentally dull, but even for an American his accuracy and exhaustiveness were remarkable. His slim books which kept appearing at respectable intervals in better and better bindings and at higher and higher prices, while they read like railway timetables, were magnificently thorough. Not a scholar could fault them. Soon they stopped trying. Every conscientious university in the States bought a copy and each was translated excellently into German—rather more curiously into French. Soon they could be seen on the most hallowed shelves in the world where they were taken out and used for reference in academic emergencies about every ten or fifteen years.

Shorty also became known for a side-line: the occasional short controversial piece about the great which he produced for one or other of the more popular literary papers—clever, sharp, always short—and though not exactly scandalous or irresponsible, with the tang of something rather nasty about it. Shorty was, I think, the first to consider Dorothy Wordsworth as anything more than her brother's beloved sister. Long before Anthony Burgess he enthusiastically launched into the syphilitic overtones in the life of Shakespeare. It was said that he had much to suggest, after the fifty years of family grace were up, about Kipling, and his piece on how far Keats had got with Fanny Brawne was discussed for many a furious week in *The Times Literary Supplement*, ensuring that every word of it was widely read. Shorty was a good scholar but his pastimes and tactics were a hyena's.

His looks however were a bull's—a bull's neck, a bull's crinkly chunk of hair, a bull's manners and a bull's dangerousness, and what in the world made me submit to him, when I was hardly twenty years old, a piece of my own unsolicited work about Jane Austen, God alone knows. It was a short piece which in my innocence I had thought might interest him about Jane Austen's only—and putative—love affair on a seaside holiday on the Dorset-Devon coast, the one or two (I forget now) contemporary hints of it and a history of the later references and theories. The piece established nothing new at all about 'this shadowy lover', but I think it was the first time the facts and allusions had been seriously set out.

It was a short report—the family summer holiday 'by some sea-side,' probably at Sidmouth, after the loss of the loved childhood home, Jane Austen's anxiety about her coming life in Bath, and the first suggestions that she felt she was growing out of her youth. Then the meeting with the delightful man 'said to be a clergyman' (some said a sailor, some a doctor), thought even by her formidable sister to have 'been worthy of Jane.' Then the man's sudden departure, 'called away on family business', and three weeks later the roundabout, astonishing news of his death. I examined all of it as best I could, then the return of the family to Bath and the final move to Chawton; Jane Austen's eventual new strength there after three years of utter silence; her increased interest in and love for her young nephews and nieces as they grew up, the desk in the window of the unremarkable sitting room looking out at the unremarkable view; the procession of the five great books, the new spectacular sympathy and good sense about love which have ever since comforted the world.

I called the thing something too pompous—*Jane Austen— Love and Privacy*—I dare say, and it was no doubt as bad and unscholarly as the title. I lost it long ago so I can't tell. But, no doubt through Shenfold's training, I believe it was thorough and properly set out, and when he handed it back to me with only a tick and 'interesting' on it and passed me out with a very poor grade at the end of my year and hardly—though I was his own particular choice of student from England—hardly a goodbye, I was very disappointed.

I was surprised, therefore, about a year later, to read under the title *Jane Austen at Sidmouth* and over his name, my article word for word with just the added hint that the lover's disappearance was a little mysterious, more of a getaway than a death. Don't ask me how this was done, but the suggestion was certainly there and his, as the rest of the work was undoubtedly mine.

I watched Shorty's flight up the ladder with some interest after that. I even met him again once or twice in England over the years. The first time was by chance outside the London Library. It was about five years after his piece on the Sidmouth lover, but he recognised me and I think would have pretended not to had I not called out 'Oh!'

He invited me to his flat at Brook Street—a party that same evening—where Fellows of All Souls put their fingertips together and stared into space, and several lady novelists looked out of windows.

He was as ebullient as ever—the perfect host, eyes everywhere. Food, drink, waiters all superb. His clothes—never a whiter shirt, a suit more English—must have cost a bomb and had pretty clearly not been paid for out of his grants and scholarships and awards, though even when I first knew him his powers of negotiating an award would have been of use to any multi-national oil company. All—I heard from one of the lady novelists—had been provided by a series of wives.

Now at first looking at Shorty one was a bit uncertain about wives. It was not that he looked homosexual—he had a big brown juicy glare for any woman who came his way—but he had the homosexual's awareness of himself and his image that does not go with conventional sexual diversion. His big, slow, lumbering frame making its way across the Ritz or Claridges— I was invited to meet him there now and then after he had begun to hear of my books—spoke of a spiffing physical and mental health, a supreme self-confidence, but not what my cousin Enid calls, 'the life upstairs.' For to Shorty—so they said in *Private Eye* and I am sure to his delight, 'Excitement means the pen.'

There must have been a certain type of woman who responded to him, however, because several of them married him. I met one in Brook Street, then there was a second—I saw her pictures in the evening papers sometimes—and then there was Lois. All three were much the same—tall, dreamy, bony, American good-looking with a tiny bewildered voice and a gigantic bank balance. Women who had the air of people needing a good rest. How he got hold of them nobody knows but it was surmised by the same private and industrious bludgeoning he accorded the short story or the sonnet. A short story or a sonnet bludgeoned by Shorty looked as if it needed a good rest, too, and usually got one.

One Thursday, two days before our outing to Chawton down the Portsmouth Road and three days before my mission with the thousand pound cheque, I had met Shorty again after another long interval. It was a summer afternoon meeting of the Royal Society of Literature in Hyde Park Gate with all the trees blowing leaves along the Bayswater Road and the clink of teacups on the terrace. There he stood—not aged a bit—a great block of a man still, perhaps slightly heavier, perhaps a shade more authoritative if that were possible. He towered above Lord Butler. Lord Snow became a flake. His bold brown eyes stuck out, the brains almost bursting from the bull's forehead. When he spoke it was still with the surprising coarse, slow snarl so different from the rest of him that it seemed an affectation.

Near him, looking out over the balustrade, hung Lois, more raddled than I remembered but bird-boned, huge-eyed, expensive still. Her fingers were knobbed with rings, her old frail feet were in crocodileskin, like prickly silk. As I saw her she turned and began to walk towards the lecture room where people were beginning to settle on the canvas chairs. I followed and said, 'Lois.'

She said, 'Well, hi,' and slid to the floor in the path of the Duchess of Kent. (For it was a big occasion and prizes were being handed out.)

'I'm pissed,' said Lois loud and clear as the Duchess stepped over her, and Shorty and I got her back to Claridges where we called a doctor, had a bit of a battle with the gin bottle and eventually put her to bed.

Shorty managed splendidly. Not even whilst holding his poor wife's head in Hyde Park Gate—I at the other end with the crocodile shoes—did he lose his dignity, and afterwards he rang me up and in the same grating, metallic voice as of old asked me if I would go out with them on Saturday. Yep—she was quite better. Yep—it happened often. It was an illness, poor Lois. He preferred to treat it as an illness. Now then. Lois had especially asked for me to go. Also, I would be useful, Lois not being able to be left at home. We would be going with a very famous man—a literary journalist often to be seen on the box. Yep—that's the man. And lookit—I knew the guy he was sure. He suspected that I knew all the big names now lookit (and here I did just wonder if I felt the slightest pause), we would be going to Chawton, near Winchester. To photograph some handwriting. Ya. Yep. Thassit. Jane Austen's cottage. And we'd have lunch somewhere.

I had not the least wish in the world to go. I felt that in some mysterious way Shorty Shenfold was haunting me. Why, of all the people I had met in my life, was it Shenfold who kept turning up? And what had happened to all the dear old friends, the ones who in novels are suddenly there in the street beside you, dancing to the music of time? Why for me was there only unspeakable Shenfold? And why could I never say no?

The photographic session was to be at the Chawton cottage on the Saturday morning before it was open to the public—a pre-arranged and rather stately affair. A senior member of the Jane Austen Society was in attendance. We were warmly welcomed and Lois and I allowed to watch the whole ceremony. I was allowed to hold the MSS, touch the old writing paper, smell it, look close at the lovely, diamond-sharp, unmistakable hand.

Lois was soon bored and wandered away into the living room, and I heard the clatter of an Austen-type vegetable dish displayed on the Austen-type dining table and thought I'd better go after her.

She stood by the writing desk in the window drawing an old woman's finger over the old blotched wood. Only the hands showed her to be twenty years older than Shorty—her figure was ageless, American East Coast, face fragile, cherished, painted; she looked out at the Chawton pub across the village street and blinked her wet blue eyes. She said, 'So she jus' sat here, did she? Writin' away?'

I said that this was what was said.

'So she looked right in at the pub, did she?'

I said that I supposed so. It was an old pub. The cottage

itself had once been a pub, but the pub across the road was quite old too. She might have sat at an angle, I said, facing the pond that used to be over towards what was the car park now—on the right.

'The pond or the pub,' said Lois. 'Like me, it's the pond or the pub.'

'Not with Jane Austen,' I said. 'She never despaired.'

'Don't they say she sat in a hood? Right over her face? Near the end? When her face—her terrible discoloured face . . .?'

I said that I had read about that somewhere. It had been a caul not a hood.

'The pond or the pub in a caul. Jesus,' said Lois. 'Poor bitch. Y'know, Annie, I wonder what she really felt?'

She took a scent bottle out of her bag and swigged at it.

'She never met anyone like me, did she? Don't seem to me she knew a lot. I bet she'd never even looked inside that pub.'

She began to cry.

'Someone ought a write a book about me,' she said, 'not about this bitch. About me. Dare say they will. Some hard-mouthed boring bitch. Some frienda Shorty. Shorty likes a hard-mouthed bitch. Write her up. Lot this bitch knew—'

Shorty and the literary editor were coming towards the living room. Before they had seen us I heard the literary editor say in the little connecting lobby, 'My dear—this is going to be *utterly* exciting.'

Then we got Lois back into the Mercedes and to London. She was not well enough for luncheon in Hampshire and nobody seemed to mind except me—I was hungry. Shorty and the literary young man had much to say to each other in the front of the car and I spent the mercifully fast journey in the back trying to command the scent bottle. It was a long afternoon. The following morning Shorty rang to say Lois was dead.

I had been afraid that when I got to Claridges I would not be able to stand him—or anything. I expected possessions in heaps, splayed suitcases (she had been hideously untidy), even twisted sheets—the Manager with hooded eyes, Shorty calm as ever but ashen, and a smell—her scent, her gin, her cigarettes, her hectic presence still about.

It was almost as unnerving to meet with no shadow or breath of a memory of her. Through the door of the suite leading to the bedroom I saw twin beds at a distance from each other under splendid dark quilts. The flowers were fresh, cupboards all firmly closed, an ice bucket and polished glasses on a tray. The *Observer* neatly folded.

Shorty, dressed for the city though in rather an unusually dark tie, opened the door. He was in great command. I saw as he kissed me—the kiss for funerals, excusable now if never again—that he had carefully considered the coming interview. Everything was ready in his head, another part of his work dealt with and completed. 1.—he had thought—Ring Annie. 2. Look up trains for Axminster. 3. Notes for Annie, payment etc., 4. Kiss on arrival.

'She died in the night. It had been expected,' he said. 'Sit down. Have a dr—coffee?'

'I'm very sorry, Shorty,' I said when the coffee had come.

He said, 'It was bad, but quick.'

'Quick? I thought perhaps years.'

'Oh—she'd been—ill—for years. But quick last night. They dealt with it very well here. Very well. Better at night of course. Hotel. It's gotta cost somethin'—'

I shut my eyes.

'Stretcher. Ambulance. Christ.'

'Yes.'

'Now of course I get the rough stuff. Cables. Funerals.'

'Haven't you *sent* cables?'

'Oh ya. Yep. Comin' right over. Big family. New York.

Comin' here. There's goin' to be big troubles with the will. I've had a lot to do there.' He looked quickly at me, bewildered and I saw in him the confusion I had felt yesterday. He was thinking, 'Why her? Why does she keep cropping up? Why do I tell her?'

'Was Lois—did Lois have children?'

'Nope. Give thanks. Only child, too. Said she'd always wanted a sister. You'd not have thought, to look—

'Lookit,' he said, 'could you do somethin' for me? I don't want journalists in on this, so I ask you.'

I thought of the tick and 'interesting' and the poor degree he had given me—his scant goodbye. Then of *Jane Austen at Sidmouth*. But then of the brave crocodile shoes, the fragile old feet, the trembling old hand on the Austen dinner service. She had wanted a sister. I said, 'Anything I can.'

He sat down at the desk and became at once the professor. He moved papers about, sighed, touched a pen, a pile of notes. He straightened them. His bulging eyes looked only down.

'It is right up your street, Annie, if I remember. Something that cropped up. I'll let you in on it. I've let a newspaper in on it—that chap yesterday who talks on the box—but only up to a point. They're paying expenses so you can make 'em high. The American and European rights are about fixed up. I've already spat it at my publisher.'

'What is it?'

'Well, it's Jane Austen. Jane Austen again. I've been doing a bit of work lately. Lois—Lois and I—we spent a bit of time down in Sidmouth, Devon. Teignmouth, Lyme, Starcross, Portsmouth—those places. We found—lookit, Annie, this is just between ourselves and naturally you gonna get paid—we found a link with Sidmouth. The Sidmouth holiday. 1801. The Sidmouth lover.'

'A link?'

'Yes.' The quick, uneasy look again as if there were something more to be said, something missing he felt he should know. 'There's a link. There's still a link. Near Sidmouth. The three silent years. The "shadowy lover".'

'You have found that he existed?'

'We have found—' said Shorty Shenfold—he spread great big pink pads of hands on the desk and leaned back. His huge face looked hot. After the rigours of the night he had shaved perfectly, his teeth shone. Tie, collar, hair, everything were immaculate but he seemed sweaty. 'There is every probability,' he said, 'that there are several letters by Jane Austen to the lover still in Devonshire and for sale.'

I said nothing and he went on, 'For sale today. At an address I'll give you, Annie. I've arranged to meet the woman at three o'clock and to pay a thousand pounds. I've worked up to this for more than a year—longer. Then the whole thing gels in a week. It had to be this week.'

'Gels?'

'I got an answer—a favourable answer—from the woman who looks after the—owner of the letters. In the end I got her to say the owner—it's her grandmother—would see me. She says there is a small bundle of Jane Austen's letters—they've always been called that—her grandmother keeps in some box. The grandmother is the great granddaughter of the woman who kept the Sidmouth—or whatever it was—lodging-house. Presumably they were letters from Austen sent to the lover to wait his return. He died and they were never delivered. The bundle is only known within the family. It's become some sort of talisman—household god.'

'If they're unopened,' I said, 'how do you know they're not a laundry list?'

'Yep. It's a risk. But worth it. The money is—was—not all that important. Get it paid over today—it's predated—and we'll not have to put it in the estate. Lois was loaded.

'So would you go, Annie? It's not Sidmouth any more. It's

Charmouth—just down the coast. Probably why they've not been discovered—dead-an-alive place. Worse than the rest, which is pushin' it. You can see Lyme from there. It's Austen heartland. Maybe you'll like it. All you do is explain why I can't be there myself. I'll give you a letter. I'll telephone, too, if it's possible to get a moment.'

'Do you want me to read them?'

For the first and only time I felt sorry for Shorty. He took almost half a minute to reply. The look came again—maybe if he had not just passed the night he had passed he would have been able to hide it, but he looked quickly, sharply at me as if he were afraid. Afraid that there were something that for once in its career his splendid computer's brain had missed. And there was something else that made me for that quick moment like him—he was genuinely, genuinely longing to see the bundle, to be the first to hold the beautiful, live writing in his hand.

Yet if they were nothing? A laundry list?

A thousand pounds was from today going to be a thousand pounds. Lois's tired old claws would be writing no more cheques.

'Well, you'd better look at them,' he said at length. 'Read them. They'll be all right. I'm pretty sure. They say they've never been read. Don't sound so likely, but you never know. Sound a queer lot, this family.'

'Get back tonight if you can. Bring them here. Take a taxi soon as you get back to Waterloo. Here's twenty pounds in case you have to stay over, but try to get back. There'll be other pay later of course.'

'I shan't need paying, Shorty.'

He looked at me with utter hatred because I did not need paying and because I was going to see the letters—and again the troubled look. A ripple of pure annoyance went across the big bumpy forehead, not a thought, nor even quite a feeling; a sort of intuitive shadow that there was something he had missed, something he should have spotted all those years ago when he had looked in to my background before giving me the scholarship to his college in America; when I had written my piece on *Love and Privacy*.

Which there was. He had forgotten that on my application form it had said where I was born and had lived with my family for twenty years. In 'Austen heartland'. At Sidmouth.

Enid saw me through the window before I even rang the bell and I saw her purse up her lips in the old way as she made for the door. She said, 'Well, Annie,' mouth still tight. There was a fan of lines round her mouth now. She had always pursed her lips when she was trying not to show excitement. It had left a map.

She had grown fatter. Her hair was grey but very neatly permed and set. She wore a home-made linen dress over an acreage of bust. Pearl earrings and a brooch. Presumably all for Shenfold.

'We expected an American professor and we get you. Well Annie. It's a very long time.'

'Did he telephone?'

'Who? Telephone? Oh—no. This is some mad American professor trying to offer us a fortune for Gran's bundle.'

'He said he'd try to telephone.'

'You know him? Goodness, Annie, you're not something to do with it? Anyway, come in.'

The tremendous noise of a racing commentary at full throttle came through the closed sitting room door. 'Come in the kitchen,' she said. 'I'll make tea. I'm not waiting for this scrounger any longer.'

'Is Auntie—?'

'In the sitting room. Sleeps there too now. She feels the cold. And the telly's in there. I never bother with it.'

'Feels the cold *today*!'

'Yes. You look hot, old Annie. D'you want to go and wash? Did you come by car?'

'No. Train and bus. The train was late. And boiling.'

I saw her think that I had no car and that I probably hadn't much of a life otherwise. No proper job, no marriage, only four or five novels in goodness knows how many years. Bits of reviewing. Something insignificant and part-time for the British Council. And after such a good start. Cambridge, then America. She, Enid, had left school at sixteen. She touched her pearls and said, 'We liked your last book. Well, we've liked them all, Gran and I. Why don't you write more? Something easy and rambly. People round here like them very much you know. They often try and get them out of the library, but it takes so long.'

'I'm slow too.'

'You usen't to be. I'm sure you could write a big book. D'you remember what a lot you used to write when we were little? Uncle couldn't keep you in notebooks.'

'Those were the days. Whizzing along with nothing to say. And no problems.'

'Problems?' Her eyes asked me to tell her my problems and then looked away with understanding that they were mine. I thought how much I liked my cousin and had always liked her. I wondered why I didn't come down here often—her comforting goodness, this quiet house, sideways to the sea in the seaside garden, the same french doors still open on to the unpainted, bleached balcony where we had poured sand out of our shoes before meals when I had been over to stay as a child. The sound of the sea loud and lively down the lane.

'No—I mean writing problems. There were none then. At ten you just go on and on. It's not like later. It's fuss, fuss, later—a few pages. Then disgust. Looking out of the window, up at the soles of all the feet going by.'

'*Up* at the feet! Good gracious, it's time you were down

here, Annie. Whyever don't you come back? For a good long time? We're very quiet. I'm rather—' she put out cups and saucers on a trolley with the greatest appearance of self-sufficiency and produced a huge home-made cake from a tin, 'I'm rather lonely I suppose really. Gran's a jolly good laugh of course.'

'She must be ninety,' I said.

'She's ninety-six.'

'Is she well?'

'She's very well. The memory comes and goes a bit. Patchy you know. Like a loose connection. But yes, she's very well. Why don't you come back? Home and family and all that. After all, they meant a lot to our own famous loose connection didn't they? Her family never stopped her from writing books—she lived for them, didn't she? Made all the jam.' I noticed Enid's great big bossy jaw again. I said, 'The Austens weren't just any family,' and felt penitent at once when she blushed, hurt.

'Neither are we just any family. The Austens were very clever—Oxford and Cambridge and Admirals and so on—but nothing out of the way socially. The story goes that to meet them they were nothing out of the way at all.'

I said, 'You're like the Irish, still going on about a hundred and fifty years ago. The Austen thing's a legend, Enid. Thank goodness we've always kept it to ourselves and never got shown up about it. It's nonsense. We've all been told for generations that Jane Austen's lover once put up at some old auntie's boarding house. There are one or two anecdotes and the famous unopened bundle. Years ago someone should have written a monograph. It's all probably rubbish.'

'I always thought you would write a monograph.'

'I did write something once. If anyone had taken any notice of it I suppose I'd have written more. I didn't put anything in it that was family gossip though.'

'What?'

'I gave it to my American professor. The year I was out there. I hoped he'd ask to talk about it but he just put a tick and said "interesting".'

'Well, it was quite good of him to do that if you put nothing new in it.'

'I didn't know anything new. Nothing definite. Just yarns. "Jane Austen was so happy"—that stuff.'

'"Merry",' said Enid, 'not happy. They always said merry. That's what I was brought up on. "Miss Austen and Miss Jane Austen called and Miss Jane Austen was merry."'

'Maybe she'd been at the bottle.'

'Annie!'

'There you go,' I said. 'Jane-worship. And I'll bet you haven't read one of the novels in years.'

'Jane Austen at the bottle! She never had any experience of that sort of person.'

I thought of Lois and said, 'Then she was extremely fortunate.'

'She was sensible about misfortune,' said Enid. 'She was thankful for compensations. She was a respectable woman and at a guess I'd say she was very sensible about all the excesses— love and passion and that sort of thing. It's one of the reasons I would—yes, I don't care what we've always said—I would like to read what's in Gran's bundle.'

'Which is why you've decided to sell it to Shorty Shenfold?'

'I didn't decide. He pestered away—you never saw such letters he wrote. Solid paragraphs. Bright blue type and paper half an inch thick.'

'Enid, you don't *need* the money.'

'No. But he sounds respectable. Scholarly. He wrote from Claridges. And he seems to think it is very important. Well, haven't we a duty when you think about it to read what's in the packet? But I certainly hadn't made up my mind.'

'He told me,' I said, 'that you had. And the sale was as good as made.'

'Rubbish. I've hardly mentioned it to Gran yet. I said he could come down and see her if he liked. Anyway, it seems to me that you must have a lot to do with this yourself.'

'You won't believe it, but he hasn't the faintest idea I even know you.'

'You mean,' said Enid, looking down her nose as she had done when telling me that the Austens were nothing socially out of the way, 'you mean that he doesn't know that we are *cousins*!'

She pushed the trolley ahead of us in to the sitting room where two exhausted horses were neck and neck and the commentator on the verge of apoplexy. A huddled person pounded the arms of its chair with small blotchy brown claws. The heavy curtains were drawn across the window for a better appreciation of Sandown Park and a huge fire roared in the grate. My great aunt, Enid's great grandmother, was surrounded by her tools and weapons—a couple of walking sticks, a long picker, several rugs, a box of sweets and a huge black handbag bulging like some old ship come home from the wars. Its ancient cracked sides and loose old tortoiseshell handles brought such a rush of memory I had to sit down— (Annie, here blow your nose. Stop crying, Annie, here's a Mars bar. No need to run for plasters, Enid, here's my bag. Yes, *and* iodine.) I sat down quickly close to her.

'Here's Annie, Gran.'

'Good,' said my great aunt, 'I'd five to one on that one.' She wrote something in a notebook. 'Did well in the Oaks,' she told me looking across. 'What's this then? The American professor?'

'No—it's Annie. The professor isn't coming. His wife died.'

'Why should Annie come then? She looks poorly. Smokes

too much. Can't think what she wants with London. Writing those books.'

'She's come about your bundle.'

'Why can't she write her books down here, that's what I want to know,' said Auntie and looked deep in the black bag. She came up with a queer-looking packet of sweets. 'D'you want a humbug, Annie?'

'No thanks, Auntie.'

'That professor sounds a humbug. What d'you want to be working for a humbug for? You could have been a professor yourself if you'd wanted. Could have been anything. I often tell Enid, Annie was the clever one. Could have been anything. She used to write that easy. She might have been writing really well-known books by now, full of descriptions.'

'Annie's not exactly working for him—'

'I dare say she writes *clever* books. Though I've never agreed with that either—for all the *Times Littery Whatsit*. They can't be that clever, I said to Enid, or I wouldn't understand them. Turn the sound down, Annie dear, till the next race. I can't do with him splurging and yattering.'

I turned it down and the quiet was a blessing.

'Jane Austen didn't leave home,' said Auntie chewing a humbug and watching the commentator's silent agitations. 'Never too grand to go and stay with her relations. That's the tale we were always told anyway.'

'There were plenty of them,' I said. 'Everyone could take turn and turn about. Nowadays—'

'What's nowadays?' said my great aunt. 'I've seen a good deal of nowadays and it's never any different. What's this professor after? Does he want to marry you?'

'*No!*'

'All right. I've never thought it much mattered anyway. Enid never married—never wanted to. She's all right. I married and I never stopped wishing I hadn't. Mind, Annie should have married. She never tells us anything. I tell her it doesn't matter. She'll always be Annie.

'I always liked Annie,' she said to Enid. 'I wonder what happened to her? Why don't she ever come and see us?'

'She's here, Gran.'

'This?' She looked at me. 'No, this young woman is an American professor.'

'It's Annie.'

'Annie was always my favourite,' she told me. 'Here. Come here.' She jerked her wispy head backwards a couple of times for me to come closer. She looked like a cunning old bookie. 'Enid's a good woman,' she said. 'We get on and she's a very good girl to me, but Annie—oh Annie was the clever one. It's a tragedy about Annie. I don't know who it was or what went wrong. All she does is write these very good books. Books that get wonderful mentions. The kind you'd never see in any shops—'

'Gran!'

'I'm leaving the money to Enid,' said Auntie, 'and I'm leaving the letters to Annie.'

'Gran, this is what Annie's here for. The professor's sent her with some huge cheque—a thousand pounds. I told you about it.'

'I never agreed.'

'No. I know you didn't. Neither did I. I never said we'd sell the things but—'

'I should hope not. They've been in this family since Lizzie's mother's gran.' She stretched out with the long picker and twitched the television into life. The sound of the next race shook the room. A board stating odds filled the screen. Gran said, 'Anyway, a thousand's under-priced.'

When the race was over—it seemed again to have been to her advantage—she said, 'Trying to get them cheap. American professor!'

I said, 'Auntie, it's very good of you. It would be wonderful to have the letters.'

'Not to sell, mind. We've never sold them. It's a tradition. And it's a tradition we've never looked at them.'

'No. Of course not.'

'They're not to be read.'

'Gran,' said Enid, 'Annie might take advice about that. You know it may be the time has come—'

'No. No. They're not to be read. It says on the packet who they're for. He never came for them. You don't read other folk's letters. Postcards maybe.'

'Auntie—'

'It says who they're for on the envelopes.'

'Then you've looked?'

She began to show the bag again.

'Gran, have you opened the bundle?'

'I've read the fronts of the envelopes, that's all,' and she brought out a very small and thin paper package wrapped in oilskin.

'It's been wrapped in oilskin since long since. Like a baccy pouch. Ever since Lizzie's mother's gran. Nobody came for it. Mind you she moved soon after, Lizzie's mother's gran. She moved here from Sidmouth. She kept it on her mantelpiece a long while, troubled about it. Lizzie's mother grew up with it. She always thought of it as something to do with the sea, being in oilskin.'

I said, 'Maybe they were written to a sailor. Some people say the young man was a sailor. Jane Austen loved sailors,'— and was surprised by a shining hard look, steady and shrewd from under Auntie's eyebrows. My heart began to beat fast. I said, 'It's terribly hot in here. I'm sorry. Look I must go outside,' and she said, 'Well here then, Annie,' and tossed the little packet in to my lap. 'It's yours by rights,' she said. 'I've always felt it. That American can do without it. Have it now. Why wait till I'm dead? It's yours, Annie, being book-ish.'

'Will you come back, Annie?'

Enid and I were on the verandah. I was writing to Shorty—very fast to catch the next post—saying that it had all been a mistake. The letters if they still existed were not for sale. They had been given to a relative and—lost track of. He might like to come and talk about it to the family but I felt it was too late.

'You are writing fast. Like old times.'

I said I was just enclosing the cheque, saying it was all off and that if he liked—did she mind?—that he could come down and see for himself.

'Yes of course,' she said. 'There's probably nothing in the packet you can still read anyway. Poor Gran. And poor Annie! It's not much of an inheritance. All this secrecy and I'll bet it's a hoax. I mean she'd have got them back, wouldn't she—Jane Austen? She'd have moved heaven? Her love letters?'

'You'd think so,' I said. 'It depends what sort of a state she was in. We can't tell—there was a family silence about it. We won't find the truth about that now.'

'If they are Jane Austen's letters, Annie, will they—would they—honestly mean anything much?'

'They would be a terrific find,' I said.

'Would they?'

'Yes. Written when she was in love. The critics would go wild. Her sister burned everything to do with that time you know. There's not a letter, not a scratch of Jane Austen's pen for three years. We don't even know the man's name. It was Jane Austen's wish—so it's said. She wanted no speculation. No sharing.'

'But d'you think anyone—the sister, us—has the right to destroy—?'

'Cassandra knew her sister.'

'She didn't know her sister was a—well, a genius. She didn't know how famous she was going to be.'

I said I didn't think that would have made the least difference.

Enid came to the gate with me and stood leaning on it. The honeysuckle hedge beside her smelled of nutmeg. Behind her the verandah doors stood open and beyond them and within could be heard the fanfare announcing the television evening news, full strength for Auntie.

'I wish you were nearer, Annie.'

'I wish I were, too. I've loved today. It's just that in London there's more chance—oh, of meeting up with old friends I suppose.'

'A melancholy situation. Depending on people from the past.'

I said, 'Could I come down in the autumn—for a long time, three weeks or so?' and she looked so thrilled that I at once felt hostile, manipulated. I said, 'Well anyway a fortnight,' hating myself. The old guilt was back, the old problem, the hostility, the fight between love and privacy.

Enid blew her nose very thoroughly and said, 'There's a good little hairdresser down here, too. You could get your hair done properly. And there's quite a lot of Bridge.'

She touched the pearls.

When she had gone in I walked to the end of the lane, but then I turned left to the sea instead of right to the bus-stop which would direct me somewhere or other for the night. I walked along the sands, weaving through the sandcastles and spades, the families gathered together in clumps on rugs, over splendid drains and moats and driftwood bridges, over and beyond the spatter of paper cups and tin cans spilling from litter bins, beyond the tussocks of grey-green grass, towards the sand hills and the cliffs.

The sand hills were nearly empty now—people were dragging back to their high tea, tired and sandy and hot. I sat looking at the sea as it tilted slowly from the sun. The ripples thickened and the waves seemed to grow slow, soften, breathe more deep. I opened the old seaweed envelope and read the two envelopes within, the unmistakable handwriting clearer even than yesterday's at Chawton. I opened each envelope and read the signature which was as expected and then I burned both letters and both envelopes with my cigarette lighter.

Then I sat for goodness knows how long, but the sun was nearly gone by the time I came back to myself, so I think it must have been several hours. I took the half-handful of ash down to the water's edge and paddled a fairway out and scattered it. Jane Austen had very much liked Charmouth Bay. 'The happiest spot,' she said, 'for watching the flow of the tide, for sitting in unwearied contemplation.' I let a very small wisp of her melt into it.

That night I fell asleep in a bed-and-breakfast place at Sidmouth utterly certain that I had done right. I woke in the night and I still felt certain. And I have not changed my mind. I have felt very happy ever since that I of all people have had the chance of paying back a little of a great debt.

I haven't seen Shorty again. He didn't answer my letter, though he did go down to Charmouth to try his luck with Auntie. Enid said it was not a success. He got nowhere, Auntie insisting that he was a member of the C.I.A. or the President of the United States for whom it seems she has little time.

Nor has he written to me, but he is alive and well, for last Christmas, when I was down with Enid, she suddenly spotted him in an old *Tatler* and *Queen*. She sat upright and said 'Gracious!'—and there he was, unchanged, after all these years. He was in Dublin, lecturing on something unpleasant he had discovered about Yeats, and beside him, in the glorious parkland surrounding her house, was a gaunt and beautiful American-Irish widow.

Shenfold looked splendid—hair a thought longer, just a touch of grey, still vigorous, vibrant, an Olympian. Good for another thirty years.

'He's attractive,' said Enid. 'Powerful. You can see he's never missed a thing. Doesn't the woman look tired?'

A Spot of Gothic

I was whizzing along the road out of Wensleydale through Low Thwaite beyond Naresby when I suddenly saw a woman at her cottage gate, waving at me gently like an old friend. In a lonely dale this is not very surprising, as I had found out. Several times I have met someone at a lane end flapping a letter that has missed the post in Kirby Thore or Hawes. 'It's me sister's birthday tomorrow. I near forgot' or 'It's the bill fort telephone. We'll be cut off next thing.' The curious thing about this figure, so still and watchful, was that it was standing there waving to me in the middle of the night.

It was full moon. I had been out to dinner at Mealbeck. I had only been living in the North for two months and for one month alone. I had joined my husband near Catterick camp the minute he had found us a house, which was only a few days before he found that the regiment was being posted to Hong Kong. The house he had found was beautiful, old and tall in an old garden, on the edge of a village on the edge of the fell. It was comfortable and dark with a flagged floor and old furniture. Roses and honeysuckle were nearly strangling black hedges of neglected yew. There was nice work to be done.

It was the best army house we had ever found. The posting to Hong Kong promised to be a short one. I had been there before and hated it—I hate crowded places—and I decided to stay behind alone.

He said, 'But you will be alone, mind. The camp is a good way off and most people will have gone with us. It's the North.

You'll make no friends. They take ten years to do more than wag their heads at you in the street up here. Now, are you sure?'

I said I was and I stayed and found that he was quite wrong. Within days, almost within hours of my miserable drive home from Darlington Station to see him off, I found that I was behaving as if I'd always known the people here and they were doing the same to me. I got home from the station and stopped the car outside my beautiful front door and sat still, thinking, 'He has gone again. Again he has gone. What a marriage. Always alone. Shall I forget his face again? Like last time? Shall I begin to brood? Over-eat? Drink by myself in the evenings—rather more every evening? Shall I start tramping about the lanes pretending I like long walks?' I sat there thinking and a great truculent female head with glaring eyes stuck itself through the car window.

'D'you want some *beans*?'

'Oh!'

'Some *beans*? Stick beans?'

'Oh I don't—? Can you spare—?'

'Beans, beans. Masses of beans. They're growin' out of me ears. Grand beans. Up to you.'

'I'd love some beans.'

A sheaf of them was dumped on the seat beside me. 'There's plenty more. You've just to say. So 'e's off then? The Captain?'

'Yes.'

'Well, yer not to fret. There's always a cup of tea at our place. Come rount back but wear yer wellies or you'll get in a slather int yard.'

In the post office they asked kindly for news. Of how I was settling, of where I had come from. The vicar called. A man in a Land Rover with a kind face—the doctor—waved his hat. A woman in the ironmonger's buying paraffin in gloves and a hat invited me to tea in a farmhouse the size of a mill with a ha-ha and a terrace at the back, gravel a foot thick and a thousand dahlias stalked like artillerymen and luminious with autumn. The tea cups must have been two hundred years old.

I was asked to small places too—a farm so isolated that the sheep and cows looked up aghast when I found my way to it, and the sheep-dogs nearly garrotted themselves on the end of hairy ropes.

'You'll be missin' the Captain,' the farmer's wife said as she opened the door. Her accent was not the local one.

I said, 'You talk differently,' and she said, 'Well, I would do. I come from Stennersceugh. It was a Danish settlement long since. It's all of ten miles off.'

Never in my life had I had so much attention paid to me by strangers, nor been told so many intimate things from the heart—of marriages, love and death; of children or the lack of them, fears of sickness, pregnancy; of lost loves and desperate remedies. Three old ladies living by the church, I heard, drank three crates of sherry a week ('It's the chemist delivers'). A husband had 'drowned 'isself in Ash Beck for fear of a thing growing out of the side of his head'.

There seemed to be total classlessness, total acceptance, offence only taken if you gave yourself airs, offered money in return for presents or didn't open your door wide enough at the sound of every bell. There was a certain amount of derision at bad management—'She never gets out to the shops till twelve o'clock.' 'She hasn't had them curtains down in a twelvemonth'—but I met no violence, no hatred. There were threats of 'bringin' me gun' to walkers on the fells with unleashed dogs, but not one farmer in ten possessed a gun or would have known how to use if he had. Language addressed to animals was foul and unrefined, ringing over the fells and sheep dips and clipping sheds—but bore no relation to conversation with humans or at any rate not with me. 'Come 'ere yer bloody, buggerin' little— 'ello there, Mrs. Bainbridge, now. Grand day. Comin' over for yer tea then?'

Alan had told me that when he came home I'd be used to my tea as my supper and then more tea just before bedtime and I would forget how to cook a steak. However he was wrong again, because it had been dinner I had been invited to at Mealbeck the night of the waving woman, and a much better dinner than I'd ever have got in Aldershot.

Mealbeck is the big Gothic house of two sisters—a magnificent cold, turretted, slightly idiotic house, something between the Brighton Pavilion and the Carpathians. We ate not in a corner of it but the corner of a corner, passing from the tremendous door, over flagged halls, a great polar-bearskin rug and down a long cold passage. At the end was a little room which must once have been the housekeeper's and crammed into it among the housekeeper's possessions—a clock, a set of bells, a little hat-stand, a photograph of servants like rows of suet dumplings, starched and stalwart and long ago dead— were a Thomas Lawrence, photographs by Lenare and haunted Ypres faces in 1914 khaki. On the housekeeper's old table where she must have handed out the wages was some fine silver and glass fit for emperors.

Good wine, too. The sisters, Millicent and Gertie, knew their wine. They also knew their scotch and resorted to it wordlessly after the best pheasant and lemon pudding I think I've ever eaten.

I said, 'Oh this has been lovely. Lovely.' We stood under the green moon that did not so much light the fells as isolate them in the long clean lines of the faded day.

'You are from Sussex,' said Millicent. 'You must find this very bare.'

'It's wonderful. I love it.'

'I hope you'll stay the winter,' said Gertie. 'And I hope you'll come here soon again.'

The two of them walked, not too steadily to the iron gates and I roared off in the little Fiat down the drive and out on to the fell, between the knobbly blocks of the stone walls flashing up in the car lights. I felt minute between the long lines snaking away, the long low undecorated horizon, the clear hard pencil lines cut with a very sharp hard point. Gigantic lamp-eyes of sheep now and then came shining into the headlights. It was midnight. I did not meet a single car between Mealbeck and Naresby and the road rippled up and down, narrow and sweeping and black and quiet. I thought of Alan in Hong Kong. It would be breakfast time. I wished he were with me. Then I forgot him in the emptiness of the road under the moon and the great encircling ball of the stars.

I went flying through High Thwaite, hurtling through Low Thwaite and the same landscape spread out still in front of me—endlessly deserted, not a light in any cottage, not a dog barking, not a cry of a bird. It was just after what appeared to be the loneliest part of the road that I took a corner rather faster than I should and saw the woman standing in her garden and waving at me with a slow decorous arm. You could see from the moonlight that her head was piled up high with queenly hair. I think I was about two miles on before I really took this in and I was so shaken by it that I stopped the car.

I was not many miles from home now—my village, my new house, my heavy safe front door. The road had dropped low to a humped bridge, and after a moment when I had switched off the engine I could hear the clear quick brown water running deep and noisy below it. I thought, 'There can't have been anyone. I'm drunk.'

I got out of the car and walked about. It was cold. I stood on the bridge. Apart from the noise of the beck everything was absolutely quiet. There was not a light from any house in any direction. Down here by the beck I could see no horizons, not the fell's edge, not even the sweet nibbled grass beside the road. The air smelled clean like fresh sheets.

This was the pedlar's road. For five hundred years, they had walked it with packs of ribbons and laces and buttons and medicines, and a great many of them according to all the stories had been murdered for them or disappeared in the snow in winter—often not found until Martinmas. If my car doesn't start now, I thought I shall be very much alone.

Had the woman been asking for help? I wondered whether to go back. I felt absolutely certain—and it is amazing how much even at midnight under only the palest moon the eye can know from the angle of a moving arm—that she hadn't.

She had been waving kindly. Not afraid. Not asking. Not even beckoning. She had been waving in some sort of recognition.

I had never been so frightened in my life.

'I went to Mealbeck last night.'
'Y'd get a fair plateful there.'
'Yes.'
'And a fair skinful.'
'We—yes. Lovely wine.'
'Wine, eh? And mebbe a tot?'
'I had a lovely time. They're very nice. Very kind.'
'That's right. They're kind. Home boozers. Did you get back safe? They say the police sits outside Mealbeck when there's entertaining. When they can spare't time.'
'I'm not saying anything against them'
'That's right then.' He—it was the farmer who had the demented dogs and whose wife came from the Danish settlement—he looked satisfied. I could see he had been wondering if I was too fancy to answer back. 'They're all right. Old Gertie and Millicent. There's nowt amiss wi' them. Did you have a fair drive home?'

'Fair,' I said. 'One thing wasn't though. I passed a place—I saw a ghost.'

'Oh aye. Y'd see half a dozen after a night out at Mealbeck.'

'No, I don't think it was that. I saw someone at a gate. It was a woman waving.'

'Oh aye.'

'Well—it was nearly one o'clock in the morning.'

'Did yer stop?' He was clipping. The sheep was taut between his legs, its yellow eyes glaring. The clippers snapped deep into the dirty heathery wool.

'Well, no. I didn't believe it till I was miles past. It took a minute. Then I thought I'd dreamed. Dropped asleep.'

'Woman was it? Dark-haired?'

'I didn't see the colour. Just the shape.'

'Did yer go on back?'

'No—well. She didn't seem to be in trouble or anything. I hope I did right. Not going back.'

He said nothing till the fleece of the sheep fell away and the animal sprang out of his clutches like a soul released and slithered dizzily light into the yard.

'Watch now or yer'll get yerself hiked,' he said as I stood clear. 'The Missus'll have a pot of tea if you fancy it.'

'*Was* it a ghost?'

'Missus!'

She appeared at the door and looked pleased to see me—this really was a wonderfully friendly country—'Kettle's on,' she called. 'I hear yer've bin gallivanting at the Hall.'

'Was it a ghost?' I asked again before I went in to tea.

'I'd not think so,' he said.

I went back along the road the very next day and at first I could find no sign of the house at all. Or at any rate I could not decide which one it was. The fell that had looked so bare at night, by daylight could be seen to be dotted with crumpled, squat little stone farms, their backs turned to the view, two trees to each to form a wind-break, grey with white stone slabs to the window and only a tall spire of smoke to show they were occupied. It was not the townsfolk-country-cottage belt so that there was not much white paint about, lined curtains, urns on yard walls—and any one of several little isolated farms could have been the eerie one. In the end I turned back and found the bridge where I'd stopped. I got out of the car again as I had before, and walked back a mile or two until I came to a lane going alongside a garden end. All I could see from the road was the garden end—a stone wall and a gate quite high up above me and behind that a huge slab-stoned roof so low that the farmhouse must have been built deep down in a dip.

Now nobody stood at the gate—more of a look-out post, a signalling post above the road. There were tangled flowers behind it. There was no excuse for me to go up the lane that must have led to the house and it was not inviting. I thought of pretending to have lost my way or asking for a drink of water but these things you grow out of doing. I might perhaps just ask if there were eggs for sale. This was quite usual. Yet I hung back because the lane was dark and overgrown. I sat down instead on a rickety milk platform meant for churns but all stuck through with nettles and which hardly took my weight. It must have been years since any churn was near it. I sat there in the still afternoon and nobody passed.

Then I felt I was being watched. There was no sound or snapping twig, no breathing and no branch stirred but I looked quickly up and into a big bewildered face, mouth a little open, large bright mooning eyes. The hair was waved deeply like an old Vogue photograph and the neckline of the dress was rounded, quite high with a string of pearls. The hands of the woman were on the wall and I think they were gloved—neat pretty kid gloves. The trappings of the whole figure were all the very soul of order and confidence. The figure itself, however, almost yearned with uncertainty and loss.

'Whatever *time* is it?' she said.

'About three o'clock.' I found I had stood up and turned to face her. For all the misery in the face there were the relics of unswervable good manners which demanded good manners back; as well as a quite curious sensation, quite without visible foundation, that this body, this dotty half-bemused memsahib had once commanded respect, inspired good sense.

'It's just after three,' I said again.

'Oh, good *gracious*—good gracious.' She turned with a funny, bent movement feeling for the wall to support her as she moved away. The face had not been an old woman's but the stance, the tottering walk were ancient. The dreadful sense of loss, the melancholy, were so thick in the air that there was almost a smell, a sick smell of them.

She was gone, and utterly silently, as if I had slept for a moment in the sunshine and had a momentary dream. She had seemed like a shade, a classical Greek shade, though why I should think of ancient Greece in bleak North Westmorland I did not know.

As I stood looking up at the gate there was a muffled urgent plunging noise and round the bend of the road came sheep— a hundred of them with a shepherd and two dogs. The sheep shouldered each other, fussing, pushing, a stream of fat fleeces pressed together, eyes sharp with pandemonium. The dogs were happily tearing about. The shepherd walked with long steps behind. The sheep new-clipped filled the road like snow. They stopped when they saw me, then when they were yelled at came on careering drunkenly round me, surrounding me and I stood knee deep in them and the flat blank rattle of bleats, the smell of sheep dip and dog and man—and petrol, for when I looked beyond I found a Land Rover had been crawling behind and at the wheel the doctor with the tweed hat was sitting laughing.

He said, 'Well! You look terrified.'

'They were so sudden.'

'They'll not hurt you.'

'No. I know—just they were so—quiet. They broke in—'

'Broke in?'

'To the silence. It's very—silent here, isn't it?' I was inane.

He got down from the car and came round near me. 'You've not been here long, have you? We haven't been introduced. I'm the doctor.'

'I know. I'm—'

'Yes. I know too. And we're to know each other better. We're both to go dining out at the good sisters' in a week or so. I gather we're not supposed to know it yet. We are both supposed to be lonely.'

I said how could one be lonely here? I had made friends so fast.

'Some are,' he said. 'Who aren't born to it. Not many. It's always all right at first.' We both looked together towards the high gate and he said, 'Poor Rose. My next patient. Not that I expect to be let in.'

'Is she—?'

'A daughter of the regiment like yourself. Well, I mustn't discuss patients. I call on her now and then.'

He walked up the side lane waving the tweed hat and left me. As he reached the point where the little lane bent out of sight he turned and cheerfully waved again, and I turned too and walked the two miles back to my car. As I reached it the Land Rover passed me going very fast and the doctor made no signal and I could not see his face. I thought he must be reckless to drive at that lick on a sheep-strewn road but soon forgot it in the pleasure of the afternoon—the bright fire I'd light at home and the smell of wood smoke and supper with a book ahead. No telephone, thank God. As I turned into my yard I found I was very put out to see Mrs. Metcalfe coming across it with yet another great basket of beans.

'Tek 'em or leave 'em,' she said. 'But we've more than we'll want and they'll just get the worm in. Here, you could do wi' a few taties too from the look of you. Oh aye—and I've just heard. That daft woman up near Mealbeck. She's dead. The doctor's just left her. Or I hear tell. She hanged herself.'

It was no story.

Or rather it is the most detestable, inadmissable story. For I don't yet know half the facts and I don't feel I want to invent any. It would be a story so easy to improve upon. There are half a dozen theories about poor Rose's hanging and half a dozen about the reason for her growing isolation and idleness and seclusion. There is only one view about her character though, and that is odd because the whole community in the fells and dales survives on firmly-grounded assessment of motives and results; the gradations and developments of character are vital to life and give validity to passing years. Reputations change and rise and fall. But Rose—Rose had always been very well-liked and had very much liked living here. Gertie and Millicent said she had fitted in round here as if she were country born. She had been one of the few southerners they said who had seemed to belong. She had loved the house—a queer place. It had been the heart of a Quaker settlement. Panes of glass so thick you could hardly see out. She had grown more and more attached to it. She didn't seem able to leave it in the end.

'The marriage broke up after the War,' said the doctor. We were sitting back after dinner in the housekeeper's room among the Thomas Lawrences. 'He was always on the move. Rose had no quarrel with him you know. She just grew—well, very taken with the place. It was—yes, possession. Greek idea—possession by local gods. The Romans were here you know. They brought a Greek legend or two with them.'

I said, 'How odd, when I saw her I thought of the Greeks, though I hadn't known what I meant. It was the way she moved—so old. And the way she held her hands out. Like—well, sort of like on the walls of Troy.'

'Not Troy,' said the Doctor. 'More like hell, poor thing. She was quite gone. You know—these fells, all the little isolated houses, I'm not that sure how good for you they are, unless you're farming folk.'

Millicent said rubbish.

'No,' he said, 'I mean it. D'you remember C.S. Lewis's hell? A place where people live in isolation unable to reach each other. Where the houses get further and further apart?'

'Everyone reaches each other here,' I said. 'Surely?'

The doctor was looking at me. He said, 'What was it you said?'

'Everyone reaches each other—'

'No,' he said. 'You said you saw her.'

'Yes I did. I saw her on the way home from here, the night before she died. Then I saw her again the next day, the very afternoon. That's what is so terrible. I must have seen her, just before she—did it. I must be the last person to have seen her alive.'

'I wonder,' he said, 'if that could be true.' Gertie and Millicent were busy with coffee cups. They turned away.

'"Could be true?" But it is certainly true. I know exactly when. She asked me the time that afternoon. I told her. It was just after three. She seemed very—bewildered about it. You called upon her hardly a quarter of an hour later. She'd hardly been back in the house a quarter of an hour.'

'She'd been in it longer than that,' he said. 'When I found her she'd been dead for nearly three weeks. Maybe since hay-time.'

I went to Hong Kong.

THE TRIBUTE

Fanny Soane rang Mabel Ince and Mabel Ince rang old Lady Benson to say that poor Dench was dead.

'Who?' screamed Nelly Benson.

'Dench.'

'Dench?'

'Yes. Poor darling Denchie.'

'Thought she'd died years ago. Must have been a hundred.'

'Nonsense, Nelly.'

'She was old in the War.'

'She was *wonderful* in the War.'

'Wonderful means old. I've been wonderful for years.'

'Nelly—' Mabel was hoping to be brief. Calls cost money. She was ringing Kensington from Berkshire. Certainly after six o'clock, but still—

'Nelly, I think we ought to do something. Put in a tribute—'

'*The Times* has gone. No sense in a tribute. No tributes now. Nobody getting born. Getting married. Getting tributes. Or dying—more's the pity.'

'Well, Dench has died.'

'In *The Telegraph* I suppose?' . . .

'Yes. Nelly—'

'Sorry. Can't go on. Too expensive.'

'But Nelly, I'm the one who's paying—'

But Kensington, like Dench, had died.

Dear Fanny, wrote Mabel next, I rang Old Nelly Benson

but she's daft as a brush and didn't seem the least bit interested in poor dear Dench. What do you think? I'm quite ready to do something—just a short one. In *The Telegraph* which I suppose is the paper Dench would have wanted now *The Times* seems to have gone for good. Oh dear, I hope Dench went before *The Times*. D'you remember how she always read it, smiling? I don't think she could have borne life without the Court Circular. 'It rivets me,' she used to say. 'Rivets me.' Though lately I gather she hadn't been well and hadn't been reading anything any more. The last Christmas card I had a year or so ago was very shaky. In fact I seem to remember there was only a signature and the little message was written in by some niece. Did you by the way get a sort of begging letter about Dench? That was from the niece too, but I didn't keep the address. I always wished I could have done something. She wanted to get poor D. into a private nursing home. Did you do anything? I feel a bit dreadful about it and if we could do this tribute now I think I'd feel a bit better. Shall we ring round? There must be half a dozen families who would want to come in on it. I can think of three Denchie nannied myself.

> *Dear Mabel,*
>
> *Oh my dear—I could have told you Nelly Benson is impossible now. Quite batty. She must be absolutely gaga not to want to go in with a tribute—or it's kindness to think so—when one knows how much Denchie did for those awful children, and grandchildren too come to that, for simply years. She saw the famous Charlotte through virus pneumonia you know. Nelly just went off to Geneva to join Charles and left Dench to it. And it wasn't as if Dench was ever paid or anything. At least I never paid her, did you? Just her keep. Well, you just couldn't. She never asked. Poor as a church m. I'd guess. But being a gent—Dench I mean—one just fed her. She 'came to stay'. To 'stop' as she called it, bless her.*

Yes, I did get a letter from some niece and I meant to answer it and send a fiver or something but it was just before we went to Penang. I felt a bit awful when I remembered about it long afterwards—too late because I'd lost the address by then, too. I do rather hate that kind of letter. Embarrassing all round. You don't feel you can possibly do enough and so you do nothing. Now of course like you we have just the Service pension. My dear, we need a whip round for ourselves now. Wish we had a niece!

Yes, of course I'll go in with a tribute. If we get say three more people it won't kill us. It's about two pounds a line I think. Something like 'In Memory of dear "Dench", beloved Nannie and friend for many years of . . .' and names of families. Will you get in touch with the rest or shall I? I suppose it shouldn't come to more than, say, 75p each?

The telephone rang in Berkshire and Mabel Ince heard a lot of muttering about tangled wires and then old Lady Benson.

'I've had a letter. From some niece. Hello?'

'Hello? Yes? Nelly? What niece?'

'Old Dench's . . .' peep, peep, peep, peep.

'Nelly, are you in a phone box? Hello?'

'Yes. It's in the hall. To stop the lodgers. She wants to meet us . . .' peep, peep, peep.

'Nelly, for goodness sake! Can't you put in a ten?'

'Hello. Tuppences are better. You get too long with a . . .' peep, peep, peep.

'Hello?'

' . . . to meet us with some things old Dench left us. In her will. Wants to meet us . . .' peep, peep.

'Can you write? Can't you write about it, Nelly?'

' . . . on Thursday. Fortnum and Mason's.'

'Fortnum and—Nelly, *would* you write?'

'I *could* write,' peep, peep, peep.

*

'Whether she'll back out of it of course,' said Mabel, 'is another matter. She says she's not been out of the house for years.'

It was Thursday morning—Thursday fortnight morning, for this was not precipitate. Mabel had set forth from Newbury by car leaving Humphrey with the television and a tray, and picked up Fanny Soane. Together they were now proceeding to Kensington and Nelly Benson. It was not as early in the morning as Mabel would have liked as she had lost time looking for Fanny's house which, being in a maze of identical streets and in Raynes Park and not Wimbledon as she had been led to believe, had proved elusive. Fanny's husband in a darned cardigan had seen them to the door as they left, waved perfunctorily and disappeared. His eyes, which as attaché in Tiflis had been interestingly hooded, now had deep swags beneath them, suggesting gin. He was losing his hair. The tiny front garden Mabel noticed had been put down to Brussels sprouts, and an elephant's foot, converted to a boot scraper, stood near the mat.

'A far cry from the Lion Palace,' said Fanny noticing Mabel noticing. 'Sometimes I wonder why we didn't Stay On— though when you read that funny little man—'

'Funny little man?'

'The one who wrote *Staying On*. The one who came out to India for five minutes and wrote all those huge books about us though goodness knows how. I never met a soul who knew him, did you?'

'At least,' said Mabel, 'Dench never knew. What's become of us all I mean. She was such a romantic. She talked about "love of country", d'you remember? Actually used the words. And d'you remember how she stood for the Queen?'

'Oh well, we all did that. We still do. Don't you?'

'Well—not to make it obvious. It depends where we are. And not like Dench did, to attention—quite eccentrically really as if it was almost a joke. Humphrey and I just sort of hesitate now, getting the coats from under the seat. We just stop talking for a moment.'

'Like vicars wondering about Grace when you ask them to dinner.'

'*Do* you ask vicars to dinner?'

'No. Well I don't know that we ever did. We don't ask anybody to dinner now. Can't afford it. Nobody asks us—we're all in the same boat. I mean the people who ask us to dinner now are not the sort one knows. Spaghetti bolognese and cheesecake.'

The two women looked back on half a life-time of invitations—battlefields, of notes, menus, first guest lists, second guest lists all professionally conceived, negotiated, carried through. Jousts, tournaments, ritual murders—masked by smiles and decorations.

'D'you remember the Bensons' invitations?'

'Lord yes—"gloves"! Bottom left-hand corner, "Gloves will be worn". Poor Nelly.'

'D'you remember Prague? The high ceilings? So beautiful. Somebody told me the other day why embassy ceilings are always so high. It's to take the noise of the cocktail parties.'

'I'd have thought Prague was older than cocktail parties.'

'Nothing's older than cocktail parties. Of one kind or another. Didn't old Dench love cocktail parties? And Prague? I used to let her stand with the children just out of sight on the landing—the Ambassador was so good about Staff—and watch all the people. The children were such angels with Dench.'

'And she *had* them so beautiful.'

'Oh yes. My word she must have cost us something. I mean H.M. Government something. Those little dresses—always Harrods or The White House. The smocking always going round across the back. Round-toed shoes. Like little conkers!'

'Oh—and the herring-bone tweeds! With the little velvet collars—Mabel, I'm going to cry. Dear old Dench. Didn't she iron and press well?'

They picked up Lady Benson rather uncertainly at an address near Notting Hill, not at first recognising her. The house was dilapidated with dirty window panes, the upper floors partitioned down the middle of windows with plaster-board and covered with stickers saying 'Capital Radio' and 'I Still Love Elvis'. A grubby-looking woman peered from a downstairs front room and turned out to be Lady Benson herself, ungloved. She appeared on the top step wearing bedroom slippers and carrying a leather shopping-bag. Her hair was extremely untidy and a smell of onions which hung about the hall accompanied her. There was still an imperial look to the eyes.

'You're not going to Harrods in bedroom slippers, Nelly!'

'I thought it was Fortnum and Mason's?'

'No—we changed it. Harrods is less flashy. But you'd hardly go to Fortnums—'

'They're all I can get my feet into, except Wellingtons. I don't go about much now. I have the house to run.'

Big flakes of plaster had come away from around the rain-water pipes. The desolate February garden was full of broken, purple edging-stones and dead hydrangeas.

'I use my wellies for gardening,' said Nellie Benson looking out suspiciously at the damp day. 'I have a pair of Dr Scholl's somewhere.'

Fanny said with fortitude that they would be better.

'Come in,' said Nelly.

'It's all right. We'll be in the car.' Mabel, who had dressed carefully in a powder blue suit and a hat of green-black feathers with a veil—bought once for the Queen's Birthday in Dar-es-Salaam—got quickly into her car and looked into the distance. Heaving the shopping bag ahead of her, Nelly climbed in alongside and said, 'I remember that hat. Always reminded me of a dead blackbird,' and laughed at this all the way along Kensington High Street.

Fanny said, 'I think perhaps we are out of the fourth form now, Nelly,' and Mabel did not speak.

'Where are you now?' Nelly asked when she had stopped laughing. 'What's become of you, Mabel? I heard you'd had to sell the castle.'

'Yes.'

'Suppose old Humphrey lost his money.'

'Oh Nelly, be quiet,' said Fanny in the back.

'Horses, I suppose. He always lost. I remember the Marsa Club in Malta. My word he flung it about. Where d'you live now?'

'Newbury.'

'Bit near the course, isn't it?'

'He watches on television,' said Mabel, negotiating the Kensington traffic lights with knuckles of ice.

'You can do that anywhere—watch the television. Unless you're like me—can't afford one. Where d'you live, Fanny?'

'Wimbledon.'

'Oh dear, that's a pity. A long way from London. Further than Newbury in a sense.' She began to laugh again.

'We're very comfortable.'

'Do be quiet, Nelly. Fanny lives in a charming house in Fethney Road. Delicious red brick. I wouldn't be surprised if it was Norman Shaw. I thought all your little things looked lovely there, Fanny.'

'Norman Shaw?' said Nelly, 'Wasn't he A. D. C. Pankot? Terrible old pansy. Dench couldn't bear him. Have you got any of *his* little things?'

'Oh for goodness sake!' said Fanny. 'Don't be so foul, Nelly. Mabel means the things we've all got—brasses and elephants' feet, the things we've all got and can't bear. I like Fethney

Road. I don't know the locals but there's the Diplomatic Wives. I go to those in London.'

'Dench would have approved of that. Poor Dench, she was never a Diplomatic Wife. Or any wife at all. I wonder why?' said Mabel.

'We were always wondering why. So pretty she must have been. Men loved her.'

'Yes. I don't think they ever got very far with her though.'

'Not that she was a puritan—my word no. Just—withdrawn somehow. Deep down. Knew how to stop things going too far. My word she'd have been a marvellous Diplomatic Wife. Complete gent of course.'

'Oh, complete.'

'And knew her place.'

'Oh yes, she knew her place.'

'There had been some man once, you know. D'you remember? The children used to tease her. Mr. Santas-something-or-other. Some Argentine millionaire. Some widower—'

'No. Not a widower. Very much married. Catholic. What was his name? The children used to call him Mr. Salteena.'

'She didn't like jokes about him. D'you suppose he existed?'

'No idea. But it is funny she didn't marry. D'you think she was a Lesbian? A lot of nannies are. Subconsciously of course,' said worldly Mabel.

'Certainly not,' said Nelly, outraged. 'Dench a subconscious!'

'And she wasn't a nannie either,' said Fanny. 'She was a gent. She was a romantic.'

'She was damn useful,' said Nelly. She eased her legs out of the car and felt for Hans Crescent with the Dr Scholl's. 'We're lucky to find a parking place I suppose, but this is a good long way from Harrods.'

'We'll go in at door ten,' said Mabel. 'Past the children's

hairdressing and the rocking horse. Then through the children's clothes to get to the lifts. In memory of Dench. She brought all my children here, Fanny, at one time or another.'

'She brought all mine,' said Fanny.

'I dare say she brought mine,' said Nelly, 'though I can't say I knew anything about it. I just handed the lot of them over to her. They were happier with her anyway. My place was with Charles.' She waddled ahead.

Hatted and handbagged, not to say shopping-bagged, talking in piercing, old-fashioned Kensington voices, the three old women watched children pitching on the rocking horse, waiting for their hair to be cut. The ones with nannies all had dusky skins. The white ones were mostly with tired-looking mothers wearing anoraks and reading *Cosmopolitan*. The dusky ones wore herring-bone tweed, the white ones space-suits. White or dusky they all screamed a good deal.

'What would Dench have thought of this!' said Fanny.

'She'd have borne it. Perhaps improved things.'

'Oh, she'd not have gone to Arabs!'

'Oh I don't know. Look at *Anna and the King of Siam*.'

'Dench didn't care about money,' said Mabel. 'That was the really lovely thing about her.'

'Yes,' said Fanny, 'Dench was cheap.'

Up in the lift the ladies rose, to the fourth floor and the big airy restaurant where they had booked a table. The head-waiter on seeing Lady Benson's shoes found that the table was after all another table—one in a corner and rather behind a screen. Mabel's long finger summoning him back took a little time to be regarded.

'A young woman will be joining us. A Miss Dench.'

'Yes, madam.'

'Show her to this table, will you?'

'Yes, madam. Sherry, madam, while you are waiting?'

There was an uneasy, negative movement, a slight sliding away of eyes.

'Not yet, thank you.'

'How will we know her—the niece? She's quite young, isn't she?' said Fanny. 'She sounded quite young in the letter. I suppose she's a great-niece. How are we going to know her? I mean, any of these women might be nieces,' she looked about, 'eating their lunch.'

'Well, a lot of people are nieces. And eat lunch. We have been nieces—'

'Not primarily,' said Fanny. 'We were never primarily nieces. All these women look primarily nieces. It's very depressing. It's rather a test when you think about it—looking a niece. Dench herself for instance would never have looked a niece. Mr. Salteena would never have fallen for a niece. We don't look nieces—'

'Don't know what you're talking about,' said Lady Benson, munching a roll.

'Well, I dare say we'll spot Niece Dench,' said Mabel. 'I believe I once saw her as a matter of fact. I went to East Molesey to see Denchie—oh, seven or eight years ago. She must have let me in. A nice little woman. I expect she'll come back to me. There was masses of ironing about.'

'Ironing?'

'Yes. On airers. You know those old-fashioned standing airers. All round the sitting room. Beautiful ironing it was—I remembered the smell—lovely warm clean clothes, and Denchie in a bed in the corner. She did look small.'

'Yes. I think she must be a very good sort of woman, the niece.'

Fanny said uncertainly, 'I suppose that's what she meant about a nursing home,' but Mabel said, 'Oh, come on—Dench was no trouble. And she ate like a bird. Don't you remember in the War? If ever we got anything on the Black Market and there wasn't enough to go round Dench never minded being left out. There were some eggs once—it was when we were in Lincolnshire and she was cook-house-keeping—six beautiful eggs and we had them boiled for a treat. There were Humph and I and the children and some child staying—little Polly Knox. D'you remember? Pretty baby thing—Dench adored her. Seven of us and only six eggs and someone said, "What about Dench?" Polly Knox said, "You can have half mine, Denchie"—and Dench said straightaway, "Thank you, dear, but I don't take eggs."'

'She used to say that about cream in the War, "No thank you, I don't take cream. Not since Canada."'

'She'd been a hero in Canada, you know. Nursed a typhoid case nobody else would touch—and caught it and nearly died. She'd volunteered—it was in all the Canadian papers. It was while we were over there. She got flowers from all over the place. Rather marvellous for her—except for being so delicate afterwards, no cream and so forth. Oh and having no money—otherwise she had a pretty good life I'd say, Denchie. I wonder if she had the OAP—I never paid her stamp, did you?'

'No.'

They fell silent. No niece appeared. The waiter drew closer holding pencil and pad.

'D'you think we should have sherry?' said Fanny.

'All right. All right, yes. She's very late. We'll have sherry. Three sherries please. Very dry and—well what about ordering some wine? I mean this is to be a tribute, isn't it—instead of the first idea of putting something in the paper. More lavish. And romantic. And very much nicer for us. I want to do it properly. I want the niece to feel we've done things properly. Do they have half bottles?'

'We can't order wine,' said Nelly, 'until we know what the niece is going to eat.'

The sherries came as they considered. Lady Benson decided she had lost her shopping-bag, then, finding it, wondered if she had time to go downstairs to the Food Halls for a pound of Finnan Haddock which though expensive was more certain than in Notting Hill not to be coloured cod.

Dissuaded by the others she sat on, and at last when the niece was more than half an hour late they ordered.

'It seems,' said Mabel to the waiter, 'that our friend is not coming. We will have three chicken à la king.'

'Anything to start with, madam?'

'No thank you.'

'Vegetables?'

'Er—perhaps a green salad.'

'I'd like vegetables,' said Lady Benson. 'I seldom seem to eat vegetables.' But a chill stare from Mabel sent him off.

'D'you remember the lovely vegetables in Hong Kong?' said Nelly. 'They used to fly the lettuces from America.'

'That was Jamaica.'

'Do you get vegetables, Fanny?'

Fanny said they had good Brussels sprouts.

'I don't see any point in spending money,' said Mabel, 'if the niece isn't here.'

'We were never in Jamaica,' Nelly said. 'Nor Africa. I'm glad to say we never had to go through Africa, Charles was always too senior.'

'I can't see how he can *always* have been too senior.'

'The place none of us ever got to,' said Mabel, 'senior or otherwise, was South America. D'you know that Dench knew South America? Very well. I first found her in Jamaica on her way back from Buenos Aires sitting all by herself at a table at The Mona—eating lettuce, I dare say. Perhaps Brussels sprouts. I thought, what a charming little woman and how sad she looks. I suppose she'd just left Salteena.

'So fragile. So sad. Not a bean. The children took to her and

I thought well, she might be just the thing, and I took her on. And that was over forty years ago.'

'Devoted,' said Fanny. 'Utterly reliable.'

'More than the niece,' said Mabel, looking towards the door where a dazzling woman had just come in wearing a tightly-belted Persian lamb jacket with mink lapels. Her long legs wore long grey suede boots. Her coat and skirt said Paris. Not young, she made youth seem a triviality.

'Not,' said Mabel, 'that I ever felt we were real favourites with Dench!'

Fanny said, 'I thought you were. I never really felt we were. She talked of your children all the time.'

'To us she talked of yours.'

'She never talked to anyone about mine,' said Lady Benson, 'and neither did I.'

'Used to send her good presents though,' she added. 'Pound of tea at Christmas. When we were in Ceylon.'

'The child she really did love more than the rest was that child Polly Knox,' said Mabel, 'the one who tried to share the egg.'

'Yes, but then that *was* an easy child. My word she was a clever girl, too. She did do well for herself.'

'Yes—Charles and I paid to go over that place once. Chateau. They weren't there. Somewhere else in another chateau I dare say. Rolling. My dear, that woman is coming over to this table. You don't think it could be the niece?'

'Not if the niece is bringing presents. This one's not carrying presents.'

A uniformed chauffeur, however, walked behind with parcels and they both approached. The woman, who looked more beautiful as she came nearer, spread Persian-lambed arms and cried, 'Dears!'

The three ladies sat like rocks.

'I'm so terribly sorry. We found it so difficult to park. Chetwode couldn't stay with the car because of the parcels. I'm so fearfully late. Oh I do hope you haven't waited. Oh good—you haven't. Thank you, Chetwode, just here on the window-sill. I'm afraid they're nothing. She said in the will you were to have mememtoes, but she had so little. You'd not believe how little. So few possessions. There—well—' She looked round. The chauffeur melted. Her hair was the colour of very pale sunshine, her eyes enormous, clear and contrite. She took off her gloves and revealed beautiful long-fingered hands which she first clasped and then undid and waved about.

'Champagne,' she cried. The head-waiter who had come close came closer. 'Champagne. We are here to celebrate,' she told him, 'the life, the *happy* life of the dearest, dearest old— No I won't call this an In Memoriam. Denchie couldn't bear going on about the past. She had the happiest life and she died peacefully and thinking about us all. A good dry—yes that one. Number six.'

Mabel said faintly that she was very glad about Dench's happiness. Nelly Benson said nothing and Fanny Soane shut her eyes and opened them again.

The niece. The niece so good at ironing.

'I believe she talked of you three,' said the niece leaning forward, 'more than anyone else. Day after day, year in year out. All the places she had seen through you and how you rescued her, Mrs. Ince, when she was in very low water and let her have an absolutely free hand with all your children—let her nurse them when they were ill. And even *grand*children, Lady Benson.'

Bewildered at being recognised and so warmly, and unable to keep her eyes off the niece's sapphire and diamond ring Mabel said stiffly, 'We grew to rely on her very much.' Lady Benson began to say that Dench knew her pl—, but stopped to watch the niece's easy greeting of the champagne and the arrangements to make the bill for it separate and hers. Fanny watching the niece draw from her silky handbag a silky tenner said that all three had known Dench for a very great number of years. Probably better than anyone else. The quality of the niece's pale silk shirt made her flush suddenly with fury (By God, nursing homes!).

'Dench was an excellent servant,' she said.

The niece raised her glass. 'To Dench,' she said.

They drank.

'D'you remember *The Times*?' said the niece.

'Only just. We gave up our idea of that sort of tribute. *The Telegraph* is somewhat not—'

'No, no—I mean Dench and *The Times*? How she wrapped herself in *The Times* all the way from Perth when there was no room for her with you in the first class and there was no heating in those days in the thirds?'

'I don't think—' said Mabel.

'I never really believed in that frost-bite business,' said Fanny.

'Do you remember the roses?' said the niece.

Nobody remembered the roses.

'I think it was one of your daughters, Lady Benson, when Denchie had been looking after Simon and Sara and Simon kicked her. Your daughter said, "Denchie, you must have some roses" and took the secateurs and a basket and led her out into the gardens and cut three. Three roses—wasn't it priceless? D'you remember those gardens—there were two thousand rose trees. One of the sights of Persia. Oh how Denchie laughed!'

'I don't suppose,' said Nelly Benson, 'that Dench had much room for displaying roses.'

'Oh no. No, no of course not. She was in the attics. She wasn't minding. It just made us both laugh.'

'I felt personally very sorry,' said Mabel after a moment, 'about the business of the nursing home. I would have liked to help Dench, even taken her myself for a week or two, just to help the family out. But we were abroad.'

'Oh, but she refused. Didn't you know? You mustn't worry. It was all arranged for the nursing home without your kind help but she was so miserable. She said, "Oh do let me stay at home." She liked being in the sitting room. So of course we let her. I promise you she never knew you had been asked.'

Lady Benson who had let the Dr Scholl's stray under the table tried to retrieve them and said, 'She always had my shoes. It's the thing I miss most if you want to know—good shoes.'

'The shoes are still there,' said the niece. 'Rows and rows. They are very old-fashioned but if you wished I could let you have them back I'm sure. Dear Denchie never wore them— they were too big, though she was a lamb and I'm sure she never told you.'

'And these,' she said stretching out to the window-sill (the waiters leapt) 'are the little mementoes—all I could find and I do feel so sorry, just little brass things, Benares trays, a hand bell, an elephant's foot—it could be adapted as a boot scraper.'

They held their gifts.

'It is very good of you to bother,' said Mabel at last, 'to bring them all this way.' The full horror of the presents had made her turn quite pink. Pink with triumph. She knew that had she discovered Dench to have had anything really—

'I feel very *honoured*,' she said. 'To think that this sort of thing was all she had. All Denchie had.'

'Well, except for the money,' said the niece.

'Money?'

'Yes. The South America money. Mr. Salteena's money as we children used to call him.'

'Did he leave her—? You mean he did exist?'

'Oh yes. Mr. Salteena existed. He left her four hundred.'

'Oh but how nice!'

'Thousand, that is. He left her four hundred thousand. She left two hundred thousand of it to me and the other two hundred thousand to her niece.'

'You,' said Lady Benson with a void and wallowing noise in the throat. 'You then are not the niece?'

'The niece! Darling, darling Lady Benson—didn't I say? Didn't you recognise me? Oh dear I thought you'd recognise me. I was fussed being late. Oh how silly! I forgot to say—the niece said no. She couldn't face it, she said, not Harrods. And—the money's not altered her a bit—she said she had the ironing.'

'But who then—?' said Mabel.

'Well, but I'm Polly Knox. You must remember me. I'm Polly Knox. I've never lost touch with Dench. She left me half and I've been astounded and quite speechless ever since. He only died a short time before she did, Mr. Salteena, but she was absolutely in her right mind and all that, when she heard. She quite understood. Her niece said she just lay there in bed with the solicitor's letter on the counterpane and she smiled. And she said—to the niece—the niece told me—she's very straight and she told me this—she said, "Why Polly Knox, Auntie?" and Denchie said and, well, we've all been wondering what on earth she meant, she said—'

'What did she say?' asked Mabel Ince with unmoving lips.

'Well, she said a funny thing. She said, "Tell Polly she shall have half my egg."

THE PIG BOY

Veronica smelled the pig boy before she saw him and the smell was the essence of her loathing and hatred of Hong Kong.

A wet, grey, bad-tempered, blowy day and cold. She was wearing a new warm jersey under her white summer suit. Back at the hotel were all the thin summer clothes she had brought with her, still unworn. She had felt the room-boy's disdain as he unpacked them. Here was a first-time-out wife. She didn't know a thing. Didn't know that as late as March it could be cold and wet and bleak. Colder than England.

Colder than Barnes, she thought. She had left London with the grass on Barnes Common brightening and long and all the candles shining on the avenue of chestnuts that crosses the pretty railway line. London had had the smell of summer—airy and fresh. Here there was grit in the air and rubbish blew about the streets like rags.

Her husband was at work. He would be at work tonight until eight o'clock. Then there would be the usual drinks party. Perhaps two parties. Then the usual meal in a restaurant with friends. Then the usual wander in the streets among the stalls. Then bed. At the weekend—her last weekend—the firm had offered them a hired car.

But it wasn't being much of a holiday, alone all day. Well, of course it was not meant to be a holiday. She was just there. There as a wife. A brought-out wife, paid for by Geoffrey's firm. She was to be brought-out (tourist class) every six months for a few weeks until he finished the job. Like most other wives with husbands working abroad she was safety-valve procedure against executive breakdown.

The air must be full of flying wives, thought Veronica—airlines to Singapore, Hong Kong, the Philippines, Colombo, heavy with wives flying husbandwards: oil wives, lawyers' wives, army wives—complacent on the journey out, glum or tense or relieved on the flight home again, leaving their husbands not necessarily to any great amusement. Geoffrey had said, 'Look round. Look at all the men sitting eating alone. Not exactly the glossy life, is it?' 'Yes—my wife's at home,' said the husbands. 'No—well she can't really. Children's education.' Or, 'No. She can't. She has her job. No, it's not much fun, but it's not forever. You learn to manage.'

And the world was full of people pitying the wives, thought Veronica. In Barnes the drinks parties glittered with sharp eyes—if you were lucky enough to be invited to any without a man. 'Yes, I'm married,' you said, 'my husband's working in Hong Kong. Oh yes—but I do get out there you know. Several weeks twice a year.'

'That sounds terrible.'

'It's very usual. Very usual nowadays. After all, it's not new. Look at army wives and sailors' wives—they've always done it. One's independent after all.'

'Not much fun though.'

'Oh, I don't know.'

The guarded look behind the eyes which said, 'Is she faithful? I'll bet she's not. I'll bet he's not either. Asking too much—alone six months of the year.'

Then would come the invitation—or no invitation. Whichever happened, it was insulting.

And for Veronica, even in the liberated streets of Barnes, staying at home was harder to explain than for many because she had no children. Being a painter she could have worked anywhere.

'No—we have no children.'

'Don't you think of being with him then?'

'Oh—I think I'd hate Hong Kong. And there are things here I can't really leave.'

'What is it she can't leave?' they thought. 'She's probably just found that she could never really stand him. There's probably trouble. I wonder what her lover's like?'

But there was no lover and there had never been trouble, and it was a surprise to find that when she arrived in Hong Kong this first time she found herself thinking, 'What if he's changed? What if I don't like him?' Dazed still by the idiot film she had watched on the flight and a couple of magazines the woman sitting next to her had loaned her, she thought, 'I wonder what his woman's like? Chinese? They're very pretty. Doting, too. Everyone will know about her except me. They'll think nothing of it. It's the custom of the job, the times. Probably always was. Insane to be chaste. I wonder why I am?'

'I don't want to see him,' she thought, waiting for her luggage to lumber up on the roundabout. 'I'm frightened.' The roundabout went hypnotically, smoothly round, black and quiet like a roulette wheel. The Englishwoman with the magazines came up to her looking fuzzy and excited—little suit and brooches. 'Forget—did you say you were army? Are you an army wife? Are you going to the married quarters?'

'No I'm not.' Suddenly angry, Veronica said, 'I work. I do a job.'

'Oh,' said the woman eyeing her, unbelieving. 'I thought if he wasn't here to meet you we could share a taxi.'

'I'm staying at the Peninsula.'

'Oh my! I'm sorry.' She looked hard at Veronica, not believing that a woman she had seen looking so uncertain could be staying at the Peninsula, though—Geoffrey had let his flat and was spendthrifting weeks of pay—this was true. They went through Customs together. An aggressive Chinese man-woman

in police-type uniform shouted at them and glared. It was cold
and the wind whined.

'I hadn't expected this,' said Veronica.

'First time out then?' The woman perked up.

'Yes.'

'Oh—you'll love it. I've been out five times. Lovely shopping.'

And there was Geoffrey, a tireder looking Geoffrey, rather
redder in the face and flabbier, his shirt bloused out a bit over
his trousers, but his eyes bright. Looking for her.

At once all thoughts of mistresses and lovers became ridiculous, their recognition of each other complete. Hurtling in the
taxi through up-and-down rivers of lights, they held tight to
each other's hand, and all the old pleasures flowed back.

It was the day time without him that had become so deadly
boring. She felt so ashamed—the first time in the East—to be
bored.

Geoffrey got up at seven-thirty and they had breakfast in
their room—a great trolley wheeled in by two waiters, like an
old film. The trolley had huge silver dish-covers, omelettes,
mountains of croissants, huge pots of coffee, a pyramid of butter (which Geoffrey because of the blousing out of the shirt did
not eat. 'Chinese call it cow's grease. Puts you off.
Convenient.'). And there were shiny cloth napkins the same
colour as the cloth and fresh flowers in a glass.

When he had gone to work she would dress slowly and
wander about. Then she would go down in the lift with its
bowing attendant and leave the room-key in the lobby. Then
she would walk purposefully out of the great white and gold
hall into the street and let the crowd sweep her along.

For the first days, just to be in the marching streets was
something, being swept up with the rest into a whirlpool at
traffic lights, then like water, surging across. She crossed to
Hong Kong Side and the crowds at the ferries nearly trampled

her under. She loved this at first. It was like going out further from the shore where the bigger waves might knock you down and bear you away and nobody know.

But after a week or so she grew used to it—used to the pace and the impersonality. It was just a richer, madder Oxford Street on a Saturday afternoon. She began to notice a pair of shoes in a display window in the side of the Peninsula hotel. Two hundred pounds. The first day the price of the shoes had seemed ludicrous. After a week or so of Hong Kong it seemed just the price of shoes.

She grew used to the legless woman who shuffled her way about the pavement under the shoes, and around the corner, among the little clutch of street stalls that appeared by magic every morning. People stepped over the woman as if she were a moving sack. Food from the stalls dropped on her as she held up her tin cup for money. 'She has to pay for that pitch,' said a lawyer friend of Geoffrey, 'like the door-man at Claridges.'

Veronica got used to the Hakkar gypsy woman with the two-year-old squatting beside her and the sharp professional gypsy wag of the head as she sent the child running after her down Nathan Road to pull at her skirt. 'Money, money, money,' the child said—angrily, like the Customs official. Its mouth was covered in sores. She grew used to this.

One day she took the harbour cruise and sat in a cold greenhouse of a boat to see the city from the sea. The lunatic, concrete growths stuck up in a forest of sharp-edged temples. They looked pushed into holes in the hills, and at their feet, among the dark little tents of the squatters was the noise of more cranes, more drills, more bulldozers, tearing away, knocking down, building yet more. It seemed like no country.

Another day she took a taxi and watched the boat families at Aberdeen from another glass greenhouse. She watched the chickens and babies and birds in cages on the decks and the screaming women in huge shields of hats all tipping and tossing over the choppy cold waves. All looked an exhibition, put on for the brought-out wives. It was not real. She was bored.

Lunch somewhere, if she remembered, and then back to the hotel for a rest (a rest from what? She was twenty-five, healthy and a full-time painter), then maybe an invitation from one of the resident wives to go shopping. They might be Chinese or French or American or English, but the conversation was always the same. Then the noisy, boozy, sociable evening in the glaring streets with Geoffrey and friends. All in the streets at night was self-consciously wicked—the transvestite street, the blue-film and massage-shop street, the nude-photograph street. Thousands of tourists.

And she was bored.

It might have been Soho except for the crazy zig-zag glitter of the lights—soft yellow and pink and gold and white and green. 'It's the pale green ones that make it Chinese,' said Geoffrey. 'The rest could be anywhere—though nowhere so many. I love the pale green.'

It was the first time he had said that he loved something here.

'D'you not long for proper green?' she said. 'You said you did. In letters.'

'Proper green?'

'You said you'd started watching television just for the scenery. Watching Westerns to see the grass.'

'Oh—there's grass here if you look. Up in the New Territories grass all the way to China. You can walk for miles. We'll go at the weekend in the car. And there's green on the islands. It's wonderfully beautiful. You can sunbathe on Cheung Chau. Next time you come out it will be really hot.'

'I think you're beginning to like it.'

'Oh—yes. What?' He was watching five little boys spooning what looked like baby snakes into their mouths from blue and white egg-cups. The naked light-bulbs over the stalls swung in the wind. They looked like Christmas tree fruits. They made shadows come and go across the five pale faces. Hair shone like tar.

'You aren't beginning to want to stay? I mean *stay*? Not go home—stay here permanently?'

'God no,' he said, 'I'm here for quick money like everyone else. You know that. We can earn more here in six months than in ten years at home. It's why we did it. Hell!'

They walked back through the packed midnight. The tenement walls hung above the narrow streets like the flanks of galleons, dressed over-all, night and day, with long poles of washing. From the lamp-lit rooms behind came the soft shuffling knock of the mah-jong games, floating out over the night until it was part of the night, like cicadas in Italy.

So now, towards the end, Geoffrey had an all-day meeting and would not be in until after eight o'clock and Veronica was to have lunch with the wife of his boss—an Englishwoman from Kent who had come out to live in Hong Kong permanently. She and the wife would then go shopping for silk and perhaps some jewellery which the wife would advise about and get a good discount. Veronica took a taxi from the Hong Kong Side ferry and it wound up the Peak, round flower beds and gardens. But cement piles were going up even among these. A shining building that looked scarcely finished was being pulled down again to make way for something more modern. A speeded-up film of the building of Hong Kong, thought Veronica, would be like the waves of the sea, rising and breaking to rise again. The gardens were certainly doomed, she thought. However much must this land be worth? The Cathedral must be sitting on a fortune. A thousand pounds a centimetre. Ten thousand pounds a geranium.

The taxi swung off the road into a tunnel of expensive white tiles and cork-screwed up it to a double meshed door. A servant in a long black dress answered it—hair screwed back, waxed yellow face, tight cheek-bones, greying hair and a sweet smile. She seemed uncertain though about letting Veronica in and disappeared for quite some time. Veronica stood in the windy tunnel.

Then down in a flurry came the lady from Kent, by no means so flawlessly dressed as at the party where Veronica had met her. Her hair flopped about. The fingernails of one hand were painted and held a brush for the fingers of the other hand which were still plain. She embraced Veronica wildly with both arms. Veronica hoped the lacquer wasn't spilling down her back.

'My dear! But it's terrible! I'd forgotten.'

'It doesn't matter at all.'

'Sit down. A drink. Oh but this is awful. I've never done it before. That party—so noisy. I do this. I *throw* invitations about. But I've never, never forgotten. Ever. I could die.'

'It's quite all right.' Veronica wondered why she couldn't just stay. 'There's heaps I can do instead.'

'Are you here for a nice long time?'

'Another week.'

'Look, I'll get the diary. We'll fix something now. Wednesday—no, I can't do Wednesday. Say Friday and I'll cancel my hair. Or Sunday—what about this Sunday and Geoffrey can come too?'

'We were—hoping for a car this weekend. To go to the New Territories.'

'Oh dear, well Monday then?'

'I'll be gone by Monday. Look—don't worry. It's nice to be here now. Nice to come for a drink.'

'You see I have a Bridge.'

Veronica thought for a moment of teeth. Perhaps new teeth making lunch difficult.

'A Bridge—the wife of—well, it's a Royal Command sort of

thing. There are two tables—a French table and an Anglo-Chinese table. And tea. Look—do you play Bridge?'

'No I'm afraid—'

'Of course not. You work, don't you?'

'I'm a painter.'

'Oh, a *painter*. Oh wonderful. I'm sure there are a lot of painters in Hong Kong. Well, I believe there's a wife at Jardines—does Chinese heads. Makes quite a little business of— Look, why don't I take you to the Bridge? It'd be quite an experience for you. It's quite serious stuff you know. It might amuse—It's *real* Bridge.'

'No, no—'

But the woman had decided. She was stretching for the jade green telephone and talking ten to the dozen. They ate some biscuits and drank some more gin.

'You don't want to bother with lunch, do you? The food here is the big danger. We get as greedy as the Chinese. Aren't you loving the restaurants?'

'Yes, loving them.'

'I hope Geoffrey's doing you proud? We hardly see him. I hear he's moved to the Pen. With you?'

'Yes.'

'Oh, rather fun.'

A taxi took them to a house even higher up the Peak—servants, glass, marble floors, rare pieces of curly black ebony and small figurines of jade. The French table was already under way—tight mouths, severe hair-cuts, fast conversation. The sharp faces on the cards looked back. The Chinese/English table was more relaxed except at moments when a deep silence fell and eyes became filled with intent. Veronica sat apart on a silk sofa beside a silk screen and watched the rings shining on the confident international fingers. Outside the window birds tipped and soared on the cold wind.

An older, Chinese woman came across to Veronica when

tea was brought and sat by her. She said, in a Knightsbridge voice, 'How are you liking Hong Kong? I believe it is your first time?

'Oh very much. Yes, it is.'

'You are from London?'

'Yes. From Barnes.'

'Ah—from Barnes.'

A louder Chinese lady came across. She had round red spots painted on her cheeks and corkscrew curls. She spoke in a high, rather cockney sing-song.

'You will be going to London soon? Then you must stay in my flat. In Ken Sing Tong.'

'But I live in—'

'You like Hong Kong?'

'Oh, yes, very—'

Little cakes made of chestnut puree wrapped in pale green marzipan were handed out with the tea. The puree was piped in little worms like the things the boys were eating at the street stalls. The pale green marzipan was like the green of the neon. 'The pale green that is Chinese.'

'But it isn't,' thought Veronica. 'It is just pale green. I've seen those cakes in Fortnums, just as, come to think of it, I've seen that queer stuff on the street stalls. It was noodles. This place isn't any more foreign than London. None of it.'

The lady who had offered her a flat in Kensington took three little cakes, ate them greedily and licked her painted fingers heavy with diamonds.

'Nothing Chinese here,' thought Veronica, looking at all the ebony and jade and silk and the Chinese carpet on the floor. 'It is the Finchley Road.'

'I am hating it,' she thought, and got up.

'I must go,' she said. The women were going back to the tables. 'Oh dear,' said the Boss's wife. 'Oh hell—I did bish it up didn't I? Must you go?'

'I must, I'm afraid. I'm meeting someone Kowloon Side.'

It was the most inconvenient moment to leave and she knew it. The hostess was trying to get the tables back together again against a lot of fast talking by the French in corners. Servants were gliding about trying to gather unobtrusively the remains of the tea. 'So glad you could come,' said the hostess with a far-away calm that did not disguise her alertness to developments in more significant parts of the room. 'We'll meet again—won't we?' said the Boss's wife. 'We've all so wondered what dear Geoffrey's wife would be like.'

Two of the French women stopped talking then and looked at Veronica quickly.

Looking round, Veronica thought, 'They are all devious. Every one of them. What are they really thinking about behind all the witty talk and the picking up of the cards and the laying down of them?' Laughter followed her out of the room and she thought that it did not sound very kind. I liked the noise of the mah-jong players better than that, she thought. Getting off the ferry Kowloon Side, it was still not five o'clock. Over three hours to go. She had not a thing to do.

When she reached the Peninsula she found that she could not go in. She walked instead along the side of it, past the little inset shop windows and the two hundred pound shoes. She thought of the rings and the earrings and the even more beautiful shoes of the women playing cards on the Peak. As she stood a woman passed her, bouncing and busty. She was coming from a hairdresser, the hair raised up in a cushion, stiff with lacquer. She was the woman from the aeroplane, the army wife. She walked jauntily past Veronica, not recognising her. It might be Barnes, thought Veronica, or Ken Sing Tong.

Then she found that she was walking away and away from the hotel and away and away down Nathan Road. At first she walked quite slowly, but then she began to walk fast, watching for the traffic, but beginning to walk in and out of it. She began to march at the same quick, steady pace as everyone else in the crowded street.

And soon she found that she was caught up with the people on the pavement. She was in a marching army. Nobody looked at her, touched her, jostled her. Nobody in the street ever seemed to touch anybody else. And they made way for you without noticing you. You began to melt through the crowd like a spirit. There were no collisions. It was like radar, like bats. Up on their toes they all walked, their faces looking straight ahead, their arms to their sides. Perhaps, thought Veronica, if you live so closely, so densely together, you have to develop this isolation. Nobody noticed her, walking, walking, marching, marching. And, as she turned off into a side street for no real reason and marched on she realised that she had stopped being unhappy.

On a corner a minute old woman sold purple chrysanthemums and Veronica bought six. They seemed very cheap. The old woman with little yellow hands wrapped the stalks in yellow paper. Her hands were like fans. Ivory fans. They had no pictures on them. No faces.

'I think I'm a bit mad,' said Veronica. 'What shall I do with these flowers?'

The wind blew and it began to rain. The rain was cold on her face and the paper round the flowers grew sopped and useless. She let it float away into the gutter with other rubbish, and walked on.

'I think I must be hungry,' she said, 'I ought to have eaten some of those Mr. Kipling chestnut things. I'll find a street stall. Geoffrey said, "Never a street stall. Never in Hong Kong," he said. "Singapore yes. Hong Kong never. Look at the pots they cook in. Slopped round with a greasy cloth. Never washed up."'

'I'll eat at a street stall,' she said.

But there seemed now to be no stalls. She had walked since leaving Nathan Road down a dozen small streets and got back to a main road again—dirtier and greyer with only a faint glitter from the tram lines and overhead wires tossing with rain and wind. Traffic screamed by. The people thinned. The trams and buses were packed with those going home from work and other thousands arriving for the evening shift. She didn't know whether to try and cross this road or not, and realised she was quite lost. Also, it seemed—but this must surely be because there was a storm coming—to be getting quite dark.

Then she was out of the street and on a great motorway, a huge clover-leaf junction. The crowd had disappeared and there was no one about. Only traffic—mostly big square lorries—streamed by. It was an enormously wide road, two triple carriageways and a scruffy central reservation. At the far side there seemed to be grass and a large, low, sad-looking building, a sort of club house. Maybe she could get a taxi back from there?

All alone in the ridiculous white suit she ran from the edge of the motorway to the central reservation and stood there between the whizzing lorries, waiting for the second dash to the far shore. And there she smelled the pig boy.

He was in a lorry—a lorry still far away up the road, but the smell was so huge and terrible that she looked about her, up and down the road, to see if some great sewer were leaking near her feet. The wind then carried the smell in a blast into her mouth so that she retched and dropped the flowers and pressed her hands over her face. Her eyes streamed with water. She struggled to get her handkerchief—anything—out of her bag, and with a clashing, cranking roar the lorry came up beside her.

The back of it was filled to the brim with screaming pigs—dark with dirt, tossed in a writhing mass, suffering, fighting with pathetic, inadequate feet to get somehow steady and in control of their great bodies. The pigs at the bottom of the heap—their gaping faces pressed into the slats—seemed already dead.

But it was the smell. It made her nearly faint.

'You want help?'

It was the driver. The pig boy. High above her head he looked down. She turned away sick, 'No, no.'

'You lost? English? You want help?'

He was not Chinese like the flower-seller, or the servants on the Peak, or the ivory-carved room-boys at the hotel, or even the red faced Hakkar professional beggar. He had a broad face, laughing cheek-bones, long, bright Mongolian eyes and curly hair.

'Thanks,' she gasped. 'No. It's fine, thanks. I'm just going— over there. To get a taxi.'

'That place shut there now over there. That place shut. For new building. Re-settlement. Old English tennis club. Nobody now. Where you stay?'

'The Peninsula.'

'Four-five mile soon dark.'

'It's all right. Please go.' She—still nearly fainting—tried to cross the road behind the lorry.

But he had jumped down and came towards her. He took her wrist and pulled her to the front of the lorry and tumbled her up and in. She retched again and her forehead fell down against the dashboard.

'You ill?' He had started the engine though it could hardly be heard against the screaming of the pigs. He turned on the radio. Chinese music wailed through the cab, too.

'The smell, the smell!'

'Oh, *smell*,' he said and began to laugh. 'Terrible, terrible smell.' He laughed with his eyes and his shoulders and his mouth and with every bit of him. Clusters of good luck charms hung across the windscreen of the cab—tokens, ribbons, silly animals dangling from strings, and several photographs of girls. Veronica turned from all of them and leaned her head against the rattling, vibrating door. 'Terrible smell!' He laughed with pride. She remembered how the room-boys had laughed and laughed, Geoffrey had told her, when he had hurt his back soon after he arrived and had had to lie down on a hard board. 'Terrible pain,' they had laughed. And someone else, telling her of a visit to a Chinese dentist—and on the Peak at that—had asked, 'Is this going to hurt?' 'Oh yes—it going to hurt all right,' and had roared with laughter. Something at last was different here.

The lorry had turned off the motorway and down a drab road, seeming to turn away from the Centre again. It rattled past warehouses and long grey sheds. By one of them it stopped. Some people came out, wearing cloths across their faces. The driver jumped out and went over to them and they all went into the shed. Veronica, still holding the handkerchief to her mouth, sweating with sickness, struggled with the door but it wouldn't open from the inside. She felt utter terror now through the sickness and began to cry.

Then the door was opened and she fell out into the pig boy's arms. He jumped back at once. He looked shocked and only when he was sure she was safe on her feet did he shout above the pigs, 'Please—come with me now.'

She could think only of getting away from the hell of the lorry and as he turned she followed, out of the filthy yard, along a wire-fenced road, then down an alley that led to another alley that led to another that led to a busy road again. They walked, one behind the other along this road until they came to an iron bridge. Under the bridge were some stalls selling kites—sharp yellow and red and blue. Around them people were eating and talking and shouting and under the bridge a man was squatting in vest and underpants playing an instrument balanced with a spike like a miniature cello on the pavement. It looked like something between a guitar, a cello and a lute and the noise that came from it was like chalk drawn across a blackboard and in its way hurt like the smell of the pigs.

As Veronica watched, the musician looked up and smiled at her and the sun came out. All the coloured kites blazed for a moment in the sunset.

'Quick, quick,' said the pig boy and walked lithe and fast under the bridge and into a dark street. As they reached it, out came the sun again and Veronica saw the street crumbling before her. A lumpish, medieval machine, very different from the mechanics on the Peak, slowly swung a huge iron ball at a tall, papery old building. The whole front of the building slipped quietly to the ground and the sun went in again.

'I am being shown things,' said Veronica, 'like Faust.' They went on down the dark and filthy street. 'Or maybe I am being kidnapped. Perhaps I am about to be raped. Or knifed. Geoffrey—all of them, said, "Never go Kowloon Side alone." I am mad.' But she walked quietly on behind the pig boy.

He stopped and said, 'Tea?'

'No—no. Please—I want to go home. Can you find me a—bus or a taxi or something? I must get back.'

'You are ill. Tea first and then home.'

They were standing outside a dirty, blackened house with a very narrow, dark doorway. It was the oldest house she had seen in Hong Kong. Outside it, on two ancient basket chairs there sat an old woman and a very, very old man dressed in black tunics and black trousers. They sat very straight, like royal people. The woman looked at Veronica and bowed. The man looked gravely at her for rather longer, and then bowed. Nobody spoke, and in the quiet Veronica could still hear the piercing music of the lute player that now sounded the only right music for the scene.

Then, from across the road, next to the house that was being pulled down, people came running and gathering round a queer, high car, piled high with paper flowers—pink and red and yellow and white. They chattered and laughed and fussed and took no notice of Veronica or the ancient royal personages or the demolition.

The pig boy had disappeared, but he now came out of the dark doorway between the two basket chairs with a painted Chinese girl who looked at Veronica and smiled. From the thickness and symmetry of the paint Veronica saw that the girl was a prostitute. Several other girls came out who looked like her sisters. They seemed dolls from a box. Then someone else came and laid a cleanish sheet of white paper on the pavement and bowed to Veronica to sit on it. Then an older woman in a thick woollen suit and a gold bangle round her ankle brought a tiny bowl of tea.

Veronica drank it, and caught the eye of the old people. The old woman smiled, showing a mouth full of gold teeth. The old gentleman touched first one side of his long moustaches and then the other before smiling, too. Across the road the wild party surged about the car, filling and covering it with more and more paper flowers. The pig boy, who had been talking to the painted girls, came over and said, 'You happy and well?'

She drank the tea.

'It is a funeral,' said the boy. 'You have come to a funeral.' He repeated this to the others in some sort of language and everyone laughed tremendously. He said, 'You are dressed in white for the funeral.' Their laughter mixed with the laughter and shouts of the funeral party across the road, as it moved off.

The sun had gone in now. The dust from the demolished building hung heavy. The pig boy stank. Rubbish was piled in the gutter. The woman brought more tea. The queer music went faintly on.

'You happy and well?'

Veronica said, 'Oh I am happy. I am well.' This was translated, and the old aristocrats bowed. There was silence.

Veronica realised sadly that they were expecting her to go. She stood up and said to the pig boy, 'I wish I had kept my flowers, my flowers to give them. I let them drop.'

This was translated and there was more bowing. Veronica shook hands with everyone. They took her hand with a very slight hesitation. Following the pig boy, she turned at the end of the road to wave to them, but there was no one on the street at all except the two old people and they seemed to be sitting thoughtfully looking in another direction.

The pig boy walked ahead and then after a while beside her, saying nothing. She could hardly keep up. He had fallen quite silent and she said, 'Please—can I get a bus or taxi now? I thought I saw a taxi just then.'

'No taxi,' he said. 'You are back hotel.'

'Where?'

'One minute now. Two minute.'

'It can't be.'

Yet the streets were different, noisier, busier. There were tourists about. Then all at once, there was the Hakkar beggar with her child, but now, the pig boy beside her, the child did not come after her crying, 'Money.'

'I should tell you,' said the pig boy, 'that you must not take hands. You must not take hands here or embrace.'

'I'm sorry. I just wanted to say thank you to them.'

He walked on, filthy and beautiful and rough in the rich street. The crowd was changing every moment, growing smarter, faster, better dressed. He wove expertly among them.

'What are you? Who are you?' she said.

'A pig boy. I bring pigs every day out of Red China into Hong Kong. Chinese pigs. Big trading.'

'Yes, I see.'

'Good job,' he said. 'Sweet and sour'—he laughed. 'Only for strong men.'

'Oh goodness,' she said—here were the shoes, 'oh good-

ness, we're back at the Peninsula. Oh thank you, thank you.'
She turned to the pig boy and not able to help it held out to
him both her hands. He looked at them unsmiling.

'You took my wrist,' she said, 'to pull me into the cab.'

Briefly he touched her hands with his own and was gone.

'My God!' It was Geoffrey beside her getting out of a taxi.
He carried a brief case and a pile of papers. 'You just back?
You've had a long day. It's past nine. God, this bloody place. I
hate it. Let's get a bath and—heavens, you smell dreadful.
Wherever's the memsahib been taking you?'

'*Do* you hate it?' She could not move one step until
Geoffrey had answered. If she moved she knew that something
would break. 'Do you hate it here?'

'Well—no. But you do.'

'Do I?'

'You know you do. I know you do. I've known all the time.'

They stood on the pavement and the crowds washed effort-
lessly by. 'You couldn't live here, Veronica.'

'I might,' she said, 'I might.'

M arjorie Partridge at the end of her garden savaged the earth around the hydrangeas and wept for her child, Olivia.

Wimbledon gardens can be venerable. Even Tudor. Marjorie's garden was only nineteenth-century but it had had a hundred years of care, seventy-five of them from a chain of full-time gardeners, now forgotten.

Wimbledon is not the suburb of the plastic greenhouse, tomato plant, sunflower and prize marrow; the squirl of coloured glass in the vestibule window, permanent-wave and coffee morning, of wife-swopping and vodka. This is folklore. It is—or the enclave of red roads round the Common is—one cannot speak for down the hill—a serious, rich and confident place which does not follow fashion.

The enclave is the old town and as in the old town in Rabat or Delhi or Paris or Dublin it breathes its own air. Like many old towns there is still money there—the best sort of money: old, invisible, slow-burning, undiscussed and never used in idiot beautification. Marjorie had not had a new coat in years. Her shoes were funny. Her drawing room curtains were very old and her Turkey rugs, though nearly priceless, were worn and frayed down to the knots. In Hampstead a house with a Picasso in its safe has grilles to its windows when the owners are away. In Old Wimbledon, when there is a Braque on the wall (the Partridges had a Kandinsky) there is only the most antique of burglar alarms hidden in the creeper. There is however a Veronica or a Phyllis or a Mrs. Something who moves in until the holiday is over to keep things looking occupied. These people cost more than grilles in the end and are not so smart, but they are more effective. They are also interesting, being the last trickle of the Edwardian servant class which staffed and enlivened these twenty or so streets until the Wars. The Partridges' house—and it was not ostentatious—had five indoor servants until 1939, Marjorie had been told, not to mention gardeners. Now, as she was fond of saying, 'There is only me—and Maureen. And of course Mr. Jackson who sees to things outside.'

Maureen and Mr. Jackson were not only better dressed than the Partridges. They had more comfortable and warmer houses, more ready cash, more holidays, more laughs, more sex, more entertaining lives. But there existed between them and their employers a queer mutual confidence, a feudal equality and a genuine loyalty that was very like love. They had stayed—Maureen and Mr. Jackson—for years.

Thus Mr. Jackson would crash into Mrs. Partridge's conservatory when she was reading Solzhenitsyn and roar, 'Your boiler's done for. It's new central heating now. Can't complain. Old in the sixties—and before that. We're none of us what we were.' Maureen the cleaner—who called herself housekeeper on the telephone but was otherwise without vice—knew Majorie's most inward thoughts, could say anything to her. 'You look better the less you try,' she would observe through the bedroom door as Marjorie gazed sternly at herself in some old fur; and, 'You and I understand each other, Mrs. Partridge.' She had known Mrs. Partridge's daughter Olivia since the shawl, and although Maureen's days were Mondays, Wednesdays and Fridays (mornings) and Olivia killed herself on a Tuesday afternoon it was Maureen who was first at the house. She lived in Morden—a good three-quarters of an hour.

Mr. Partridge had left the previous morning for Thailand

via the Middle East and Dacca, and was just about arriving in Bangkok as Maureen reached Rathbone Road. He was a civil servant in high office, a tiny, yellow-faced, pre-aged man, not clubbable. He seldom spoke at the few Christmas drinks parties he attended in the enclave but was very welcome at them and would have been very sorry not to have been asked. He was known as 'old Jack Partridge—bloody clever'. He read a great deal—Descartes—in the French of course—Hobbes, Keynes; but Thomas Hardy too, and Brecht, and Beckett. At the cinema—the Partridges did not watch television and did not have a set—he very much enjoyed Woody Allen. Unstuffy Jack Partridge, immensely able, up to date, seeing both *Private Eye* and *The Times Literary Supplement*.

And no one could say that he had ever expected too much of Olivia. He had never pushed her in any way. There had been no need. Dreamy and cool, Olivia had always seemed to live without stress. Yes, Jack Partridge knew that he had the measure of nearly all his colleagues at work. Yes, he had got a First at Cambridge and later at Harvard. Yes, he could run rings round his Minister and such members of the Cabinet as dared present themselves before him; and when he dined on high table at his old college, such Fellows as were forewarned sharpened themselves up in advance. Yes, he knew that only Marjorie who had also taken a First—in English at Oxford—very much the woman's subject in those days, but still—yes, he knew that only Marjorie could stand up to him in rational day to day logic; and yes, he knew that the pair of them must be rather formidable parents for an only child.

But not for Livie.

Jack Partridge had loved his daughter from the day he first met her in St Teresa's Maternity Hospital along the Ridgway. In those days it was run by crackling long-skirted nuns, and quite cheap, not as later the resting place for millionaires, often foreigners. It was the unquestioned lying-in place for the memsahibs of the enclave and many of them had met there and long friendships had begun. In the private room at St Teresa's Jack had noted for the first time his daughter's silky hair, her bland reflective sleeping face, had moved a sensitive finger, later that evening used to turn the pages of official reports, along her cheek. 'Olivia,' he had said.

'"Olivia Partridge",' Marjorie had said, looking down at the cot. Marjorie was rosy and large—an awfully nice woman—huge-bosomed on the high bed, for she was of course going to breast-feed. A Double First was by the way in the sixties. Educated women were fulfilled by their memories and moved on with intensity and dedication to bring up their children themselves. They read the FT with the baby on their shoulder, kept up *The Times* crossword and at least one foreign language. They baked cakes, wrote letters to each other and when the children were old enough to be at school all day had pleasant times at Hatchards and the University Women's Club for lunch. Feminism's self-awareness, self-love, was in Wimbledon strictly for the future—though less than ten miles away in Richmond it was already knocking on the Georgian doors, seeping through the wisterias and round the glossy dining tables. Richmond women were rushing upstairs weeping and packing suitcases, or asking young men to lunch and to stay the afternoon. But a curious class of person has always lived in Richmond.

'"Olivia Partridge",' said her mother, eighteen years ago at St Teresa's in her sensible long-sleeved nightdress, surrounded by the garden flowers of local friends and a photograph of Jack doing his army service in the Education Corps, '"Olivia Partridge"—oh dear, it does sound rather like a don.'

'She's beautiful,' said old Jack and put her in the paper, which is to say *The Times*: 'To Jack and Marjorie Partridge, a daughter, Olivia,' and entered her name for Sherborne School and took out another couple of insurance policies. The satisfaction he felt about Olivia became the deep part of his life. He was unconcerned that no other child followed her. Neither parent was young.

Olivia went first to Mrs. Parsons's nice little school on the Common which didn't fuss about examinations like the High School. The little girls spent a great deal of time doing Nature, with Miss Phillips puffing behind them up to Caesar's Camp. Twice a week they played Rounders under the twisted chestnut tree opposite South Side, which had given shelter to generations of Wimbledon nannies even before Robert Graves was patted under it in his pram by Swinburne. It was gentle Rounders, and consisted largely in Miss Phillips's calling out encouragement and shaking tidy the heap of brown cardigans that were used as bases; and in the making of daisy chains. Marjorie, striding by on a walk with the dog, used to pretend not to see Livie, thoughtfully fielding, for she knew that a child must develop its private life at school.

Which—the Partridges never put a foot wrong, ever—Livie did. She was clearly very clever, and so self-reliant that at seven she was making two or three trips a week to the Public Library down the hill.

The parent Partridges, living in Rathbone Road, had no need of down-the-hill themselves. Jack was a member of the London Library which took care of books. Friends, shops, restaurants, fresh air, exercise, Church (Livie was not deprived of the chance of Christianity though her parents were not believers and they explained this to her) were all available within the enclave. Jack did not even have to walk down the hill to the station but took a bus to Putney and then the tube. Chauffeurs were for foreigners and the media people on Drax Avenue and Parkside.

But Olivia devoured books so fast that the down-the-hill library was vital to her and she was found sitting—aged eight—in the Reference Room in Compton Road among all the

hackers and spitters and tramps clinking bottles and old creatures taking grey sandwiches out of paper bags, and looking
very happy. It shocked her mother who rousted her out. 'My
dear!' she said to her friends. 'She was oblivious. You know,
she is off this earth!'

'Oblivious Olivious,' said Jack. 'Oblivia Olivia!' It became
quite a joke.

Marjorie did occasionally go down the hill to meet Jack in
the car off the Waterloo train when he was late and this was a
quicker way home. She hated it—sitting in the station forecourt, a place nobody has ever loved (waiting-time mercifully
restricted to ten minutes) watching the army of pale men
emerge from the underground like souls from hell. Over the
years she saw known faces growing greyer, lines between nose
and mouth cut deeper, good suits become more expensive, less
noticeable, briefcases more importantly battered. Some talked
to themselves, head down, turning for the hill to walk, for
health's sake, home. 'So alike,' thought Marjorie. 'Some day I'll
drive off the wrong one.'

'Jack,' she said. 'I'm finished with down-the-hill. When you
come home by train you'll have to get a taxi.'

'Why?'

'Oh they are such awful people down there. Or else just
those poor tired men.'

'The country's run by us. The poor tired men,' he said. 'You
ought to thank God for us. We watch over governments, the
tired men. And I suppose women. A few. We're the protectors.
Didn't Cromwell live at The Crooked Billet?'

'Nonsense. Cromwell was Huntingdon.'

'It's said.'

'I expect it was Thomas. He probably once walked over the
Common. You only have to have a cup of tea in Wimbledon
for them to put up a blue plaque to you.'

'There isn't a blue plaque for a Cromwell.'

'I don't suppose dear old Wimbledon ever heard of either Cromwell while he was alive. It's always been pretty private.'

The Crooked Billet is the pretty, countrified pub near the green end of Rathbone Road. It faces a famous seventeenth century house—famous of course only within the enclave: protected from general acclaim—which never has its windows washed and where there are said to be Rembrandts. It is alongside the site of a mansion pulled down the year Livie was born where Pitt the Younger used to spend his country weekends. Pitt the Younger, like Jack Partridge and the hosts of the grey-faced men on the underground, is on record as saying that he would have cracked without the blessedness of Wimbledon Common at weekends. It stretched gently then, unchangingly, to Roehampton, smelling of hay and flowers as it does still. 'Thank God for the Common,' Jack would say, whistling up the dog. 'Coming, Livie?' and they would walk to the windmill and down into the woods. 'It sparkles,' said Livie on a windy, watery day. 'Like a Corot,' said her father, and Livie nodded. At eight she knew what a Corot was.

The woods had a pool in them called Queensmere where Wimbledon gentlemen (Jack had not met any of them) were allowed to bathe naked before eight o'clock in the morning. It was all very respectable and sylvan, and the three Partridges laughed about it sometimes for fun. But Livie, writing of it in an essay for Miss Phillips, 'The Place Where I Live', had this part crossed out in broad, green ink.

Queensmere after that, a murky place, was bewildering to her. She couldn't like it anyway because quite soon after the essay her father had told her that someone—some 'poor, uncertain lady'—had drowned herself there long ago. 'It was winter. They found her in the morning and her hair was spread out in spikes, frozen in the ice. Unpleasant business.' Jack was a Wimbledonian—born in the enclave. He knew the legends.

'I never told you that,' he said years later. 'It was your

mother I told. "Uncertain lady"—really Olivia! As if I'd say that to a child.'

But he often tended to get his two women mixed up.

On June the fifth every year a Fair comes to Wimbledon Common and you can hear its thump and beat as far away as Putney Hill. First come the big caravans, shuttered and huge. They arrive by night, as they have done perhaps since Pitt the Younger. One morning they are found resting there like birds from Africa. For two days they sleep, then spring to life the third evening, blazing and blaring and whirling with lights like musical fireworks. The ring of houses of the enclave sits darkly by, for the Fair people have nothing to do with the people of the enclave (their evening customers come from Tooting, even Streatham) and the enclave pretends that the Fair is not there, even when the lights play over their faces as they lie in bed. For two weeks the flickers and strains of the Zharooms and the Bumpums and the Tunnel of Love and the wonderful Golden Horses ('Rode by all with Pride') take charge of the Common's central platform near the War Memorial as they did the day Marjorie brought Olivia home in her arms from the hospital run by the excellent nuns. For years Olivia thought that the Fair was some demonstration in honour of her birthday and had been so old when she had realised that this was not so (maybe ten—even eleven) that she blushed to think of it.

At eleven Olivia did not go away to Sherborne School after all as she won a magnificently important scholarship to a famous London day school. The decision to accept it had been entirely hers, said the Partridges, and she was doing special subjects there—Greek, Russian—in no time at all. 'It seems young,' they said. 'But the school think she's up to it. We don't interfere.' She was keeping up her Music too—begun at Mrs. Parsons's—and attending the Royal College in Marylebone on Saturday mornings. On Sundays for nearly a year, she took

Confirmation classes, and then did voluntary work through the local church—there was an old lady she went to see in Bathgate Road and a spastic boy in The Drive. 'My dear, we never *see* her,' her mother said to friends at lunches. Jack, dining in Geneva or Berlin, said, 'Yes. One girl. No—London day school. More in touch we think. Doing Russian—and it's to be Chinese next I hear. Yes—very young. Well—Cambridge, we rather hope.'

But he never boasted, was never excessive, never mentioned Olivia without being asked. Marjorie, digging her Brussels sprouts or writing a little monograph on *George Eliot at Southfields* for the Wimbledon Lit. and Sci. (Literary and Scientific Society, founded 1891) was sensible likewise. She would smile down at her spade or out of the study window at the gate, watching Olivia coming home (she looks tired, thought Marjorie, but you do look tired in your O level year)— Marjorie would smile and indulge in quick fantasies that it would be Oxford Olivia plumped for—that her first term, leaves falling, green lawns, sloping to the river—she would settle Olivia in at her own old college. Perhaps into her own old room.

Livie didn't do particularly well in the O Levels, though the school said that this hardly mattered. O Levels are no test of a mind. Marjorie and the Headmistress had quite a smile about how much better some of Livie's contemporaries had done with not a tenth of Livie's brilliance. Livie proceeded to Russian, Greek and Mathematics at Advanced Level. She continued her Music. Her piano playing was now astonishing. 'I wouldn't say exactly *concert* standard,' said Marjorie, laughing as if she were lying a little. Livie took on secretaryships of many societies and became Head Girl. She organised dances to which boys were invited, though she did not meet any of them socially—or dance. She stood gravely by the disco looking beautiful but in heavy, low-heeled shoes.

She looked tireder—but no wonder. Marjorie took to making lightning dashes to the school to fetch her home—sometimes finding that there was a long wait when she got there. But she had the car radio and a heater and her petit-point. Often she found that she and Livie had missed each other and Livie was at home before her—head back, eyes shut on the porch seat having forgotten her keys. Livie was vague now about her time-table, vague even about where she had been. Marjorie gave up the petit-point at the school gate. Livie had never been enthusiastic about her mother coming to fetch her anyway. Not even at Mrs. Parsons's.

'Is she overdoing things?' Marjorie wanted to ask the Headmistress. But Livie was seventeen. The Headmistress was statuesque and looked as if she had never needed a mother. Anyhow, Marjorie hated women who fussed to Headmistresses.

The Fair arrived during the Advanced Levels. It was louder than ever this year with some new and wilder variety of music. Marjorie—Jack was away—almost thought of moving up into London, near to the school during the examinations—perhaps to a private hotel—but Livie looked amazed. She was used to the Fair's arrival during examination days. The noise was familiar to her, washed beautifully over her. It had never interfered with sleep or work. And it was part of her birthday. She opened her bedroom windows wide and the night before the Greek Unseen paper Marjorie went up with milk and glucose to find Livie's curtains flapping, books put tidily away and Livie not there. It was past ten o'clock. Livie came in after midnight.

'Livie! Where were you?'

'I went round the Fair.'

'Alone?'

'Yes, Pride of the South. "Rode by all with Pride." It says it in scrolls.'

'Have you been in The Crooked Billet? Are you drunk?'

'I've been to the Fair. The Golden Horses aren't there. They've been smashed up. He said it would be too expensive to repair them. "Rode by all with pride."'

'Are you well? Are you all right?'

'They were Italian,' said Livie. 'Very old. Lovely wrong grammar. All gone. It was vandals.'

But she seemed herself in the morning.

She did all right in the A Levels. All right. Nothing spectacular. There were some spectacular results that year and some girls were even given university places unconditionally. One of these girls was also found to be pregnant, not in favour of abortion and desirous of keeping the baby. Her mother—a Kensington woman—had a nervous breakdown and took herself off to the South of France, so that one unconditional university place was going to be wasted. 'There are people with *real* problems,' wrote Marjorie to Jack in Tokyo, and Jack went straight out and bought Livie some pearl stud earrings (Minimoto, like her mother's) and wrote her a delightful letter saying how little he worried about her. She was splendid. She had to remember that she was a really splendid person. 'For Oxford,' he said (it *was* to be Oxford), 'it is the entrance examination and the personal interview that counts. I confidently predict—and remember, Livie, I am not unastute at prediction though I dare say it is a thing I would only admit to you or your mother—I confidently predict that no tutor in his right mind could ever turn you down. You are very special.' And he went on to talk about the economy of Japan.

He added a post-script. She was to remember the triviality of examinations. The hazards of being accepted by Oxbridge were to her trifling. The real assessments of her, the true tests of the brain were to come. Quality was after all—except for the bourgeois—only apparent after the first Degree, at postgraduate level. 'So it won't all be over by Christmas, old girl. Don't think you're at the end yet.'

The Partridges were parents in a million, loving, kind and good. They spoke eye-ball to eye-ball, man to man.

The Oxford entrance examination was still an autumn away and so Marjorie made a great point of seeing that Livie had some fun during the summer holidays. She arranged for her to go to some of the private dances in the enclave arranged by the Wives' Fellowship. These were by invitation only to big houses in Marryat and Bathgate Road and even one in a quaint house over towards Raynes Park belonging to a woman married to a Greek (an unfortunate result of reading Modern Languages at Hull) but who was third-generation Wimbledon and a super girl. 'One knows simply everyone at these dances,' said Marjorie, 'that's what's so nice, and if some of them speak in common voices and wear one earring one knows that it is just showing off. They'll be sending their own children to Wives' Dances one day. You could tell just to look at them— pink hair, earrings and the lot. As Robert Graves said in *Goodbye to all That*—and Robert Graves of course was born just off the Ridgway, down the road from Livie—you can always tell a gentleman. These young people were gents. It would have been none of them for example who had smashed the stone lions which had stood for a hundred years outside the vet's in the High Street. Heaven alone knew who those people might be.'

Livie was writing something slowly across the kitchen window as her mother's view of Robert Graves and the vet's lions was being put forward. She had just come home from one of the dances—she always came home alone. She turned eyes of such desolation on Marjorie that Marjorie stopped laying the breakfast.

'Livie?'

'The vet's lions,' said Livie. 'My God.'

'Now Livie—'

'My God.'

'Aren't you pleased that the people at the dance didn't smash the vet's lions?'

'My God.'

'Livie! They've been repaired by the John Evelyn Society.'

'Do you see John Evelyn on the vet's lions?'

'Now Livie—Well, no Livie. No Livie, of course I don't. They used to stand on some gateposts about then—Evelyn's time—I believe. Some great house. I don't think he actually lived in Wimbledon you know. Just passed through.'

'A lot of them,' said Livie. 'Did that.'

'The Thackerays would have known them of course. I expect Anne Thackeray must actually have sat on them. You all sat on them of course, *all* the children at Mrs. Parsons's.'

'Rode by all with pride.'

'Livie—whatever's wrong? Just get out the marmalade, would you? Swinburne must have known them of course. He'd have passed them every day on the way to The Rose and Crown before getting his newspaper from Frost's. At the second door. Did you know, Livie—Frost's had two doors. Until just last year when they pulled it down they called the second door "Mr. Swinburne's door". Isn't it killing?'

'Killing.'

'Livie—'

But Livie had walked away.

'Olivia's getting a bit cantankerous—just a little bit difficult,' wrote Marjorie to Jack. 'It's natural I suppose. We have been so lucky—and looking round we still are so lucky. Sometimes you might almost think it was something to do with this place, the disasters there are on all sides. And yet I'm sure there's no place more caring. I suppose there is always disaster with the young. "Youth is a blunder"—Disraeli. Did I tell you about Michael B. in Bicester Crescent? He's had something they call a breakdown (drugs?) and he's in The Priory. *Brilliant* A Levels. He's been sleeping rough on the Common.' Later she wrote, 'Those poor Smiths on Ridgway Hill. Ophelia has gone off to Tooting to live with an Iranian. She's been in trouble with the police. She met him in this so-called wine-bar. And do you remember little Duffy Duff? Apparently he left Cambridge without a Degree. Went in to each exam and just walked out again. He's so good they say they would have given him something if he had only written his name on the paper. All he wrote was 'not to be classified'. Oh, isn't it sad—do you remember him reciting that lovely little ballad at the end-of-term Christmas concert? He looked like a little angel himself. He's helping to run a Meditation Centre in the Lake District now and when he rang his father up the other day to wish him happy birthday—which is something I suppose: Mrs. Parsons's training!—he was talking in broadest Cockney! I don't suppose anybody understands a word he says, especially in the Lake District. Oh how lucky we are with Livie.'

Livie, the day of the Oxford entrance papers, had the composure and quietness of the day she was born. Her tall figure in good skirt and jersey, her hair well cut—she went to Marjorie's girl at Peter Jones—delighted some of her mother's friends who passed her on the way to the bus. 'Dear Livie,' they said. 'Her smile hasn't changed since they were all at dancing class.'

'I'd not say that,' said Maureen, passing through the Partridges' hall—jumble was being sorted—'Keeps herself to herself. Always did. But I'll not say she's never changed. There's different bits to Olivia. I'll not forget when I used to take her to watch the Fair.'

'Oh, she always liked the Fair.'

'Made me go on that Ghost Train. Sick as a dog.'

'Were you, Maureen?' Marjorie carefully avoided her friends' eyes in case someone laughed. Maureen was a card. 'You shouldn't have given way to her.'

'No—*I* weren't sick. She were. Olivia was the one sick. She didn't care though. She loved them rotors, too. Stuck to the side of the drum she was with her skirt above her head. And she got me to take her up on them golden horses too—them things with barley sugars skewered through them diagonal and their heads tossed back and their teeth glaring out. Both arms round their necks and her hair all streamed out like Godiva.'

'Maureen is sometimes quite coarse,' said Marjorie to Jack over carré of lamb from the butcher in the High Street who delivered, and put frills on the cutlets. Olivia was out—probably something to do with the spastic or the old lady—not church, which she had given up. She had been uncommunicative that morning and since the Oxford entrance papers. 'Maureen said that Livie used to scream at the Fair with her skirt over her face.'

'Not much harm in that. And very long ago if it was when Maureen used to take her. By the way, which day does she hear?'

'Oh quickly. The interview is this week. On Wednesday—Oxford is quite quick.'

'Oh Lord—then I shall be away?'

'Yes of course. Didn't you know?'

'At Cambridge I think they took longer to tell us. Or was it shorter?'

'I don't think you need worry about not being here. She's much less fussed than either of us. And we're only fussed because—well, not because she might not get in. That would be ridiculous. I suppose we're really just excited. It's an emotional time. It doesn't seem a minute since this was happening to me. After all—it's a very big moment, getting into Oxbridge.'

'You know,' said Jack, 'I don't remember it. It was taken for granted. Just part of life then if you were any good at all. Less pressure then.'

'Oh—Livie's had no pressure. Not from us. Good heavens, she knows, even if there were some lunacy and she didn't— well, as if we'd think any less of her!'

'Well, of course. Marjorie—I suppose she *will* get an interview?'

'Well, of course she'll get an interview. It's only the absolute unknowns who don't. And heavens, I've always been very close to Mabel Pye. It'll cause a great deal of surprise if she doesn't, I must say—I've written round several people to say that she may be looking in on Wednesday afterwards for a cup of tea. Goodness, at school they say she's the best they've had in ten years. It's not the possibility of interviews they're all thinking about. It's the kind of Award she'll get. Just wait till we're all hearing that she's the first woman at All Souls.'

'Now then Marjorie. This letter—the letter giving the time of the interview comes when?'

'It doesn't come. They all have to be at the college on Wednesday *unless* there is a letter. If a letter comes it's to say they're not wanted.'

'A pretty devastating business. Rather cruel.'

'It's fairly new, I think. Oh, I don't think we need worry about letters.'

Jack trickled perfect mint-sauce over his lamb. 'We should chop back the mint,' he said. 'It's tending to get above itself.'

'I've done it. I've had the parsley out, too. Time to re-sow.'

'It's time to divide the irises. And bring in the dahlias.' He looked at his disciplined garden, programmed for Spring. It was getting near Christmas. Next door a neighbour, a fashionable lawyer, was giving one of his drinks parties. The women could be heard screaming in gusts as the front door opened and shut. 'I'd rather my women screamed at the Fair than next door,' said Jack. 'Just listen to them—baying for gin. The road's changing.'

'Oh—I don't know.'

'Oxford we're going to find changed, too, you know. I warn you. I was talking—'

'Oh well—of course we are. It must. To a certain extent. But there'll always be some like us. A nucleus—'

'Feminism,' said Jack. 'Lesbianism. Free love or whatever they call it nowadays. This pill business.'

'We needn't worry about Livie.'

'Over-work—'

'Livie's *never* over-worked. Her mind's not even been stretched yet. She's not a worrier. Livie's the most peaceful person I know.'

They walked, Jack and Marjorie, on the Common that afternoon meeting several friends. Most of these also walked in pairs, for divorce and early death are remarkably rare in the enclave. Most were without children. Their children were grown and flown. The Partridges called out to them and they called back in similar pleasant old-fashioned voices. 'Any news of Adrian?' 'Is Francesca still at the BBC?' 'I hear Camilla's in at Girton—not a bit surprised.' 'Good luck to Livie on Wednesday.'

The calls were passwords, codes, the names of the measures of a dance. They meant more than they seemed to mean. They meant, 'We are a tribe. A club. We think alike. We have done our best. We have brought up our children to follow us on, which is ancient and natural but nowadays courageous. We act for the common good.'

The calls said that there had been many shared years—first with prams, then push-chairs, then small bikes, then ponies from the riding school: changeless Miss Thompson's dancing class, Guy Fawkes parties and Hallowe'ens; that there had been year after year of birthdays on the Common, the cake carried, with candles separate, to be assembled in the long grass with the flowers in it by The Causeway or The Pound or in the secret, woody parts round Queensmere. The calls said that all nice children have clean hair, that to Christmas tea parties they bring small presents, prettily wrapped, and the boys wear bow ties and the girls long white socks and pretty dresses, not jeans.

The words said, 'We and our children belong to a time before the Beatles, before the recession, before we all drank wine every day although it was so cheap, to a time when you could buy cakes like you make at home in the High Street and none of us had heard of a video centre or seen a launderette; a time when you could drive down Church Road in tennis fortnight and even park there. And the tennis players were still gentlemen like Robert Graves. When at the Fair the Golden Horses flew.'

The words said, 'We are the elect. By many we suppose we are considered dreadful. We are all true blue, even if we are radicals, or the odd eccentric socialist. We are staunch, we are loyal, we are innocent in a way, bless us. We are rather happy people and when bad times come we comfort one another.'

The enclave was out in force that afternoon, their dogs bounding round them. Such people and dogs not of the enclave who passed, passed like shadows. Marjorie, contented, thought, 'This is my landscape,' and uncharacteristically took Jack's hand, as the sun went down suddenly behind Queensmere in a scar of white light.

On Tuesday after the second post and the last nonsensical thought of a rejecting letter was past, Marjorie went down the hill to the station to buy Olivia's return ticket to Oxford for the next day. She had decided, rather wisely she thought, not to drive her there. 'It is Livie's day,' she said to herself on the hill, 'Livie's life. I have always seen to that.' She remembered all at once the long-ago Rounders game by the twisted chestnut tree on the corner of South Side, and Livie, reflective in the long grass; how she had turned away from the child, not wanting Livie to feel that she was watching to see whether or not she caught the ball. 'And Livie knew,' she thought. She stopped in surprise. 'Livie knew—Livie has always known all about me. And Jack. She's never said anything. Never said that she—loved us, for instance. We never said these things to each other, any of us. We never said it to her even when she was a baby.

'She'll be touched, though, that I've been down to get the ticket,' she thought. 'When I get home I will put it into her hand.'

But when Marjorie got home Livie was not about. The enclave was silent. Marjorie made herself tea and sat by the telephone to wait for Jack's call to say that he had safely reached Bangkok. Rathbone Road was still. Marjorie slept.

Later, two waited with her, Maureen in the kitchen in her coat, motionless, and Mr. Jackson outside, standing like wood beside the bleached and undivided irises.

Marjorie at the end of the garden savaged the earth around the hydrangeas. She wept and dug, dug and wept.

THE EASTER LILIES

M iss White, who was a dotty little woman with a queer, grinning glare and had long ago taught kindergarten at a good school, came back from Malta full of the lilies.

'They grow everywhere. Like weeds. At the roadsides in clumps. All among the stones,' she said.

She was talking at the church lunch.

Mrs. Wellington, a warden's widow munched.

'They would,' she said. 'Why not? They are weeds in other countries. In Australia they are called pig lilies.'

'But they're free. They just grow anywhere. Beautiful.'

'I know.'

Mrs. Wellington's husband had been RN, stationed on Malta in the great days. They had had a house between Marsa and Siggiewi among orange and lemon trees, a paved court-yard where they had held cocktail parties, with fairy lights and dance music on a gramophone. Three adoring, barefoot Maltese maids had looked after her and there had been a full time gardener. The lilies round the courtyard had had to be hacked. '*Hacked* away,' said Mrs. Wellington. 'To make room for the roses.'

'But think of Easter,' said Miss White.

'Easter?'

'The Easter lilies. Didn't they have Easter lilies in Maltese churches?'

Mrs. Wellington looked into space for a moment, or rather

she looked across the church hall at other champing women in brave feathery hats who were consuming rolls and paté and a single glass of claret—a pre-Lent treat. This was a progressive church. 'There were lilies,' she said, 'in the Anglican cathedral. But they were not the pig lilies. They were gigantic, waxy things, like swirled up flags. Several hundred of them we had up in the chancel. Sheaves of them, specially grown. They were—d'you know I suddenly remember—they were a penny each.'

'And the wild lilies were free?'

'We never picked the wild lilies. Weeds. Of course they were free.'

'But they are lovely. They're as good as the Easter lilies here. Just a bit smaller. And we give fifty pence each here, just for one.'

The bowl in fact was coming round the tables for the Easter lily money. A bowl had come round earlier for the luncheon expenses. The lunch cost fifty pence too. Now the second bowl approached.

'Lily money,' said the Sunday School teacher, rosy faced and good.

The coins clonked onto the felt bottom of the bowl. When she reached Miss White, however, there was a pause. Mrs. Wellington dropped her money in—there were a lot of half p's. Mrs. Wellington kept half p's in a jam jar in the kitchen since the Captain died. They were for this sort of occasion. She brought them all to church in an envelope and showered them in. The bowl then hovered beside Miss White and Miss White peered down at it for quite a time and then said, 'No. No. I think not, dear.'

It was a surprise. A surprise to the Sunday School teacher and a greater one to Mrs. Wellington. She knew that Miss White was poor but she was notoriously generous. In the seventy-odd years she had been a member of this church she—or her family, now all dead—could never once have failed to pay for an Easter lily.

'Is anything wrong?' asked Mrs. Wellington.

Miss White said, 'Yes. It is ridiculous.'

'Ridiculous! At Easter?' (The Church was High.)

'The roof is coming in. The Hall is leaking. Father Banks couldn't live if he didn't eat Irish stew round half the parish four times a week, poor soul. And we spend fifty pence each on Easter lilies. I shall get some from Malta.' She gave her dotty grin, the grin which at school they had all imitated in the cloakrooms. In the breathy, high voice that had not changed in all the years and which they had also imitated, in the playground and even in front of her if she had come out to clap her hands for quiet (and she had never minded and they had always obeyed), she said, 'I'll write to Malta and get some sent.'

In the pink, tipsy-looking house built under the walls of Rabat, half-covered with ramshackle clematis and dark red roses, old Ingoldby read Miss White's letter.

Then, holding it, he walked into his garden and stood by the well and read it again, looking up at last to regard the great clumps of lilies all about his feet. 'Gone crackers,' he said.

Then he went in and poured himself a bowl of cornflakes and took it into the garden to eat. It was one of the things the Maltese knew about him and rather respected. The old Maltese, that is, the ones who remembered the eccentric pink-faced English roaring about. They often ate cornflakes in the garden, played bagpipes on their roof-tops, blustered over whisky and became obsessive about the difficulty of growing sweet peas, while their thin, sweet-natured wives talked over tea-trolleys. Malta had been gentle to the English wives. For some mysterious reason the Maltese women and the English women had loved and understood each other, respected each other's religion, liked each other's children. Mistresses and maids had wept at parting when terms of Service were up and the ships had gone sailing home.

But old Ingoldby had never had a wife. He'd been RN until the end and been about a bit of course, but he'd kept away from women. Kept away from most people after retirement. Lived in the lop-sided ancient house and painted. He knew Malta better than any Maltese. He knew a stream on it, a small river, though all the guide books said there was none. He painted on the south shore, taking his gear in the back of a battered old Ford, walking laden with it over little plots of vineyard above the threads sewn over the earth to keep the birds away, leaping on now rather stiff old legs a chasm between rocks with purple sea beneath them, totally alone, watched only by one or two men lying on their stomachs with guns, hunting larks, he painted endlessly the sea. Miss White's fortnight's visit, just over, had disrupted his life very little. She had stayed at a good, quiet hotel in St George's Bay, meeting him for supper now and then. Twice he had taken her for a drive. He was not actively missing her.

'Crackers,' he said again at lunch time on the rock, taking out a packet of old-fashioned egg sandwiches wrapped tightly in greaseproof paper with envelope ends. 'Off her rocker. It's not allowed.'

He was scarcely younger than Miss White. He had been one of her first and older pupils. He had never forgotten her and had written to her all his life, at sea, during the First and Second Wars, from his shore-station, from Malta in his retirement—always for Christmas and Easter. She sent him teacloths on his birthday and handkerchieves and a copy of the school magazine. He had never found her female or attractive or even wise but nevertheless, though he did not know it, he loved her and she was the only woman he had ever felt his own.

'What's the ruling on sending flowers to England these

days?' he asked in the shop in the village—to very great amazement.

'*Exporting?*' they said.

'No. Sending a present.'

'You're allowed to take a bunch,' they said. 'People do sometimes. Just like you can still sometimes bring in pheasants.'

'There was English families over St Julian's who used to take in potatoes.' Everyone laughed and smiled.

'Wouldn't happen now,' said an old Maltese lady in Maltese, swelling in a dark corner like bread. She blinked straight ahead of her, looking at old tourists and their babies, now parents themselves who never came back, remembering all the blonde hair and the buckets and spades and how the English children had loved the Maltese sticky sweets. The streets had been packed then, not only with holiday people but with the proper English Maltese who had loved Malta.

'I want to send a parcel of Easter lilies to England,' said the Captain. 'I thought I would send them with someone going over. Someone might consent to carry a bundle just over the arm. Not many—say fifty. Packed tight they would be no trouble.'

The shop was bewildered, but being Maltese did not show it. They smiled dazzlingly and agreed that it was a beautiful idea. Somebody said that the Captain ought to find out about a permit. He ought to go in to Valletta, they said, glittering happily at him, knowing that he had not been to Sliema for years, let alone Valletta.

The Captain said yes, and went away so helplessly that an old man sitting on a kitchen chair outside the shop playing patience, looked up and said that if the Captain liked, his son could drive to Valletta tomorrow and a woman—the granddaughter of the shop, huge with a great-grandchild to come, ran after him and said, 'No—you leave it to us, Captain. Leave it to us. We have a nephew in the Customs and Excise. Buy the lilies and tell us when.'

Dear Miss White,

Thank you for your letter. I am more than glad that you enjoyed your holiday here and found Malta still pleasant after so many changes and so long. We must not let so many years pass before you visit us again. For my part, seeing you again, you who taught me manners, was as always a very great pleasure.

As to the query about lilies, although at first very doubtful that there would be any chance of export, owing to the cool relationships between governments and the endless formalities in such matters, I hear from Maltese friends that one bunch of flowers, taken as a gift, is in order. A difficulty might obtain at your end as plants are prohibited imports to Britain. If however we make sure that there are no bulbs attached to the lilies and I can get the necessary note from the Powers that Be, I think I might be able to arrange something.

Certainly fifty pence per bloom sounds very ridiculous even for England and one would like to do something to help.

Will you write and instruct me exactly when the lilies will be needed? I imagine that you will want them on Easter Saturday. I shall probably be able to send them via my old friend Sir Henry Hatt—they travel home annually on Easter Saturday as he likes to attend his old church on Easter Day and afterwards spends the summer at home. His wife I have to admit may not be co-operative but I shall do my best with Henry. I should like precise details of the arrangements for collection at London airport and will send details of the estimated time of arrival of the Hatts' flight. Fortunately there is still time for us to make all our plans water-tight.

The weather here is continuing to be beautiful and I have been painting unhindered all week. Your visit in no way ham-

pered the picture's progress and this is being a most successful spring. Your stay, as ever, brought only pleasure.

Sincerely yours, Paul Ingoldby.

My dear Paul,

How very good of you to take my request for Easter lilies so seriously. Alas, here at All Saints they are very uncertain of the sense of it and proceeding with the purchase of expensive lilies as before. I feel more and more that there is a great lack of imagination, spirit and 'GO' about this country nowadays and I have therefore stuck to my guns in the hope of a change of policy in future years. I am enclosing a cheque for £1 (one pound) and intend to meet the lilies myself on Easter Saturday and bring them directly back from the airport to arrange them in the church. I shall have completed my church work for Easter Day before I set out.

This will not be a particularly joyful Easter at All Saints incidentally, as the new Team Vicar has told us—just this week—the sad news that the church is to be closed down. The main reason is that the roof needs several thousand pounds spending on it. There are several other churches in the town and poor Father Banks is worked off his feet. Or so they say. He seems to me to be very seldom on them on account of all his committee meetings. I often wonder how these parsons would get on if they had had to stand before a class of children for six hours a day—and take games and supervise dinners. Better perhaps. But as to All Saints, we are all fairly poor now and we have given all we can over the past years— our jewellery, silver bits and pieces and between ourselves I have even given away the needlework picture of my great-grandfather the admiral. I know that I have bored you with all this for far too long when I was with you, and you are not, dear Paul, and never were even as a child, in any way religious. I remember to this day your stony stare when we were *doing the Sermon on the Mount. But you will understand because you have a kind heart that the closure of All Saints where I was baptised as were my parents and grandparents (my grandfather of course was the first churchwarden) and where so many of us, and not only the old, spend a very great deal of time and prayer, will be a blow. It is not a beautiful building but it stands in blocks of identical suburban streets, all so dull, all so tasteful, all with the same expensive curtain linings to the windows and the same flicker of the television screen, all silent of life otherwise as one walks the dog late at night, that it stands out as something different and serious and I truly believe that temples of worship are needed by man as I said when we spent the delightful day driving to the golden temples of Hagar Qum.*

Well, dear Paul, I am nearly eighty years old so that I shan't be in need of the building or any building much longer in any case, but I am very glad to be able to make some gesture of—well, of positive farewell in the matter of the lilies, and I am grateful to you for that. As to your kind remarks about it being I who taught you manners that is rubbish. It was your Nannie taught you manners—a very nice woman. I remember her. A very good sort. Many Methodists of course can be good Christians.

Your sincere friend, Clara White.

'Lilies?' said Lady Hatt.

'Just a bunch of lilies.'

'What—to carry? *Hand* baggage?'

'Yes. Nothing at all really,' said Sir Henry nervously. His skin was like old porridge and he was hunched up in an ancient arm chair at the Xara Palace Hotel where he had lived for twenty years in a daze of memory and for five years trying not to see his new wife who slept in another room. She had been his nurse, and their marriage those few years ago had seemed a good arrangement. Vermilion trouser-suited, with spectacularly waved hair and a face painted into a 1940s mask, she was flinging pearls round her neck and prodding earrings into her ears. She twisted her face about in mimic agony and stared with fierce eyes at him through the mirror.

'Who will carry them? Whatever is it all about?'

'Well, you will hardly have to carry them at all. Nobody will. Someone will hand them to you at the airport and the steward will put them on the rack for you. At London the steward will get them down again and you will simply have to carry them through customs and hand them to this old friend of Ingoldby. There's a permit—all has been seen to. They're for a church at Easter.'

'And all is left to me?'

'I intended to take them. I can't help being unable to come. It is the doctor—'

'I don't dispute you can't come. Just as you don't dispute I have to go—'

'No, no.'

'I have to open up the house. For when you are well. I am ready to do this for you and to come back and fetch you. But I don't see why I should take these—bloody—lilies.'

He drooped in the faded velvet chair and the Maltese light shone through the window and the leaves of a vine. His paper-pale face sagged. Her brilliant trouser-suit and white frothy blouse glared in the old room, with its old stone walls. 'The car has come,' he said.

She kissed the top of his shiny, freckly head in a businesslike way and straightened his rug. 'Old Ingoldby'll come and see you. You'll be all right.' She fiddled at the catch of her pearls round the front of her neck, and then with a big diamond brooch. He said, suddenly urgent, shaky, 'Take the lilies.'

Miss White at about the same moment was settling her dog with a bowl of water and checking windows and doors. She then put on her gloves and hat and walked down the hill to the station. She changed to the underground at Earls Court—a long wait—and at last got on to a train direct to London Airport. It was an excellent train, new and bright and clean, and she was in no way over-excited by it for it had served her very well earlier in the year on the way to her holiday.

She felt odder, though, than then. Rather weak. Her feet prickled. They did not quite touch the floor. Her heart beat very loud and to try both to still it and to distract attention from her distress—as she had done since she was a child—she grinned her zany grin about the carriage. The few people lolling opposite, this Easter Saturday afternoon, took little notice.

She reached the airport far too soon and thought that she would find a cup of tea, and it was while she was standing with her tray for the tea that the pain hit her in the chest like the piercing of a sharp knife. She bent over the tray and had to stand still. There was a wide space between her and the cash desk, but she could not go on. People behind her—it was quiet at the airport today—the rush had been yesterday (Good Friday—to travel on Good Friday!)—people behind her took their trays round her back, not looking at her. 'I could die here,' she thought, 'and no one would notice.' She thought of a newspaper report of how somebody had died in London Airport and no one had noticed for seven hours.

'Though why should it matter where one died?' she thought. 'To Christians at any rate—taught at All Saints.' 'Dying is only moving into another room,' she said to the triangles of chocolate cake behind the glass boxes on the shelves.

After a while she slid the tray along to the cash desk and paid for the tea. Then, tottery, she made for a near table. The tray seemed heavy. She felt very small. 'I am very small,' she thought. 'I have always been small. I have always thought of myself with—she paused, facing secret sin—well, with some sort of tall man near me.'

She sat on the plastic orange bucket seat and her feet again did not quite touch the ground. She thought of Paul Ingoldby. Such a nice boy. She hung on to the safe thought that he was one of her boys. Her pupils. He must be ten years younger. She had been a new teacher of twenty and he had been a little boy of ten. They were now eighty and seventy. She thought of her letter to him. How that in some way it had not been proper. She had shown too much of her heart in it, she thought.

Then she thought, 'Oh dear Lord God, if I had only sometimes shown more of my heart.' She closed her eyes.

When at last the little letters made of green lights on the board above her head swam into place and said that the Malta flight had at last landed, she noticed how late it was. She had been sitting at the table for over an hour. She must have slept. At some point she must also have drunk the tea for her cup was empty.

'Landed' said the green lights, so she got up and went down the huge hall and, holding the rail, she climbed the stairs and walked back along the long stretch to the railing where people waited for the passengers.

There were not really many people but it was not easy for her to get up against the rope rail, so she walked back to the place where the airport attendants were keeping a space clear for the people coming off the plane to pass.

'Now then, Gran,' said one. 'Keep back now. You don't want to be trampled under. You'll get lost.'

'I have to stand at the front,' said Miss White. 'You see, I'll know her but she won't know me.'

'How you going to know her?'

'She'll be carrying lilies.'

'Lilies. I doubt that,' said the man. 'Not allowed—lilies.'

'There is a permit,' said Miss White. 'It has all been properly cleared. It was arranged by a Captain in the Navy.'

'Navy, eh?' said the man watching Miss White's queer grin. 'Ah—boyfriend.'

Miss White's eighty-year-old lips set firm. Shocked, she turned away and saw Lady Hatt coming towards her, lurching a little, brick-red in the cheeks and vermilion in the body and on her face an expression of fierce malice. She was carrying her big bottle of duty-free whisky, a large crocodile handbag and her frothy blouse was escaping from the waist of her trouser suit, her hair untidy. Her over-thin legs above wobbly ankles tottered pathetically above high heels. In her arms as well as the whisky was a clutter of parcels, and between them and below the dangle of unsteady-looking earrings was a huge sheaf of newspaper from which stuck the heads of many tight-foiled, greyish lilies.

'Oh, how kind, how kind!' Miss White leapt forward. 'Oh how very kind of you!'

Lady Hatt glared. She shuffled the lilies off her heap of belongings and let them fall very heavily into Miss White's arms. An earring swung. She marched on.

Miss White ran after. 'Oh, please. I do want to thank you. I've brought some chocolates—'

'Oh—certainly not. *No* thank you.'

'I don't even know your name, so can't write—'

'I hardly think that's necessary at all.' Lady Hatt smelled of gin. Her eyes were hard blue, the whites reddish. She had released the lilies like a package of poison, and not quite knowing the source of her hate she seethed against them as she might have seethed at the touch of an angel's wing. She had been manipulated into the lilies—uncharacteristic emblems of other people's worlds. She had been manipulated into them by her husband whom she despised and for a cause she despised. Easter, she thought. 'Churches. Women like this. Chocolates—

my God!' She strode away—a chauffeur appearing from some-where and taking her belongings and her overnight bag and her whisky. She disappeared leaving Miss White with the chocolates and the bundle.

'I so hope they weren't a trouble,' Miss White called—and at once realised that they must have been, for the bundle was large and bony and really extremely heavy. She cradled it in her arms and found that she could scarcely see over it. Going down the stairs, buffeted about—the airport was getting more crowded now—she found she could only go a step at a time as she could not spare a hand for the hand rail. Waiting at last on the platform for the underground train again, she tried to peer in to the top of the sheaf round the tight-packed pages of *The Times of Malta*, secured with firm string and excellent naval knotting. She thought, 'They don't look so beautiful after all. I hope—' and then the knife twisted in her chest again and she stood very still and closed her eyes and grinned very wide. When it had passed she said, 'I hope they'll improve when they're put in water.'

She took a taxi when she got to her own station. It was a dreadful extravagance but she felt unequal to the hill and it was now dark. A sweet, spring darkness and the cherry blos-som smelling in all the pleasant gardens. The blossom whitened in the April evening. In some rooms in the decorous streets lights were coming on. In some—really rather prettily, she thought, 'I don't know why I ever despised them'—the lights of television sets flickered blue. Dark as it was someone was giving his patch of grass the first mowing of the year in St Agnes Road and the wet, summery, heartbreaking smell of the sap hit her as she stepped from the cab at the door of the church. It seemed the smell of all her life—the essence of the best of all her life—a new moon, she thought, suburban grass and summer coming. She thought how happy she had been in this place.

She had—as Sacristan of course she had—a key to the church and went in and felt for the light switches. She switched on the chancel light and the lady chapel and the light of the vestry. Looking at all the great arrangements of flowers shining to themselves through the night waiting for Easter morning, she grinned her grin and switched on every light in the place. There seemed, she thought, to be a great many lilies—two great vases on the altar and two more on the chancel steps. Pounds and pounds worth. Well of course they'd all gone silly. Bravado, she thought, sentimental bravado because the church was going to be closed.

They could have saved fifty pounds, she thought, towards the roof.

She put down the heavy pig lilies on the steps of the lady chapel and went looking for a vase or two behind the organ. There wasn't much left. Only the old green bucket thing that was always left till last and was usually stuck up at the back of the bookstall where it didn't show. She rummaged and found a great old glass jar—something to do with the Guides. She swilled both these out with water and took them back to the lady chapel.

Feeling now very tired, she undid—not easily—the traceries round *The Times of Malta* and let the lilies fall out loose, scatter and breathe on their hard dark stalks. She shook them and spread them until they lay released across the blue chapel carpet. Lying in their midst was a magnificent string of pearls.

'Her pearls!' thought Miss White. 'They must be Paul's friend's pearls. They must have dropped off. Oh, how very dreadful!'

She touched them with her fingertip. 'They are beautiful,' she thought. 'How dreadful. I must put them in the safe. She won't know what's happened to them.'

The pearls glowed among the lilies. The light of the vestry where the safe was, looked far away. Miss White looked at the lilies and then at the pearls and thought, 'The pearls are more beautiful. It ought not to be so. The lilies are weeds after all. And they are dead. I am old and a fool.'

Tears came into her eyes. For safety, she picked up the pearls and fastened them round her neck. 'I'd like to see them on,' she thought, 'I love pearls.' But the glass where Father Banks looked at himself and his vestments over in the vestry before service, swinging about, handsome and grand (How different from Paul. If I had had Father Banks to teach he would not—), the glass was far away in the vestry, too.

'Vanity,' said Miss White to herself, and twisted the pearls out of sight under the collar of her old jersey. Then, feeling tireder still, she put down her round head among the pig lilies, and died.

She had left everything to the church, of course, and there was practically nothing except her small flat—and the pearls, which everyone was astonished to hear about. They were spectacular, said a sympathetic local jeweller, and he gave two thousand pounds for them. Lady Hatt, by the time Miss White's body had been found lying peaceful among the dead lilies on Easter morning, had had her hysterics, mounted her first wave of accusation against the airline and was well on the way with her claim to the insurance company, which was unfriendly but at length paid up. Paul Ingoldby did not hear for some time of his old teacher's death on Easter eve for she had left him no bequest, thinking it inappropriate. He felt satisfaction, however, when he heard that the lilies had reached their destination.

The church with its new roof survived.

THE FIRST ADAM

My woman's made of paper. She's spread on the bed. She's figures and drawings. She's called The Tender, and she's not my wife. She's not young, neither—she's knocking on.

She's my mistress, this one. My tender mistress. Wife's at home in Welwyn and this sweaty midnight, whilst I'm sitting on the hotel bed, looking across at the other one, with the whisky on the floor and a mosquito pissing around and God knows how at seven floors up and netted windows—this moment, damp evening, Moira's waking to the Welwyn thrushes and a cold dawn.

She's lying under the Danish goose-down duvet and waiting for the Teasmade. Dead centre she's lying in our Heal's king-size, dead centre on the winter side of the mattress. Alone.

Faithful? Yes she is. God knows why she is or why I'm sure she is. She's past fifty, mind, and men never meant that much to her. I never meant that much to her. I meant more I'd say as time wore on and I was abroad more. She likes being on her own. Less mess. Can take her time washing chair covers. Doesn't have to cook. Less washing up. And plan! How she plans. She's planned the Extension two years—ever since we came home together from KL with all the cane furniture. 'All that beautiful cane furniture,' she says, 'still in the roof. Crying out for that Extension. Can't you build that Extension now you've retired?'

'Can't afford extensions now I've retired.'

Digging in the garden. Mending stuff. Round the super-market with her to help lift out the boxes. 'Not that loaf. You know we don't have that loaf, Bull. Put it back.' I put it back. Other old buggers trailing round likewise. Giving a hand. Retired. Other wives marching ahead like Moira. Rat-trap wives. Holding the reins. Holding the purse.

Well, there was pruning the roses.

And the decorating.

Walking the dog last thing round the block. Always the same walk. Your feet flap flap in front of you and you remember run-ning, moving fast on your toes and dancing, long since—well, not that long since. I danced on the runway job at Heraklion.

Only sixty.

Christ, when the telex came, I said yes. 'Reply immediate,' it said. I replied immediate, 'Accept'. I accepted two years in Drab, for godsake. Back again in Drab, sorting out a mess and getting out a new tender. Back at the old Drab Intercon. Sixty? What's sixty? Heart? What's heart? That was two years back in KL. Bad, leaving KL. Bad moment. When you've worked out East thirty years there's limits to Welwyn.

Different for her. She never came out a lot. KL was the last, and she was only there three months and she never liked it. Not a woman for places, Moira. Things for Moira—cane fur-niture, carpets, lamps made out of animals' skins. There was Hong Kong one year—twittering on about jade. There was Kuching. Not much to be got in Kuching. Kuching nearly bust us apart and she was only there three weeks. Maybe better if it had bust us. She never got over Kuching.

'Well, it's a man's world,' she says in Welwyn. 'Bull's in a man's world out there. I'm just intruding. Construction work—well, it's not for women. Oh no—Bull's not lonely. Not the lonely type. "Do whatever you like," I say, "so long as you don't tell me." It's what we all say—all the wives. The English wives—I'm sure I can't speak for the French or American. The

Japanese wives of course, they don't think about men once they've got a husband. He meets his old cronies, don't you, Bull? Wherever he goes. Best of everything. Best hotels when he's not working on site. Car and driver. Do this, do that. All expenses. And the pay's good—not the pension unless you've thought ahead—and that's not Bull—but the pay's very comfortable and Bull's not extravagant. He loves his work. Never bored. Well, half of them, it's all they ever talk about, work. On and on, late at night, in one of their bedrooms like as not. I've seen them at it. It stops you going to bed. Well, you get bored watching them. I'd sooner be home—a woman—and have everything nice when he gets back.'

She doesn't even face—not even in dreams if she dreams—the possibility of a lack of her, a need for her. She turned away her thoughts a long time ago from what needing is. She doesn't need me any more.

She's right about the work, though. It's what I need most. They don't know what you're on about in England—work—but it's true. There's a number of us. It's not booze that's vital, or girls. No night-life to speak of, not in Drab at any rate. Not for my lot, and there's plenty like us up and down the world. Up-country work. Getting buildings up in a swamp. Getting plant out to a desert. Getting pylons fixed. Digging through a cliff. Scooping out a reservoir. Keeping the work-force sweet. Just about the only power the bloody country's kept since the Empire—big, overseas construction work. Like the British Army used to be but a bloody sight more useful. You're looking to a constructive conclusion. Years ahead you have to look, and you can see them stretched before you—satisfying. There on the bed—the figures, difficulties, options, all laid out. My willing mistress. 'Construction work.' They think nothing of engineers at home—think of wireless mechanics or something. Yet it's work where you see the world change. You see something that'll be there when we're all dead, up and finished. You see something completed—wipe your hands on a rag, nod and go away, knowing it'll outlive you. I saw Plover Cove, Hong Kong, right through, start to finish—the cove become the lake and all the villages rebuilt better on the hills and the people still putting little dishes of food out around it, to appease the dragons. I saw through the Singapore land reclamation—planes flying off a runway scarcely months ago was water. I worked with the Eyties on Abu Simbil and saw the great old faces of the kings moved up the slope. The Eyties thought nothing of them—wouldn't cross the road to look at them, they said—carrying on about the Pantheon. 'I'd have a shot at moving that Pantheon,' I said and they screamed.

It's a club. Same folks turning up year in, year out—black, white, yellow—makes no difference. They're mates. Internationals. Intercontinentals. Always the Intercon. Hotels. They're our level—not a suite, of course: a good double room, private bath, couple of beds, one for work and one for Bull. Papers—my tender mistress—first things seen when you open your eyes in the morning and last thing when you close them at night. Wake—stretch for drawings, like Moira for the Teasmade and the Today Programme on the BBC. Well, I'm clear of the Today Programme, anyway.

I'm not unhappy.

No kids, mind.

Though maybe that's a blessing, when you look round. There's engineers I've known never seen their kids two, three, five years. Then kids get sent out for holidays and don't know their fathers. There was Abbott, walking jaunty—embarrassed—through the Olde English restaurant at the Shangri La somewhere (Jakarta?) with a bird all paint and legs. 'Nice work, Abbott,' say I. He says, 'Meet my daughter.' What sort of sense is that?

You get to act set ways. You take set parts. You're one feller to the World Bank crowd, another feller to the UN lot, another to the legal buffs, another for the oil men. You have your set jokes for nights out. Keep a supply—nucleus—for new acquaintances. Best is the Intercon. joke—goes down anywhere.

'Who is the happiest man?'

'The happiest man is the man with the Japanese wife, the Chinese cook, the English house and the American income.'

'So okay—who is the unhappiest man?'

'The unhappiest man is the man with the American wife, the English cook, the Japanese house and the Chinese income.'

You swop the nations about a bit, depending on the company, but it's a winner most parties. Only trouble is it's been around a bit now. It's knocking on. Like my tender mistress.

She's an airport, this mistress, and she's a demon. A year or so ago she looked a treat, but she's gone down lately—literally down for it turns out she's based on mud. The big jumbos would have disappeared in her. Then we found she had, in addition, a heart of stone—and her heart, as is sometimes the way with mistresses—was not in the right place. Now neither mud nor stone need spell amen to a runway, but there was a particular set of circs. in this one that meant that they might.

So we got round that.

Then there was the typhoon. That swept most of the bitch away and we put her back again, piece by piece.

Then we had the cholera and that very nearly killed her, and it did kill a lot of men whose faces I don't forget that easy. In Singapore, Hong Kong, if there's a couple of cases of cholera, it's headline news. In Drab it's a couple of lines at the foot of the back page if there's two hundred, and no mention on the television. Just as nobody bothers to mention the malaria down the Old City. And I'd not rule out smallpox, whatever they say.

Then we had the murder. Drunken Scottish clerk-of-works shot a Sikh who'd taken his woman. Well, it was the Sikh's wife. Everything stopped then. My mistress stayed spread on the bed. In a coma. We're still just beginning to ease her out of it. This week the trucks started coming back—slow. There's men on the job again—clumps here, clumps there. Quiet still. No singing. But working again. And it's one hundred degrees.

You can't swear and threaten too much at one hundred degrees.

I never swear and threaten anyhow. Tend instead to watch and walk quiet. Being on the site dawn to dark does better than threats and temper. They see you coming, see you standing, see you camping out there all night often as not. See you not noticing heat, not noticing cholera, not scared of Ferguson blowing the Sikh's head off—so drunk you'd never think he'd hold a gun, let alone aim it; let a man—me—take it out of his hand like a baby. Put him to bed—get police, ambulance. You get through and beyond fear, through and beyond surprise, through and beyond heat.

Now and then, mind, there's a flutter in the old loins. Like today—Sunday—here at the hotel. We're suddenly off the site, not working—not because it's Sunday this being a Muslim country—but because some bugger delivers the wrong stuff. No plant arriving. Blinding, beating silence. Men sleeping rolled in rags and sacks like parcels. In the gravel heap—the factory they call it—where they hit the big stones with the smaller stones and then the smaller stones with smaller stones and the smaller stones with smaller—and so on, for the cement. Some of them had dug holes for themselves in the gravel, crawled in like mites in cheese. A few lay about on top, like dead birds. A few still worked, tapping slow, under umbrellas. They were dotted in the grey shale like currants in a pudding. Living skeletons. Nothing moved.

'In Bengal
To work at all
Is seldom if ever done'

—nor yet in Drab.

They'll do this sudden, men. Anywhere out East. Just as they'll go mad, sudden, too. Like Penang, that calm, warm Monday with the rain falling and they all began to throw bricks off the Ong skyscraper down on the Minister of Works on a state visit.

I couldn't manage that one. It was Chinese/Malay trouble and there's no Englishman equal to that. There's degrees of foreignness you'll never fathom—like the way in Bengal the husbands and wives shave the pubic hair off each other every Thursday night. Off each other! Then it's Holy Friday and they sit and itch. Then Saturday it's Bingo! It's as good a story for the restaurants as the one about the happiest man, but by God, it's when you feel foreign.

That day—the warm, rainy day of the fight at the Ong Tower—I left the lot of them to it and went off to the Botanical Gardens and watched the orang-utang they've got there hanging like a sweet-chestnut in its cage. Dying. It was dying, the orang-utang. It was a present from the President of Korea or somewhere to the king of Malaysia. He'd given them two, but the woman orang-utang had died already. This feller left—it just hung there. By one hand. Its eyes bloody lonely. Malays no bloody good with animals. I stood there half the day looking at its tired little red eyes. 'Not a bugger to talk to,' I said. 'You've not got a bugger to talk to,' and it just looked back. Then it gave a great swing, away and up, and sat looking up into the trees, across towards the Straits, north towards the jungles where it was born. Like Adam. The first Adam. It didn't throw things down on me. It sat quiet. Not that interested. It mourned. It observed me and thought, 'This is where you feel foreign.'

So—today, no work, and I get into my bathing trunks and out into the Intercontinental Hotel gardens. They bring me a blue mattress for my slatted long-chair and there I lie on the green lawns among the mallow bushes, purple and white flowers on the same bush—and God, the beautiful smell of them. There's great mountains of sweating bodies take the magic off, mind. All around. Bodies almost as big as mine. Australians, airline pilots resting. The size with them's just food and flab. Me—I'm hard as iron. Neck two foot round, growing low out of the shoulders. Thrusting. Hence, Bull.

Lie there.

Watch roses high above swinging from cement pergola above swimming pool and crows sitting in among them, looking down. When a lad comes out dressed in baby blue, hips like a girl, with a coffee tray, you see crows glitter.

They flap down like floating black newspapers. They sit by you. All round you. They move up and take the sugar, or page of your paper, or coffee spoon. Sharp, evil beaks. Like grey candle grease.

But the sun's hot, the sky's blue, the roses red and—hello. Loping over the grass with two waiters running behind there's this woman six feet tall with bangles round her ankle and arms and in a shouting-pink jellaba, kaftan, whatever. Stalking high-heeled. Looking nowhere. Points at long-chair beside yours and waiters lay out blue mattress. Bow again. Coffee? She pays no attention. They depart. Crows watch. Even crows fall silent.

You almost close your eyes. Slide eye-balls sideways under lids as with one sweep off comes jellaba and she collapses gentle along mattress in pink bikini—green bangles, blue bangles, pink bikini, huge smoked glasses like a skull. Her stomach's not what it was. Droops a bit. Flat breasted but lean as a crane—the machine on the site, not the bird. She's bloody tanned—narrow boned. Proud. Face pretty terrible—mingy, disappointed. Like a hen.

But the face you needn't look at. She's got legs all right. Well, fairly all right. The more you look the less you see is all right. It's just the general impression. Big glamour. She's European. Or American. And alone.

She brings out letter and she reads and reads it. She folds it up and then lies back. Then she opens it again. And reads it. Two short deep lines appear above the glasses and below the line of the scraped back bleach of hair. She is in a trance with the letter.

He's left her. Or he isn't coming to find her. Or he's not been in to Cartier lately.

So the end of it is she's in my room after dinner, me on my bed and her on the chair and the tender mistress spread out with both of us looking at her.

'You mean you live with these? All the time? With these papers?'

'All day. All night.'

'You are alone?'

'There's the men. The management. The Intercon. lot. We all come and go. We meet up all the time—the world over.'

She looks around. I suppose the room has got fairly squalid while I'm on and off the site. The room-service knows my ways. Knows what they haven't to touch. Drawers have got left half open. Clothes about. Inside-out socks. Laundry list still on the floor. Tipped-over photograph of Moira on dressing table.

'Your wife?'

'A long time ago.'

'You have been married long?'

'Thirty years.'

'Thirty years. To the same woman?'

'Yes.'

A sigh. She goes to the window.

'Whisky?'

I have to get new bottle from back of my sweat-shirts and dislodge old tea-making machine. It's a cable with two wires sticking out like adder's tongue at one end, and metal ring the other. Bought it Kowloon, years back. You fix it in the shaving plug marked shavers only. Once fused the whole of the Doha Hilton and nearly killed myself, but I was young then. Get out my box of Brook Bond tea bags—Moira sends them out from Safeways. 'Maybe tea?'

She sighs again. Turns. She's a great shape. Like Katherine Hepburn. But God—the moment goes.

I remember her in the garden—the way she got them to put her mattress next to mine. Remember the letter—how old it looked. The folds were dirty. At dinner downstairs tonight I saw the poor old hands below the blue bangles and the neck inside the swathes of necklaces patched brown with maps of Asia.

No tenderness here. No more tenderness than in the waitresses—all saris and buttocks and insolent stares. Why should she be? She's knocked about. And she could be sixty. Well—sixty's nothing.

But not tonight.

So, it's a drink only and I take her out and leave her at the lift and then I go down the stairs and walk in the hotel gardens in the hot night. The crows'll still be up there watching. If I took off my watch and swung it, they'd swoop. If I listen, they will speak. 'Keep off her, Bull. There's no future. She's lost. She's one of the wanderers. She'll be there some form the next place. You've the Extension to build.'

Letter from Moira as I pass desk. Forgot to ask before. Tap letter first one corner, then another on desk. Looking down. So easy—'Anything further, Mr. Bull? Can we get you anything?' asks the Bell Captain. So easy. Just push dollars over. Ask for her room number.

She'll be in bed now, staring at ceiling, tired eyes deep in fragile bones of thin face. Earrings, bangles, rings lie on bedside table. Dry skin washed clean of paint is creased with years.

It is not kind or tender in me to leave her alone.

I insult her, standing here, not asking for her room number—old Bull, fit as a bull, except for the occasional twinge in the rib-cage. Poor old Bull, holding the corner of his wife's letter. How many years left? Ten? Not likely twenty. Nor for her neither, her with the bangles. It is Bull's duty to tap on her door.

But, here is Bull on his bed, looking across at his tender mistress, thinking that if he had any sense he would go through some of the preliminary tarmac figures and the War Clause before sleep. Here's knock on door and in come Bob and Kassim. Just as well she's not still here. Would have put up 'do not disurb' I guess.

'Now then—you're late, Bob. Thought you'd both not be coming.'

'Thought maybe if we'd any sense, Bull, we'd go over the preliminary tarmac figures. And look at the War Clause.'

'You've got a bloody mosquito in here, Bull.'

'They do no harm. We're immune. We're old.'

'Don't see where it came from. Seven floors up. They don't breed here. The water's too dirty.'

'Like us. Whisky?'

'Tea if we're doing the figures.'

Bull fills three tea cups with cold water and attaches wires to shaving plug.

'You'll blow us all sky high one day, Bull.'

'You've been glad of it often enough, Kass. Decent free cup of tea.'

'You've a letter there unopened.'

'It'll keep till we've done the figures.'

So we gather round the far bed, the bed of the mistress, one on each side of her and one at her feet. We touch and pat her, moving pieces of her about. Gradually we grow interested. We put down our tea cups on the floor and as people sleep and wake around the spinning world we scrutinise this creature with gratitude, with love.

THE PANGS OF LOVE

It is not generally known that the good little mermaid of Hans Christian Andersen, who died for love of the handsome prince and allowed herself to dissolve in the foam of the ocean, had a younger sister, a difficult child of very different temper.

She was very young when the tragedy occurred, and was only told it later by her five elder sisters and her grandmother, the Sea King's mother with the twelve important oyster shells in her tail. They spent much of their time, all these women, mourning the tragic life of the little mermaid in the Sea King's palace below the waves, and a very dreary place it had become in consequence.

'I don't see what she did it for,' the seventh little mermaid used to say. 'Love for a man—ridiculous,' and all the others would sway on the tide and moan, 'Hush, hush—you don't know how she suffered for love.'

'I don't understand this "suffered for love",' said the seventh mermaid. 'She sounds very silly and obviously spoiled her life.'

'She may have spoiled her life,' said the Sea King's mother, 'but think how good she was. She was given the chance of saving her life, but because it would have harmed the prince and his earthly bride she let herself die.'

'What had he done so special to deserve that?' asked the seventh mermaid.

'He had *done* nothing. He was just her beloved prince to whom she would sacrifice all.'

'What did he sacrifice for her?' asked Signorina Settima.

'Not a lot,' said the Sea King's mother, 'I believe they don't on the whole. But it doesn't stop us loving them.'

'It would me,' said the seventh mermaid. 'I must get a look at some of this mankind, and perhaps I will then understand more.'

'You must wait until your fifteenth birthday,' said the Sea King's mother. 'That has always been the rule with all your sisters.'

'Oh, shit,' said the seventh mermaid (she was rather coarse). 'Times change. I'm as mature now as they were at fifteen. Howsabout tomorrow?'

'I'm sure I don't know what's to be done with you,' said the Sea King's mother, whose character had weakened in later years. 'You are totally different from the others and yet I'm sure I brought you all up the same.'

'Oh no you didn't,' said the five elder sisters in chorus, 'she's always been spoiled. We'd never have dared talk to you like that. Think if our beloved sister who died for love had talked to you like that.'

'Maybe she should have done,' said the dreadful seventh damsel officiously, and this time in spite of her grandmother's failing powers she was put in a cave for a while in the dark and made to miss her supper.

Nevertheless, she was the sort of girl who didn't let other people's views interfere with her too much, and she could argue like nobody else in the sea, so that in the end her grandmother said, 'Oh for goodness' sake then—go. Go now and don't even wait for your *fourteenth* birthday. Go and look at some men and don't come back unless they can turn you into a mermaid one hundredth part as good as your beloved foamy sister.'

'Whoops,' said Mademoiselle Sept, and she flicked her tail and was away up out of the Sea King's palace, rising through the coral and the fishes that wove about the red and blue seaweed trees like birds, up and up until her head shot out into the air and she took a deep breath of it and said, 'Wow!'

The sky, as her admirable sister had noticed stood above the sea like a large glass bell, and the waves rolled and lifted and tossed towards a green shore where there were fields and palaces and flowers and forests where fish with wings and legs wove about the branches of green and so forth trees, singing at the tops of their voices. On a balcony sticking out from the best palace stood, as he had stood before his marriage when the immaculate sister had first seen him, the wonderful prince with his chin resting on his hand as it often did of an evening—and indeed in the mornings and afternoons, too.

'Oh help!' said the seventh mermaid, feeling a queer twisting around the heart. Then she thought, 'Watch it.' She dived under water for a time and came up on a rock on the shore, where she sat and examined her sea-green finger nails and smoothed down the silver scales of her tail.

She was sitting where the prince could see her and after a while he gave a cry and she looked up. 'Oh,' he said, 'how you remind me of someone. I thought for a moment you were my lost love.'

'Lost love,' said the seventh mermaid. 'And whose fault was that? She was my sister. She died for love of you and you never gave her one serious thought. You even took her along on your honeymoon like a pet toy. I don't know what she saw in you.'

'I always loved her,' said the prince. 'But I didn't realise it until too late.'

'That's what they all say,' said Numera Septima. 'Are you a poet? They're the worst. Hardy, Tennyson, Shakespeare, Homer. Homer was the worst of all. And he hadn't a good word to say for mermaids.'

'Forgive me,' said the prince, who had removed his chin from his hand and was passionately clenching the parapet. 'Every word you speak reminds me more and more—'

'I don't see how it can,' said the s.m., 'since for love of you and because she was told it was the only way she could come to you, she let them cut out her tongue, the silly ass.'

'And your face,' he cried, 'your whole aspect, except of course for the tail.'

'She had that removed, too. They told her it would be agony and it was, so my sisters tell me. It shrivelled up and she got two ugly stumps called legs—I dare say you've got them under that parapet. When she danced, every step she took was like knives.'

'Alas, alas!'

'Catch me getting rid of my tail,' said syedmaya krasavitsa, twitching it seductively about, and the prince gave a great spring from the balcony and embraced her on the rocks. It was all right until half way down but the scales were cold and prickly. Slimy, too, and he shuddered.

'How dare you shudder,' cried La Septieme. 'Go back to your earthly bride.'

'She's not here at present,' said the p., 'she's gone to her mother for the weekend. Won't you come in? We can have dinner in the bath.'

The seventh little mermaid spent the whole weekend with the prince in the bath, and he became quite frantic with desire by Monday morning because of the insurmountable problem below the mermaid's waist. 'Your eyes, your hair,' he cried, 'but that's about all.'

'My sister did away with her beautiful tail for love of you,' said the s.m., reading a volume of Descartes over the prince's shoulder as he lay on her sea-green bosom. 'They tell me she even wore a disgusting harness on the top half of her for you, and make-up and dresses. She was the saint of mermaids.'

'Ah, a saint,' said the prince. 'But without your wit, your spark. I would do anything in the world for you.'

'So whats about getting rid of your legs?'

'Getting rid of my *legs*?'

'Then you can come and live with me below the waves. No one has legs down there and there's nothing wrong with any of us. As a matter of fact, aesthetically we're a very good species.'

'Get rid of my *legs*?'

'Yes—my grandmother, the Sea King's mother, and the Sea Witch behind the last whirlpool who fixed up my poor sister, silly cow, could see to it for you.'

'Oh, how I love your racy talk,' said the prince. 'It's like nothing I ever heard before. I should love you even with my eyes shut. Even at a distance. Even on the telephone.'

'No fear,' said the seventh m., 'I know all about this waiting by the telephone. All my sisters do it. It never rings when they want it to. It has days and days of terrible silence and they all roll about weeping and chewing their handkerchieves. You don't catch me getting in that condition.'

'Gosh, you're marvellous,' said the prince, who had been to an old-fashioned school, 'I'll do anything—'

'The legs?'

'Hum. Ha. Well—the legs.'

'Carry me back to the rocks,' said the seventh little mermaid, 'I'll leave you to think about it. What's more I hear a disturbance in the hall which heralds the return of your wife. By the way, it wasn't your wife, you know, who saved you from drowning when you got ship-wrecked on your sixteenth birthday. It was my dear old sister once again. "She swam among the spars and planks which drifted on the sea, quite forgetting they might crush her. Then she ducked beneath the water, and rising again on the billows managed at last to reach you who by now" (being fairly feeble in the muscles I'd guess, with all the stately living) "was scarcely able to swim any longer in the raging sea. Your arms, your legs" (ha!) "began to fail you and your beautiful eyes were closed and you must surely have died if my sister had not come to your assistance. She held your head above the water and let the billows drive her and you together wherever they pleased.'"

'What antique phraseology.'

'It's a translation from the Danish. Anyway, "when the sun rose red and beaming from the water, your cheeks regained the hue of life but your eyes remained closed. My sister kissed—"

('No!')

'"—your lofty handsome brow and stroked back your wet locks ... She kissed you again and longed that you might live." What's more if you'd only woken up then she could have spoken to you. It was when she got obsessed by you back down under the waves again that she went in for all this tongue and tail stuff with the Sea Witch.'

'She was an awfully nice girl,' said the prince, and tears came into his eyes—which was more than they ever could do for a mermaid however sad, because as we know from H. C. Andersen, mermaids can never cry which makes it harder for them.

'The woman I saw when I came to on the beach,' said the prince, 'was she who is now my wife. A good sort of woman but she drinks.'

'I'm not surprised,' said the seventh mermaid. 'I'd drink if I was married to someone who just stood gazing out to sea thinking of a girl he had allowed to turn into foam,' and she flicked her tail and disappeared.

'Now then,' she thought, 'what's to do next?' She was not to go back, her grandmother had said, until she was one hundredth part as good as the little m. her dead sister, now a spirit of air, and although she was a tearaway and, as I say, rather coarse, she was not altogether untouched by the discipline of the Sea King's mother and her upbringing. Yet she could not say that she exactly yearned for her father's palace with all her melancholy sisters singing dreary stuff about the past. Nor was she too thrilled to return to the heaviness of water with all the featherless fishes swimming through the amber windows and butting in to her, and the living flowers growing out of the palace walls like dry rot. However, after flicking about for a bit, once coming up to do an inspection of a fishing boat in difficulties with the tide and enjoying the usual drop-jawed faces, she took a header home into the front room and sat down quietly in a corner.

'You're back,' said the Sea King's mother. 'How was it? I take it you now feel you are a hundredth part as good as your sainted sister?'

'I've always tried to be good,' said the s.m., 'I've just tried to be rationally good and not romantically good, that's all.'

'Now don't start again. I take it you have seen some men?'

'I saw the prince.'

At this the five elder sisters set up a wavering lament.

'Did you feel for him—'

'Oh, feelings, feelings,' said the seventh and rational mermaid, 'I'm sick to death of feelings. He's good looking, I'll give you that, and rather sweet-natured and he's having a rough time at home, but he's totally self-centred. I agree that my sister must have been a true sea-saint to listen to him dripping on about himself all day. He's warm-hearted though, and not at all bad in the bath.'

The Sea King's mother fainted away at this outspoken and uninhibited statement, and the five senior mermaids fled in shock. The seventh mermaid tidied her hair and set off to find the terrible cave of the Sea Witch behind the last whirlpool, briskly pushing aside the disgusting polypi, half plant, half animal, and the fingery seaweeds that had so terrified her dead sister on a similar journey.

'Aha,' said the Sea Witch, stirring a pot of filthy black bouillabaisse, 'you, like your sister, cannot do without me. I suppose you also want to risk body and soul for the human prince up there on the dry earth?'

'Good afternoon, no,' said the seventh mermaid. 'Might I sit down?' (For even the seventh mermaid was polite to the Sea Witch.) 'I want to ask you if, when the prince follows me down here below the waves, you could arrange for him to live with me until the end of time?'

'He'd have to lose his legs. What would he think of that?'

'I think he might consider it. In due course.'

'He would have to learn to sing and not care about clothes or money or possessions or power—what would he think of that?'

'Difficult, but not impossible.'

'He'd have to face the fact that if you fell in love with one of your own kind and married him he would die and also lose his soul as your sister did when he wouldn't make an honest woman of her.'

'It was not,' said the seventh mermaid, 'that he wouldn't make an honest woman of her. It just never occurred to him. After all—she couldn't speak to him about it. You had cut out her tongue.'

'Aha,' said the s.w., 'it's different for a man, is it? Falling in love, are you?'

'Certainly not,' said Fräulein Sieben. 'Certainly not.'

'Cruel then, eh? Revengeful? Or do you hate men? It's very fashionable.'

'I'm not cruel. Or revengeful. I'm just rational. And I don't hate men. I think I'd probably like them very much, especially if they are all as kind and as beautiful as the prince. I just don't believe in falling in love with them. It is a burden and it spoils life. It is a mental illness. It killed my sister and it puts women in a weak position and makes us to be considered second class.'

'They fall in love with us,' said the Sea Witch. 'That's to say, with women. So I've been told. Sometimes. Haven't you read the sonnets of Shakespeare and the poems of Petrarch?'

'The sonnets of Shakespeare are hardly all about one

woman,' said the bright young mermaid. 'In fact some of them are written to a man. As for Petrarch, (there was scarcely a thing this girl hadn't read) he only saw his girl once, walking over a bridge. They never exactly brushed their teeth together.'

'Well, there are the Brownings.'

'Yes. The Brownings were all right,' said the mermaid. 'Very funny looking though. I don't suppose anyone else ever wanted them.'

'You are a determined young mermaid,' said the Sea Witch. 'Yes, I'll agree to treat the prince if he comes this way. But you must wait and see if he does.'

'Thank you, yes I will,' said the seventh mermaid. 'He'll come,' and she did wait, quite confidently, being the kind of girl well-heeled men do run after because she never ran after them, very like Elizabeth Bennet.

So, one day, who should come swimming down through the wonderful blue water and into the golden palaces of the Sea King and floating through the windows like the fish and touching with wonder the dry-rot flowers upon the walls, but the prince, his golden hair floating behind him and his golden hose and tunic stuck tight to him all over like a wet-suit, and he looked terrific.

'Oh, princess, sweet seventh mermaid,' he said, finding her at once (because she was the sort of girl who is always in the right place at the right time). 'I have found you again. Ever since I threw you back in the sea I have dreamed of you. I cannot live without you. I have left my boozy wife and have come to live with you for ever.'

'There are terrible conditions,' said the seventh mermaid. 'Remember. The same conditions which my poor sister accepted in reverse. You must lose your legs and wear a tail.'

'This I will do.'

'You must learn to sing for hours and hours in unison with the other mermen, in wondrous notes that hypnotise simple sailors up above and make them think they hear faint sounds from Glyndebourne or Milan.'

'As to that,' said the prince, 'I always wished I had a voice.'

'And you must know that if I decide that I want someone more than you, someone of my own sort, and marry him, you will lose everything, as my sister did—your body, your immortal soul and your self-respect.'

'Oh well, that's quite all right,' said the prince. He knew that no girl could ever prefer anyone else to him.

'*Right*,' said the mermaid. 'Well, before we go off to the Sea Witch, let's give a party. And let me introduce you to my mother and sisters.'

Then there followed a time of most glorious celebration, similar only to the celebration some years back for the prince's wedding night when the poor little mermaid now dead had had to sit on the deck of the nuptial barque and watch the bride and groom until she had quite melted away. Then the cannons had roared and the flags had waved and a royal bridal tent of cloth of gold and purple and precious furs had been set upon the deck and when it grew dark, coloured lamps had been lit and sailors danced merrily and the bride and groom had gone into the tent without the prince giving the little mermaid a backward glance.

Now, beneath the waves the sea was similarly alight with glowing corals and brilliant sea-flowers and a bower was set up for the seventh mermaid and the prince and she danced with all the mermen who had silver crowns on their heads and St Christophers round their necks, very trendy like the South of France, and they all had a lovely time.

And the party went on and on. It was beautiful. Day after day and night after night and anyone who was anyone was there, and the weather was gorgeous—no storms below or above and it was exactly as Hans Christian Andersen said: 'a wondrous blue tint lay over everything; one would be more inclined to fancy one was high up in the air and saw nothing but sky above and below than that one was at the bottom of the sea. During a calm, too, one could catch a glimpse of the sun. It looked like a crimson flower from the cup of which, light streamed forth.' The seventh mermaid danced and danced, particularly with a handsome young merman with whom she seemed much at her ease.

'Who is that merman?' asked the prince. 'You seem to know him well.'

'Oh—just an old friend,' said the seventh m., 'he's always been about. We were in our prams together.' (This was not true. The seventh m. was just testing the prince. She had never bothered with mermen even in her pram.)

'I'm sorry,' said the prince, 'I can't have you having mermen friends. Even if there's nothing in it.'

'We must discuss this with the Sea Witch,' said the seventh mermaid, and taking his hand she swam with him out of the palace and away and away through the dreadful polypi again. She took him past the last whirlpool to the cave where the Sea Witch was sitting eating a most unpleasant-looking type of caviar from a giant snail shell and stroking her necklace of sea snakes.

'Ha,' said the Sea Witch, 'the prince. You have come to be rid of your legs?'

'Er—well—'

'You have come to be rid of your earthly speech, your clothes and possessions and power?'

'Well, it's something that we might discuss.'

'And you agree to lose soul and body and self-respect if this interesting mermaid goes off and marries someone?'

There was a very long silence and the seventh mermaid closely examined some shells round her neck, tiny pale pink oyster shells each containing a pearl which would be the glory of a Queen's crown. The prince held his beautiful chin in his lovely, sensitive hand. His gentle eyes filled with tears. At last he took the mermaid's small hand and kissed its palm and folded the sea-green nails over the kiss (he had sweet ways) and said, 'I must not look at you. I must go at once,' and he pushed off. That is to say, he pushed himself upwards off the floor of the sea and shot up and away and away through the foam, arriving home in time for tea and early sherry with his wife, who was much relieved.

It was a very long time indeed before the seventh little mermaid returned to the party. In fact the party was all but over. There was only the odd slithery merman twanging a harp of dead fisherman's bones and the greediest and grubbiest of the deep water fishes eating up the last of the sandwiches. The Sea King's old mother was asleep, her heavy tail studded with important oyster shells coiled round the legs of her throne.

The five elder sisters had gone on somewhere amusing.

The seventh mermaid sat down at the feet of her grandmother and at length the old lady woke up and surveyed the chaos left over from the fun. 'Hello, my child,' she said. 'Are you alone?'

'Yes. The prince has gone. The engagement's off.'

'My dear—what did I tell you? Remember how your poor sister suffered. I warned you.'

'Pooh—I'm not suffering. I've just proved my point. Men aren't worth it.'

'Maybe you and she were unfortunate,' said the Sea King's mother. 'Which men you meet is very much a matter of luck, I'm told.'

'No—they're all the same,' said the mermaid who by now was nearly fifteen years old. 'I've proved what I suspected. I'm free now—free of the terrible pangs of love which put women in bondage, and I shall dedicate my life to freeing and instructing other women and saving them from humiliation.'

'Well, I hope you don't become one of those frowsty little women who don't laugh and have only one subject of conversation,' said the Sea King's mother. 'It is a mistake to base a whole philosophy upon one disappointment.'

'Disappointment—pah!' said the seventh mermaid. 'When was I ever negative?'

'And I hope you don't become aggressive.'

'When was I ever aggressive?' said Senorita Septima ferociously.

'That's a good girl then,' said the Sea King's mother. 'So now—unclench that fist.'

STONE TREES

So now that he is dead so now that he is dead I am to spend the day with them. The Robertsons.

On the Isle of Wight. Train journey train journey from London. There and back in a day.

So now that he is dead—

They were at the funeral. Not their children. Too little. So good so good they were to me. She—Anna—she cried a lot. Tom held my arm tight. Strong. I liked it. In the place even the place where your coffin was, I liked it, his strong arm. Never having liked Tom that much, I liked his strong arm.

And they stayed over. Slept at the house a night or two. Did the telephone. Some gran or someone was with their children. Thank God we had no children. Think of Tom/Anna dying and those two children left—

So now that you are dead—

It's nice of them isn't it now that you are dead? Well, you'd have expected it. You aren't surprised by it. I'm not surprised by it. After all there has to be somewhere to go. All clean all clean at home. Back work soon someday. Very soon now for it's a week. They broke their two week holiday for the funeral. Holiday Isle of Wight where you/I went once. There was a dip, a big-dipper dip, a wavy line of cliffs along the shore, and in this dip of the cliffs a hotel—a long beach and the waves moving in shallow.

Over stone trees.

But it was long ago and what can stone trees have been?

Fantasy.

So now that you are dead so now—

Sweetie love so now that you are dead I am to spend the day with the Robertsons alone and we shall talk you/I later. So now—

The boat crosses. Has crossed. Already. Criss-cross deck. Criss-cross water. Splashy sea and look! Lovely clouds flying (now that you are dead) and here's the pier. A long, long pier into the sea and gulls shouting and children yelling here and there and here's my ticket and there they stand. All in a row— Tom, Anna, the two children solemn. And smiles now—Tom and Anna. Tom and Anna look too large to be quite true. Too good. Anna who never did anything wrong. Arms stretch too far forward for a simple day.

They stretch because they want. They would not stretch to me if you were obvious and not just dead. Then it would have been, hello, easy crossing? Good. Wonderful day. Let's get back and down on the beach. Great to see you both.

So now that you are dead—

We paced last week. Three.

Tom. Anna. I.

And other black figures wood-faced outside the crematorium in blazing sun, examining shiny black-edged tickets on blazing bouquets. 'How good of Marjorie—fancy old Marjorie. I didn't even know she—' There was that woman who ran out of the so-called service with handkerchief at her eyes. But who was there except you my darling and I and the Robertsons and the shiny cards and did they do it then? Were they doing it then as we read the flowers? Do they do it at once or stack it up with other coffins and was it still inside waiting as I paced with portly Tom? Christian Tom—Tom we laughed at so often and oh my darling now that you are dead—

Cambridge. You can't say that Tom has precisely changed since Cambridge. Thickened. More solid. Unshaken still, quite unshaken and—well, wonderful of course. Anna hasn't changed. Small, specs, curly hair, straight-laced. Dear Anna how we sat and worked out all. Analysed. Girton. We talked about how many men it was decent to do it with without being wild and when you should decide to start and Anna said none and never. Not before marriage you said. Anna always in that church where Tom preached and Tom never looking Anna's way, and how she ached. So now that—

Sweet I miss you so. Now that you are— My darling oh my God!

In the train two young women. (Yes thanks Anna, I'm fine. Nice journey. First time out. It's doing me good. Isn't it a lovely day?) There were these two women talking about their rights. They were reading about all that was due to them. In a magazine.

'Well, it's only right isn't it?'

'What?'

'Having your own life. Doing your thing.'

'Well—'

'Not—you know. Men and that. Not letting them have all the freedom and that. You have to stand up for yourself and get free of men.'

We come to the hotel and of course it is the one. The one in the dip of the cliffs almost on the beach, and how were they to know? It's typical though, somehow. We didn't like them my darling did we, after Cambridge very much? We didn't see them—dropped them in some way. We didn't see them for nearly two years. And we wondered, sometimes, whatever it was we had thought we had had in common—do-good, earnest Tom, healthy face and shorts, striding out over mountains singing snatches of Berlioz and stopping now and then to pray. And you were you and always unexpected—alert, alive, mocking and forever young and now that you are—

But they were there again. In California. You at the university and I at the university, teaching a term; and there—behold the Robertsons, holding out their arms to save America. Little house full of the shiny-faced, the chinless—marriage counsellors, marriage-enrichment classes oh my God! And one child in Anna and one just learning to walk. We were taken to them by somebody just for a lark not knowing who they'd turn out to be and we said—'Hey! Tom and Anna.'

And in Sacramento in a house with lacy balconies and little red Italian brick walls and all their old Cambridge books about and photographs we half-remembered, we opened wine and were very happy; and over the old whitewashed fireplace there was Tom's old crucifix and his Cambridge oar. And I sat in the rocking chair she'd had at Girton and it felt familiar and we loved the Robertsons that day in sweaty, wheezing Sacramento because they were there again. This is no reason. But it is true.

We talked about how we'd all met each other first. Terrible party. Jesus College. Anna met Tom and I met you my darling and it was something or other—Feminism, Neo-Platonism, Third World—and there you were with bright, ridiculous, marvellous, mocking eyes and long hard hands and I loved you as everyone else clearly loved you. And the Robertsons talked sagely to one another. They were not the Robertsons then but Tom and Anna. We never became the anythings, thank God. There was no need because we were whatever the appearance might be one person and had no need of a plural term and now that—

Sweetie, do you remember the *smell* of that house? In Cambridge? And again in Sacramento? She liked it you know. She left dishes for a week and food bits and old knickers and tights in rolls on the mantelpiece and said, 'There are things more important.' Under the burning ethic there was you know something very desperate about Anna. Tom didn't notice her. Day after day and I'd guess night after night. He sat in the rocking chair and glared at God. And meeting them again just the same, in Sacramento, you looked at the crucifix and the oar and at me, your eyes like the first time we met because there we both remembered the first time, long ago. Remembering that was a short return to each other because by then, by America, I knew that you were one I'd never have to myself because wherever you were or went folk turned and smiled at you and loved you. Well, I'd known always. I didn't face it at first, that one woman would never be enough for you and that if I moved in with you you would soon move on.

Everyone wanted you. When we got married there was a general sense of comedy and the sense of my extraordinary and very temporary luck.

It is not right or dignified to love so much. To let a man rule so much. It is obsession and not love, a mental illness not a life. And of course, with marriage came the quarrelling and pain because I knew there were so many others, and you not coming home, and teasing when you did and saying that there was only me but of course I knew it was not so because of—cheap and trite things like—the smell of scent. It was worst just before the Robertsons went away.

But then—after California—we came here to this beach once and it was September like now, and a still, gold peace. And the hotel in the dip, and the sand white and wide and rock pools. And only I with you. You were quieter. You brought no work. You lay on the beach with a novel flapping pages and the sand gathering in them. We held hands and it was not as so often. It was not as when I looked at you and saw your eyes looking at someone else invisible. God, love—the killing sickness. Maybe never let it start—just mock and talk of Rights. Don't let it near. Sex without sentiment. Manage one's life with dignity. But now that you are dead—

And one day on that year's peaceful holiday we walked out to the stone trees which now I remember. They told us, at the hotel, that in the sea, lying on their stone sides, on their stone bark and broken stone branches, were great prehistoric trees, petrified and huge and broken into sections by the millenia and chopped here and there as by an infernal knife, like rhubarb chunks or blocks of Edinburgh candy, sand coloured, ancient among the young stones.

Trees so old that no one ever saw them living. Trees become stone. I said, 'I love stone,' and you said, 'I love trees,' and kicked them. You said, 'Who wants stone trees?' And we walked about on them, a stone stick forest, quite out to sea, and sat and put our feet in pools where green grasses swayed and starfish shone. And you said—despising the stone trees—there is only ever you—you know—and I knew that the last one was gone and the pain of her and you and I were one again. It was quite right that you loved so much being so much loved and I am glad, for now that you are dead—

I shall never see you any more.

I shall never feel your hand over my hand.

I shall never lean my head against you any more.

I shall never see your eyes which now that you are—

'The sandwiches are egg, love, and cheese, and there's chocolate. We didn't bring a feast. It's too hot.'

'It's lovely.'

'Drink?'

'I don't like Ribena, thanks.'

'It's not. It's wine. In tumblers. Today we're having a lot of wine in very big tumblers.'

(Anna Robertson of evangelical persuasion, who never acts extremely, is offering me wine in tumblers. Now that you are dead.)

'It's nice wine. I'll be drunk.'

The children say, 'You can have some of our cake. D'you want a biscuit?' They've been told to be nice. The little girl pats sand, absorbed, solemn, straight-haired, grave like Tom. The older one, the boy, eats cake and lies on his stomach aware of me and that my husband has died and gone to God.

And you have gone to God?

You were with God and you were my god and now that you—

The boy has long legs. Seven-year-old long legs. The boy is a little like you and not at all like Tom. He rolls over and gives me a biscuit. I'm so glad we had no children. I could not have shared you with children. We needed nobody else except you needed other girls to love a bit and leave—nothing important. You moved on and never mind. I didn't. I did not mind. The pain passed and I don't mind and I shall not mind now that you are dead.

The boy is really—or am I going mad altogether—very like you.

The boy is Peter.

Says, 'Are you coming out on the rocks?'

'I'm fine thanks, Peter. I'm drinking my wine.'

'Drink it later and come out on the rocks. Come on over the rocks.'

See Anna, Tom, proud of Peter being kind to me and only seven. They pretend not to see, fiddling with coffee flask, suntan oil. 'Wonderful summer,' says Anna.

'Wonderful.'

'Come on the rocks.'

'Peter—don't boss,' says Anna.

'Leave your wine and come,' says Peter, 'I'll show you the rocks.'

So I go with this boy over the rocks my darling now that you are dead and I have no child and I will never see you any more.

Not any more.

Ever again.

Now that you are—
It is ridiculous how this boy walks.

How Anna wept.

'Look, hold my hand,' says Peter, 'and take care. We're on old trees. What d'you think of that? They were so old they turned to stone. It's something in the atmosphere. They're awful, aren't they? I like trees all leafy and sparkly.'

'*Sparkly* trees?'

'Well, there'd be no pollution. No people. Now just rotten stone.'

'I like stone.'

He kicks them, 'I like trees.'

And I sit down my love because I will not see you any more or hold your hand or put my face on yours and this will pass of course. They've told me that this sort of grief will pass.

But I don't want the grief to change. I want not to forget the feel and look of you and the look of your live eyes and the physical life of you and I do not want to cease to grieve.

'Look, hey, look,' says Peter and stops balancing. 'The tide is coming in.' The water slaps. The dead stone which was once covered with breathing holes for life takes life again, and where it looked like burned out ashy stone there are colours, and little movements, and frondy things responding to water, which laps and laps.

'Look,' says Peter, 'there's a star-fish. Pink as pink. Hey— take my hand. Mind out. You mustn't slip.' (This boy has long hard hands.) 'The tide is coming in.'

How Anna cried.

The tide is coming in and it will cover the stone trees and then it will ebb back again and the stone trees will remain, and already the water is showing more growing things that are there all the time, though only now and then seen.

And Peter takes my hand in yours and I will never see you any more— How Anna cried. And things are growing in the cracks in the stones. The boy laughs and looks at me with your known eyes. Now that you are.

AN UNKNOWN CHILD

The bandaged della Robbia babies stretched their arms in blessing towards the piazza. Across the piazza the Englishwoman sat on a high window seat of the pensione and looked at them in the autumn evening light.

Her husband said, 'Come for dinner.'

'It's a wonderful evening. Look at the della Robbia babies. It's a pity about the traffic in between.'

'They'll want us to be in time for dinner. It's a pensione.'

'I'm glad the della Robbias are still there. They were there when I was twenty.'

'They were there when your grandmother was twenty. And her grandmother. And hers. We ought to go in for dinner.'

'Yes. Wait. I'm glad they haven't hacked them off the walls yet. They took the frescoes off the walls you know. Some sort of blotting paper. We'll see the marks where they used to be tomorrow. When I was here you could actually touch the frescoes. With your hands. Just going down the street. Like in the Renaissance. They survived the war but not the tourists. I'm glad they haven't hacked off the babies.'

Every bit of the journey there had been babies. From London to Calais, Calais to Milan, Milan to Florence. A baby had watched them from the next quartet of seats on the Intercity. Babies had screamed and chatted and roistered and roared, been carried and rocked and coaxed and shouted at on the boat. Larger, older ones had rushed about the deck, pushed their heads over the side between the spume and the seagulls, all the way to France. Two Swiss six-year-old babies with the heads of financiers had been absorbed in pocket calculators across the carriage from them all the way to the frontier. The night, from Switzerland to Chiasso, had been made sleepless by the wailing of an Umbrian infant with the toothache. From Milan, the corridor had been solid with nursing mothers.

He had said, 'Evelyn, why the hell are we not travelling first class?'

'I didn't last time.'

'My heaven—nearly twenty years ago. And you were fit then. You could have just about walked to Italy then.'

'I'm fit now,' she said. 'A miscarriage isn't an illness. It's usual. A blessing. We know it.'

He was a doctor. That her miscarriage of a child was a blessing was a fact that he had levelly insisted upon since it happened, two weeks ago. The child, he had told her, had certainly been wrong. For the rest of their lives they would have been saddled with—

She had lain on the bed and said nothing. They had been married twelve years. For fifteen she had been doing medical research, as busy as he in the same teaching hospital. On her marriage she had made it clear that she had no intention of wasting herself—her youth, her training—in childbearing. Her brain was at its best. Children could come later. Good heavens, you could have a child at forty now. There was that top Civil Servant woman who had had a child—perfectly healthy child—at fifty. It had always been so—able women often produced children late. Mrs. Browning—(For Evelyn was properly educated: literary as well as medical.)

And she looked so young for her age. It had become a joke at parties, how young Evelyn stayed. 'I'm Mrs. Dorian Grey,' she said, though few of Mick's colleagues knew what she meant. Mick had loved her first (it sounded crude) because of her health—her health, energy and bright eyes and shiny sea-side hair and out-spoken Yorkshire good sense. In a rare moment of imagination—it had made up her mind to him—he had called her 'The Scarborough Girl'. It had been her lovely, apparently indestructable youth and health and sense that had given him the courage to tell her at once after the miscar-riage—directly after his consultation with her gynaecologist—that, at her age, there must be no more. To conceive a child again must be out of the question.

'Why?'

He told her. She listened thoughtfully, with a careful, con-sulting room expression, not looking at him but at the waving top of the silver birch outside their bedroom window, for the miscarriage had taken place at home as they had so dashingly planned that the birth should do. The foetus had been between four and five months old. It had lain with her for an hour in the bed. It had had small limp arms. There was no tele-phone by the bed and she had waited an hour for him to get back from the hospital. The only sound in the empty house had been the whimpering and scratching of the dog at the bed-room door and her terrified, thumping heart fearing that it might get in. She had bled a good deal and had watched the birch tree turn its topmost leaves first one way and then the other in the evening light, had fainted as Mick arrived. As she fainted she had seemed to see his eyes in a band of brightness, separate from his face and filled with raw dismay. Afterwards—he had been so steady—she thought that this must have been a dream.

'I'm sorry,' he said now, 'I didn't know this place was oppo-site the Innocenti baby place. You should have let me book a good hotel. Just because you were here before— It's no good trying to live things over again.'

'I don't try. It's lovely here. I knew it would still be lovely, even with all the traffic now. When I was here before, the piazza used to be almost empty. In the early morning there'd be just one donkey and cart going across, and someone spreading out a flower stall round the feet of the statue. Now this huge great car park. But the light's the same. And the buildings—the columns of the orphanage.'

'Come and have dinner.'

'And along here,' she said, walking ahead of him down the narrow corridor with the old slit windows, 'the floor used to crackle with the heat as if the boards were on fire.

'And you could see mountainous great cedars—look. See them. Look. And just the top of the dome where the Michelangelo David is. Look how solid the trees are.

'Oh—and the dining room's exactly the same. Exactly. Look. Pure E. M. Forster. There's even the same long table down the middle.'

They were shown, however, past the long table to one of the empty side tables. The long table, though fully laid, stayed empty.

'I was here twenty years ago,' she said to the waitress—who exclaimed and rejoiced. Afterwards Evelyn must come and see the old Signora—the very old Signora now. *At once* the girl would go and tell her. The old Signora loved people to return.

'I was still a student,' Evelyn told her as she came with the soup, 'under twenty. Oh, it was wonderful to have free wine put on the table, just like a water-jug. We hardly drank wine in England then.'

'You speak beautiful Italian,' said the waitress. 'Students have been coming here and learning good Italian, the old Signora says, for a hundred years. When were you here? Ha!' (she clapped her hands) 'Then I was the baby in the kitchen. Now' (she stroked her stomach) 'soon there shall be another baby in the kitchen.'

'I'd like to be at the long table,' said Evelyn over the pasta, which seemed very plain.

'Nobody's sitting there.'

'Everyone used to sit there. All together. Like in *A Room with a View*. D'you think we could ask? Nobody's sitting there.'

'If nobody's sitting there we might as well stay over here by the window.'

'No—if we sat there, then other people would come. We could talk. Oh Mick—I wore such a dress. Tartan taffeta! Can you imagine? I thought you had to change for dinner, you see. I'd never been anywhere. Just read Forster and Henry James. All the others were in beads and rags. It was the new fashion—rags. I hadn't met it. I was terribly behind the times.'

'This wasn't the time when you were with The Love of your Life?'

'No. I told you. It was just after Finals. Waiting for the results. I was with a girl who was chucking Medicine and going to be a nun. She went into a nunnery as soon as we got home. It was her last holiday.'

'Must have been a jolly little outing.'

'Mick'—Her laughter warmed him more than the eye-watering wine. He leaned across and took her hand. 'I'm glad you didn't go into a nunnery,' he said.

'Oh, I was pretty boring. I hadn't even got hooked on Medicine then. I only wanted everyday sort of things.'

The door of the dining room opened and an English family—mother, father and five children—filed in and sat at the long table. The older children folded their hands. The younger ones sat still and good. The youngest, a girl about seven, sat on her hands, her short arms stiff at each side of her until the father turned bleak wire spectacles on her and said, 'Elizabeth.' Then she took her hands from under her thighs and folded them in her lap like the rest, but the corners of her mouth became very firm. She was unusually beautiful.

'What a beautiful child,' said Evelyn. Other people at side tables were looking too.

'Yes. Come on, love, what shall we have next?'

'No choice. It's a pensione. Osso bucco every night. I told you. Mick—just *look* at that child.'

'Yes. Let's have some more wine. Leave them be.'

'Why should I? I'm all right you know. You don't have to worry. For heaven's sake, look at them all. Aren't they beautiful?'

'The mother's not,' said Mick. 'She looks worn out.'

'Yes.' Evelyn looked vaguely, but then back at the children, especially at the child Elizabeth.

'What a father,' said Mick, seeing the glasses gleam from one child to another, then the order given for all to say Grace. Five pairs of eyes shut around him. Five pairs of hands were folded together. The wife moved spoons about the cloth.

'"For what we are about to receive,"' said the father—

'I don't believe it,' Mick said. 'They must be ghosts. I'll bet they're from Hampstead.'

The children began to drink soup which had been rather laconically slapped down by the young Signora. The child, Elizabeth, looked round as the young Signora pranced by and the young Signora tickled the top of the child's head. Again the father said, 'Elizabeth.' The mother continued to stare into space.

'Shall we go to bed now?' Evelyn was across the dining room almost before she had said it.

'Aren't we going out?' He hurried after her. 'For a walk? See the Duomo and all that? I think they floodlight it. It's too early to sleep.'

'No. You go and see it if you like. I'm tired. We'll be out all day after this—every day from tomorrow morning. When Rupert comes there'll be no cloister left untrod.' Her face had lengthened and her eyes looked tired.

*

In his bed across the room from her he said, 'You're not sorry we came? It's a busy place for a convalescence.' He was staring at their painted ceiling, shadowy with carved angels.

She said, 'I remember this ceiling. D'you know, I think we were in this same room. I wonder if—the girl who became a nun, goodness, I've forgotten her name—I wonder if she remembers this ceiling.'

'You're not sorry, Evelyn? It maybe has been a bit soon.'

'Don't be a fool. God—*children* have miscarriages these days. Abortions, abortions—you hear of nothing else. A clinical fact of life now. Unless you're a Catholic. Even Catholics aren't what they were. Catholic *doctors* now are doing abortions in Africa. In the famine places. It's a rational matter.'

They both thought of the abortion reform posters they had passed, slapped over ancient buildings—church walls, palazzos—and modern banks and municipal offices, on the way from the station.

'Not my line of business, thank goodness.'

'Well, no—nor mine.'

'You're not trying to persuade yourself,' he said, 'that this is the same? This was no *choice* for heaven's sake.'

After a time, as the old wooden room cooled and crackled in the early night she said, 'No.' Then, 'What do they mean—choice?'

Rupert's arrival was like a salt breeze. He bounced into the mahogany and plush entrance hall, arms astretch and talking, before the young Signora had finished opening the inner door for him. He was fresh from Cyprus—the archetypal, unwed, ageless English academic, rich, Greece-loving, sexless—all passions channelled into deep concern for friends: the man you meet at college who turns up about every five years looking exactly the same and remembering every last thing about you and telling you nothing of himself. One's lynch-pin, one's strong rock. 'My dears—dears! Out. Out. Out we go at once before we're eaten by the aspidistras.' He wrapped Evelyn in his arms, gazed adoringly at the smiling young Signora over her shoulder and grabbed hold of Mick's arm. Like many men with secret lives he touched people often and bravely, hating it.

'What a place you've found. Is it real? I saw a troupe of little Nesbitts making for the Boboli Gardens with hoops and kites—a neurotic Mama and a father from the Iffley Road.'

'We think Hampstead.'

'My dears—Oxford. They can only be Oxford. Mum is a lecturer in—let's see—Thermo-Dynamics and Pa is—Pa is—ha! He is a Biologist. He reads *Peter Rabbit* at home and picks apart little pussy cats in the day-time. He glares down microscopes at the death agonies of gnats. One day the children will all silently pack their bags and away to California. And Mama will take a tiny pistol out of her poche and shoot him through the head.'

'You know them, Rupert?'

The three of them were clattering down the pensione's stone stairs under the vaulted archway to the piazza.

'But dozens of them. Whole families of them.'

'Oxford rather than Cambridge?'

'Oh—masses more of them at Cambridge. Cousins and cousins. But in Cambridge, dears, they don't dress their children in Greenaway-yallery. It's filthy tee-shirts and shaven heads. All reading Stendhal at six. Shall I tell you what happened to me last time I went to Cambridge?' He was sweeping them along the Via Servi. The crowds smiled at him, parting before him. 'Drinks,' he said, 'with a Fellow of Queen's. Sitting there talking (Coffee? Coffee? Let's stop here.)—oh, post-structuralism, Japanese realist fiction, usual stuff. Out from behind a sofa comes youngest child wearing nappies and smoking a cigarette.'

'Pot?' said Mick.

'No no no—Russian Sobranie. Twenties stuff.'

Evelyn was laughing. 'You made that up, Rupert.'

She sat back at the cafe table, looked at the small coffee cups, the glasses of water, the sugar lumps wrapped in paper decorated with little pictures of Raphael's Virgin and Child. She lifted her face to the sun.

'Come on Rupert, you did,' said Mick. 'These children were History Man children. University of E.A.'

'Certainly not, dear. History Man children have nothing to do with Oxford. Nowadays they're churchgoers—1662. Learning their Collect for the day. The parents toy with communities—not communes, communities. Firmly, firmly in their own beds most of the time. If not it's away to the confessional and deep discussions over an evening milk drink. All terribly sweet. The children terribly ugly.'

Evelyn became still. She watched the sugar lump as the coffee turned it amber. 'Those pensione children weren't ugly.'

Rupert began to talk of Giotto saints and San Miniato, all of which he said if they hurried they could see before lunch. Evelyn wondered what he and Mick had said when Mick had telephoned Cyprus last week to say that their holiday together was now going to be a convalescence. Rupert stood right outside this area of loss, outside all areas of marriage. On Rupert's part the conversation would have been no more than a quick exclamation of regret—then details of his time of arrival.

Yet, as the days passed, it seemed odd how skilful Rupert was being at making Evelyn smile, in directing her away from precipices. As Mick stood vague before the Michelangelos, Rupert kept at Evelyn's side. While Mick made no plans, Rupert had pages marked each day in maps and guide books. It was Rupert who saw to it ('My dears, this is a holiday—not a penance') that they ate all their meals away from the pensione except for breakfast which they ate alone in their bedrooms.

The admirable English family faded as if they had been the miasma they had looked.

On Rupert's last day, in the woods above Fiesole, they picnicked and talked and sunbathed and slept and Evelyn awoke feeling brisk and well. In her old, incisive mood she talked of packing and, back in Florence, Rupert even allowed her to do some of his for him. He smiled at her with love as they all three struggled through the screaming rush-hour traffic to the railway station in one of the painted, horse-drawn carriages he had insisted upon.

'Dotty things,' said Evelyn. 'Sentimental, Rupert.' When she had been here before they had been the only sort of taxi. It had been different then. Pretty. Romantic. But now they were going to miss the train. Times change. You have to face reality.

'Don't you, Rupert dear?'

'No,' said Rupert, kissing her, waving goodbye, scattering largesse to porters, leaping the train as it began to move out. 'Not all at once at any rate,' he called. 'Give it time. Let it face you.'

It was quiet without him that evening. They were tired and the pensione was dark and still and nearly empty. The long centre table was no longer made up and they sat in their alcove with only one old lady, bent like a leaf over her library book, at another. The food was a little less staid than on their first night, the wine kinder, the noise of the traffic less disturbing. There had been one of the frequent Florentine power cuts and the stately young Signora had placed a candle inside a bell of glass on each table so that shadows made the white-washed walls serene. Evelyn and Mick sat long over their coffee. The old lady closed her book and crept away.

Then the door opened and the English family, very slightly flushed in the face, swept steadily in like a river and sat down at the long table without a word. The young Signora, coming through to remove the old lady's plate and blow out her candle, stopped and gasped. It was past nine o'clock. Over two hours late. It was as clear as if the Signora had shouted it that the kitchen was empty, the cook abed, the ovens cold. She said nothing, stood still, then after a pause went away and the family sat staring straight ahead. After quite a few minutes the Signora returned and asked, with a catch in her voice, whether they would take soup.

'Please,' said the father, candlelight on his glasses.

In the considerable time that then passed, the father said once, 'Is something wrong?' and nobody answered him.

Soup came. The Signora could manage no smile. She did not even look at the child, Elizabeth. She handed the basket of bread to each of them and, turning her big body about, disappeared through the door with head high. 'Shall we go?' said Mick to Evelyn, who was looking all the time at the child, but Evelyn said, 'No. No. Wait please.'

'Oh, Evelyn.'

'No. Just wait a bit longer. Please.'

From the shadows of the centre table somebody suddenly said very high and clear, 'The soup is cold.' The mother pushed hers away.

'I think,' said the father, 'that it must nevertheless be drunk, don't you?'

Two or three of the children put down their spoons. Elizabeth went on with the soup until it was finished.

'Shall we all finish the soup?' asked the father slowly, turning his head about. The children one by one picked up their spoons again, getting the soup down somehow with the help of the hard bread. The mother turned sideways and looked at the floor.

'Come along now, Elizabeth, eat your bread.'

'I have drunk the soup,' said Elizabeth, 'but the bread is too hard.'

'Then we shall hope that you can eat it later, shall we not?'

Pasta came, freshly made, the Signora hot in the face. Evelyn and Mick asked for more coffee and the Signora, serving it, suddenly blazed her eyes at Evelyn and poured forth a whispered torrent of Italian with backward movements of the head at the centre table. Evelyn nodded but did not take her eyes from the child.

'We shall not take meat or fruit,' said the father, 'we shall go to bed. "For what we have received—" Elizabeth?'

She did not look up.

'You have not eaten the bread.'

'It's too hard. I drank the soup.'

'Come along. Eat the bread.'

She did not move.

'"For what we have received the Lord make us truly thankful." Come along. We shall go. And Elizabeth shall stay here until she has eaten the bread.'

They went out, one of the older boys giving Elizabeth a push in the back with a friendly finger, but nobody else paid any attention, the mother leaving the room first without a glance. All their feet could be heard receding down the corridor, crackling like a forest fire, and doors were heard to close.

Suddenly, all the electricity in the pensione came on in a flood and the child was revealed like a prisoner under a searchlight, all alone at the long table. She sat stalwartly, with small, round, folded arms, looking at her hands, her mouth dogged, the bread untouched on the tired cloth.

'Shall we go now?' asked Mick, loudly and cheerfully, coughing a little, squeaking back his chair.

'No. No. Not yet. I want some more coffee.'

'We can't have *more* coffee, it's much too late.'

The Signora came in again and stopped to see the child sitting alone in the glare. She turned astonished eyes on Evelyn and Mick and started towards the centre table, but the dark, fierce air hanging around the child made her shy.

'You—finito? Everyone now?'

The child did not answer.

'Could we have more coffee? I'm sorry—I know it's terribly late,' called Evelyn and looking back over her shoulder at the child all the way to the door, the Signora made for the kitchen again.

Mick began to hum and pace the floor a little. He looked out of the window where the colonnade of the Innocenti blazed patchily above the whirling lights of the cars. Above was the starry sky. Turning in to the room again, he said, 'Hard old bread, isn't it?' and went and sat down by the child. 'Enjoying your holiday?' he said. 'Expect it's all a bit of a bore, isn't it? Churches and stuff. I expect you'd rather be at the sea.'

Then he put out his hand and let it stay for a moment above the child's head. He let it drop and began slowly to stroke her hair. She flung up her chin and pulled away as though she had been stung and simultaneously the door to the corridor opened and the father stood in the dining room. He said, 'What is this?'

'I was talking to your daughter.'

'I'm afraid my daughter is not allowed to talk to strangers.'

'Isn't it rather unwise then to let her sit alone, long after her bedtime, in a room with only strangers in it?'

'She knows how to behave. She knows that she has to stay there until she has eaten the bread.'

'That's your affair—'

'It is.'

'It's your affair, but suppose that the strangers had not been us? To leave a small child alone. Late at night. In a foreign restaurant.'

'Hardly a restaurant I think.'

'You treated it as a restaurant tonight. Over two hours late for dinner. Never a word of apology. The one and only wait-ress tired out. Pregnant. Behaving like lord and peasant—I'm sorry. I'm sorry, but my wife and I have been horrified. Disgusted. Disgusted with you. Never seen such idiocy. Quaint. Victorian play-acting. You need a psychiatrist—not fit to have children.'

'Are you an authority on children?'

'I—yes. I am a doctor. I know a lot about children.'

'And how many have you?'

'That's not the point. I see a child being studiously, insanely—'

'Shall we continue this outside?'

'By all means. If you will send this child at once to bed.'

'I shall consider it when we have talked. Outside this room if you please. I don't believe in discussions of this sort in front of children.'

'Very well.'

As the father swung out of the room and Mick swung after him, Evelyn saw in her husband's eyes the remote, terrible band of dismay she thought she had dreamt before. He was blind to her. She put her head in her hands and thought, 'I never knew how much he wanted children. In all the years, I never asked. I never thought of him.'

Lifting her face, she found that the little girl was looking at her with interest. The bread uneaten on the cloth. Her face was serious. She said to Evelyn, 'Don't cry. It doesn't matter.'

'I'm not. I wasn't—'

'It was a puncture. We got late. He's terribly ashamed. It's all right.'

'I—I just didn't—'

Tramping feet, loud voices were to be heard returning and the child, looking kindly at Evelyn, sighed and picked up the bread in both fists.

'Oh no—oh no! Please don't,' cried Evelyn. 'Please let me

have it—please. I'll hide it in my bag.' She held out her arms. 'Throw it me. Throw it me.'

But Elizabeth, shocked, turned away. 'It's all *right*,' she said, and began to munch.

The two men as they returned, saw first this loyal munching and then Evelyn in her corner, weeping at last.

SHOWING THE FLAG

The boy with big ears, whose father was dead, kissed his mother with a sliding away of the eyes, heaved up his two immense suitcases and loped up the gang-plank. At the top he dropped the cases briefly to give a quick sideways wave, keeping his face forward. He jerked the cases up again, grimaced, tramped on and his mother far below, weeping but laughing, said, 'Oh, Pym! It's the size of the cases. They're nearly as big as he is. Oh, I can't bear it.'

'He is going for a sensible time,' said her elderly woman friend. 'Three months is a good long time. The cases must necessarily be heavy.'

'I can't bear it,' wept the other, dabbing her streaming cheeks, laughing at her weakness.

'Of course you can. You must. It's not as if he's never been away before.'

'Since six. He's been away since he was six. Oh, boarding-schools. Oh, children—why does one have them? Children—it's all renunciation. Having them is just learning to give them up.'

'It is the custom of the country,' said the elderly friend—unmarried. She was a Miss Pym. 'It is in the culture of the English middle class. We teach our children how to endure.'

'He has endured. He has learned.'

'Oh, he scarcely knew his father, Gwen. Don't be silly. His father was hardly ever at home.'

"He missed him. Not of course as I—'

'You scarcely saw him either,' said sane Miss Pym. She was a plain-spoken woman.

'I loved him,' said Gwen, impressive in her heavy hanging musquash coat and flat velvet bandeau (it was the nineteen-twenties). 'And now I have lost Philip. Oh, can we find tea?' She held her tightly-squeezed handkerchief in her fist, out in front of her like a blind woman, and her friend led her away through the crowds, among the crates and high-piled luggage and the other fluttering handkerchiefs. Arm in arm the two women disappeared, slowly, floppily in their expensive boat-shaped shoes, and Philip who had found a good position for the suitcases beside a long slatted seat, hung over the rail and waved to them in vain.

When the last flicker of them had gone he blew through his teeth a bit until a whistle came and swung his feet at the bottom rail along the deck, scuffing his shoes like a two-year-old, though he was nearly thirteen. As the ship got away towards France he hung further over the rail and called down at the seagulls who were wheeling and screeching round the open port-hole of the galley. A bucket of scraps was flung out. The seagulls screamed at it and caught most of it before it hit the foam. They plunged. 'Hungry,' thought Philip. 'I'm hungry. I hope the food's going to be good. Messy French stuff. They all say it's going to be good, but it'll be no better than school. It's just disguised school.'

'The seagulls eat like school.' He watched enviously the birds tearing horrors from each other's beaks, flying free. Were they French or English seagulls? Where did they nest? They spoke a universal language, seagulls. And all birds. All animals. Presumably. Didn't need to learn French. 'They're ahead of people,' thought Philip, covering his great red ears.

It was bitterly cold. Maybe it would be warmer in Paris.

He was to get to Paris on the boat-train by himself and would there be met by a Major Foster. They would know one another by a small paper Union Jack pinned to a lapel on each of them. Philip was keeping his Union Jack in his coat pocket at present, in a small brass tin. Every few minutes he felt the tin to make sure that it was still there.

He left the rail and sat on the long seat beside the suitcases. He could not remember actually having seen the flag in the tin, only hearing about it there. He had seen it when it was part of a small packet of Union Jacks, tied in a bundle. He had heard nothing else but Union Jacks it seemed for weeks: his mother's search for just the right one, the dispatch of the Major's identical one to Paris with the instructions to him about the lapel. The (rather long) wait for the letter of confirmation from the Major that the Union Jack had been safely received. Then a further letter about the positioning of the Union Jack on the *right* lapel, in the centre and with a gold safety-pin.

Philip however could not remember the act of placing the Union Jack inside the tin. After all, she might just have forgotten. Not that it was the sort of thing she ever did do—forget. But during the last few months—after the funeral which he hadn't gone to, and which she hadn't gone to, being too ill in bed and her friend Miss Pym paddling about nursing her and bossing her in a darkened room—after the funeral there had been some sort of break. Only a short break of course. His mother wasn't one to break. She was terrific, his mother. Everyone knew she was terrific. She kept everything right. Never made a mistake. Ace organiser. He'd heard them saying in the kitchen that it was her being so perfect had killed his father, though goodness knows, thought Philip, what that meant.

Oh, his mother was a whizz. Organising, packing, making decisions. 'These are your gifts. These are your life-blood,' had said Miss Pym. 'You are by nature an administrator—quite wasted now as a mere mother.' His school matron always sighed over his trunk at the end of term. 'However did your mother get so much in?' she said. There was not a shoe not filled with socks, not a sock that did not hide a card of special darning-wool or extra buttons. Bundles of Cash's name-tapes would be folded into a face flannel. Soap in a little soap-shaped celluloid box would rest inside a cocoa mug, and the cocoa mug would rest inside a cricket cap and the cricket cap would be slid into a Wellington boot.

No. She'd never have forgotten the Union Jack.

'I think it's rather a lot to expect of a Frenchman,' had said Miss Pym. 'To wear the English flag.'

'The Fosters are French-Canadian,' had said his mother. 'They're very English. Very patriotic, although they live in the Avenue Longchamps.'

'I hope their French is not patriotic. If so there's very little point in Philip going.'

'They are patriotic to France as well.'

'How odd,' said Pym. 'That is unusual.'

Philip took the tin out of his pocket and shook it and there seemed to be no rattle from inside. But then when he opened the lid, there lay the little paper flag quite safe beside its pin and the wind at once scooped it up and blew it away among the seagulls.

Philip ran to the rail and watched it plucked outwards and upwards, up and up, then round and down. Down it went, a little bright speck until it became invisible in the churning sea.

'*Calais*,' said the fat French lady along the seat beside him. 'You see? Here is France.' Philip immediately got up and walked away. He looked at the scummy waves slopping at the green jetty, the tall leaning houses. There was a different smell. This was abroad. Foreign soil. In a moment he was going to set foot upon it.

And he was lost and would never be found.

'*Le petit*,' said the French lady coming up alongside him at the rail and stroking his hair. He wagged his head furiously and moved further away. 'Tout seul,' and she burst into a spate of French at her husband. Philip knew that the French meant that the barbaric English had abandoned this child. Not able to consider this concept he shouldered the suitcases and made for the quay, and there was approached by a ruffian who tried to take them both from him. He hung on to them tight, even when the man began to scream and shout. He aimed a kick at the man and tramped away, the cases grazing the ground. Not one person on the crowded quay paid attention to the attempted theft.

Philip showed his passport and was swirled into the crowd. 'Paris,' cried the fat lady, swinging into view, 'Paris—ah, le petit!' and she held her rounded arm out boldly but shelteringly in his direction, leaning towards him. Her husband who had a sharp nose and black beret and teeth began to talk fast and furiously into the nearest of Philip's vulnerable ears.

But Philip behaved as though he were quite alone. He climbed into the train, found his seat, took off his gaberdine raincoat, folded it onto a little rack and looked at the huge suitcases and the higher luggage-rack with nonchalance. The rest of the carriage regarded them with amazement and several people passionately urged that the racks were unequal to the challenge ahead of them. Another ruffian came in and seemed to want to remove the cases altogether but Philip with a vehemence that astonished him and the ruffian and the whole carriage and a stretch of the corridor, flung himself in the man's path and across his property. He turned bright red and his ears redder and cried out, 'No, no, no.'

This caused more discussion and the ruffian, lifting his gaze to the ceiling and his hands near it, went shouting away. The suitcases were then successfully stowed on the racks, two of the Frenchmen shook hands with Philip and an old woman wearing a long black dress and a lace headdress like some sort of queen, offered him a sweet which he refused. Huddled in his corner seat he looked out of the window and wondered what to do.

Rattling tracks, bleak cement, scruffy houses all tipping about and needing a coat of paint. Shutters. Railway lines insolently slung across streets, all in among fruit-stalls, all muddly. Rain. No Union Jack.

Rain. Fields. Grey. Everything measured out by rulers. Small towns, now villages. Gardens. Allotments. No Union Jack.

Men in blue overalls. More berets. Black suits. Stout women with fierce brows. Men standing looking at their allotments, very still and concentrated like saying their prayers. Vegetables in very straight rows. Men carefully bending down and plucking out minute, invisible weeds. Mix-up of muddle and order. Like Mother. No Union Jack.

What should he do? Major Foster would be wearing his Union Jack and Philip would go up to him and say— But in all the hundreds of people getting off the train at Paris there might be a dozen boys of twelve. Perhaps a hundred. The Major would go sweeping by. 'Oh no. I'm sorry. They were very particular. The boy I am to meet will be wearing—'

And he'd be speaking in French of course. Probably French-Canadians spoke no English. It hadn't been clear. Miss Pym had written all the letters to the Foster family because she could write French, and the replies had been in French. Miss Pym had taken them away to translate with the dictionary under her arm. No Union Jack.

How stupid. How stupid of his mother. Why hadn't she sewed the Union Jack on his raincoat in the first place? She loved sewing. She was always mending and sewing, not even listening to his father and Miss Pym scrapping away about politics, just looking across at them now and then, or looking over, smiling, at him. His socks were more darns than socks because she so loved darning. Loved making things perfect. Loved making everything seem all right.

So then she sends him away with a rotten little Woolworth's Union Jack out of a cheap packet of them, loose in a tin. And not waving either when she'd said goodbye. Not crying at all. He knew about that crying-and-laughing-together she did. He'd never thought anything of it. He wondered if it had been the laughing-and-crying and all the darning and soupy Miss Pym and her French that had killed his father.

After all, she hadn't really seemed to mind his father dying. Gone off to bed for the funeral. Perhaps she'd really wanted him to die. Wanted to be free of him so that she could have long, cosy chats with Miss Pym. Horrible Miss Pym speaking her mind all the time. Not liking his father and showing it. Not liking boys. Not liking him. Goopy-goo about his mother. Organising these Fosters. Very glad he was going away. Making no secret of that.

Perhaps his mother also was glad that he was going away.

Philip when this thought arrived concentrated upon the colourless, hedgeless, straight-edged French fields. Rattle-crash the train went over the level-crossings that sliced the roads in half. Long poles hung with metal aprons. Funny people. Lots of them on bicycles, clustered round, waiting to cross. Very dangerous. Very daring. People full of—what? Different from home. Full of energy. No, not energy—what? Fireworks. Explosives. Confidence. That was it. Not as if they needed to keep private their secret thoughts.

If they suddenly discovered for instance that their mothers did not love them they would not sit dumb and numb in a corner.

People in the carriage were now getting out packets of food. One of the hand-shaking men offered Philip a slanted slice of bread, orange and white. Somebody else offered him wine. He shook his head at all of it and looked out of the window. When the talk in the carriage began to get lively he got up and took down the raincoat and took from the pocket the packet of lunch his mother had made up for him herself, with her own fair hands, ha-ha. He sat with it on his knee. He was too sad, too shy to open it.

Also he didn't really want it. His mother had packed it up so carefully. Like a work of art. Greaseproof corners turned into triangles, like a beautifully-made bed. The package was fastened with two elastic bands, criss-cross, making four neat squares. And even his name on it in clear black pencil, PHILIP. How silly could you get? Who else would it be for? *Madly* careful, that's what she was. And then she goes and leaves the Union Jack loose in the box.

And she knew how flimsy it was. She must have expected it to blow away. She expected everything. She'd expected a wind. She'd gone on at breakfast-time about him getting seasick. And she knew he'd be more than likely to open the box.

Oh, she'd known what would happen all right. She'd gone off without even waving, her yellow fur arm on the yellow fur arm of Pym. She did not love him, want him, know him and she never had. It was all just darning and being perfect.

She wanted him lost.

All that about flags was just a blind. She *wanted* him to miss the Major. Wanted rid of the bother of him. Wanted him to disappear. She was a wicked woman who had killed her husband. All that laughing as she cried.

One night when he was young Philip had come downstairs after being put to bed, to get a book from the morning room and through the dining room door had heard his father singing at table:

Oh me and oh my
Oh dear and oh dear
I ain't gonna drink
No more damned beer

and Miss Pym had come sailing out of the room with her lips pressed together. 'Coarse,' he had heard her say. 'Coarse,' and then, seeing him standing in his pyjamas at the foot of the stairs in the summer evening light, 'Go to bed, Philip. Don't look so stricken. There is a point when every child sees through his parents.'

But his father's singing hadn't made Philip think any less of him. He'd always rather liked his father, or what he saw of him. He'd not been able to talk to children, just looked awkward and done card-tricks. Once in the town, seeing his son walking on the other side of the road, his father had raised his hat to him. What did she mean 'see through'?

But now he was seeing through his mother. He was seeing through her all right. He knew her now. The stupid woman. All that fuss trailing about for flags in Canterbury and then she gets one that blows away. Accidentally-on-purpose-ha-ha. She'd be free now. Free for life. Free to be with Stinkerpym. They'd got rid of him together, making sure the flag was really flimsy. Brilliantly they had evaded the law and there would be no evidence of their plot. Philip the only son would simply disappear.

Well, he wouldn't. At least he would, because he'd never go back. Not to Canterbury, never. Thirteen was all right. He'd manage. Look at *Kidnapped*. Look at *Treasure Island*. You can get on without your mother. When he'd got to Paris he'd— He had some money. He'd just put up in a hotel for a few nights. Get work. He could probably get work somewhere as a kitchen boy or—well, somewhere where there was food.

He was very hungry now. Probably Major Foster and his sisters would have got a good dinner ready for him. This dinner he would never eat, never see, as he would never see the beautiful house they all said would be like a little palace near the Bois de Boulogne. Too bad. He'd go to the Paris stews. At least they sounded as if you didn't go hungry.

And since he was so hungry at the moment he would eat his mother's sandwiches. She could hardly have poisoned them.

Could she?

As he opened the greaseproof paper he considered the enigma of his mother, how she flitted in and out of his life, always waving him away on trains. Sending him to boarding school at six.

'And even now I could fox her,' he thought. 'Even now I could tear a bit off this greaseproof and draw a union-jack on it and pin it on the lapel with the pin in the box. I could write my name on it too. I could borrow a pencil.'

He looked round the carriage wondering which of them he might ask. It would be an easy sentence to say. He'd even done it at school. And he had begun to like the look of the French faces.

But no. He'd go to the stews.

He opened the sandwiches and there was an envelope on top and inside it a piece of paper and his mother's huge hand-writing saying 'Oh Philip, my darling, don't hate me for fussing, but I do so love you.'

Pinned to the paper was a spare Union Jack.

SWAN

Two boys walked over the bridge.

They were big boys from the private school on the rich side of the river. One afternoon each week they had to spend helping people. They helped old people with no one to love them and younger children who were finding school difficult. It was a rule.

'I find school difficult myself,' said Jackson. 'Exams for a start.'

'I have plenty of people at home who think no one loves them,' said Pratt. 'Two grandparents, two parents, one sister.'

'And all called Pratt, poor things,' said Jackson, and he and Pratt began to fight in a friendly way, bumping up against each other until Jackson fell against a lady with a shopping-trolley on a stick and all her cornflakes fell out and a packet of flour, which burst.

'I'm going straight to your school,' she said. 'I know that uniform. It's supposed to be a good school. I'm going to lay a complaint,' and she wagged her arms up and down at the elbows like a hen. Pratt, who often found words coming out of his mouth without warning, said, 'Lay an egg. Cluck.'

'That's done it. That's finished it,' said the woman. 'I'm going right round now. *And* I'll say you were slopping down the York Road Battersea at two o'clock in the afternoon, three miles from where you ought to be.'

'We are doing our Social Work,' said Pratt. 'Helping people.'

'Helping people!' said the woman, pointing at the pavement.

'We're being interviewed about caring for unfortunate children,' said Jackson.

'They're unfortunate all right if all they can get is you.' And she steamed off, leaving the flour spread about like snow, and passers-by walked over it giving dark looks and taking ghostly footprints away into the distance. Pratt eased as much of it as he could into the gutter with his feet.

'She's right,' he said. 'I don't know much about unfortunate children. Or any children.'

'They may not let us care for any when they see us,' said Jackson. 'Come on. We'd better turn up. They can look at us and form an opinion.'

'Whatever's that mess on your shoes?' asked the Head Teacher at the school on the rough side of the river, coming towards them across the hall. 'Dear me, snow. It is a nasty day. How do you do? Your children are ready for you, I think. Maybe today you might like just to talk to them indoors and start taking them out next week?'

'Yes, please,' said Jackson.

'Taking them *out*?' said Pratt.

'Yes. The idea is that—with the parents' consent—you take them out and widen their lives. Most of them on this side of the river never go anywhere. It's a depressed area. Their lives are simply school (or truanting), television, bed and school, though we have children from every country in the world.'

'It's about the same for us,' said Pratt. 'Just cross out television and insert homework.'

'Oh, come now,' said the pretty Head Teacher, 'you do lots of things. Over the river, there's the Zoo and all the museums and the Tower of London and all the lovely shops. All the good things happen over the bridge. Most of our children here have scarcely seen a blade of grass. Now—you are two very reliable boys, I gather?' (She looked a bit doubtful.) 'Just wipe your feet and follow me.'

She opened a door of a classroom, but there was silence inside and only one small Chinese boy looking closely into the side of a fish-tank.

'Oh dear. Whatever . . . ? Oh, of course. They're all in the gym. This is Henry. Henry Wu. He doesn't do any team-games. Or anything, really. He is one of the children you are to try to help. Now which of you would like Henry? He's nearly seven.'

'I would,' said Pratt, wondering again why words kept emerging from his mouth.

'Good. I'll leave you here then. Your friend and I will go and find the other child. Come here Henry and meet—what's your name?'

'Pratt.'

'Pratt, HERE'S PRATT, HENRY. Henry's not deaf, Pratt. Or dumb. He's been tested. It is just that he won't speak or listen. He shuts himself away, PRATT, HENRY,' she said, and vanished with an ushering arm behind Jackson, then closing the door.

Henry Wu watched the fish.

'Hello,' said Pratt after a while. 'Fish.'

He thought, that is a very silly remark. He made it again, 'Fish.'

The head of Henry Wu did not move. It was a small round head with thick hair, black and shiny as the feathers on the div-ing-ducks in the park across the river.

Or it might have been the head of a doll. A very fragile Chinese-china doll. Pratt walked round it to try and get a look at the face, the front of which was creamy-coloured with a nose so small it hardly made a bump, and leaf-shaped eyes with no eye-lashes. No, not leaf-shaped, pod-shaped, thought Pratt, and in each pod the blackest and most glossy berry which looked at the fish. The fish opened their mouths at the face in an anxious manner and waved their floaty tails about.

'What they telling you?' asked Pratt. 'Friends of yours are they?'

Henry Wu said nothing.

'D'you want to go and see the diving-ducks in our park?'

Henry Wu said nothing.

'Think about it,' said Pratt. 'Next week. It's a good offer.'

Henry Wu said nothing.

'Take it or leave it.'

Pratt wondered for a moment if the Chinese boy was real. Maybe he was a sort of waxwork. If you gave him a push maybe he'd just tip over and fall on the floor. 'Come on, Henry Wu,' he said. 'Let's hear what you think,' and he gave the boy's shoulder a little shove.

And found himself lying on the floor with no memory of being put there. He was not at all hurt—just lying. And the Chinese boy was still sitting on his high stool looking at the fish.

Pandemonium was approaching along the passage and children of all kinds began to hurtle in. They all stopped in a huddle when they saw large Pratt spread out over the floor, and a teacher rushed forward. The Head Teacher and Jackson were there, too, at the back, and Jackson was looking surprised.

'Oh dear,' said the teacher, 'his mother taught him to fight in case he was bullied. She's a Black Belt in judo. She told us he was very good at it. Oh Henry—not again. This big boy wants to be kind to you.'

'All I said,' said Pratt, picking himself up, 'was that I'd take him to the diving-ducks in the park. What's more, I shall,' he added, glaring at Henry Wu.

'Why bother?' said Jackson. They were on their way home. 'He looks a wimp. He looks a rat. I don't call him unfortunate. I call him unpleasant.'

'What was yours like?'

'Mine wasn't. She'd left. She was a fairground child. They're always moving on. The school seems a bit short of peculiar ones at the moment. I'll share Henry Wu the Great Kung Fu with you if you like. You're going to need a bit of protection by the look of it.'

But in the end Jackson didn't, for he was given an old lady's kitchen to paint and was soon spending his Wednesdays and all his free time in it, eating her cooking. Pratt set out the following week to the school alone and found Henry Wu waiting for him, muffled to just below the eyebrows in a fat grasshopper cocoon of bright red nylon padding.

'Come on,' said Pratt and without looking to see if Henry followed, set out along the grim York Road to a bus-stop. Henry climbed on the bus behind him and sat some distance away, glaring at space.

'One and a half to the park,' said Pratt, taking out a French grammar. They made an odd pair. Pratt put on dark glasses in case he met friends.

It was January. The park was cold and dead. The grass was thin and muddy and full of puddly places and nobody in the world could feel the better for seeing a blade of it. Plants were sticks. There were no birds yet about the trees, and the water in the lake and all round the little island was heavy and dark and still, like forgotten soup.

The kiosk café was shut up. The metal tables and chairs of summer were stacked inside and the Coke machine was empty. Pigeons walked near the kiosk, round and round on the cracked tarmac. They were as dirty and colourless as everything else but Henry looked at them closely as they clustered round his feet. One bounced off the ground and landed on his head.

Henry did not laugh or cry out or jump, but stood.

'Hey, knock that off. It's filthy,' shouted Pratt. 'They're full of diseases. London pigeons. Look at their knuckles—all bleeding and rotten.'

A large black-and-white magpie came strutting by and regarded Henry Wu with the pigeon on his head. The pigeon flew away. Henry Wu began to follow the magpie along the path.

'It's bad luck, one magpie,' said Pratt. 'One for sorrow, two for joy,' and at once a second magpie appeared, walking behind. The Chinese boy walked in procession between the two magpies under the bare trees.

'Come on. It's time to go,' said Pratt, feeling jealous. The magpies flew away, and they went to catch the bus.

Every Wednesday of that cold winter term, Pratt took Henry Wu to the park, walking up and down with his French book or his Science book open before him while Henry watched the birds and said nothing.

'Has he never said anything?' he asked the Head Teacher. 'I suppose he talks Chinese at home?'

'No. He doesn't say a thing. There's someone keeping an eye on him of course. A Social Worker. But the parents don't seem to be unduly worried. His home is very Chinese, I believe. The doctors say that one day he should begin to speak, but maybe not for years. We have to be patient.'

'Has he had some bad experiences? Is he a Boat Person?'

'No. He is just private. He is a village boy from China. Do you want to meet his family? You ought to. They ought to meet you, too. It will be interesting for you. Meeting Chinese.'

'There are Chinese at our school.'

'Millionaires' sons from Hong Kong I expect, with English as their first language. This will be more exciting. These people have chosen to come and live in England. They are immigrants.'

'I'm going to meet some immigrants,' said Pratt to Jackson. 'D'you want to come?'

'No,' said Jackson to Pratt, 'I'm cleaning under Nellie's bed where she can't reach. And I'm teaching her to use a calculator.'

'Isn't she a bit old for a calculator?'

'She likes it. Isn't it *em*igrants?'

'No, immigrants. Immigrants come *in* to a country.'

'Why isn't it innigrants then?'

'I don't know. Latin I expect if you look it up. Emigrants are people who go out of a country.'

'Well, haven't these Chinese come out of a country? As well as come in to a country? They're emigrants and immigrants. They don't know whether they're coming or going. Perhaps that's what's the matter with Henry Wu.'

'Henry's not an immigrant. He's a *ninny*grant. Or just plain *innigrant*. I'm sick of him if you want to know. It's a waste of time, my Social Work. At least you get some good food out of yours. You've started her cooking again. And you're teaching her about machines.'

'Your Chinese will know about machines. I shouldn't touch the food, though, if you go to them. It won't be like a Take-Away.'

'D'you want to come?'

'No thanks. See you.'

'Candlelight Mansions,' said the Social Worker. 'Here we are. Twelfth floor and the lifts won't be working. I hope you're fit.'

They climbed the concrete stairs. Rubbish lay about. People had scrawled ugly things on the walls. On every floor the lift had a board saying 'out of order' hung across it with chains. Most of the chains were broken, too, so that the boards hung crooked. All was silent.

Then, as they walked more slowly up the final flights of

stairs, the silence ceased. Sounds began to be threaded into it; thin, busy sounds that became more persistent as they turned at the twelfth landing and met a fluttery excited chorus. Across the narrow space were huge heaps. Bundles and crates and boxes were stacked high under tarpaulins with only the narrowest of alleys to lead up to the splintery front door of Henry Wu's flat. A second door of diamonds of metal was fastened across this. Nailed to the wall, on top of all the bundles were two big makeshift bird cages like sideways chicken-houses and inside them dozens of birds—red and blue and green and yellow making as much noise as a school playground.

'Oh dear,' said the Social Worker, 'Here we go again. The Council got them all moved once but the Wus just put them back. They pretend they don't understand. Good afternoon, Mrs. Wu.'

A beautiful, flat Chinese woman had come to the door and stood behind the metal diamonds. She did not look in the least like a Black Belt in judo. She was very thin and small and wore bedroom slippers, a satin dress and three cardigans. She bowed.

'I've just called for a chat and to bring you Henry's kind friend who is trying to help him.'

Mrs. Wu took out a key and then clattered back the metal gate and smiled and bowed a great deal and you couldn't tell what she was thinking. From the flat behind her there arose the most terrible noise of wailing, screeching and whirring, and Pratt thought that Jackson had been right about machines. A smell wafted out, too. A sweetish, dryish, spicy smell which sent a long thrill down Pratt's spine. It smelled of far, far away.

'You have a great many belongings out here,' said the Social Worker climbing over a great many more as they made their way down the passage into the living room. In the living room were more again, and an enormous Chinese family wearing many layers of clothes and sitting sewing among electric fires.

Two electric sewing-machines whizzed and a tape of Chinese music plinked and wailed, full-tilt. Another, different tape wailed back through the open kitchen door where an old lady was gazing into steaming pans on a stove. There were several bird cages hanging from hooks, a fish-tank by the window and rat-like object looking out from a bundle of hay in a cage. It had one eye half-shut as if it had a headache. Henry Wu was regarding this rat.

The rest of the family all fell silent, rose to their feet and bowed. 'Hello Henry,' said Pratt, but Henry did not look round, even when his mother turned her sweet face on him and sang out a tremendous Chinese torrent.

Tea came in glasses. Pratt sat and drank his as the Social Worker talked to Mrs. Wu and the other ladies, and a small fat Chinese gentleman, making little silk buttons without even having to watch his hands, watched Pratt. After a time he shouted something and a girl came carrying a plate. On the plate were small grey eggs with a skin on them. She held them out to Pratt.

'Hwile,' said the Chinese gentleman, his needle stitching like magic. 'Kwile.'

'Oh yes,' said Pratt. (Whale?)

'Eat. Eat.'

'I'm not very . . .'

But the Social Worker glared. 'Quail,' she said.

'Eggs don't agree . . .' said Pratt. (Aren't quails snakes?) He imagined a tiny young snake curled inside each egg. I'd rather die, he thought, and saw that for the first time Henry Wu was looking at him from his corner. So was the rat.

So were the fish, the birds, Mrs. Wu, the fat gentleman and all the assorted aunts. He ate the egg which went down glup, like an oval leather pill. Everyone smiled and nodded and the plate was offered again.

He ate another egg and thought, two snakes. They'll breed.

I will die. He took a great swig of tea and smiled faintly. Everyone in the room then, except the rat, the fish and Henry, began to laugh and twitter and talk. The old woman slipper-sloppered in from the kitchen bringing more things to eat in dolls' bowls. They were filled with little chippy things and spicy, hot juicy bits. She pushed them at Pratt. 'Go on,' said the Social Worker. 'Live dangerously.'

Pratt ate. Slowly at first. It was delicious. 'It's not a bit like the Take-Away,' he said, eating faster. This made the Chinese laugh. 'Take-Away, Take-Away,' they said. 'Sweet-and-Sour,' said Mrs. Wu. 'Not like Sweet-and-Sour,' and everyone made tut-tutting noises which meant, 'I should just hope not.' Mrs. Wu then gave Pratt a good-luck charm made of brass and nodded at him as if she admired him.

'She's thanking you for taking Henry out,' said the Social Worker as they went down all the stairs again.

'She probably thinks I'm a lunatic,' said Pratt, 'taking Henry out. Much good it's done.'

'You don't know yet.'

'Well, he's not exactly talking is he? Or doing anything. He's probably loopy. She probably thinks I'm loopy, too.'

'She wouldn't let you look after him if she thought you were loopy.'

'Maybe she wants rid of him. She's hoping I'll kidnap him. I'm not looking after him any more if he can't get up and say hello. Or even smile. After all those terrible afternoons. Well, I've got exams next term. I've got no time. I'll have to think of myself all day and every day from now on, thank goodness.'

And the next term it was so. Pratt gave never a thought to Henry Wu except sometimes when the birds began to be seen about the school gardens again and to swoop under the eaves of the chapel. Swallows, he thought, immigrants. And he remembered him when his parents took him out to a Chinese restaurant on his birthday.

'Oh no—not those,' he said.

'They are the greatest Chinese treat you can have,' said his father. 'Quails' eggs.'

'Aren't they serpents?'

'Serpents? Don't you learn *any* general knowledge at that school? They're birds' eggs. Have some Sweet-and-Sour.'

'The Chinese don't have Sweet-and-Sour. It was made up for the tourists.'

'Really? Where did you hear that?'

'My Social Work.'

The exams came and went as exams do and Pratt felt light-headed and light-hearted. He came out of the last one with Jackson and said, 'Whee—let's go and look at the river.'

'I feel great. Do you?' he said.

Jackson said he felt terrible. He'd failed everything. He'd spent too much time spring-cleaning old Nellie. He knew he had.

'I expect I've failed, too,' said Pratt, but he felt he hadn't. The exams had been easy. He felt very comfortable and pleased with himself and watched the oily river sidle by, this way and that way, slopping up against the arches of the bridge, splashy from the barges. 'What shall we do?' he asked Jackson. 'Shall we go on the river?'

'I'd better go over and see if old Nellie's in,' said Jackson. 'I promised. Sorry. You go.'

Pratt stood for a while and the old lady with the shopping-trolley went by. 'Lolling about,' she said.

'I'm sorry about your flour,' said Pratt. Filled with happiness because the exams were over he felt he ought to be nice to the woman.

But she hurried on. Pratt watched her crossing the bridge and found his feet following. He made for Candlelight Mansions.

'Does Henry want to come to the park?' he asked a little

girl who peered through the diamonds. Her face was like a white violet and her fringe was flimsy as a paint-brush. There was a kerfuffle behind her and Mrs. Wu came forward to usher him inside.

If I go in it'll be quails' eggs and hours of bowing, thought Pratt. 'I'll wait here,' he said firmly. Mrs. Wu disappeared and after a time Henry was produced, again muffled to the nose in the scarlet padding.

'It's pretty warm out,' said Pratt, but Mrs. Wu only nodded and smiled.

In the park Pratt felt lost without a book and Henry marched wordlessly, as far ahead as possible. The ice-cream kiosk was open now and people were sitting on the metal chairs. Pigeons clustered round them in flustery clouds.

'Horrible,' said Pratt, catching up with Henry. 'Rats with wings. I'll get you a Coke but we'll drink it over there by the grass—hey! Where you going?'

Henry, not stopping for the pigeons, was away to the slope of green grass that led down to the water. On the grass and all over the water was a multitude of birds and all the ducks of the park, diving-ducks and pelicans and geese and dab-chicks and water-hens and mallards. Old ducks remembering and new little ducks being shown the summer for the first time. Some of the new ducks were so new they were still covered with fluff— white fluff, fawn fluff, yellow fluff and even black fluff, like decorations on a hat. The proud parent ducks had large V's of water rippling out behind them and small V's rippled behind all the following babies. Henry Wu stood still.

Then round the island on the lake there came a huge, drifting meringue.

It was followed by another, but this one had a long neck sweeping up from it with a proud head on the end and a brilliant orange beak and two black nostrils, the shape of Henry Wu's eyes.

The first meringue swelled and fluffed itself and a tall neck and wonderful head emerged from that one, too.

Suddenly Henry pointed a short padded arm at these amazing things and, keeping it stiff, turned his face up to Pratt and looked at him very intently.

'Swan,' said Pratt. 'They're swans. They're all right, aren't they? Hey—but don't do that. They're not so all right that you ought to get near them.'

'Get that boy back,' shouted a man. 'They'll knock him down. They're fierce, them two.'

'Nasty things, swans,' said someone else.

But Henry was off, over the little green hooped fence, running at the swans as they stepped out of the water on their black macintosh feet and started up the slope towards him.

They lowered their necks and began to hiss. They opened their great wings.

'Oh help,' said Pratt

'It's all right,' said the man. 'I'm the Warden. I'll get him. Skin him alive, too, if they don't do it first,' and he ran down the slope.

But the swans did not skin Henry Wu alive. As he ran right up to them they stopped. They turned their heads away as if they were thinking. They shifted from one big black leathery foot to another and stopped hissing. Then they opened their wings wider still and dropped them gently and carefully back in place. They had a purple band round each left leg. One said 888. White swans, purple band, orange beaks, red Henry Wu, all on the green grass with the water and the willows about them, all sparkling and swaying.

'Bless him—isn't that nice now?' said the crowd, as the Warden of the swans gathered up Henry and brought him back under his arm.

'You'll get eaten one day,' said the Warden. 'You'll go getting yourself harmed,' but he seemed less angry than he might.

On the way home Henry did not look at Pratt but sat with him on the long seat just inside the bus. It was a seat for three people and Henry sat as far away as possible. But it was the same seat.

Then Pratt went on his summer holidays and when he came back the exam results were out and they were not marvellous. He stuffed miserably about in the house. When Jackson called—Jackson had done rather well—he said that he was busy, which he wasn't.

But he made himself busy the next term, stodging glumly along, and took the exams all over again.

'Aren't you going to see your Chinese Demon any more?' asked Jackson afterwards. 'Come and meet old Nellie.'

'No thanks.'

'She says to bring you.'

'No thanks.'

But when the results came out this time, they were very good. He had more than passed.

Pratt said, 'How's Nellie?'

'Oh fine. Much better tempered.'

'Was she bad tempered? You never said.'

'How's Henry Wu? Did you ever get him talking?'

'No. He was loopy.'

But it was a fine frosty day and the sun for the moment was shining and Pratt went to the park and over the grass to the lakeside where one of the swans came sliding around the island and paddled about on the slope, marking time and looking at him.

It dazzled. The band round its leg said 887. 'Where's your husband?' said Pratt. 'Or wife or whatever? Are you hungry or something?'

The sun went in and the bare trees rattled. The swan looked a bit lonely and he thought he might go and get it some bread.

Instead he took a bus back over the bridge and went to Candlelight Mansions.

They've probably forgotten me, he thought as he rang the bell. The bundles and the bird cages had gone from the landing. He rattled the steel mesh. They've probably moved, he thought. They'll have gone back to China.

But he was welcomed like a son.

'Can I take Henry out?'

Bowings, grinnings, buttonings-up of Henry who had not grown one millimetre.

'Where's the rat?' Pratt asked.

'Nwee-sance,' said Mrs. Wu.

'Neeoo-sance,' said the fat gentleman. 'Nee-oosance. Council told them go.'

But the flat was now a jungle of floating paper-kites and plants with scarlet dragons flying about in them, mixed with Father Christmases, Baby Jesuses and strings of Christmas tinsel. In the kitchen the old lady stirred the pots to a radio playing *Oh Come All Ye Faithful*. Henry, seeing everyone talking together, sat down under a sewing-machine.

'Has he said anything yet?' asked Pratt, eating juicy bits with chopsticks. Everyone watched the juicy bits falling off the chopsticks and laughed. Now and then, when anything reached his mouth successfully, they congratulated him. They ignored the question, which meant that Henry had not.

It was cold in the street and very cold as they stood at the bus-stop. Pratt had forgotten that the days were now so short, and already it was beginning to get dark. Far too late to go to the park, he thought. The bus was cold, too, and dirty, and all the people looked as if they'd like to be warm at home in bed. 'Come on—we'll go upstairs and sit in the front,' said Pratt and they looked down on the dreary York Road with all its little half-alive shops and, now and then, a string of coloured

Christmas lights across it with most of the bulbs broken or missing. Some shops had spray-snowflakes squirted on the windows. It looked like cleaning-fluid someone had forgotten to wash off. Real snowflakes were beginning to fall and looked even dingier than the shop-window ones.

I should have taken him over the river to see some real Christmas lights in Regent Street, thought Pratt. There's nothing over here.

But there came a bang.

A sort of rushing, blustering, flapping before the eyes.

The glass in the window in front of them rattled like an earthquake and something fell down in front of the bus.

There were screeching brakes and shouting people and Pratt and Henry were flung forward onto the floor.

As they picked themselves up they saw people running into the road below. 'Something fell out of the sky,' said Pratt to Henry Wu. 'Something big. Like a person. Come on—we've got to get out.'

But it was not a person. It was a swan that sat heavy and large and streaked with a dark mark across its trailing wings in the very middle of the road.

'Swan, swan—it's a swan!' Everybody was shouting. 'It's killed itself. It's dead. Frozen dead with fright.'

'It hit a wire,' said someone else—it was the woman with the shopping trolley—'I saw it. An overhead-wire from the lights. They oughtn't to be allowed. They're not worth it. They could have electrocuted that bus.'

'It's killed it, anyway,' said Jackson, who seemed to be with her. 'It's stone dead.'

But the swan was not dead. Suddenly it decided it was not. It heaved up its head and wings and lollopped itself to the side of the road and flopped down again, looking round slowly, with stunned wonder, opening and shutting its orange beak, though with never a sound.

'It was migrating,' said the man from a chip-shop.

'Swans don't migrate, they stay put,' said a man from a laundry.

'Anyone'd migrate this weather,' said a man selling whelks and eels. 'Look, it's got a number on it. It's from the park. Look, it's put itself all tidy on the yellow line.'

'Out of the way,' said a policeman. 'Now then. Stand aside. We'll want a basket.' A laundry-basket was brought and some-one lent the policeman a strong pair of gloves.

'Clear a space,' he said and approached the swan which proved it was not dead by landing the policeman a thwacking blow with its wing.

'Have to be shot,' said a dismal man from a bike-shop. 'Well, it's no chicken.'

'Course it's no chicken,' said the woman with the trolley. 'If it was a chicken it'd be coming home with me and a bag of chips.'

And then a girl with purple hair began to shriek and scream because she didn't believe in eating animals, which included birds.

'Anyway, all swans belong to the Queen,' said the trolley-lady. 'I heard it on *Gardener's Question Time*.'

'I'm going crazy,' said the policeman who had withdrawn to a little distance to talk into his radio-set. 'If they all belong to the Queen I hope she'll come and collect this one. I'm not sure I can. Move along now. We have to keep the traffic moving. We can't hold up London for a swan.'

One or two cars sidled by, but otherwise nobody moved. It was a strange thing. In the middle of the dead dark day and the dead dark street sat the open laundry basket and the shining, mute bird with its angel feathers. The road fell quiet.

Then Henry Wu stepped forward, small inside his padding, and put short arms round the bulk of the swan's back and lifted it lightly into the basket where it fluffed up its feathers like rising bread and gazed round proudly at the people.

'Heaven on high!' said everyone. 'The weight!'

'His mother's a Black Belt,' said Pratt proudly.

'That Chinese'll have to be washed,' said the trolley-lady. 'They'd better both come home with us, Jackson, and I'll give them their tea.'

But Pratt and Henry did not go home with old Nellie on that occasion because the policemen asked them to go back to the station with him and the swan. If Henry would be so kind as to assist him, he said. And Henry stroked the swan's docile head twice and then folded it down with its neck behind it— and a big strong neck it was, though very arrangeable—and quickly put down the lid.

The Park Warden came to the police station and he and Henry and Pratt and the swan then went on to the park, where the swan took to the water like a whirlwind and faded into the dark.

'Off you go, 888,' said the Warden. 'There's your missus to meet you. You wouldn't have seen her again if you'd not dropped among friends.'

'They can't take off, you see,' he said to the two boys, 'except on water. They're like the old sea-planes.'

Pratt watched the two white shapes fade with the day.

'They're strange altogether, swans,' said the Warden. 'Quite silent!'

'Is it true they sing when they're dying?' asked Pratt. 'I read it. In poetry.'

'Well, that one's not dying then,' said the Warden. 'Gone without a sound. It's funny—most living creatures make some sort of noise to show they're happy. Goodbye, Henry. There'll be a job for you with creatures one day. I dare say when you grow up you'll get my job. You have the touch.'

On the bus back over the bridge to Candlelight Mansions

Henry sat down next to Pratt on a double seat and staring in front of him said in a high, clear Chinese-English voice, 'Hwan.'

'Hwan,' he said. 'Hwan, hwan, hwan, swan. Swan, swan, SWAN,' until Pratt had to say, 'Shut up Henry or they'll think you're loopy.'

DAMAGE

S he terrified me. She looked like a fly. Threadwire arms and legs arranged all anyhow across a slatted seat in the Jardin Anglais: the lake cold and thrashing about against the quay, the wind squealing in the shrouds of the wintering boat-yard. Why should a fly terrify? How can a woman on a park bench be a fly? Something mingy about her. Bothersome. Unhealthy. Not poor—rich, rich. Look at her shoes! And all so small, and twisted sideways. Wearing black. Not young. Skinny. And sobbing, sobbing, sobbing.

January. Geneva. And, unusually for me, Geneva on Saturday. For years I have been coming to work in Geneva, flipping back and forth from London. I go to other places—Prague, Berlin, Lisbon, The Hague—but to Geneva mostly. I am a translator. I translate at international conferences and arbitrations, simultaneously with the spoken word. I have four languages and am in much demand. As the speaker spouts out the message from the podium I drink his words into my head and ears and fountain them out again, translated. Tensely but steadily, smoothly, almost unhesitatingly they flow out of my mouth on to a disc at the end of a microphone which is enclosed with me inside a glass bubble fitted over my desk.

My voice is transferred about the room to the ears of those delegates whose language I am speaking. It passes through holes in similar discs fitted to their ears by a band across the head. One day this will be thought very comical and antique. One day there will be a machine and not me beneath the bubble. Perhaps one day we shall all have our brains nipped about at birth and there will be one universal language. Later still there will be perhaps a miraculous speaking in tongues and our heads surrounded not by plastic earphones but by points of fire, and there shall be a new heaven and a new earth and fewer arguments. But, until the ultimate machine or the Apocalypse, they must have me, and those like me.

We sit in a row—four of us at this arbitration—along the foot of the stage, our lips constantly moving. I have no way of knowing which ones in the audience are listening to me and which to my colleagues. Delegates select their own channels. Once I translated into German for a whole morning not having been told that the German delegates had missed their plane, and my words, my tens of thousands of words, had been passing into air. Or rather they had never existed, as at the beginning of the world when volcanoes, tidal-waves, hurricanes happened in silence for want of an eardrum against which to sound.

Once when I was young and frisky and new to my profession I used to long to take the microphone into my power, spread mischief. 'Here is an important announcement. Her Majesty, Queen Elizabeth the Second of England, is filing a suit for divorce.' 'Mr. Gorbachev, having recently contracted the AIDS virus, has announced his intention of seeking the comforts of the Russian Orthodox Church.' 'Nude bathing is to be allowed from tomorrow morning along the Swiss shore of Lake Leman. Delegates interested in forming bathing-parties should assemble by the Jardin Anglais at eight o'clock. In the buff.' Heads would jerk. Mouths fall open. These things are dreams.

I plug on, hard at it, thinking only of words and words.

It is tiring, especially if the case is technical, has its own specialised vocabulary which has had to be worked up for weeks before a session begins and often revised during the hearing in the evenings.

By Friday afternoon at four o'clock I am always exhausted and try wherever I am to get home for the weekend. I have a pretty cottage in Putney, bought with my alimony. I have a very old father in South Wimbledon. On Sundays I go to see him, cook our lunch. He expects me, though he does not greet me. After lunch he sleeps, with the *Sunday Telegraph* over his face, while I wash up the dishes. In summer I mow his small lawn. In autumn I sweep up and burn the leaves from his trees. In winter I may bake him a cake. He is disappointed in me. He liked my husband.

I go back to Putney after tea—washing, ironing, hair, nails—and late at night or on Monday morning catch a plane that will have me attached to my discs again by ten-thirty their time, nine-thirty ours.

I am always put in good hotels. The very best—and this in Geneva means in one of the best hotels in the world. I am also, I suppose, well-paid, though not so especially well when you consider where the world would be without me. I am usually with the same group of translators, but it happens that we none of us talk much about such things as the pay. We are a curious breed and, though a breed, we do not stick together. Translators have little in common except the kink in the brain and the teaspoonful of heredity that has given us our eerie linguistic memory—though we ourselves find nothing eerie in it. It is simply the ability to sing in tune in different keys. A gift. We tend to be solitaries. Mynah birds. You seldom see Mynah birds roosting together.

At the end of each day's session we vanish separately from the chamber, each to his bough.

Mine is always the hotel—my bedroom, with its en-suite bathroom and sometimes sitting room; its marbled basins, its coloured telephones—one even upon the bath—its clutches of lights. When I arrive at each new hotel I make solemn acknowledgement of all these, and of the presents: the soaps, the foam-baths, the shampoos, the bath-caps, the scents, the talcs, the bowl of fruit done up in thick transparent paper with the note saying 'Welcome', and, every night, the three round chocolates wrapped in silver paper on the pillow.

And six great fat white bath towels every day!

I pad across the fleecy carpet and open the fridge full of drink—all the little bottles of spirits and liqueurs looking like free samples. I hardly drink, not even the frosted wine crammed in discreet half-bottles on the shelves below, ready for romance. I take it all out sometimes and look at it. And all the soft drinks and bags of nuts! Years of these treats now—ever since my husband left—but I've never grown used to such bounty. Such gifts—and nobody looking!

I lie back and gaze at the television. It is nondescript in every country but Britain, but I gaze. I yawn with langour. I twirl my naked foot. I play the switches at my bedside one after another—all the music channels. 'And when I leave,' I tell the ceiling, 'I don't even have to pay the bill.' I am thirty. It is my retarded area. My secret sin.

The big hotels I stay in differ very little from one another wherever they are and I am not very interested in what goes on outside them. Countries are countries. It's a small world. My time and money are given to my appearance. Concerts, theatres, dinners are expensive and there need to be two of you. So I work at my clothes, my figure, my skin. For health I walk about a little. I listen to my feet in their Gambazetti pumps making hollow clops about the lunch-time picture galleries. In Geneva, in the evenings, I walk in the Old Town, looking at the lighted shop-windows: spotlight, gold and diamond cluster, twenty yards of velvet backcloth. I examine the *objets d'art* in the antique shops. They seldom change. They seem covered in golden dust.

The streets of Geneva are quiet at night, exposing it for the little provincial town it is. At midnight on the wide deserted streets all that move are the jujube traffic-lights dotted here and there into the distance. The few people patiently waiting near them—the slowest-changing lights in the world: they seem always to be standing at red—cross over at last. Over they go, left-right.

People who walk alone in Geneva keep their eyes wide and unsmiling. Nobody touches. Ladies sit easily alone, or maybe two or three, very quiet. Very confident. There is gold about. A good many necklaces, bracelets, watches. A great many rings. Always earrings. Always painted faces, however old. A formal city. Waiters—the emblems, the daemons of Geneva, cold, colourless, rich—keep their distance, watchful as policemen. At a loud voice or laugh they look sharply across.

Once or twice a year the waiters stand guard over the empty restaurants as the rest of the city pays to watch from its own streets the millions of dollars-worth of fireworks exploding over the lake in cascades of chrysanthemums, peacock-tails, palms. These are greeted with a drifting, respectful murmur, a shifting of feet, a ripple of milk-and-water clapping, and never a coarse hurrah. Everything is superbly sane, superbly balanced in Geneva. It is a careful city. Careful of its heart. It suits me well.

But on the seat by the boats, on the clipped and colourless grass, in the middle of the evening crowds sat this fly-person, weeping.

I passed her, as everybody else was doing, all of us well-dressed as she was, in her hat and fur coat and gloves and beautiful shoes. After I had passed I heard her start to shout and swear, the sobs separated by foul words in a language we none of us quite knew, but all recognised. We all forged ahead, step, step. Two children were walking with a nurse, the little girl hanging back to stare, the boy marching on. The nurse called to her.

'But what is it? What is it, nannie?'

'Oh, come on.'

The child watched but, seeing me watching her, turned and ran to the nurse's hand. The bark of the woman's voice knocked about behind us in the trees, and I hurried along the scoured paths, past the dry fountain and the clock which in summer is planted with flowers but today was two metal pointers clamped together against raked earth. She was yelling like Clytemnestra, a hymn of death.

I asked for my key at the hotel foyer and today on duty behind the desk was the head-porter himself, a famous man in Geneva, accustomed to kings. He took his time. I watched the people in the foyer and the lounges, the professional internationals who live with no abiding place, with nothing for every day; whose lives slip off and drop to the ground like a coat as the aeroplane takes off for the next place, who listen with less than half an ear, to messages about the unlikeliness of the aircraft landing on water. Bland and secure. I depend on them for my life.

'Your key, Madame.'

I found that I was looking at the key in the magisterial hand. I said, 'Not just at present,' and left the hotel, crossed the bridge, waited at the time-warp lights, passed the floral clock without flowers and the dead fountain. Only one or two people were left from the short rush-hour, skimpy earwig-people standing watching the choppy lake, the whippy boats. Her bench was now empty.

My father said he didn't call this twelve o'clock. He liked his Sunday dinner at twelve o'clock. He liked *Gardeners' Question Time*.

'I only got back last night, we were working Saturday.' (I thought; to anyone else I'd say 'on Saturday'.)

He said, 'Working, you don't know the meaning of working.'

In the kitchen he had laid out the usual meat and potatoes

and one vegetable—a huge cabbage—flour for the gravy and the pastry, apples to peel for a pie. The oven was not lit. He said, 'It'll be teatime by the time I get my dinner.'

'I've brought the pudding.'

'Is it one of them French things?'

'I've been in Geneva, it's a cherry pie.'

'Then I'll miss my tart.'

He turned the radio up loud so that there was no need to converse. I cooked and tidied after myself—peelings, cabbage stalks—in the threadbare kitchen, opened the back door to see to the dustbins that had to be carried through the house.

His cats slid under my feet. He began methodically, unnecessarily to remove furniture, clear a path for me and the rubbish to pass through to the front-door. I said, 'I think I'll do them when I've finished cooking. I don't want to touch food with rubbishy hands.' He said, 'Good God, it's in bags, isn't it? You know it's your first job, the rubbish,' and went back to the fire. 'I'm powerless in my own house now.'

Flour and fat congealed in the bottom of the meat-tin, slowly thickened; slowly re-liquified as I added cabbage-water. 'Bring the wireless in,' I yelled. 'It's ready.'

'I don't like listening and eating,' he said, stumbling forward, carrying the radio by its strap on the front of his walking-frame, placing it before him on the table, adjusting the volume upwards. We ate, meat, gravy, cabbage, potatoes to the accompaniment of the instructions about the heating of greenhouses. He said, 'It's not a bad pie.'

I said, 'You don't have a greenhouse.'

He said, 'Pastry's a bit oily. It's not your mother's pastry.'

I said, 'Pity you never told her you liked her pastry when she was alive.'

He said, 'I dare say I'll be getting a greenhouse. Maybe a couple. I've a mind to take up market-gardening.'

I wash up. Make him a sponge-cake. Do the rubbish. Wash

his clothes. Put them in the drier and it throbs gently. The fire crackles, the 1930s wedding-present clock ticks.

He says, 'Driers. Your mother never gave the time of day to one of them things. Hung them all across the yard. Sweet they smelled, like her French childhood.'

'It's snowing. Anyway, there's not the time.'

'Off again, are you? I've had my ration. Flying off to Monte Carlo. Some people know how to make out. Me all alone. I'm a great age, you know. You'll be sorry when it happens. Never see a soul one week to the next.'

'There's hundreds come to see you. All the neighbours.'

'Fools. Loads of rubbish.'

'Meals on wheels.'

'Loads of filth.'

'I must go now.'

'Aye, aye.' He sits rocking forwards on the walking-frame, crouched over it, like me in my translator's kiosk. The enclosing bubble is invisible but it's there. Not looking at me he says, 'If I sold this house I could go round the world.'

'Goodbye, Dad.'

'Off again. First-class in the morning then, eh?'

'Club-class.'

'Might go on a cruise. I'm thinking of it. Goodbye, then.' Still not looking at me but vaguely toward the door, sliding a glance he says, 'Bye, you're getting fat.'

'I'm eight stone.'

'Putting on a fair load of weight. All the rich living.'

As I close the front-door I say, 'I may not be able to come next week.' I say it every Sunday, and every Sunday I try not to turn and wave to him from the gate.

All the next week I avoid the Jardin Anglais but on Friday afternoon I am given a ticket for *Un Spectacle* which is to be held in the Parc La Grange and can only be reached by walking along the quay. For weeks, posters have been attached to most of the lamp-posts in Geneva advertising this function, and as the arbitration has not risen until five o'clock today, just too late for the evening plane, I accept it. In my room I telephone to change my flight for a Saturday one and find that all are full. So I must stay the weekend. I bath, change, manicure my nails. I had lunch so that I do not need dinner. Nothing to do. There is still an hour before I need leave for the concert and I telephone my father, direct-dial, to tell him that I shan't be home unless I can get a cancellation tomorrow evening. There is no reply. I decide to help myself to gin and tonic from the magic supply. I eat nuts. I ring again. Nothing.

I set off for the *Spectacle*, which is to be held in the Orangerie of the park. In the dark the cold lake splashes. There is snow about in the Jardin Anglais, triangles of it swept up against the boles of the thin trees. Ice bulges out of the fountain. All the park-benches are empty and I pass the fly's bench carelessly, the singing boats, the gates in the walls of the park, and see the Orangerie shining out across frosted flower-beds.

Inside is the nest all the lamp-post banners flew from: UN SPECTACLE, in bunting, all around the stage. The audience doesn't seem to be very large. It seems in fact to be composed of visitors to Geneva, perhaps all stuck here for the weekend. They have a hangy look and seem to be searching each other's faces to find out why they are here. The great glasshouse is boiling hot but glitters cold. The audience is very quiet.

Potted palms. White flowers. A white piano. MOZART HAYDN BRAHMS on white posters. Silence. Coughs. Whispers. A man in evening-dress walks upon the stage. We clap. He holds out a beckoning hand and a woman in evening-dress walks out to join him. He sits at the piano and she prepares to sing. She wears a long black dress and her arm is in a sling. A white sling.

The woman next to me takes off her glasses and looks at

me. 'A broken arm!' she says, eyebrows high. After the woman has started to sing she turns to me again, and says, 'In a sling! She must be German. She could not be Swiss.'

As the woman sings—smooth, faultless, bland, douce—I see that she is small and thin, so thin, and her mouth opens in a cave. I get up and make for the door, then out of the glasshouse, down the dark paths, through the tropical trees weeping for the sun. The iron gates are locked.

'Who's there?' cried the gate man.

'I want to get out.'

'Were you at the *Spectacle*?'

'Yes. I have to get out.'

'Sorry, Madame, nobody is allowed to leave the *Spectacle* until the end. The gates are locked until the end of the *Spectacle*.'

'Is there some other way out?'

He shrugged with a Swiss shrug that has to do only with the neck and jaw.

'Only the wall.' He goes back in his box.

Beside the locked gates the wall is low, for the earth for the park has been banked up against it. I step up on it in my Emil Rodin boots, then sit with legs dangling. The other side of the wall drops ten feet and I drop down.

But it is farther than it looks and I have drunk from the fairy-godmother fridge and I feel the heel of my boot break under me. I lie twisted on the grass in my black-silk dress and fur jacket. People passing along through the Jardin Anglais look at me quickly and do not stop. After a time I get up and hop along, slowly, stopping often, holding on to railings, to benches, at one time to the back of the bench on which the fly had sat and wept. In the hotel foyer the concierge sees me and busies himself about his desk. Back in my room I shake, stagger as I try to run a bath, make a grotesquerie of undressing, hobble to the phone to ring my father. There is still no reply so

I send for a room-service omelette, turn on the television, watch unseeing. Later I go to bed and my ankle plays a steady tune. Very much later I sleep.

I wake at five-thirty by the lighted digits on the bedside clock and there is another little light, a message-light, beside them; a red dot pulsating from the bedside telephone. Here then it is. It has come.

Dial three for front desk.

'Hello? There is a message for me?'

'Message, Madame?'

'On the telephone. My message-light on the telephone is showing.'

'Ah, just one moment, Madame. This is still the night staff.'

How long I wait, sitting upright on the bed in the dark. I feel about for the light-switch but it turns on a blast of music. 'Hello—hello? Yes?'

'Yes, Madame, there was a call for you last night. While you were out.'

'While I was out—but I was in before ten o'clock.'

'I'm sorry, Madame, this is only the night staff. Shall we send it up, Madame?'

'Yes please, at once.' My voice is steady. Most commendable.

I take the message as it is flicked under the door. 'Shall you be attending the party today? If so I shall call for you, Helmut.' (Another translator.)

But I must ring my father, for this is a crossed line. It has some meaning. Party? What party? There is no party that I've heard of. I don't go to parties. I must find the real message.

The phone rings and rings among the tables and chairs, the sideboard, the lithographs, the brass ornaments, the big black group-photographs of my dead mother's dead relations. The hearth-rug is turned back against sparks. Ashes are fallen in the grate. Cold. The tap drips as it has since my childhood.

Cats lift their heads, eyes alight at the noise in the dark. Cold. Wind under the front-door. The passage cold, the staircase cold, his bedroom cold and fusty, piled high with his clothes and old boots and old newspapers and gardening magazines. The familiar smell in it of them and of him. In the bed the small hump, the old man gone.

'Hello—what in hell—?'

'Pa!'

'Who the hell? It's four o'clock in the morning.'

'It's me. I'm sorry. It's nearly six here.'

'It's four o'clock!'

'Are you all right?'

'What? Yes, I'm all right. I need my shopping doing. Mrs. Aylesford's going to do it if she doesn't forget. She's a very funny woman. You have to watch your step with her. I'm in her power of course. If she forgets, I'm finished. Finished. Her and Myrtle. If they've turned funny you'll have to do it tonight, or tomorrow morning at a Sunday-shop. Better get yourself over here this morning. You can stop over the night.'

'I'm in Geneva. I've rung because—'

'You're ringing from Geneva? It'll be twenty pound.'

'I've hurt my foot.'

'You mean you won't be coming?'

I say with assurance and release, 'No.'

'So who's to get my dinner?'

I have fallen silent.

'Hello? Hello? Well—this is the finish, isn't it? You won't be home the weekend. You won't be home for another week. I'm out of Fairy Liquid.'

'Father—where you are is not my home.'

'Oh, we know that. No two ways about that. Your mother and I realised that long ago. You made your mother very unhappy.'

'I'll see you next week. I rang because I was worried.'

'Eh?'

'I thought you were dead. You weren't answering last night.'

'No, I wasn't. It was the Euro-Vision Song Contest.'

'Goodbye. I've had about enough.'

'Oh, I'm sure of that. We're not good enough for you now, your mother and I.'

'But Mother's dead.'

'Eh?'

Helmut is waiting for me in the foyer at twelve o'clock, drinking brandy and staring at the floor. He is a solemn man, a failed barrister, failed everyone thinks because of a profound seriousness that affected the clients. It is said that he insisted on settling every case however clear-cut its impending victory on the grounds that victory in this world is as dust. He is clever, quirkish, can translate into Farsi and, from the gathering gloom on the faces of the unmistakably Iranian delegates in the arbitration in which we are at present engaged, it is possible that his interpretation of some of the admissions carries a whiff of judgment more terrible than this earth can compass. He is a devout Christian and hates travelling on a Sunday, a dear man, of enchanting contradictions. At present one hand is knocking back the brandy and the other holding a book of meditations.

We stand waiting for a taxi. Overnight, Geneva has swept up to a peak of cold. A pitiless wind blows the snow and only a few people are about, walking hunched and head down under a white sky. 'What is the party, Helmut? I didn't know about a party. Are you sure I'm invited?'

'He said "all the translators". I think we're the only two here, though.'

'Who is it?'

'The Austrian. The expert-witness. He lives here.'

'What does he do when he's not being an expert-witness?'

'Adjusts his monocle. Remembers happier days as inter-rogator first-class, *Sieg Heil*, out with the fingernails. God knows what they all do with themselves, the ex-pat Genevois. Machinate. Fornicate. Play Bridge. The English arbitrator was at church this morning,' he added approvingly.

The taxi is taking us out of the city towards the French side of the lake. Near the frontier it veers inland and we are among trees. Large houses stand in clearings, their windows protected by steel mesh. We turn down a narrower road, then a lane, then a gravel drive and at the end of it stands a perfect gingerbread cottage gleaming with fresh paint under the snow, shutters ripple-striped and glossy, window-boxes with heart-shaped rustic cut-outs, burglar-alarms clamped to the eaves. The front door has a peep-hole in it and is surrounded with leaves and berries so highly scarlet they look enamelled. Fabergé. A hen's egg in diamonds. A butler opens the door and from behind him floats the sound of the international Diplomatic elite at play.

We are in the midst. Silk walls, shiny floors, Persian rugs, cherry-wood fires, waitresses with trays of crystal, women in suede as soft as silk and silk as rough as straw. Helmut says, 'You'll be all right here, Krista. You will fit like a glove.'

'I won't. I'm a wreck. I didn't sleep.'

'Always I think, Krista, that you are dressed ready at any time to meet the Queen.'

'Ah!' A broad, powdered woman looms in muted tartan. Experienced mouth, experienced eyes. A face that has quelled wars. That has countermanded the launching of a thousand ships.

'We are the translators.'

'Ah!' She looks expertly about for the right people for us to meet. It will not be easy. She smiles conspiratorially at Helmut, in a way that means I shall provide for you in a moment, and I am led towards a group where the men are languidly inclining their heads and the women exhaustedly moving their mouths.

A man turns to me—vermilion-cheeked, collapsed old mouth, ageing, not well. The woman beside him turns away towards a looking-glass and is gone. A sad smile, mouth turned down at the corners, some hint of a white triangle . . .

'Oh! Was her arm in a sling?'

The red-cheeked man looks puzzled.

'I believe I heard her sing yesterday.'

He looks alarmed.

'Oh, I hardly think so. Not many musicians at these do's of ours you know. She's nobody we know. Visitor here. You're English, aren't you? Good guess. Translator at this jamboree at the Metropole?'

'Yes.'

'Well—very well paid, isn't it? Jolly good. Like Switzerland, do you?'

'Yes, very—'

'Get a bit of skiing on the side? Jolly good. Know the Mitfords? Not many of them left now. I'm W.H.O. Great place. Air so good. Feel so well. Just married again, how about that? Sixty-six. She's about your age. Heh? Come and meet some people. Here's Sergei.'

Glasses are re-filled. Laughter is louder. Sergei looks Slav. Tall. With eyelids. He holds one arm bent at the elbow across his back. He bows from a great height. He and the vermilion cheeks converse. I am nowhere.

'You are leaving?' the Slav says, surprisingly beside me at the door. 'It is soon.'

'Yes, I must.'

'I too.'

He kisses the powdery woman's hand. I thank her but she is looking over my shoulder. At the door we stand for a moment, watching the snowflakes as his car slides up and his chauffeur approaches with an umbrella. We sink in soft cushions and lie back.

'You are going to a luncheon appointment? Where may I drop you?'

'No. Oh, anywhere near my hotel.'

'Certainly not. You shall lunch with me. Have you your passport? Then we shall go to France.'

Near Yvoire we leave chauffeur and car beside a bistro at the edge of a village and walk up the middle of an empty street, snow gathering in chunks on the toes of our boots, to the gateway of a chateau. One great gate leans from a broken hinge. Snow paints its delicate iron roses and plumes. Fastened across the back of the ironwork is old wire-netting and a menu behind a yellowing plastic sheet is tied to it with string. The menu, all but the word MENU, has faded away.

Across the courtyard the door of the château is being opened by the oldest maître d'hotel in the world. He bows. There is a marble and wrought-iron staircase, a black and white marble floor, a desk with a Meissen vase of French graveyard flowers, a dozen clocks—long-case, short-case, ormolu, bell-jar, enamel and gold. Their ticks are water-drops. There is a harp standing outside the dining room door, two strings gone.

And this dining room must once have been a ballroom. It has long windows looking at the white lake and three tables near them, round, large, all arranged in one corner, thick damask cloths (darned) to the floor. We have a bloomy field of parquet to cross to get to our chairs. The silver forks were forged for Titans, the napkins, small counterpanes dimly patterned with lilies. There are no other diners, no sound of life, no smell of food but a tiled stove with little eighteenth-century scenes of Vaud reaches the ceiling and the great room is alive from it, pleasant and warm. Pad, pad across the parquet comes the ancient with wine upon a tray. We talk of Sergei's childhood home in old Bohemia.

And then the caviar. And then the borscht. And then woodcock. And then a camembert. And then a cream pudding. And then a glass of candied fruits that shine in the snowy light. And then coffee and a bilberry liqueur.

And then, I supposed, bed.

But this is my misfortune. I do not now like bed.

I go to find a cloakroom. I sit at a dressing-table with silver brushes, look at my face in a glass so old that it is exploding with bronzy stars. A flattering, greeny light. This is a brothel for international moguls, for giants, for great white whales (I am woozy with wine) and I am a minnow, a sprat, a wafer of plankton to float almost invisible through their jaws.

Not that he looks like a whale. He looks a gentle man.

He is waiting for me on a sofa in the hall and there is nobody else anywhere to be seen. He gets up, takes my elbow, draws me down beside him. He says, 'I believe that the answer will be no.'

I say, 'I'm afraid so,' through a wave of disappointment. And memory.

'Let's sit here a moment until the car comes. Where may I take you home?'

We sit on in silence. He is looking at me all the time and says that I am beautiful. 'Beautiful,' he says. 'But so frightened. I understand it,' and he stretches out his left hand. 'You must look.'

'I—yes, I noticed.'

'You didn't like seeing me eat.'

'I—no. I don't mind—'

'Some women of course like it. It thrills them. Hold my hand.'

I stretched out and took the gloved hand and under the leather it is hard and wooden. Hard and dead.

'It is the result of Stalingrad.'

'It's wonderful,' I said. 'How could it be made?'

'It's an old miracle now. A German miracle. Before its time, like Ming china.'

I close my eyes and try to think of things that are living and complete. Un-secretive and open. My father's face keeps getting in the way. I stroke the hand and he says, 'You are thinking of the contraption at the wrist when I take it off. And what happens at night.'

'I was thinking nothing of the sort,' I say and hold the glove all the way back to the hotel. As he kisses my living hand on the steps of the hotel he says, 'I believe you to have been very unhappily married.' Then he kisses my cheek and the snow-flakes swim past us, large and light and lacy in front of the glitzy revolving doors.

There are four carrots in a row, nose to tail. Six potatoes. Four rashers of bacon and a gigantic chicken on a plate. Nearby stands a jelly-square upon a saucer. The old linoleum on the kitchen floor, the cupboard tops, sink, look as if they have been scrubbed daily for several hours. Cats sit outside on the sill with frantic dinner-time eyes. I unpack the food I have brought, light the gas.

'You may as well know—' he calls through.

'Yes?'

No reply.

I go back to the sitting room. He doesn't move. 'Did you see the chocolates I brought you?'

'You may as well know—'

'What?'

'I'm getting married.'

'Oh yes. Who to?'

'Mrs. Aylesford.'

There is a tapping at the back door. It is Mrs. Aylesford with pots of marmalade. 'How d'you find him?' She leans forward, bright-eyed.

'He says you're going to be married, Mrs. Aylesford.'

'Me? Whoever to?'

'To him.'

'Yes. He's getting worse. I've brought you some marmalade. He ought to be cared for, Krista.'

'But he's perfectly all right. He's very well.'

'Not if he thinks he's getting married to me.'

'But he doesn't. Not really. He has to say things like that. It's boredom—boredom. Look how he's arranged all those carrots.'

We survey the line of carrots.

'Last week,' I say, 'he was thinking of going on a cruise. Oh, I do wish he would go on a cruise.'

'You ought to take him off foreign with you,' she watches me. Interested. Examines my clothes. 'Eh. Krista?'

He appears in the kitchen doorway and seeing Mrs. Aylesford says, 'Oh, God,' and shuffles off again.

'Can't even keep away when I've got my daughter here,' he says. 'My only daughter. My only child. It's a pity you weren't a boy. Where's my dinner?'

'If I was a boy you wouldn't have me cooking your dinner. You wouldn't get a son doing what—'

'And what's this about me going off foreign? I can't do with foreign stuff,' he says, scooping away at Movenpick Black Forest cake.

'She says I should take you with me abroad.'

'The trouble with this world is,' he says, taking more cream, 'the way people can't be satisfied with being in one place. If people all kept to their own homes—'

'If they kept to their own homes you'd never have met Mother.'

'Well. That was a mistake. My marriage to your mother. All these foreign languages. Foreign tongues. Everything better somewhere else—that's it, isn't it? Grass in the next field. Going off to these chocolate-box places.'

He examines the chocolates I've brought, prodding them

for the soft ones. 'They can't even print a key to these things now. They used to put a card in.'

'Switzerland isn't really chocolate-box.'

'It's picture-postcard.'

'It's full of—full of pain. Like everywhere.'

'Now I've got a bloody Brazil.'

'I went out with a man last week who'd had a hand burned off. At Stalingrad.'

'Now Stalingrad. That was a very terrible thing. Month after month. How old was the bugger? Must have been my age.'

When I have carried out the rubbish he says, 'Full of pain, is it? Switzerland? I went there once. Faces like emery-boards. Hard-mouthed Nazis. You're over-sensitive, that's your trouble. You're like me.'

I sit down behind him and cover my face with my hands. I hang on to one good thing—that he cannot mention my marriage.

After a time he says, 'Where've you gone? What you sitting behind me for? I'm in everybody's clutches.'

On my way to work on Monday I saw the fly again. We met head on, on a corner of the Rue Verconnex outside the shop with the glassy pillars. I side-stepped a moment, avoiding somebody and suddenly there she was, loping forward towards me with her black lost eyes. She was not this time crying but there was all the frenzy there, lashed down but as fierce as at the first encounter. She looked hard at me and passed.

Under my bubble the words flow out. We are on one of the last few witnesses now. This one drones on and on about the wrongs and rights of a machine-tool being employed to dig a dam in Baghdad. 'As we have stated before'—endless parentheses—'As we have stated before, in a way quite incontrovertible, whereas the statements submitted on Day Sixteen by Mr. Bronx concerning point number two hundred and forty-seven on the question of costs of the extra-hyper-digger equipment and in conjunction with Mr. Jinx's evidence concerning point number three hundred and eighty-six, of statement number nine hundred and five on Day Thirty-Six, I will submit that, notwithstanding ... '

The words pour from him. The words pour from me, from Helmut, from the other two. The clock on the wall with its twelve dots, its stubby fingers, never seems to move.

Towards the end of the week Helmut is waiting by the door for me at lunch time. 'You all right? Like some lunch?' We go over towards the Old Town and passing along the Versonnex, towards the shop with the glittering pillars, suddenly two great lymphatic people appear holding the hands of a retarded child, and I reach out and grab Helmut's sleeve.

He looks surprised. Nobody touches Helmut. As we go through the Place des Eaux Vives he looks at me again and draws quite close to me. 'You don't often see those in Geneva. They keep them off the streets. What is it?' He takes my arm and we go up over the cobblestones to a restaurant under the arches, warm and dark, red and white table-cloths, Italian, almost empty. As we wait, Helmut takes out a Missal. When the spaghetti comes he puts the book carefully away in his pocket and says, 'You are beginning to look a little better.'

'I'm all right. Why?'

'You look so ill. Is it money, sex or sickness?'

'It's none of them. I have no reason ... It's just that there's so much damage. So much pain.'

'Geneva? Damage? Pain?'

'Yes. All kept under wraps. Everywhere in the world.'

He pauses with a forkful of carbonara and says, 'But it's you who keep yourself under wraps.'

'I don't know how not to. But it's not just fancy. Haven't

you noticed here? It's a crime to be miserable in public. It is indecent. Indecent to be open.'

He says, 'You know, I think it is this most bloody of all arbitrations. You need a rest. But I like Geneva.'

'I'm frightened, Helmut.'

'Of what?'

'I keep seeing this woman. She's like a fly.'

He regards me, courteously.

After the hearing that day I saw Helmut talking to the English arbitrator who came over to me as I left my kiosk. 'Bear up,' he said, 'not much longer.'

'This week?'

'Oh, definitely this week. Maybe even tomorrow. Come for a drink.'

We walked, the elderly man and I, down to the lake-side restaurant on the Rue du Rhône, full of the very young— silky hair, pale suits, Patek Philippe watches. Among them the English arbitrator looked comfortable, shabby and wise. We sat silent, listening to all the talk about money and he said, 'Sorry. I thought it might be more interesting. Young and gay for you. Why do you keep looking over your shoulder?'

'Oh—I just thought—I thought I saw someone.'

'Aha, you are being followed. You are a spy. Something to do with Swedish Sergei of the wooden claw.'

'I didn't know he was Swedish. He said he was at Stalingrad. I only had lunch with him.'

'I'm sure. He's homosexual. But charming. You were very safe. Did you know that the police in Geneva have a file on every foreigner working here? There's one about me and there will be one about you.'

'There's absolutely nothing they could find to say about me. Oh—!'

The fly was there. Standing outside, looking in at me through the glass.

'Sweet child,' he said. 'What is it? You look nearly out of your wits. Come on—you're not being followed, you know. Drink your drink. Bear up. We really are almost finished now, and when it's over I am going to give us all a huge and wonderful party at the Perle du Lac.'

On the Friday—for of course the case lasted out the week: it was to resume for a final day on Monday—he came across again as I dashed for the plane and said, 'Helmut's going home with you. Right to your front-door.'

And on my front doorstep—Helmut a little disorganised by three Bloody Marys and St John of the Cross on the plane—I said, 'What do you think is wrong with me?' And he said, 'I think you know.'

'But I don't. What?'

He said, 'I don't. You do. Somewhere.'

I said, to him, 'Listen, there is a woman like a fly. I see her everywhere. I saw her this week looking through a window at me at the Rue du Rhône and if you want to know I saw her just now in the luggage hall going through the Goods to Declare. It's the first time she has followed me home.'

'I think you will understand in time.'

'She has little hands and they were clutching the handle of the trolley and her mouth was a cave.'

He said, 'Krista, all will be well.'

My car wouldn't start the next morning and I had to take the tube to South Wimbledon and walk over to my father's. It is a mile from the station so that it was half-past ten by the time I reached his gate and saw the curtains all drawn across the windows and a notice pinned to his front door.

The pulsating bedside light.

It was a typed message inside a transparent plastic bag with a drawing-pin at each corner, neat and straight. 'Dear Krista,' the message read, 'please call immediately next door, number 38, and oblige E. Aylesford.' I took out my key and went immediately upstairs to my father's bedroom.

The cats shot out as I opened the door and found him under his old satin eiderdown. He was staring at the ceiling like an effigy.

'Pa—are you ill?'

No reply. I went to the bedside and sat down and wished that I could bear to hold his hand. He had humped himself over now with his head in the corner, his knees drawn up. He began to cry.

'What is it? Pa? She said I had to go in next door first—'

At once he was sitting upright in the bed, hair on end, eyes staring.

'She, what? Who?'

'Mrs. Aylesford.'

'Where is she?'

'I don't know. She put a message on the door.'

'Which door?'

'The front-door.'

'My front-door? With glue?'

'With drawing-pins.'

'She stuck drawing-pins in my front-door? I'll kill that woman. She's not right in her mind. Where were you last night? What about the shopping?'

'Why are you lying in bed in the dark?'

He collapsed again and began to whimper into the eiderdown.

'It's because it's all a myth.'

'What is?'

'Heaven.'

'I'd better go and see Mrs. Aylesford.'

'Leave her alone. It's a myth, isn't it?'

'I don't know.'

'They all go on. Churches. Parsons. There's never anyone to prove it. Nobody's ever come back. Heaven! When you die you're dead. Look at your mother.'

'I don't know.'

'They're all gone, aren't they? All the old ones. Everyone. You stop, that's what you do. Go out. And all the things you've missed. Look at what you missed with Graham.'

And so—he had said it.

I left him and went up Mrs. Aylesford's path and saw her through her front-room window, waiting for me. Myrtle from number 32 was sitting with her and they were talking simultaneously, nodding their heads up and down. 'Come in, Krista, we've been waiting for you such a time. Would you like a cup of tea?'

It was all laid out ready, with teaspoons and sugar-lumps and a lace tray-cloth. As Mrs. Aylesford went out for the teapot Myrtle lit a cigarette and said, 'Cold, isn't it? No sign of spring yet.'

'Is it something important, Mrs. Aylesford?'

She was fussing with the hot-water jug. 'Biscuits, Krista? They're Nice biscuits. Or talking to you I suppose I should say Neece biscuits. It's funny, you never know how to say it. They always seem so English somehow.'

'Is it about Father, Mrs. Aylesford?'

She was busy with a tea-strainer. Then she put a little plate with a biscuit on it by my cup. Then she settled carefully in her chair. 'Well, yes, dear, it is. I'm afraid the time has come for me and Myrtle to speak out. And others agree, down the terrace.'

'You're worried?'

'Oh, very worried. Aren't we, Myrtle.'

'We're distracted sometimes. Distracted.'

'I know,' I said, 'you've been most terribly good and kind. I know he's very difficult—'

'Oh, it's not that he's difficult. We're quite used to difficult people, aren't we, Myrtle? There's been half a dozen in the terrace difficult but we haven't minded. There was poor Mrs. Cross who left me her china, she used to have to sleep sitting up. Well, she died sitting up and I couldn't get her flat. Her back broke right through. She was worn away to cornflakes, wasn't she, Myrtle?'

'Cornflakes. Her bones were cornflakes.'

'And we had a terrible time with next door the other side, he used to sleep by day and work by night. Do-it-yourself, and all those dogs. I daren't tell you the state the house was in when he went. Well, we were the ones that found him. It hadn't happened long. The social services commended us. They said we must have suffered, living so near. It took a fortnight to get the place clean and the bottles out.'

'How good you are. But you don't have any of that with Father?'

'Oh no. Nothing like that.' They looked in their teacups, spinning it out. The long-planned encounter.

'Well, Krista, it's his rudeness. It's his cruelness.'

'Oh, he can be cruel,' said Myrtle.

'It's the things he says. The terrible cruel things.'

'And he's a bit sexy too. I don't like telling you this and you his daughter and him so old. You'd think he'd have forgotten. I suppose it must be a sub-conscious thing like Freud. And he's so miserable. And so horrible.'

'I know,' I said, 'that he's a great pessimist.'

'Pessimist, Krista, he's in black despair. And it's not right because he passes it on. All about no heaven and this life being hell, and all about death.'

'He never leaves death alone,' said Myrtle. 'Never. He keeps appearing in that door. Standing there with his eyes blazing. Here, in Mrs. Aylesford's front doorway saying, "Where will it end? I'll tell you where—it'll end here and now and forever"—doesn't he, Mrs. Aylesford? "Here and now. Cancer or a stroke. Or an overdose or slit-my-wrists." It's terrible.'

'It's like a bad angel. We can't take any more of it, Krista. And then last night—well, that's when we knew we had to speak to you.'

'I'm so sorry. I couldn't get over last night.'

'Oh, I'm sure you're very busy. You have a very busy life with all your foreign travel. Mr. Aylesford and I always found holidays abroad very tiring.'

'What happened?'

'Well, he wandered off. I'm afraid, Krista, he wandered off and we had to call the police. That's why he's in bed today. He had quite a long session at the police-station—talking about sins and you and rubbish. He had to see a police doctor.'

'I've been up to see him. He doesn't seem very ill.'

Their four eyes were excited and hostile. '"Physically," the police doctor said, "physically, he's wonderful".'

'It's mentally,' said Myrtle, 'it's mental trouble. He went on and on to the policeman about his shame.'

'What shame?'

'Oh, I'm sure I don't know. I expect it's something private to the family.' They looked uneasy. 'But altogether—I'm afraid we had to report to the police that in our opinion—and of course we're not professionals; this is simply the opinion of the terrace—we think he ought to be Assessed. In a home. He's a damaged man.'

'In an asylum,' said Myrtle. 'Or any rate a Nerve Home.'

'Yes,' said Mrs. Aylesford, 'I mean especially, Krista, if he's going to start walking away. He went all the way to Wimbledon Park pond and started going for all the lads with their remote controls for being so noisy. He said something very disgusting to them which I'll not repeat.'

There was a welcome, though unhealthy silence.

I said, 'I'll go and talk to him for a bit. I'm so sorry.'

'I think we'll have to have something a bit more definite than that, Krista.'

'Yes, of course. The job I'm doing comes to an end on Monday. I can be here perhaps by Monday night. I'll speak to the doctor. If you could just hold the fort till then—'

'You didn't ever think, Krista, of having him up to live with you?'

'Yes. I did. I have asked him. He has always said no.'

'I expect he's just not wanting to be troublesome.'

'Well, that isn't exactly usual. And he does realise I work abroad most of the time.'

'Oh, yes.'

'But I think,' said Mrs. Aylesford, 'that we all have to make sacrifices for our parents, don't you? I mean money's not everything and it's in the Bible.'

'But I have to work, Mrs. Aylesford.'

'Yes, it's hard when you're not married. But with the money you could get for his house. Or for your house—? Another biscuit? It would break our hearts here to see him in a Nerve Home.'

The bed was empty when I went back next door but I could see him dressed and out in the back-garden on his walking-frame lunging about at a large tree with the pruning-shears. I said, 'The dinner's warming up in the oven. You'll get cold out there. Come back in.'

'I've never had a cold in my life. Mind, I'm breaking up otherwise.'

'You look very well. I hear you took yourself off for a walk?'

'I've got five black toes.'

'Have you shown the doctor?'

'I know what he'd say. And I know what he'd think, too. Corruption—that's what it is. Decay. I'm decaying. I'm getting started in good time. For my box.'

'Pa—will you promise not to go off on your own again. You're frightening next door.'

'They need frightening. They need something to get them out of bed in the morning. All they do is sit and yatter. My going off's the biggest thing that's ever happened to them. Gives them orgasms.'

'They think you should come and live with me.'

'I wouldn't live with you,' he said, 'if it was the atomic bomb.'

But, as I finished washing up and hanging up the tea-towels and putting on my coat, he was crying by the fire. 'You never liked me,' he said. 'And I never liked you.'

I said, 'Oh, Pa. I'll be back on Tuesday at the latest. I'll come over and stay with you. I'll take some time off.'

'A lot of use you'll be. What use is anyone? What's it all mean? You can't tell me. And I wouldn't come near that fancy place in Putney bought with Graham's money, not if you prostrated yourself in the road.'

'I'm going then.'

'Where? Now? Leaving me all alone? You're not going off tonight in that aeroplane? Not after all that's happened.'

Usually I call him before I leave for Heathrow but tonight, as I stood looking at the telephone, asking for strength, it began to ring and at the same moment the doorbell started ringing, too. I thought, 'Taxi—I'll get it first,' and found instead Helmut on the step muffled up and holding his usual plastic carrier full no doubt as usual with prayer-books, whisky, toothbrush, electric razor, two shirts. No one ever calls for me.

'I must just get the phone.'

'I've come to pick you up. The taxi's waiting.'

Not quite asking him in I said, 'Oh yes. Right. Hang on,' picked up the receiver and heard Mrs. Aylesford's voice. I was surprised that after the great pleasure I had just felt on seeing

Helmut I could be swept into equal distress that it was not my father.

And there seemed to be something else. Something over my shoulder, some shadow, something black and bad that was considering me carefully. 'Yes, Mrs. Aylesford?'

'I'm very sorry to have to say, Krista, I'm very sorry to be the bearer of bad news, but he's gone again.'

'But I'm just leaving to catch my plane.'

'I'm sure I'm very sorry but—'

'I have to catch it. I can't let them down. It is the last day, tomorrow. There is nobody else to do my work. He can't be far.'

'It is a very dark night, Krista.'

'Oh, Lord. I'll ring the police. How long—'

'I saw him about twenty minutes ago. I took him his tea. He was crying, Krista. I'm afraid he was saying you had been very unkind—'

'Yes, I see. All right.'

'I can't go,' I said to Helmut. 'My father's disappeared.'

He took the phone.

'This is a friend of Krista. Please explain to me the situation.'

There was an interested pause. Then I heard her voice, hesitant, then more confident, then furiously clacking.

'We shall telephone you from the airport if there is time, otherwise from Geneva. In the meantime, kindly get in touch with the police. Krista will be back as soon as possible. Goodnight.'

Clack, clack, squawk.

'Good evening.'

Halfway to Heathrow I said, 'I can't possibly go, you know.'

'The woman Aylesford said that he does this often.'

'She has never told me that.' I looked. Short-legged, tight-lipped, fierce-nosed Sir Thomas More. Archetypal immovable lawyer. He said, 'I pressed her.'

'But I can't go. Not knowing.'

Walking behind me in the cafeteria queue (the plane had been delayed an hour) he said, 'I think that we should now sit down and that you should talk to me. I am right in thinking that you are in some way obsessed with your father and he with you?'

'No, of course not. What's the matter with me is that I am going mad. I keep seeing—oh, God! I told you. You didn't take any—'

'You told me that you keep seeing a woman who looks like a fly. The name of the fly I suggest to you'—he looked at the postage-stamp-sized packet of biscuits on my tray and added a doughnut—'the name of this fly is Guilt.'

Eating the doughnut, or rather picking it up and putting it down again, I said, 'I dare say.'

'Are we, I wonder, in the areas of child-abuse, incest or cruelty?'

'Of course not.'

'Why of course not?'

'Not in the terrace.'

'My dear, you little know. Why do you feel guilty about your father?'

'I don't know. I told him something once I shouldn't have done. I said I was sorry. It was just once. I have done all I can for him. I suppose not enough. I suppose I ought to love him more—or show something more. But there seems no more that I can possibly do.'

'You feel pity?'

'Oh yes, I do feel pity. You see he is so sane. His trouble is not senility or insanity but a most rare sanity. He really does look steadily at the nature of death and is terrified. He talks about it. What he says is all true. Other people can't face it. He sounds so dotty but he says what's really in all our hearts.'

'There is no need for him however to have destroyed your happy young spirit.'

'I'm not sure I had one.'

'Yes, you did. We all did. Sometimes deeply secreted. He has been murderous. Why has he?'

'I don't know.'

'Perhaps,' Helmut said, 'the woman you see, the fly, is not your guilt but his? Is there something he may feel guilty about?'

'Plenty that he should—'

'But is there?'

And so I told it.

'It was my husband. He was thrilled by him. He fawned over him. By my marrying important Graham he had bolstered himself. He strutted. He used to say, "They'll think a bit more of me now." As if it had been my duty to do it for him.'

'Did Graham like him?'

'He loathed him. He couldn't bear to be in the same room with him. He didn't see that he was sad or frightened and he never found him funny. He made excuse after excuse not to see him. In the end he said if I couldn't free myself from my father he was going. And in the end he went.'

'Did your father know the reason for his going?'

'I told him. I told him once. I broke open. I screamed it at him. Afterwards I couldn't believe I'd done it. Since then he has been much worse to me.'

'Yes, of course he has. Your father is wanting you to leave him. To withdraw from him. Chuck him.'

'Leave him? He rules me. He devours me. He weeps to keep me.'

'He wants you to leave him alone. If he can see you free and happy, then his guilt about your marriage will go away.'

'You're saying he loves me?'

'Yes. But let me tell you, Krista, if you do not do something decisive, when he dies the fly, Guilt, will spawn a disgusting maggot called Remorse who will be with you always.'

'Since you've never met him—'

'It is not necessary. I know you.'

The plane was signalled. I said, 'You mean I must not go home tonight?'

'Your home is not with him.'

'Helmut, he is out-of-doors, alone, lost in the dark. He is very old. Can't you think what they'll all say?'

'For the love of God, forget what they'll all say. If ruthlessly, selfishly, wordlessly you do not leave for Geneva now, tonight, you will be damaged forever, destroyed, and he will die a guilty and unhappy man. You have to set him free. Get your passport.'

On the plane he said, 'All right?' but I didn't answer.

At the hotel he said, 'And now I am coming with you to your room.' The concierge's hand paused over the keys. 'From which we shall telephone together.' At my bedroom door he said, 'And be prepared for anything.'

'You mean—the fly?'

'Fuck, Krista, the fly. I mean—ah yes.'

The message-light was on. Helmut picked up the phone, dialled downstairs, spoke to the operator. Then said, 'Your father has telephoned you.'

'He has telephoned *me*? Here? Telephoned Geneva?'

'Now I shall ring the neighbour Aylesford.'

I sat on a chair by the bathroom door and listened, as he listened, undoing his long scarf, removing his gloves, hat, then his coat with all the time the receiver under his chin. Then he put down the phone and said, 'Your father is safe home. He is in bed.' He went to examine the fridge, came back to the bed, sat on it and began to unpeel one of my goodnight chocolates.

'You can't stay here,' I said, 'I'm not having it said that all I needed was a man.'

'All you needed was an ally,' he said, removing his shoes. 'An expert witness. But please, you must pull yourself up,

Krista. You are looking most wild and untidy and your mouth is a hole.'

We lay side by side on the bed and I said, 'I must ring him back.'

He said, 'In a minute,' and took hold of my wrist.

'I love him,' I said.

'Wait ten minutes.'

When it was half an hour he said, 'Ring later.' And then it was much later, and too late, and then it was morning and only half an hour to get to the arbitration.

In the taxi we sat hand in hand, and the lake flying past, the throb of the terrible packed traffic on the bridge—the fact of not having telephoned was the faintest shadow. At twelve o'clock the last, the incredible, scarcely believed-in last session ended without histrionics or perorations, a simple unremarkable end to the years and years of patient argument in Teheran and Rome and here. It ended with a nodding, a relaxation between the parties, a smiling and sitting back among the arbitrators and the pause before the great pack-up of papers for shipment home about the world. The court began to chatter in its different languages, drawing away into groups. Babel once more.

'And the faces of the translators are suffused with joy,' said the English arbitrator to Helmut and me, as we stood together. 'See you in half an hour at the Perle du Lac.'

'Oh, I can't. I must get home. There's a bit of a crisis—'

'Couldn't you ring from the restaurant?'

'You would have heard if there were anything,' said Helmut.

But at the Perle, with its glass walls against the lake and sudden sunlight on the mountains and the snows, I forgot. We celebrated until the four o'clock plane. Champagne and rosy tablecloths and flowers and Helmut touching my fingers.

The house was all in darkness, but next door Mrs. Aylesford's lights were on. I was alone and walked to her window. She and Myrtle were seated facing the blank television screen, their backs solid, rather stooped. Myrtle was smoking and staring at the floor. Mrs. Aylesford had knitting idle on her lap. On the sofa facing the window and looking straight at me, sat the fly.

Br. Fish lost 420,000
7 people 200,000
Germans 500,000
Banks of the Somme River,
France

France / British
advance
8 km

Getting to Pebble
is good

THE DIXIE GIRLS

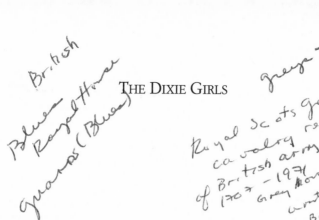

Eighty years ago, or thereabouts, Nell had shared a governess with the Dixie girls, Vi and V. and May, the daughters of a Major in the Blues and Greys.

It was V. who had been the particular friend. Vi had been five years older and bossy, May, three years younger and rather sharp. Nell, the landlady's daughter, had been in awe of all three of them and fearfully in awe of the parents; Mrs. Dixie, a remote, enduring woman sitting upright and frowning at her sewing in an uncomfortable chair, pursing her Scottish lips; and the Major, a voice, a moustache a lubricious gleam, an Olympian shadow springing down the stairs. Major Dixie had been often from home.

The Dixies had been long-term lodgers with Nell's mother in the North Yorkshire town of Pickering, a high cold blowy place near the garrison in the middle of moors. It had suited the Dixies well, for they had come from bracing Peebles. Peebles they had so loved that in Nell's ears it came to be confused sometimes with heaven. She would wonder if she would ever get there.

The governess one day went hastily home to it and after that the governess was Vi, who kept a page or so ahead of V. and May and Nell, reading everything up an hour before the lesson. Nell's mother was not charged for her daughter's education but the rent of the Dixies was reduced from twenty-five shillings a week to sixteen (family rate, food, heating inclusive) though this was never mentioned. The Dixies somehow made it clear to Nell that they were being good to her.

They saw to her Yorkshire accent for a start. Nell at over eighty, lying in the dark sometimes, and thinking of her days in the schoolroom—that is to say in her mother's dining room; cruets on the sideboard, woolly mats, a malicious, razor-toothed plant, dry as buckram on a tall jardinière in the window—Nell saw more clearly than her recent landscapes the Dixie girls all twisting and squirming with glee at her voice. 'Bread and serrip. Bread and serrip.' She remembered her blush and sometimes so intensely that she blushed again. Blushing is rare in the old. She saw again behind the rosy bobble curtains and the governess's wretched face the white light of the moors. She heard the north wind over the scratchy black heather.

The Dixies all went away, following the flag, following the Major. Nell lived on for years in Pickering and kept on with helping at home where officers' families were always coming and going. During the Great War she married a batman of one of these officers and afterwards settled with him in Leeds. He was a cobbler, a silent man who had survived the Somme. They had a baby daughter.

Nell however did not lose touch with the formidable Dixie family since the one thing that the white-faced governess had instilled in her—apart from the unacceptability of the Yorkshire accent—was the necessity of Correspondence to a civilised life. The first duty of the day for a woman—unless of course she were of the servant class—was to attend to her letters.

This as it happened was entirely to Nell's taste and she would probably have done it anyway, for she was a creature so formed that she felt nothing to have properly occurred unless she had communicated it in writing. Writing to people about other people was her relish and her huge delight and though she could not manage to write as she had been taught, straight after breakfast and for the first post, after the slop-pails, the scrubbing brush, the possing-tub, the mangle, the range, the scouring of pans with soda, the black-leading of the grate, the brasses, the making of dinner for herself and the cobbler and Hilda the robust baby and the clearing of everything up, down she would sit to her letters. She wrote with a smile upon her face or with lips tight with emotion, with frown-lines of right-eous indignation and sometimes even with tears a-flow. The most minute events of the terrace in Leeds were made radiant by Nell and born earlier or later she might well have been advised to branch out and become a novelist, brimming as she did with such immediacy.

As it was, she had a very happy time and the Dixie girls as the unselfconscious pages flowed forth from Leeds into India, Kenya, Malta, Basingstoke, Cyprus, Aden, Cheltenham and Singapore called out to each other, 'Here's dear Nell again,' raising amused eyebrows. They always read the letters, often two or three times, and V. who was the chief recipient kept many of them in a box. 'Dear Nell,' they all said to each other. 'Such excitements.' There was a slight uneasiness in their voices sometimes—or at least in the voice of Vi or May—that Nell should be so entertaining, so articulate, so full of gusto. Was it not just a bit *forward* of her to write with such self-con-fidence? But V., who was nice, said not at all. She looked for-ward to dear Nell's pretty handwriting on an envelope. 'Well, she owes that to *us*,' said Vi.

V.—it was short for Victoria—replied to Nell's letters very dutifully, as she too had been taught; never starting a para-graph with an I, always answering information received point for point before presenting anything new, always remembering to send messages to the cobbler and the baby—never forget-ting the baby's birthday. Sometimes she enclosed sprigs of colonial vegetation—a silken purple poppy-flower pressed almost transparent like a butterfly's wing, or a squelched hot orchid from Kuala Lumpur or a dry little shower of bay. The

Dixie girls communicated best in symbols, being not much hands at describing. V. alone could now and then wax voluble on the subject that meant most to her, which was her health— or rather her sickness and the sicknesses of others.

Sickness and death. These were the enemy. The Dixie girls who had so upsettingly to their parents not been boys had need of enemies, enemies through whom, though they could not be despatched by sword or shot, they could demonstrate their bravery.

How very bravely for instance V. set out to do down the onslaughts of the flesh. She ate little, she lived in cold houses, she walked far in bad weather on fragile ankles, she spent almost nothing on clothes; and after her parents' death she returned to England to a freezing address on the Kent coast spending her evenings sewing sides-to-middles of old sheets for charity, and darning for herself, and often writing her delicate letters with fingers blue and pleated at the tip. The Major had died of drink and Mrs. Dixie of desiccation. There was no money left. Said V., 'We are in penury.' Vi had taken a job as a teacher at a dubious private school near Wokingham and May had 'taken a job' moving pieces of paper about in an office that had something to do with a kind godfather, and had a bed-sit in Ealing. 'We are fallen on hard times,' wrote V. to Nell from the pretty Kent cottage beneath her father's fine portrait and before a fire of one small coal. 'It is a very good thing that we are Dixies, or we could not bear it.'

Nell found this statement totally unsurprising. She had believed for so long that the Dixies were significant that their superiority to everyone she knew was notched in her brain. Dixie to her meant Hohenzollern, Battenberg and Teck. She knew that had the Czar or Charlemagne or the Prince of Wales come riding by and stopped in front of her she would have been perfectly all right so long as the patrician Dixies had been at her side. They knew the rules.

Once, when she was thirty or so Nell was invited to meet V. in London to witness the marriage procession of the Duke and Duchess of Kent. She and V. arrived early upon the Embankment and took up positions in the front row. Nell carried a little flag to wave hurray. V. in her threadbare coat of ancient design simply stood, but as the carriages came by it seemed the merest accident that V. was on the pavement and not bowing and twirling her wrist from the inside of one of them. 'Such a pity about the hat,' she said. 'The Queen knows never to wear a big hat. She knows that we all want to see her face. Poor Marina of course is Greek,' and she led Nell off to a Lyons tea-shop for a little something. V. had to eat a little something every three hours, otherwise she fainted. 'Oh poor V.,' said plump Nell. 'And you're so terribly thin.'

'All Dixies are thin.'

'But you are really *frighteningly* thin,' said Nell. 'I do hope you've seen someone.'

'Oh, dear me yes. I've seen half a dozen. The girls took me to Harley Street.'

'That must have cost—' said Nell before remembering that prices are never mentioned. 'And what did they say?'

'They said,' said V. looking across the small sandwiches, 'they said I was to eat something every three hours.'

'But couldn't you eat *more*?' asked Nell who after twenty-four hours in May's bed-sitting room (which had turned out to be a very nice flat with three bedrooms but a kitchen with only a kettle) was famished. 'Couldn't I—well, wouldn't you let me buy you something substantial? Some baked beans?'

V.'s narrow, birdish, sweet face for a moment almost lost its stiff upper lip. 'I'm afraid there's no hope of *beans*,' she said and went on to discuss train time-tables back to Kent and her mid-week ticket which must not be wasted. She said that there was just time to see a film about Henry VIII that was on at Victoria.

During the bed scene with Anne Boleyn, V. had to leave as she felt a faint coming on, and they went to find a little something in the railway buffet. Nell went to Kings Cross and ate seven sausages and felt disgraceful. As soon as she got home to Leeds she sat down at once to thank V. for the wonderful outing.

'Particularly the film,' she wrote and paused. V. had pronounced the film shocking. 'So realistic,' she wrote with delighted malice.

'Laughing?' asked the cobbler.

'Oh no,' said Nell ashamed, 'I'm very fond of V. She's so poor you know. It's just as well she's a Dixie.'

'I'd have thought you'd have got all you wanted, down in London.'

The cobbler was a heavy man who sat slumped with a pipe and would never put a bit of coal on the fire or draw a curtain, but he was splendid in bed which had been a glorious surprise to Nell who had expected something unpleasant or just to be endured. Her one experience of sex before marriage had been a fumbling on a landing with Major Dixie in Pickering when she was twelve, an experience she had shared with the governess had she known it (Mrs. Dixie had) and with many others. Her marriage, her female self, she never dreamed of even hinting at in her letters to V. and was delighted and surprised by her confident knowledge that she should not. She had mastered an area of etiquette that would never be demanded of the Dixie girls. And much else unknown to the Dixie girls.

At this time, and it was the first time, she began to find it difficult to provide material for letters to V. about sickness and death. It was a relief when the baby came and she could announce nappy rash and gripes and the possibility of infantile thrush, even though V. replied imprecisely about these, countering them, fielding them, with her own familiar symptoms, bravely borne.

So the years passed and everyone grew old and Nell's husband died and Hilda grew to be a large, angry sort of woman very high up in local government. When Nell was eighty-four Hilda retired and they went to live at a sea-side place where Hilda had had meaningful holidays during the menopause with a woman called Audrey, now dead. She took up residence on a pink housing-estate set out in crescents on the ugly edge of a pretty mediaeval town. Gulls screamed, you could hear the waves on rough days and there was a sea-light sometimes in the sky and wide sunsets, but all you could see from the windows were identical windows opposite, very nicely painted, grass well-cut and a shaped hedge.

It was an elderly crescent. Few children played. Nobody much passed by. Nell had one side of a twin-pack semi-det, Hilda the other, an excellent scheme. 'I can hear her if she knocks through the wall,' said Hilda, 'and she's not incontinent yet.' Nell was grateful in her way and always waved as Hilda went charging down the next-door path each morning to her clean and glittering little car. Hilda, though retired from London, was becoming politically indispensable to the South-East coast. She shopped and cooked for her mother, bursting in each evening with supper from the microwave under a plastic dome. Sometimes on Sundays they ate lunch together. Nell often now called it Sunday dinner in the old way and in the old Yorkshire voice that had reasserted itself as had some nice old words she wondered at even as she spoke them. Her fitted, hot and cold bathroom basin for example had become 'the washstand' and the dustman's crunching-lorry had become a 'dray'.

When Nell had become ill with bronchial pneumonia one winter there had been a day when Hilda had stayed home from work to see the doctor who had suggested that now, or at least during the winter months, might not Nell move in with her daughter, but Hilda had said, 'Now about that I have to be very firm. No choices. To be happy and secure, old people must have no choices,' and the doctor, humbled, had gone away. He called on Nell once unexpectedly and found her writing letters in a chair by the window. 'Oh, very thankful,' she said. 'Everybody's very kind. I do just wish there was somebody in the day-time and the view is rather poor.'

Outings were suggested. Minibuses filled with doleful invalids arrived at the door. The invalids looked out at Nell on the step with little enthusiasm and Nell said to the woman in authority who was trying to lure her towards them that after all she didn't feel up to it. 'I get these little faints,' she said in a Dixie voice and went in and shut the door and despised herself. 'Your mother needs mental stimulation,' the authorities told Hilda.

So one day when it was extremely dark and wet, dark and wet as it can only be in sea-side Kent in winter, and when Hilda had no committees, she put her mother in the car and took her for a drive. They sizzled along the sea-front, windscreen wipers going a-lick, lorries flinging spray all over them and the wind banging. Somewhere along the road beside the invisible white cliffs of Dover Nell said it reminded her of Pickering.

'Pickering?' said Hilda. 'Pickering's in the middle of moors.'

'Oh, it's quite near the sea.'

'Don't be ridiculous.'

'I like the East coast. Pickering's North East. I'm glad you brought me East again, Hilda. It's better than London.'

'I can't see you in London.'

'I've been down here before you know. V. lived down here for years. Vi and May moved down to join her. They all lived somewhere down here at the end.'

'Are they all dead now, those women?'

'I got out of touch,' said Nell, 'after V. died.'

'Awful snobs. I couldn't bear them,' said Hilda.

'I liked V.,' said Nell and found herself weeping. The tears wetted her round cheeks. She thought of the schoolroom in snow-light, the golden serrip and the Duchess of Kent. 'V. was the last person to write me a letter every week,' said Nell. 'It's a sad thing when there's nobody to write you a weekly letter.'

'Nobody writes me a weekly letter,' said Hilda.

'That's because I live with you. I'd be writing to you if I didn't.'

Hilda remained unmoved by this information.

'I have to think to find people to write to now,' said Nell. 'It's people's children I write to now, and some of them are getting old. I miss V.'

'Was she the one who was always having little rests? Frustrated spinster?' A container truck from Belgium bore down on Hilda's car and tried to fling it into the sea but she stuck to the wheel and held her course, thrusting upward her jaw. 'Those women needed a good analyst. Idle. Depressed. We're almost there. I'm not sure it's not too wet to get out.'

They were visiting Walmer castle where the Duke of Wellington had breathed his last. It was one pound fifty, seventy-five p. for old-age pensioners and open until six o'clock. Both Nell and Hilda were old-age pensioners so that it was a cheap outing, and also there were few steps, which suited Hilda who had a hip. The gloom of the afternoon had turned to the dark of evening for it was after five o'clock. The rain fell.

Hilda let her mother, whose hips were in order, unlatch herself from her seat-belt and watched her walk light-footed to the ticket-office inside the dark stone keep. Then she went to the car-park, for the tickets were to be her mother's treat.

The ticket-collector looked surprised to see Nell. There was no sign of other visitors. 'What weather,' said Nell, but he turned his shoulder from her and went on reading the *East Kent Mercury*. Nell went to wait for Hilda on the half-landing of the shallow staircase between the portraits of Wellington and Napoleon after Waterloo. 'Such a proud nose, Wellington's,' thought Nell. 'So strained you can almost see the bone shining through. It's a bit like Major Dixie's.' She turned to Napoleon who was surveying the world that had bowled him over the cliff. The pale, pale face. The wisps of blown scant hair. The plebeian neck. Too big a hat, like Marina of Kent. The eyes burned with the desolation of the eternal dark. Hilda coming up, dot and carry, said it was an upsetting picture.

They walked along a cold corridor in to the Duke of Wellington's death chamber where the shabby chair he died in stood untouched since he had last sat in it. Near it stood his iron camp-bed with its single dreary blanket. 'It's very austere,' said Nell. 'Of course, that's the Army.' Standing in the greenish shadow of the window alcove was a woman, lean, shoulderless, colourless, in faded clothes. She seemed to be part of the texture of the scoured grey wall behind her. Nell thought, 'It's V. She is not dead,' but as the woman came forward she saw that it was only May.

They stared at each other for a moment and then May said, 'Why, it's little bread and serrip. I thought you were gone long ago Nell.'

They walked together round the Duke's apartments. They examined the furniture that had belonged to an assortment of the great—William Pitt, Lord Byron. 'It's rather damp here,' said Nell. 'It needs some warmth to put the bloom back in it, and a warmed wax polish.'

May said that Queen Victoria and all her children had used the castle for sea-side holidays. 'Just think,' she said, 'all the little crinolines swinging about.' Conversation waned.

'I expect there's central-heating now,' said May. 'In the State apartments. Where the Queen Mother stays. She often comes here you know. But then, she's used to draughts in Scotland.'

'I'm sure they must have done something about a radiator for the Queen Mother,' said Nell.

'Of course the Duke had no need of it,' said May. 'The Army doesn't hear of it.'

'Well, I do,' said Hilda, 'and I think we should be hurrying up.'

The two old women went out by the draw-bridge, Hilda limping behind. 'I'll write,' said Nell. 'It has been wonderful. When did—? Did Vi—?'

'Vi went seven years ago. Two years after V.'

'Time goes,' said Nell. 'I'll write. You have my address? We're in the book.'

'Goodbye,' they all said. 'Goodbye,' and left May in the dark rain looking autocratically about for a taxi.

As Nell had forgotten to ask May for her address, nothing came of this meeting. No telephone call came to the crescent and Nell found that somehow she didn't want to look up May's address. Hilda forgot. In the Spring, though, another outing took place and as Nell and her daughter flew between the tall trees and the sea near St Margaret's Bay Nell said, waking from some dream, 'The Dixies. They used to live here. This is where I stayed with V. and Vi. Oh—in the forties. Oh, I could take you straight to the house.'

'Well, all right. Something to do,' said Hilda swinging seawards, missing a cat. Up and round the sandy curving road they went, past good houses in wide blowy gardens. 'It reminded them all of Brittany,' said Nell. 'One year the Major took them all to Brittany. It was before tourists.' She felt proud to have known people who knew where to go abroad without being told. 'Not many knew Brittany before the War,' she said.

'I suppose the Bretons did,' said Hilda. 'I don't know why you're so in love with those Dixies.'

'Not in love,' said Nell, 'I don't know what it is. Here. Up here,' she said. 'That court-yard.'

And so it was. 'You've still a memory,' said Hilda accusingly. 'But you'd better take a grip I'm afraid, Mother, because you're going to be disappointed. I very much fear,' and she crashed the brakes and hobbled from the car to ring a doorbell with authority. She gazed about her as if the courtyard needed dealing with, which it did not.

The door opened, Nell saw, on pine walls, an Aga cooker, dried herbs in bunches, a wine-rack and a girl who looked fourteen with a baby under her arm and a tail of hair swinging cheerfully about behind her as she turned to look for an address. Music and a smell of garlic and warmth floated out towards Hilda's car.

'Moved,' said Hilda, returning, buckling herself in, 'four months ago. Can't find the forwarding address but it's a nursing-home down the road. She described it. Not far from the castle. D'you want to go and find it?'

Nell, surprised by choice, said yes, she did and looked sideways at Hilda's strong profile, grateful. 'After all, nothing else to do,' said Hilda, 'unless we go back for another look at Wellington's death-chamber. Shouldn't take long.'

But there were several candidates for May Dixie's latest resting place. At least six large, gable-ended houses that could only be nursing-homes flanked the castle and the sea. Hilda disappeared inside the huge unlocked front door of one of them, a grey-green flaking edifice with shutters drawn across many windows and heavy net obscuring others. Nell sat in the car in the silent circular drive. In one window stood three drooping peacock feathers. From another a white monkey-face peeped. Nell looked at the empty flower-beds.

After some time Hilda returned, looking shaken. 'No reply,' she said. 'Nobody there.'

'Nobody?'

'Knocked on five doors. Great big doors. Golf-clubs in the hall—awful, sandy-looking old tiles. Golf-clubs had spiders' webs in them. Everything silent but after you'd knocked it grew more silent. Listened at one door first and there was a medical sort of voice. I knocked and it stopped. You could smell the hypodermics. And that other smell. That rich, geriatric smell.'

'I don't like a poor geriatric smell,' said Nell who had once lately been in a public geriatric ward. 'It doesn't sound like the Dixies. I didn't know you had such a fancy, Hilda.'

'You're never to go to a place like that, Ma, never,' and Nell in sudden joy looked at her with love and said she didn't intend to and thank goodness she had no money. 'I wouldn't mind a nice State home though, where you all sit round nodding off or watch the telly. And you get your meals brought on trays. And all the respectable ones change their characters and start swearing.'

Hilda rolled the usual hostile glance.

'And you all wear old bits, and have nips of sherry.'

'I don't know what you're talking about,' said Hilda. 'God help us all at the end, that's all. All I hope is that I go fast and soon.'

'Oh, not too soon,' said Nell. 'Not too fast.'

'Couldn't be too fast for me,' said Hilda. 'Here, what's this one? This looks more like Dixies.'

A very spruce, large house on a corner, newly-decorated in rich deep cream which showed off the red brick, stood before them. A brass plate announced The Grove and beneath it a brown plate added 'Retirement Home. No tradesmen.' Along all the pretty french windows on the ground floor only the top of one white hospital screen was sinister. Polished fat bulbs were coming up in all the borders and on one of the balconies upstairs, facing the sea, there already stood a summer basket chair. 'I remember that chair,' said Nell.

Hilda marched up the path and a smiling, very clean young man with a gold earring and holding a bright orange duster answered the door. There were two or three moments of intense conversation and Hilda came back and sat firmly and sensibly behind the wheel again. 'Bad news,' she said, 'I'm afraid, Mother. Bad news. She's only just died. About a month ago.'

'So odd,' said Nell. 'Coming to the door with a duster. She wouldn't have liked that.'

'They're very upset,' said Hilda. In her new vulnerability after the cobwebbed golf-clubs, the whispering demon doctors, she looked warily towards her mother to see how she had taken it.

'D'you know, I *thought* she might be dead,' said Nell. 'Somehow I had a feeling. I never really liked May. She had a mean little face when you come to think about it.'

They drove more slowly away. 'She didn't die there,' said Hilda. 'Not at The Grange. They'd had her temporarily moved while they were being re-decorated. They sounded genuinely upset. That man said she was one of the old school. Proud she was going to go through with something. The young man said it had been a big shock to them.'

'Well, it would be,' said Nell. 'Very expensive those places. It must be quite difficult to fill them up. I wonder if she took the old furniture. I expect she left them that chair. I wonder who got the rest? I never really liked May.'

'But a nice young man,' said Hilda and thought, 'There's something queer here: I'm beginning to talk like her and she like me.'

'Diamonds in his ears,' said Nell. 'There's a lot of that about. I'd not have thought May would have cared for it. I wonder why she died.'

'Shock. Heart. Being moved at that time of life. Too old for hotels.'

'I've always had a fancy for hotels,' said Nell. 'I never stayed in one.'

'The Grand Duke,' said Hilda. 'Good Lord—there it is.'

'That!' said Nell. It was a tall slit of a building painted purple with dark red curtains and dirty brass rails across the inside of the windows, which were grimy. A tremendous noise of shouting and bleeping, the booming of fruit-machines and a general din of youth issued from within. A second door stood beside the open door of the pub. Painted beside it with an arrow pointed upwards was the word 'Rooms'. Hilda's car had been halted outside this pub on a roundabout solid with traffic en route eastward for France and westward for the Medway towns. They were greatly intertwined. A frightful place. Nell unclicked her seat-belt and got out.

'What in *hell* are you doing?' said Hilda, reversing.

'Oh, I must just have a—'

'Get back in the car at once.' But behind her the seething lorries bellowed and honked.

'Park, dear, and come back for me,' said Nell and vanished inside the pub where she sat down at an iron table in the corner. It was awash with beer. Her feet did not touch the floor. She swung them.

A man came across to her, very fat. The rolls of fat showed through his tee-shirt like the rolls of a brisket of beef. He wiped the table. He had an old-young baby-face. Pouting, he watched the damp cloth moving. Outside, the traffic made the whole of the Grand Duke vibrate. He had to shout above it and above the clashing of the music.

'It's nearly closing time.'

'I don't really want—' said Nell. 'My friend died here.'

'Not Miss Dixie?' The fat man sat down. 'Oh, my dear! She seemed so comfortable. Such a surprise. It had been her own choice to come you know. You can't blame Gary. Something to do with Wellington. She scarcely spoke. Oh, she was a real old stager. A lady. We took all her meals up.'

'Well, she wasn't really my friend, it was her sister,' said Nell.

'She had a very old-fashioned voice,' said the fat man. 'A pleasure to hear her.'

'It was the Army,' said Nell.

A cheer went up. Somebody had won a fortune. A robot pulsated, spoke from a deep throat. Two young men began to fight on the floor and others to shout and laugh. 'That's the Army, too,' said the fat man. 'The Marines from down the road. When she was here she was on about some Blues and Greys. There's always been soldiers here. But she kept her distance. She'd only known officers. It wasn't what she'd expected.'

'I could live here,' said Nell. 'I could just live here nicely. Could I just get a look at May's room?'

Outside they went and up the steep stairs and inside. The room seemed all to be covered in delicate grey mole-skin. When you touched it, it moved, for it was dust. 'We found her just over there,' said the man. 'All huddled. Right away from the view. One of the few things she said was that at The Grange you had "the Duke's view"—whatever that meant.' He pointed a toe about on the dusty Turkey carpet. On the carpet, some of them stacked up, were a great many little red and gold chairs and a high knobbly bed. There were dried grasses in jars and great windows at each end of the room. The sea boomed. Nell said, 'I could enjoy it here.'

'It's the traffic's the problem,' said the fat man. 'The noise. There's the terrible noise of the roundabout. You can't deny it. Accidents all the time. There's one now. Can you hear it?'

She could and it turned out to have been poor angry Hilda who had gone slap into a tanker and was no more. Nell moved to the pub and became a fixture there in her corner seat, living on for some years. She drank sweet sherry all day long and grew fatter than the landlord, rejoicing in the clamour within and without. The Yorkshire accent was gentle and it flew free. She swung her foot in time to the terrible music.

Sometimes she talked to the soldiers about other soldiers

and old wars and of her husband who had never once mentioned the Somme. They asked her what the Somme was, and she was unsure.

'Who is she?' new recruits would ask. 'Her in the corner?'

'Don't know. She was one of The Dixie Girls or something.'

'What's the Dixie Girls?'

'Don't know. Some old song and dance act. Nobody's ever heard of them.'

GROUNDLINGS

I s she there?'
'Yes, she's there.'
First thing you ever do is look to see if she's there. Bundle
of clothes in the dark, pressed up close beside the ticket-office.
She's always the same, lying prone on a length of black macintosh. Nothing much around her, not even a thermos. Never
like the rest of us with camp-stool, rugs and books. I've never
seen her with a book, not in nearly forty years.

I've known old Aggie Batt in theatre queues all of thirty-five
years, anyway. She looks no different from the 1945 season at
The New. Oh my—Olivier, Gielgud, Guinness! Richardson's
Cyrano! The Old Vic—but it was in St Martin's Lane then. All
London was full of theatres that were still part of war-time,
turned into offices, or shells with the daylight shining through,
or rubble with the daisies growing.

There was good standing-room at St Martin's Lane. For a
shilling you could stand all down the side aisles, leaning your
shoulder against the wall. They didn't let you sit down, even
for *Anthony and Cleopatra* or *Hamlet* in its entirety. 'Eternity'
the actors used to call it, but I don't think we ever did. If you
slid down on your haunches, usherettes came along and hissed
at you to stand up because of fire regulations. Fire in the loins.
And they didn't let you take your shoes off because of being
alongside all the people in the stalls who had paid good money.
I don't know why the stalls didn't complain anyway, all the students in huge hairy duffles standing down the side-aisles three

feet away from them; but they didn't. It was just after the War when there was still good-temper about. Students were ever so quiet then. Shy. You wouldn't believe. Ever so thin and grey-looking. Well, it was all the poor food we'd had wasn't it? Even bread on coupons. But, oh it was a wonderful year that, '45-'46, first term at college for me, all the theatres getting going, all the actors coming back, new plays starting and the great big expensive yelling American musicals. After all the bombed indoor years.

I don't think I was ever so hungry as I was then—much worse than in the war. If you went to an evening performance you missed college-dinner, as well as the last bus, and never a penny over for a sandwich at a Lyons corner house. Two-mile walk back, the last bit through Regent's Park at midnight, but nobody worried. No muggers. We went dreaming home, stage-struck, Shakespeare-struck, *Annie-get-your-Gun*-struck. Slaughtering over. We'd won. First things first now. You should have seen Olivier's Mr. Puff.

Not that she—Aggie Batt, we christened her—ever was to be seen queuing for the American musicals or even for the Sheridan. It was Shakespeare for Aggie Batt, Shakespeare then and Shakespeare now. Shakespeare all the way. There was never a Shakespeare night she wasn't there.

That's to say she was there every night that I and my friends were there, and between us all we didn't miss much. And Aggie B. was always at the head of the queue as she was until this very year.

We laughed at her. She wore a balaclava helmet and men's socks and grey gloves that looked made out of wire, and shiny brown trousers with flies, and a queer jacket, double-breasted. Her face was sharp and disagreeable with a tight little mouth. She had small hard eyes. She looked a bit mad and she hasn't changed. She has grown no madder. She is just the same. A *little* mad. A bit bonkers.

I suppose her face is older now. It must be. It must have more lines on it. It must be more leathery. But I can't say that I can tell. I mean, you don't if it's someone you're used to seeing year in, year out, like family. My own face strikes me as being no different really, until I see the photographs. I went to an old-students' reunion once and it was terrible. Embarrassing. Most of us, if we recognised one another, just yattered on with fixed smiles and slunk off home. But that's by the way.

Aggie Batt is ageless. Ageless as the years roll on and the theatre-queues change and become stream-lined and organised and tickets a matter for scientific pre-plotting. In her way she is a famous figure, a well-known part of the London theatre scene. I mean of course well-known to the groundlings, the queuers, not to the people who only go to the theatre if they can get a good seat. She is there repeatedly, at every production. After a first-night if you don't see her in the queue for the second night you know there must be something very wrong. A performance at the National or the Old Vic or the Barbican will have to be abysmal if she's not present then, and many times more. She is a comfort, Aggie Batt, disdaining time. She is a symbol. She is homage. When we see her we grin. We say, 'There's Aggie' but we are really saying, 'There's one of us, the best of us.' Through Aggie Batt we know our tribe.

I've often tried to speak to Aggie Batt but it's not easy. For all the notice she's taken of me all these years I might be invisible. It's probably because I'm not serious enough. At the beginning, when I was eighteen, I was just one of a gaggle of girls—a first-year student. I'm not that exclusive about Shakespeare you see, and never was. I like to go to everything. As far as I'm concerned it's the only way to keep going, the theatre. Any theatre. I spend a lot of money but I don't have time as my husband says to spend money on much else, and I've got money now, having married it. I'm a very comfortable theatre-goer. I have a fur-lined mac from Harrods and a huge great tartan coat from Aquascutum. I still get my tickets mostly through the theatre-queue though, because (a) you get good seats (b) you get good company and (c) it's home.

More home than home. I don't get the same chance to talk at home. I very much like nattering on. It's a pity that these days the queue has changed a bit. There are a lot of people now not very talkative or who want to sleep. People are tireder nowadays, especially men. Well, I'm nearly sixty now. They don't notice me.

Aggie Batt doesn't sleep much. She lies there on her black macintosh sheet with her eyes open. Whatever I talk about she scarcely blinks.

The first hour of queuing, if it's a popular production— say a Hopkins *Lear* or a new *Hamlet*—Piggot-Smith or Roger Rees—the queue will start to collect while it's still dark. If it's winter it will be still the deep dark. For the first hour's queue-ing she'll be lying back to the road, her face up against the plate-glass (if it's the National) like an Arab in a Gulf airport in a sandstorm. In winter all the lights are out along the river—only the occasional window shining high up in the Shell building and the odd street-lamp on the bridge. As the dawn comes up somebody, somewhere switches on long necklaces of light-bulbs, pink and gold, all along the riverside terraces. They come on as it gets light. An eccentric idea. You'll notice then, suddenly—Aggie Batt moves very qui-etly—that she's sitting with her knees drawn up in front of her, eating biscuits out of a bag and staring straight ahead. She'll get up then and pace about a bit, flexing her fingers in the wire gloves, her nose sticking out sharp from the bala-clava if it's that sort of day. In summer it's a scarf. She'll go off somewhere—I suppose to the Ladies at Waterloo Station— and come back and stand in profile to the river. It's a tense, fierce profile. Richard III. The Scottish King. Nothing very friendly about it. She'll stand maybe half an hour like this.

Then she'll turn toward the bridge and watch The Great Procession.

I've rather stopped watching the Procession now, after so many years. It is the procession of the people of South London that takes place Monday to Friday with as great punctuality as the changing of the guard at Buckingham Palace. It is the procession that floods across Waterloo Bridge from the Station, across the river to work. It is a very fine sight. It is an army of silently tramping, non-conversing, face-forward, jerking, walking, trotting, running ants, heads held tense, hands hard-gripping on cases, umbrellas, newspapers, the coming day. It continues, a steady flow, for the best part of two hours, dwindling off at just after ten o'clock. It is the march of the disciplined, the bread-winners, the money-grubbers, the money-needers, often the dead. Over the Bridge they tramp, south to north, into the stomach of London. They don't look over their shoulder and down or they would see us, their opposites, as in a mediaeval diptych of heaven and hell—or hell and heaven: the motley bundles of the theatre-queuers looking upwards and over at them as we blink with sleep. Us, the pleasure-lovers, the pleasure-seekers, the unrepentant from across the wide world, the creatures of high holiday. Gazing and munching and blinking we sit—big loose Australians, intellectual Indians, serious Americans, antiseptic Japanese and all the mongrel English, including me in fur or plaid, the fastidious Yorkshire lad with the walk-way (another regular) and the lady with the diamond earrings and the New York accent and the Harrods deck-chair, reading a famous critic on The Scottish Play. Once there was even the critic himself. He drove right up beside us in a Rolls-Royce. He got out and locked it—you can park right down on the river-side if it's before eight o'clock in the morning—and joined the queue. He didn't speak (like Aggie Batt) even when I offered him a sandwich. He just smiled politely. He was deep in something to do with a First Folio.

I remember that I wanted to tell someone that there was someone famous and he was reading about First Folios and I went back to my place again—I'd been stretching my legs—near the top of the queue. Then I went actually to the very top of the queue and I said to Aggie Batt, 'Look who's there. He's reading about First Folios,' and—it's one of the very few times in all these years I've heard her speak—she said, 'Very fragmented.'

What can you say to that? Did she mean that the FF (it was *Ant. and Cle.*) was very fragmented? Did she mean that this critic was very fragmented? Or what I said was not cogent? That's what the remark used to be at the end of many of my Shakespeare essays—'Not cogent.' Maybe she did think that the play was very fragmented—I know I do. I've often thought you could cut a lot of those little bitty scenes at the end. Everyone—actors, audience—are too tired for them by then. Everybody knows, even if they haven't read the play they know, that everyone's having to reserve strength for the death scenes, especially Anthony. Cleopatra—well, after the asp it's all quite quiet for her. She just has to sit dead and be carried out. The asp must be rather a relief. I'd forgotten all the notes I had on it once but I think they were on this Aggie Batt line of argument, and I was grateful to her, for when I'd bought my ticket at ten o'clock—I always stand to one side while I check my seat-number and so on, even if the rest of the queue behind me has to step over my blankets—the great man looked at me, and I was able to say, 'I see you are reading from the First Folio, Sir. It's very fragmented isn't it?' He seemed to be quite surprised.

You'll probably have seen Aggie Batt in the audience many a time. She doesn't look at all as she does in the queue in the morning. Oh dear me no. She wears a black dress up to the neck, long in the arms, and her hair that is invisible under the balaclava turns out to be long and fine. From the morning appearance you'd expect what used to be called The Eton Crop—very mannish and coarse, like metal, the kind that ought to clatter when you run your hand through it. Julius Caesar hair. Nothing of the sort. It is light and downy and thin so that you can almost see the scalp through and it's not so much white as the colour of light, though I'm not putting this very well.

Oh and dear me, she is thin. Through the black dress you can see her old shoulder-blades sticking out at the back and her collar-bones at the front. She has a long shawl affair that floats about—ancient—and when she lets it go loose you can see her hip bones and her stomach a hollow below them. She could be Pavlova in extremis except for oh dear, her legs! Her legs are old bits of twig. She wears very old, cracked, shoes with broad black ribbons tied in bows, stockings with ladders, and often a pair of socks.

She's nearly always in the same seat—G25. You've seen her. Every time you've been to a London Shakespeare. You've sat next to her perhaps. It's an old joke in the queue, G25: someone saying that they'll get to the queue twenty-four hours early so they can get G25 to see what she'd do without it: see if she'd drop dead. I didn't think anything of him for saying it.

She never buys a programme, that's another thing. She doesn't seem to need one. There's a number of people don't, of course. I remember when I was young I didn't. It was a snob thing. I used to take the text instead, and a torch, and follow with my finger. It was very helpful for exams, though if there was a row of us doing it people round about got tetchy. We were like glow-worms. In those days I didn't need a pro-gramme anyway because I knew who everyone was and which was playing what. I know most of them now, but not like Aggie Batt, who I suppose breathes them all in by osmosis. As I say, she never has a book with her, she's not one for a text. It's the performance for her. It's him. Himself. William the Man she comes for. The play she wants. The living thing in action. That's what the walk-way boy says. He seldom speaks either, but he sits near her often and seems to have picked things up from her.

He says she lives in North London behind Kings Cross and walks everywhere. She even walks there and back to the Barbican—five miles each way. She walks there and back in the morning for the ticket and there and back in the evening for the performance. Isn't she afraid of walking about the empty Kings Cross streets so late at night? No. She carries in her purse the exact money for her ticket plus thirty-five p. for a cup of tea; and her pension book.

But she can't be utterly poor. Walk-way boy says she's travelled. Seen *Hamlet* in Denmark. Been to Shakespeare Festivals in Berlin. I asked her what she thought of Berlin and it was one of her answering days and she said, 'Professors of Shakespeare look like steel rats.' One day I bought her a pie. She seemed pleased. It was just a pie from the stall under the station arches but she ate it with hunger and nodded at me and even answered the question I asked her while I was gathering up her rubbish. This I have to keep doing for she surrounds herself with quite a lot of it. I asked her who was her favourite character in Shakespeare and she said Enobarbus. I asked her which was her favourite play and she said '*The Winter's Tale*, but it's getting late for it now.'

I've seen her in a *Winter's Tale* queue several times so I didn't know what she meant. I thought that maybe her memory was slipping and she was forgetting what she had seen. Not that that has ever seemed to me such a great deprivation. If you lose your memory you can experience things again as if they were new, like when you were young.

Well no. Never really like that.

Next *Winter's Tale* I told myself I'd take her a bunch of flowers. I don't suppose anyone ever gave Aggie Batt flowers. Years and years ago there was a young man used to be in the queue. Oh, he was about nineteen I'd think and she must then have been nearly forty. They used to go off together after an hour or two's queueing, leaving the black mac. They used to sit side by side on the black mac. He I remember used to leave a pair of yellow leather gloves on it to keep their places. He had that ripply, goldielocks hair you see sometimes on young men and a very soft mouth and gently moving hips. You didn't comment in those days but you sniggered. Somehow though I never sniggered.

He stopped being around after a while. One of the sniggerers heard he'd run off to be a ballet-dancer. Aggie Batt looked madder then, her face more severe. She began to carry a walking-stick and twirl it about. After I was married, my husband sometimes came to join the theatre queue with me—just at first. One day we arrived very early and we saw the poor old bundle, with the walking stick alongside, on the black mac. 'Good God, what's that? Who's that poor old man?'

'Sssh, it's Aggie Batt.'

He looked down the queue and said, 'Looks like a string of winos, but my word! The one at the top!'

My husband's full of quips. Once when I was late home from a seven-hour stint of the *Henrys* he'd put my mail out on the hall-stand re-directed, 'Not known at this address. Try The National Theatre.' But he wouldn't be bothered with jokes about Aggie Batt.

And why am I writing all this? What is so special about her? After all, she's dead now. The London theatre is going along perfectly well without her. There has been no obituary and she won't ever be mentioned in any memoir. She's not as far as I know ever been referred to in a theatre column or theatre magazine or been interviewed on television. I don't think she ever heard of television. What was she? An interesting psychiatric subject for discussion: a woman with a Shakespeare fixation. That is all.

Well, it is not all. I am writing down all that I know now about her because it is not all, and because of the wonderful thing that happened the day she died, and if you don't believe a word of it, what do I care? Shakespeare's plots were unbelievable. Larger than life. When people say to me, 'Oh, I say—another story larger than life', I say to myself, think of Shakespeare. Think for example of the story of *The Winter's Tale*, and I say, 'Things may be larger than your life but they are not larger than mine.'

Well, it was to be the first night of what promised to be a marvellous *Winter's Tale*. The preview notices had been nonpareils. The agency tickets had been sold out weeks before. We had read already in all the papers of the wonderful, ice-bound Act One and the blooming and blossoming dizzy Spring in store for us in Act Two: the songs and the sheep-shearing, the frolic, then the regeneration, the triumph over wickedness and death at the end. Huge portraits of the players were plastered against the glass sides of the National: pictures of yokels and bears, statues and queens and sages, and Perdita and her princeling—the hopes of the world.

I decided that to be sure of a seat I must leave home about 5:30 A.M. and drive to London in the car. I didn't tell anyone at home that I was going so early because there's opposition nowadays on account of my leg and the time I didn't see the Sutton roundabout.

I crept out of the house and it was already light—a warm, Spring morning. All the birds of Tadworth making a racket like Illyria. I stood for a moment thinking how much I love Tadworth. All the birds, and so easy for the theatre. I thought how much more musical suburban birds are than country ones and wondered what the Southwark birds had been like in Shakespeare's time. Thinking of Shakespeare and *Winter's Tale* I went round to our garden at the back to pick Aggie some flowers. There were some lovely primroses and still some nice daffs, though some had gone a bit brown-papery, a few primulas and six little irises. We've a nice garden. I put them in a plastic bag with a bit of blue rue we have by the gate and stowed them in the glove compartment and roared off down the drive trying not to look in case any angry heads were sticking out of bedroom windows. My daughter is a light sleeper and not just now my friend. I imagined her furious face. 'For goodness *sake*! Adolescent! Immature! Sitting with students!' and so on. My daughter is in Management Consultancy although I called her Cordelia. She doesn't understand.

It was difficult parking the car that morning. Someone had forgotten to take the chain down from across the theatre forecourt and I had to go half-way to Southwark to the carpark where you take a ticket from a sleepy man in a box and the surface is like craters of the moon. It can't have been worse in Shakespeare's time. Great puddles. I set off walking back. Ten minutes.

That can make all the difference from being number twenty and number thirty in the queue. Each person in the queue for tickets sold on day of performance is allowed two tickets. There are only forty tickets altogether unless there are returns, and there are unlikely to be returns for a First Night, so ten minutes can mean defeat.

So I went pounding along to the National, past the head of the queue where of course lay Aggie Batt, fast asleep, and for some reason feet foremost today, lying at right-angles to the glass wall, her head below the enormous chin of Edward Woodward picked out in purple. Even she wasn't first in the queue for this performance. There was a man ahead of her leaning against the glass, reading, and then the Yorkshire walkway boy sitting cross-legged, staring ahead, numbed by the secret music under the ear-muffs. 'Late,' I called out, but neither the man nor the boy nor Aggie Batt made any sign. I went to the end of the line and dumped my cushion and blankets and stood out from the wall—we all sit under a wide cement awning which shields us from the rain—very different from the

old days, humped in raincoats under umbrellas on little battered stools. I counted back and I was number 45. So I wasn't
going to be lucky.

However, you never know. Miracles sometimes happen and
other hopefuls were still gathering up behind me, thinking
likewise. I wrapped myself up and watched the Bridge. I slept
a bit I think because it suddenly seemed much lighter and the
people round about were beginning to eat things. I drank some
coffee from my thermos and wished I'd brought a book. There
were huge Germans on either side of me, fast asleep. Nobody
to talk to.

Soon the day-light began to wane again as clouds came over
and rain began. Never say die, I thought and felt in my pockets for chocolate—then remembered the flowers I'd left
behind in the glove-compartment, way down Pickle-Herring
Street. I felt tired and my leg was jumping.

However—I put my thermos on the cushion to keep my
place and set off back past the head of the queue. Aggie Batt
had not stirred, neither had the leaning man (what strength of
shin!) nor the walk-way boy. 'Just going to the car,' I called, but
I'm like scenery. They didn't speak.

When I came back again with the flowers in the plastic bag
I had an idea. I have *never* had this idea before. I have never
asked, for it is not done—to ask someone buying only one
ticket near the top of the queue if they'll buy their allowance of
two and sell one back to you. The walk-way never buys more
than a single ticket and neither of course does Aggie Batt, but
asking her would be out of the question. It would mean sitting
next to her through the play and chatting, which I knew she
would never countenance. It would be like asking a nun to
share her hassock or a fakir to shift over on his mat.

'S'okay,' said the walk-way boy, lifting off a muff an inch.
Little tinny sounds came out, like distant revels. He let it
spring back in place and I sat beside him and took out my

purse and counted the money. I felt dreadful, breaking the rules, and I said to the standing man, 'I know him. He's a very—old friend. I've never done this before.' I looked at Aggie but she was still asleep. Sleeping late. Peaceful. I took the flowers from the bag, bound them round with the elastic band from my sandwiches and the boy and the man watched.

I laid the flowers on Aggie Batt's chest for her to find when she woke. The boy paid no attention now but the man continued to watch. 'It's because it's *Winter's Tale*,' I said. 'It's her favourite.' Although he did not speak I knew that he found what I had done acceptable. I also knew that I need say no more and I went back to my place.

I am a garrulous woman. I suppose by now that's clear. I cannot help it. It is because I am not confident. I am not even confident about Shakespeare. I only got a Lower Second. I try to justify myself too much. I try to explain my hungry need for Shakespeare by trying to be learned about him—catching on to other people's stuff about First Folios and textuality and fragmentation and things not being cogent rather than just saying that when I am watching Shakespeare I am happier than at any other time. I knew as I sat down at the end of the queue again that I had no need to justify myself to that man and I felt young again. I felt rather as I had done long ago, when I was eighteen standing in the aisle at the New Theatre, famished, light-headed, looking forward. It was like falling in love.

Soon the necklaces of lights came on and the rain stopped, leaving big pools about on the concrete. A warm, quite summery breeze blew over us and I may have dropped off because all at once I noticed the welcome 9:45 A.M. signs of life inside the National's glass wall. The counter of the ticket-office was being dusted and a Hoover was being wheeled away, lights switched on.

There is a moment in the theatre queue and it is 9:59 A.M. With one accord, like the audience at Messiah with the lift of the baton for the Hallelujah Chorus, everyone rises to his feet. Everyone does a shuffling left turn and stands waiting. Hardly a sound. Then the man inside looks at his watch, comes out from his lair, undoes the bolts and opens the glass doors, and without pause the whole queue begins to flow forward, each person holding six or twelve pounds or a cheque-book like a talisman. The queue marches through and the whole thing is over in less than a quarter of an hour.

But not this morning, for when I reached the head of the queue, Aggie Batt had not got up. She lay there with her nose as sharp as a pen and the flowers on her chest.

The queue passed round her of course. As was right. I stayed with her, waiting for the walk-way boy to come with our tickets and when he did, he knelt down by her and took off his ear-muffs and began to undo her jacket and scarves. The leaning man who'd been ahead of her had disappeared—he wasn't a regular. He'd probably hardly noticed her, deep in his book. The last tail-end of the queue reluctantly stepped round her. A few stood lingering about in the forecourt, looking towards us, before going away.

I told the boy to find someone quick, to get an ambulance, but he said, 'No hurry. She's dead,' and I felt her face and it was ice-cold. 'She's been dead for hours,' he said. 'I know. I'm a hospital porter,' and he went inside, slowly, to find a telephone. 'You'd think that man would have noticed,' I said, 'standing beside her all this time. He was ahead of her. He must have been there when she arrived.' 'What man?' said the boy. 'There wasn't any man. She was head of the queue.'

When the ambulance had taken away what remained of Aggie Batt, and the walk-way boy gone off to get us some coffee, I put my ticket in my purse and went over towards the river. I watched the great procession streaming over the Bridge, swirling along like the water below. The people of Shakespeare's parish.

GRACE

Clockie Gosport had this great diamond in the back of his neck. Under the skin. At the top of the spine. In among all the wires that keep the show on the road. Just on the bone they break when they hang you. Clockie Gosport.

He was never a one to mention the diamond. Never. Very quiet and modest. A thoughtful man, born over Teesport in a street right on to the pavement, no back door or yard or running water or electric. And clean! Every part of it, including the old man, old Gosport, Clockie's father, who was made to strip in the passage every night home from the Works and bathe in the tin behind the screen.

She was a silent woman, Ma Gosport. She held the world together, packing in the lodgers head to tail in the upstairs double, the family all crammed about. She took in both day- and night-shift men, and every hour God gave she was washing and possing and mangling and hanging out bits of sheets. She hung them out courtesy of Mrs. Middleditch and the hook in her wall across the way. All was hygiene.

And this story went around. 'Clockie Gosport got a diamond in his neck.'

'Is it true you got a diamond in yer neck, Clockie?' (He was Clockie because way back someone had said: 'Like a watch. Watches has bits of diamond in them.')

Clockie always smiled. 'Now how could I have a diamond in me neck? They'd have me head off.'

That was as a grown man. At school he'd said nothing, just stared. He had these poppy eyes. The other kids said it was the diamond pushing them forwards. 'Gis yer diamond, Clockie. Come on, yer booger, gis yer diamond.' They would grab at him and Ma Gosport or the school teacher would wade in and cuff them all about.

Nobody cuffed Clockie, though. It was tradition. When Clockie had been five or six he'd been cuffed about at home for screaming and it was found to be the meningitis. There'd been silence all down Dunedin Street that night and folks coming and sitting quiet on the step and Old Gosport weeping. And Ma Gosport had been slapping and bashing the sheets in the back and then getting into her things for the walk to the Infirmary. Mrs. Armitage and Mrs. Middleditch had gone with her, the one excited, the other grim. They'd gone in order to support Ma Gosport back after the news, and Ma Gosport had stuck out her chin and never spoke once on the road, the three of them walking abreast in their hats and coats. She gave the women presents later. Mrs. Middleditch she gave a jet brooch of her grandmother's and Mrs. Armitage she gave a steak pie.

For Clockie had recovered and, before Ma Gosport left the Infirmary, the doctor had called her in—'No, just the mother, please'—and had put his arm round her.

'Mrs. Gosport, your boy will get better and he's a lucky lad. We're very interested, though, in the foreign body lodged in the neck.'

'It's a diamond,' said Ma Gosport.

The doctor brooded. 'What exactly do you *mean* by a diamond, Mrs. Gosport?'

'I don't know. It just happens sometimes in the family. There comes a bairn with the diamond. It means luck.'

'Have ...' the doctor covered his face with his hands and swirled them about, 'has anybody ever seen it?'

'No. Well, it's under the skin, isn't it?'

'We ought to examine it, you know. It is most fascinating.'

So she let them, but it was long ago before the war when X-rays were feeble, and what with air raids coming and hospitals so busy, Clockie's diamond went out of folks' minds.

Clockie was a poor scholar and slow talking. He never read. He grew very good-looking. Beautiful, really. He began work at the new chemical plant after the war, sweeping a road a mile long. He brushed with men to either side of him, a thin grey line, and every now and then a machine came along that gobbled up the dirt. Then the men stopped, drew on a fag, slung it away, lined up again, swept on. At the end of the mile they knocked off for a can of tea and walked back and started again. It didn't worry Clockie. It was regular work and you could listen. It was surprising what you heard.

''Ere, Clockie,' they said on wet days, 'how 'bout releasing this diamond and we all get off to Paris?'

They'd glance at the back of his neck now and then, but it was always covered by the sweat-rag his mother gave him, boiled clean, each morning. They'd not have thought of touching it.

When he got a girl, though, she wanted to touch it, of course she did. She was Betty Liverton, dumpy little thing, all charm.

'Welsh,' said his mother. 'Not to be trusted.' Betty had her hands round his neck second time out.

Clockie wasn't sweeping any more. He'd graduated first to the suction machine and found affinity with all forms of mechanical life. Now he was the feller with the screwdriver round the ethylene plant and everybody shouting for him.

He'd moved up to the mechanics' canteen, where Betty Liverton washed the mugs. Short little legs, lovely chest, freckles, soft eyes—she watched him with his curly hair. Big feller, Clockie.

Then down Ormesby Lane, by the bit of wood and stream that's not overlooked, they lay down beside the kingcups and put their hands on each other and she screamed.

'What is't?' He was undoing her dress.

'Stop it. Dear Lord, it's true!'

'What's true?' His blue pop-eyes were shining. He wasn't laying off for long.

'It's true. In the back of yer neck. The diamond.'

He pushed her down. (And him thought slow!)

'Get off. I want to see. It's right on the surface. I could bite it out.'

'Does it bother you, then?' He took both her wrists in one hand and held them in the grass above her head. She was amazed.

'It doesn't bother me. I just never could believe it.'

She forgot the diamond. All she could think of that night in her bed as she played back her deflowering beside Ormesby Beck was that it couldn't have been his first time.

'Was it yer first time?' she asked when they were married.

'It come natural,' said Clockie.

She became the envy of the street with her sleepy honeymoon looks.

They got a couple of rooms up the road and Ma Gosport made the best of it, taking in another lodger and then another when Old Gosport went at last, spotless, to his coffin. She never liked Betty Liverton.

Clockie stayed tranquil, so tranquil that it was a puzzle to some that after the first days of marriage were over and Betty grown brisk there were so quickly two girls and a boy, all the image of their father. It was only image, though. There was not his temperament, not the peace of him. They grew up to be rubbish.

'Well, their mother's rubbish, isn't she?' said Ma Gosport. 'She got tired of him. There wasn't a thought between them.'

Clockie grew quieter still after the kids were flown and

Betty went off with Alan Middleditch. 'That's Wales for you,' said Ma Gosport just before she died.

And Betty drank port-and-lemons down the golf club and was always well away by eight o'clock, talking of her husband who thought he had a diamond in his neck.

Clockie used to walk the beaches of the estuary in time, among the sharp sand-grasses and the grey flowers. He met folks there. Once he met a daft fairground girl, white-headed. He was an old man now and they lay quiet in the sand dunes. The girl lay beside him like a pearly fish.

She said: 'You've got this thing in the back of your neck. It'll be a diamond.'

'Have you heard tell of this, then?'

'Oh, aye,' she said, 'long since. There's them with the diamond.'

'Where you from, girl? Which country?'

But she didn't seem to know.

He fettled for himself at home till his hip went and he had it done and a date fixed for the other one, but by then he was failing. He was no great age, but old for a man of his history always living in the reek of the Works. The road he'd swept was a bit of a motorway now, the chimneys all plumed with gases. In hospital he grew poorly and they sent for his children and a son came he'd not seen for years bringing a little one with him called Meg, golden-haired. Before they left, Clockie put out a calloused old hand and touched her hair. He put his hand under the hair and at the back of the neck he felt the diamond. They looked at one another.

The doctors had wanted him to have the foreign body removed on the occasion of the first operation and they were still on about it now. 'It can't be doing you any good, Grandad. Is it First War shrapnel? You're a lucky old devil.'

'I wasn't born First War,' said Clockie. 'It's said to be a diamond.'

Well, they were full of it. Clockie lay thinking of Meg.

''Ere,' he said late one night, 'nurse. Tell them O.K. I'll have it done. They can take out the diamond when I'm under the knife for the hip. They tell me it's but a matter of lifting it off. Now then, if it does turn out to be a diamond, it's to be for Meg. She'll not need it, she's got her own. But you're to tell her I said.'

The surgeons laughed their heads off. One said he'd once had a patient with a tin of Harpic stuck up his bum. They put off the hip for a week, until the big man could come down from Newcastle.

'Let's have another look at the little lass,' said Clockie, and when she was brought he sent her father out and said: 'Meg, you and I are old friends. What's this behind the curtains?'

And she said: 'It's a diamond.'

'That's right,' said Clockie. 'You'll be grand. You'll always be grand, girl. You and me, Meg, we know the ropes of living and dying. We're safe, girl.'

The next day they did the hip successfully and nipped out the diamond from the back of the neck and they killed him of course.

The thing rattled into the kidney-dish, a vast great lump of glass. They all went mad. One doctor who was South African said he'd seen many an uncut diamond but never one as fine as this. The great man said: 'You know, this could be a diamond.'

Then Clockie began to die and it was all hands to the pump, and in the midst of the red alerts going off, and Clockie going out, a soft young nurse (she was an Armitage) cleared away the kidney-dish and washed the diamond down the sluice. It was a wide-lipped sluice without a grille and so the diamond was taken straight down into the Middlesbrough sewers and then far away out into the North Sea, where it is likely to be washing around for ever.

When she was told of her grandfather's death, Meg put her

face in the back of his chair to savour the nice salt smell of him. She put her thumb in her mouth, and the other hand she wound round to the back of her neck to make sure of the diamond.

MISS MISTLETOE

D aisy Flagg was a parasite. Nothing wrong with that. Hers is a useful and ancient profession. In Classical times every decent citizen had a parasite. There were triclinia full of them. They flourished throughout Europe in the Middle Ages, though later demoted in England to the status of mere court jesters—demoted because your pure parasite does not have to sing for his supper. Not a bar. Not a note. His function is to sit there smiling below the salt cellar; not ostentatiously below it, but as *ami de maison.*

Now and then the parasite was noticed by those upstream above the salt, among the silver platters. Sometimes he was taunted and had to pretend to enjoy it. There was a Roman parasite who was teased by his host that he had only been invited because the host was having his way with the parasite's wife, and Ha! ha! ha! the parasite had to reply.

Professional parasites turn up even today in Italy—at country weddings, sloping around at the back of the chairs, jollying people along at the wine-feast, nobody knowing who they are. The host sees they get their dinner.

Oh, the parasite was always a self-respecting fellow in his chosen profession. He knew he was easing the host's passage through this world and into the next. He was Lazarus raised up from the city gate. He was the rich man's ticket to heaven.

And there's something of him left still, especially at Christmastime, in England. We've all met him: the friend who's always at the Honeses', the Dishforths', the Hookaneyes'; who provides none of the spread, is no relation, doesn't do a hand's turn, seems to have little rapport with the rest of the company and is not particularly inspiring. Dear Arthur. Jim's friend Alan Something. Dorothy-she-was-something-to-do-with-your-grandmother. Mr. Jackson (Beatrix Potter knew all about Mr. Jackson). And it is excellent for all, because the host of any one of these people can say, 'And there'll be Mr. Jackson of course as usual, God help us. But it *is* Christmas,' and Mr. Jackson can say when the drunken invitation is at last extended at the office party on Christmas Eve, 'Oh, thanks, but at Christmas I always go to the Infills.'

And so it was with Daisy Flagg, the Christmas parasite known to the Infills behind her back as Miss Mistletoe. For years and years she had come to the Infills for Christmas, always arriving late following extensive devotions in her parish church some hundred miles away. She drew up in her ancient and decrepit car (which she maintained and serviced, patched and painted herself), its windscreen hazy, its tyres criminally worn, its back seat of rubbed-away, hollowed-out leather laden with awful presents. 'Sorry I'm late,' she would cry, springing through the back door into the kitchens, leaving the car in the middle of the frosty drive below the Renaissance urns on the terrace, all the eighteenth-century windows glittering in disdain. 'Happy Christmas, happy Christmas, all. *Terribly* sorry.' She would enter by the kitchens as a privileged member of the family, a family that now cooked its own Christmas dinner rather better, if more chaotically, than when there were cooks, and who because of the presence of Daisy Flagg/Miss Mistletoe behaved rather less badly among the bread sauce and the prune stuffing and the whirling machinery that resulted in the brandy butter than they otherwise would have done.

Daisy Flagg/Miss Mistletoe sat to table with her face in its permanent rictus grin, giving the impression of a delighted grasshopper in a paper hat. She was flat as a child, sideways almost invisible, transparent as a pressed flower. She was very clean. Her clothes seemed to have been boiled, her hair almost shampooed away. Her nails were scrubbed seashells. ('Some sort of guilt there,' said Laetitia the year she was doing Psychology.) Her shoes came from the jumble sales of her spiky church. They were often the old dancing slippers of dowagers, and once were gigantic Doc Martens found in a paper bag on the pavement in Victoria Street. Miss Mistletoe, who was very poor, had of course taken these straight to the police station. To the very top police station, Scotland Yard, just across the road. They had told her there that lost shoes were not their speciality and if they were her they'd keep them.

Miss Mistletoe wore miniskirts. Always. She must have acquired a great number of them some hot summer in the Beatles' time, for they were all very flimsy and her knees seemed to knock together beneath them in the icy wastes of Infill Hall. Her hair was always done for Christmas in a Cilla Black beehive *circa* 1975. It made her look steady and con-trolled; the permanent spinster, if the word still exists.

She ate voraciously, keeping the conversation flowing, trooping with the rest out of the dining room to listen to the Queen. She ignored the children. She didn't like children. And she never walked the dogs in the park. Long ago she had been dissuaded from helping with the washing-up, for she tended to hop and giggle and drop the Infill Spode on the flagstones. 'Just sit and be comfortable,' they said, and disappeared with the retrievers into spinneys and woodlands and to trudge round the ornamental lake in the park.

Like a little bundle of sticks sat Miss Mistletoe beside the fire in the hall, across from vast old Archie, bibulous and asleep. She kept up her merry patter—the weather, her car, her journey, the Royal Family (not the scandals), *The Archers*, any-thing. When it was teatime she stayed on. Drinks time, she stayed on. Supper, she stayed on. A sort of pallet had always been laid out for her in a remote bedroom once occupied by a Victorian tubercular tweeny who was said to haunt it, though Miss Mistletoe never complained. Grey blankets and a towel were laid across this bed and these were always left so perfectly folded the next day that everyone wondered if Miss Mistletoe had slept in the bed at all. On Christmas night about midnight someone would say, the brandy flowing pretty free by now, though Miss Mistletoe never touched a drop of it, nor any alcohol ever: 'Come on, Daisy; you'd better stay the night.' 'Would that be all right?' was the awaited reply. 'It's *terribly* kind of you.' And she grinned and grinned.

The joke for Boxing Day was how to get rid of her. You couldn't say that everyone was going hunting because nobody did now. The horses were gone and the stables rented out as craft shops and mushroom beds. Laetitia still attended the meet in the village, but in her Lagonda because she was now a hunt saboteur. Nor could you say that everyone was going to the panto in Salisbury, because Miss Mistletoe's face seemed to say to them: Why didn't you get a ticket for me?

Usually they eased her out about noon with the second turkey leg and a wedge of the pudding and a tin of Boots' Lavender talcum powder which had always been her Christmas present. After waving her off they went back into the house and gathered up the presents she had given them and put them with the stuff for the NSPCC summer fair. They shrieked and groaned about Miss Mistletoe for the rest of the day.

Over the years some Infills died and some new ones were born but the numbers for the table at Christmas stayed more or less steady between fourteen and twenty. The year old Archie died, however, spread out peacefully beside the log fire one November morning early (though they didn't realise it till after *Newsnight*), the numbers had dropped. There would be only twelve, with Miss Mistletoe making the dreaded number of thirteen, and the oft-raised but never seriously considered question began to be asked outright: Do we have to have her?

'We could ask someone else and make it fourteen.'

'Who?'

Nobody could think. 'Well, we can't sit down thirteen. I'm not superstitious but, I mean, Christmas is a religious do. That's when thirteen started.'

'It didn't,' said Laetitia, who was at present concerned with Theology.

'We could say we were all going away.'

'She knows we never go away.'

'Well, we might. We could say we are all going skiing.'

'Don't be silly. Letty and Hubert are over ninety.'

'We could say we're all going on a cruise.'

So they said they were all going on a cruise and they sent Daisy Flagg a fat cheque (ten pounds) and loving messages saying they knew that she would have much more exciting places to go than Infill Hall. Daisy Flagg wrote back on her lined paper in her schoolgirl hand to say it was quite all right, perfectly all right, and she'd be going to a friend in Potter's Bar.

Sighs of relief.

'She's such a *bore*,' they said. 'How many years have we had her? Twenty?'

'Oh no. Not twenty. It feels like twenty. Maybe ten.'

'How old is Daisy Flagg?' someone asked as the turkey was rather wearily dismembered, paper hats lying about the table and not on anybody's head. 'Forty? Fifty?'

'Could be any age. Could be only thirty-five. She was just a little girl in a first job when Mamma found her, wasn't she? Glove counter in the Army & Navy. Took a fancy to her. Isn't she still there?'

'No idea. I always thought she was something to do with Nannie.'

'Well, we needn't escape all afternoon anyway. Ghastly cold out there.' And they sat about indoors for hours, missing the Queen.

'We can hear her later,' said Jocelyn.

'If we must,' said Laetitia.

Somehow they didn't.

The evening hung heavy. Children fought over videos. Nobody would sit in Archie's splayed chair. The dogs lay around making smells because nobody would take them out. Nobody could face the second turkey leg. 'Next year,' said someone, 'better have the little creature back, don't you think?'

When, the following October, Laetitia decided to go and work for Mother Theresa in Calcutta (calling in at Rome on the way for a new handbag), the numbers came right again and the invitation was issued. Lady Infill surprised herself by saying, 'We missed you last year. You must tell us *all* you have been up to since.'

There was a little pause before the reply came, but it was an acceptance. Daisy Flagg said that she had missed them, too, and would be arriving as usual after attending the early cele-bration of Holy Communion. It was to be hoped, she added, as usual, that there would be no inclement weather for her hundred-mile drive.

And then, over the answerphone on Christmas morning— bleary-eyed Gervais pressing the button as he stood, yawning, over the kettle for the early-morning tea—came Daisy's voice saying she hoped it would be all right but she was bringing someone with her.

'Of course it's not all right,' screamed Lady Infill. 'Call her back immediately.'

'She's at church. The Early Celebration.'

'I don't care what celebration. She can't just land here with someone. We'll be thirteen again.'

'Maybe we could get in the vicar.'

'We don't know a vicar.'

'Maybe,' said Auntie Pansy hopefully, 'I could go to my London club?'

They quarrelled their way through breakfast, through the stuffing of the turkey, through the creation of gravies and bacon rolls, through the endless trimming and cleansing of sprouts. They sulked and fumed and drank a lot of wine and began to say that Daisy Flagg was a pain, always had been a pain, always would be, and why had they got her? They'd had the chance to be shot of her. They'd let it go. Who was she anyway? Nobody had ever known. It was all their mother's fault. Playing the eccentric *grande dame*. Years out of date. Egalitarian rubbish.

'Well we all know who your mother was,' said Sukey. 'Nobody.'

They sat at the table in disarray.

Turkey over, there was still no Daisy.

'Maybe she's had a crash on the motorway at last,' said someone.

But it was after half-past two by this time and nobody quite dared to say, 'Let's hope,' for they were now disquieted.

'She'll swan in with the nuts,' said someone else. 'You'll see. She's probably bringing a man. She's probably married.'

But she wasn't married. Daisy Flagg the parasite never married.

Miss Mistletoe *married*? Ridiculous!

Towards the end of the orange and lemon sugar slices and the coffee, the limp wagging of the crackers, came the sound of the motor car upon the dying winter afternoon. It came into view, spluttering and clanking, between the stark branches of the avenue and jerked to a halt below the terrace.

And out of it sprang a shining-faced and stocky Daisy Flagg with a three-month-old baby in her arms, and she took her place at table and put this baby on her knee.

'So *terribly* late,' she said. 'Such *terrible* trouble with sparking plugs,' and she grinned. 'She's *terribly* hungry. D'you mind if I do this at table?'

And Miss Mistletoe upped with her smock and her T-shirt to reveal amazing bounty beneath.

TELEGONY

I: GOING INTO A DARK HOUSE

Molly Fielding's mother had been a terrible woman born about the same time as Tennyson's Maud and as unapproachable.

Nobody knew anything much about her, Molly herself being now very ancient. Molly had been my grandmother's friend and my mother's, before she was mine, but with the demise of each generation she seemed to grow younger and freer—to take strength. Her hair, her clothes, her house, all were up to the minute. So were her investments; and her foreign holidays became farther and farther flung.

I had found the photograph of her mother before my own mother died. It was a coffee-coloured thing mounted on thick, fluffy, cream paper, unframed in a drawer, with the photographer's name in beautiful copperplate across the corner: 'Settimo'.

I could not believe it. Signor Settimo! He had taken my own photograph when I was a child. I remembered a delicious little man like a chocolate, with black hair and eyes and Hitler's square moustache. My Settimo must have been the son—or even grandson—of course. Molly Fielding's mother must have known the first. Probably the first Settimo had come over from Italy with the ice-cream makers and organ grinders of the *fin de siècle*. It was a long-established firm when I knew it and a photographer in the English Midlands with a glamorous, lucky name such as *Settimo* would be almost home and dry. All he'd need would be flair and a camera and a book of instructions—a match for anyone.

But not for Molly Fielding's mother. Oh, dear me no. There she sits, her strong jaw raised, its tip pointing straight at the lens. Very watchful. She is examining the long hump of Mr. Settimo beneath the black cloth behind the tripod. Her eyes— small eyes—are saying, 'Try—but you'll not take me. *I* take.'

Her great face, like his small one, is covered in black cloth. Hers is covered by a fine veil of silk netting, tied tight round the back of her neck by a broad black velvet ribbon. It is stitched at the top round the hat brim—a tight hat, expensive and showy, glittering with jet beads like the head of a snake. Her own head is proudly up, her eyes are very cunning. Oho, how she despises Mr. Settimo, the tradesman. She is smiling a most self-satisfied smile. She is armed with a cuirass of necklaces across her beaded front, a palisade of brooches, great gauntlets of rings. She is fair-skinned beneath the veil. She must have been a pretty young girl, and her mouth, above the chin grown fierce, is still small and curly and sexy. No lady. Like somebody's cook but in the way that duchesses can look like somebody's cook. Not born rich, you can see—but now she is rich. At this moment, seated before foreign little Mr. Settimo, she is rich. I never saw a nastier piece of work than Molly Fielding's mother. I swear it. I don't know how I knew— but I swear it.

'What an awful woman. Who is it?'

My mother said, 'Oh, dear, that's old Molly Fielding's mother. I knew her. She was a character.'

'You *knew* her! She looks before the Punic Wars.'

'She was, just about. God knows. An authentic mid-Victorian. She had Molly very late. She was famous for some sort of reputation but I can't remember what it was. She died about the time Molly married, and that would be all of sixty years ago.'

'What was the husband like?'

'Oh, long gone. Nobody knew him. Molly can't remember him. Maybe there wasn't a husband, but I think I'd have remembered if it was that. I think he was just dispensed with somehow. He was very weak—or silly. But rich.'

'She doesn't look as if she would have needed anyone, ever.'

'Well, she certainly didn't need poor old Molly. Her only child, you know, and she hated her. Molly—such a silent little thing at school. After that she was "at home with mother".'

'Didn't she ever work?'

'Are you mad, child? She had to gather up her mother's shawls and go visiting with her and return the library books.'

'Until she married?'

'Yes. And she'd never have married if her mother could have stopped it. She was always very attractive, Molly. Not beautiful but attractive. She was never let out of her mother's sight—and not let into anyone else's. They lived in hotels, I think, up and down the country. Sometimes in boarding-house places abroad. There had been a big house somewhere but they left it!'

'Were they poor?'

'Rich, dear, rich. Just look some time at Molly's rings.'

This conversation was years ago and since then I have often looked at Molly's rings. I looked at them the other day when she came to lunch with me and they still shone wickedly, catching the light of the winter dining room, weighting down her little claws. Molly was a trim, spare, little woman and the claws were smaller now and even sharper-looking than when I'd seen her last, two years ago. Her nails were tiny and beautifully manicured and the prickly old clusters below them looked loose enough at any moment to go sliding off into the chicken supreme.

'Looking at the rings?' she asked. 'You're not getting them, dear. They're for impeccable Alice. My albatrosses. She could have them now if she wanted. I hardly wear them. High days and holidays, like this. I keep them in—no, I'm not going to tell you. You never know. Careless talk ... You think they're vulgar, do you?'

'No. I was just—well, remembering them. From way back. They looked smaller then. Your rings were you. Most things look bigger when you're young.'

'I'm smaller,' she said, 'that's all it is. I keep getting them re-made but they can't keep pace with me. I get them done over every year before the insurance runs out.

'I tell the insurance people the stones rattle. They don't, but you can get them cleaned free if you say that. A jeweller cleans them better than you can yourself. A good jeweller always cleans when he secures. Gin—that's all you can do for yourself, soak them in gin. But it's a waste. You feel you can't drink it afterwards with all the gunge in it.'

The rings shone clear and sharp and there was not a trace of gunge and never had been, for Molly had a code of practice for the maintenance of goods that would have impressed a shipping company; and she had an eye for the free acquisition of necessities and schemes for the painless saving of money that many a government might envy. She also had a talent for the command of luxury. Stories of Molly sharing hotel rooms for which her friends and acquaintances had paid were in my childhood canon. She had slept on the floor of the Hyde Park, for instance, with her daughter's old nanny who had struck it rich with a (now absent) South American lover.

'Nanny had the bed of course—I insisted. Yes, she did fuss about me being on the floor, and we did change over about eleven o'clock, but I'd have been perfectly happy. Who minds sleeping on a floor if it saves two hundred pounds a night? They never notice, you know. I'd been Nanny's dinner guest and we went up to her room after dinner as if to get my coat. No one notices if you don't go home. And it was Harvey

Nichols' sale in the morning, just across the road. I felt since I'd saved two hundred pounds I could spend it.'

'But, Molly, you didn't *have* to spend two hundred pounds. You didn't *have* to go in to London the night before at all. You only live in Rickmansworth.'

'Oh, but there's nothing in Rickmansworth like the Hyde Park Hotel. Another thing, dear, did you know you can get a jolly good free bath on Paddington Station? There's a very decent bathroom in the Great Western. You just go in there for a coffee and then trot upstairs to the ladies' room and along the corridor and you're in a very nice big bathroom with marble fittings and nice old brass chains to the plugs. Thundering hot water, dear. I take soap and a towel always when I'm in London. In a Harrods bag.'

'You could be arrested.'

'Rubbish. There's not a hint of a sign saying "Private". It says "Bathroom". Nobody uses it but me because all the rooms are this ghastly thing *En Suite* now. Have you noticed on the motorway—the motels? '*24 En Suites*'. I'd never stay in a place like the Great Western now, of course. It's only for commercial travellers. But the bathroom's useful if you have to change for the evening. It saves that nonsense of belonging to a so-called Club. Deadly places—all full of old women. Victoria Station was very good, too, before the War, and at St Pancras, The Great Northern, you could always stay a night no questions asked if you knew the ropes and wore the right clothes. They used to leave the keys standing in the doors. So unwise.

'And did you know you can spend *such* a pleasant hour or so in the London Library simply by ignoring the Members Only notice? You just walk in looking thoughtful and go upstairs to the Reading Room. It's a pity they've moved the old leather armchairs. They were so comfortable and you could sleep in them before a matinée. I always picked up one of the learned journals from the racks—something like *The John*

Evelyn Society Quarterly—so that they'd think I was an old don.'

'They can see you're no don, Molly, with those diamonds.'

'I turn them round, dear. I'm not silly. They used to give you a tray of tea in the London Library once, you know, but all those nice things have stopped since the Conservatives got in. Look—an elastic band. It's the Post Office. I keep these. The postmen drop them all over England—all up the drive of the Final Resting Place. I told the postman they're worth money so now he drops them all through my letter box instead, great showers of them, like tagliatelle.'

We were walking on the common now. Lunch was over. It was a cold day and people were muffled up and pinched of face but Molly looked brisk and scarcely seventy. From the back—her behind neat, her legs and ankles skinny—she might have been forty-five. She wore a beautiful, old, lavender-mixture tweed suit and no glasses and she carried no stick. Trotting around her was a new puppy, a border collie she was training. She walked at a good speed through the spruces, as fast as I did and nearly as fast as the puppy, which she'd let off the lead. Her cheeks were pink, her eyes were bright and several people smiled at her as she went by. One old boy of about sixty gave her the eye and said he agreed about the wastage of elastic bands.

I said we should turn back as it was going to rain and she didn't want to be landed with a cold.

'I never catch cold,' she said. 'It's because I don't use public transport. I like my car. It was quite unnecessary for you to fetch and carry me today, you know. Very nice of you—but I'd have enjoyed crossing London again.'

'Do they let you drive still, Molly?' She had one of the little houses on an estate for the elderly she called the Final Resting Place.

'They can't stop me. Not yet. It's coming up of course—

next driving test. Well, yes, they do fuss a bit. I can't remember where I'm going sometimes after I've set off, and the other day I couldn't remember where I'd been.'

'That might be a warning sign, you know, Molly. That it's time to stop.'

'Oh, fish! Wait till I get properly lost, then I'll stop. I've a card in my bag with my telephone number. I haven't forgotten who I am yet.'

'That does happen—'

'Oh, that Alzheimer business. That must be a terrible thing. But it only happens to the old, doesn't it?' She roared with laughter and clipped the dog on the lead.

Molly's dogs have always been wonderfully well-behaved and obedient—never smelled or chewed things or wet things or snapped or barked. Rather dispirited animals really. She never appeared to pay much attention to them. Years ago I remembered that she had said it was her mother who had taught her how to handle dogs.

'Come on,' she cried from the traffic island in the middle of the High Street. 'You'll get run over if you hang about. Make a dash.'

At tea—she'd done well at lunch with a couple of sherries and a glass of chablis with the chicken—she settled down to a crumpet and a long and interesting analysis of her investments. As usual I forgot altogether that Molly had been my grandmother's friend. I forgot the great string of years she had known, the winters and winters and winters, the spring after spring, flowing back and back and back to the first mornings of the century. I forgot the huge number of times she had woken to another day.

When I was a girl, Molly would come breezing by to see us in a fast car, usually with a woman friend, never with a man or her husband who had been, like her father, a shadow. (She had married in ten minutes, my grandmother used to say, when her mother was upstairs in bed having measles of all things: absolutely furious, her mother was, too. In fact she died.) When I was a girl, I had always felt that Molly was empowered with an eternal youth, more formidable, much more effective, than my transient youth that seemed longer ago.

'Well, I'm not clever,' she often said. 'I'm a fool, dear. I know my limitations. No education and not a brain in my head. That's the secret. You're all so clever now—and all so good. It does age people. And also of course I'm frightfully mean. I don't eat or drink much unless I'm out.'

But she wasn't mean. When she gave a present, having said she could afford nothing, it tended to be stupendous. Once she gave me a car. And she did leave me one of the rings. But, 'I'm mean,' she said. 'And I'm not intellectual. I always wanted to be a racing driver after motor cars came in. Not allowed to, of course. D'you think I'm embittered?' (She shrieked with laughter.) 'I've struggled through. I've struggled through.'

And struggle it had sometimes looked to be—her freezing house, her empty hearth and fridge, her beautiful but ancient clothes all mended and pressed and hung in linen bags in the wardrobe. She had often sat wrapped in rugs to save coal. She had never had central heating. An ascetic pauper—until you looked at her investments, and they were wonderful. Whenever you saw her reading the financial columns she was smiling.

'And,' she said, 'hand it to me. I'm rational. That's what gets you through in the end, you know—being rational. I've no imagination, thank God. I give to charity but I've the sense not to watch the news. "Thank God" by the way is jargon. I don't believe in God and I don't believe that half the people I know who go to church and carry on at Christmas and go to the Messiah and that sort of thing—that they do either. All my Bridge lot, of course they don't believe in God. Religion's always seemed to me to be fairy stories. I go to church now and then, but it's for keeping up friendships and the look of it. And I quite enjoy weddings and funerals, of course.'

She was awesome, Molly. Awful really. But she was so nice.

She was in the midst of one of these 'I'm rational' conversations, the refrain that had threaded all my association with her, and she was eating her crumpet, and I was wondering why she was still insisting on her—well, on her boringness, and why she didn't bore me, why she never annoyed me; and I had decided it was because she never dissembled, that in my life her total truthfulness was unique. The truth Molly told showed her to be good. A good, straight being. Molly the unimaginative was unable to lie.

At which point she suddenly said, 'By the way, my mother's been seen around again.'

I looked at her.

'Around the village. And the FRP. She's looking for me, you know. But she won't find me.'

I said, 'Your *mother*?'

She said, 'Yes. You didn't know her. You were lucky. I hated her. Of course you know I did. You must have heard. She was very cruel to me. Well, she's back. Darling, are you going to take me home to the house of the near-dead? It's getting dark.'

'Yes, of course. Are you ready?'

'I'll just run upstairs.'

This she did and I waited with her coat and gloves and walking shoes and the basket with the dog's belongings and the dog.

'Yes,' she said coming down the stairs, twisting about at her knickers. 'Yes, she's been around for quite a time, a year or so. I don't know where she was before. I've managed to keep out of her way up to now. I hope that she didn't spot me leaving today, she'd have wanted to come, too.'

So, half an hour later I said, 'Molly, do you mean your *mother*?'

'Yes, dear. I'm afraid she was very unkind. I don't often talk about it. I was very frightened of her. D'you know, dear, I don't know when I've *had* such a wonderful day. Oh, how I've enjoyed it. Now if you turn left here and left again we can take the short cut and get straight to the bypass. You see I know exactly where I am. Now don't come in with me—you must get back before the traffic.'

I said, 'Molly—'

She kissed me, hesitated, and then got out. I saw her standing motionless before her mock-Georgian front door looking first at the lock, then at her key.

'Shall I open it?' I called to her.

'No, no. Of course not. Don't treat me as senile. Ninety-four is nothing. It won't be thought anything of soon. When you're ninety-four there'll be hundreds of you, with all this marvellous new medicine that's going on.'

'Goodbye, dear Molly. I'll wait till you're safe inside.'

'It's just that the lights aren't on.' She said, 'If you could just watch me in from the car. Just watch till I light everything up. It's so silly but I don't greatly like going into a dark house.'

I drove to the estate office and spoke to the lady superintendent who said that Molly was indeed still driving, though they were getting worried about it. She said that Molly was utterly sensible, utterly rational and her eyes and mind were very good. In fact she upset the younger ones by doing her stocks and shares and phoning her broker in the public common room.

'No aberrations? Does her mind wander?'

'*Never*,' she said. 'She is our star turn.'

Yet on the way home I decided to ring up her daughter,

Alice, and was walking towards the phone the next morning when it began to ring, and it was Alice calling me. There were the statutory empty screams about how long since we'd spoken and then she asked if it were true that Molly had been to lunch with me. I said yes, and that I'd fetched her and taken her back, of course.

'Not "of course" at all, ducky. Do you know she's still driving?'

I went on like the superintendent for a bit: about the beady eye that saw me look at the rings, the high-speed walk, the psychic hold over the dog, the fearlessness on the High Street, the splendid appetite. 'There was just—'

'Ha!'

'Well, she says her *mother* is about. Alice, her mother'd be about a hundred and thirty years old.'

'I know. Oh, heaven, don't I know. Did she say her mother's looking for her around the village?'

'Yes.'

'And making her clean her nails and polish her shoes and— She rings me up and asks me to bring a cake over because her mother's coming to tea. About twice a week.'

'But I've never heard her mention her mother before.'

'The doctors say it's the supply of oxygen to the brain. It's running uneven, like a car with dirty plugs. There are vacuums or something, and it's in the vacuums she really lives. Maybe it's where we all really live.'

'But all the bossy, sensible, happy years?'

'*All* the years. It was all there underneath, always. The fear.'

'Could we remind her of her mother's funeral? Would that end it?'

'She never went to the funeral. Her mother died abroad. I do say sometimes, "She's not here, Ma—she's dead and gone," but she just says, "I'm afraid not." She'll forget for a week and then remember. Then the terrors begin.'

'Whatever can the woman have done to her?'

Alice paused so long, that I thought we'd been cut off.

'Oh, I expect nothing much,' she said, in the end. 'Something quite hidden. It's just part of the horrors of old age.'

But at Molly's funeral I wasn't so sure. Among the extraordinarily large crowd—many of them young, many dog-lovers, some old, old racing-driver types, her solicitor, her stockbroker and a horde from the Final Resting Place, quite a few children—I could not rid myself of the notion that there was someone else present, just at my shoulder.

T here again,' they said in Spratpool Street. 'She's there again,' and they looked at each other and plodded on round the shops.

The horse lifted and dropped a hoof. The groom sat above on the polished seat of the trap. The trap was smarter than a carriage, quite chic and, like the County, expensive and correct but not yet a motor. It stood outside the studio of the new photographer and the groom stared ahead, knees stalwart under the rug, the Ironside groom, just about the last in Shipley.

Mrs. Ironside was attending the photographer. All of sixty, squat as the old Queen, she was again attending the photographer, she was never away.

The first visit had been only a sighting from the road when the new studio was still an amazement in the town and she had directed the trap to pause there as she passed by, to allow her to examine the window.

A low, artistic signboard of bright wood was painted with gold lettering: 'Settimo. Portraiture', and behind it stood a huge, near life-size photograph of a newly married couple, the she in a mile of heavy lace, the he in half a bale of black, ill-fitting, foreign-looking suiting. The she had her veil pulled down low over the brow with a little tight band of flowers, rather like a swimming cap. It gave her a glamorous ferocity. The sheaf of lilies across her lap lay like swords. The he stared hot-eyed, plump-cheeked, a broad silken moustache and tie, round-ended stiff collar, hair plastered flat on his head, gleaming; and on his ankles spats, grey spats above patent leathers. They were a serious, confident pair, not yet rich but determined. You could see the black ink of ledgers, the shouting and the passions, little leisure, and the children not having it easy. Mrs. Ironside felt a liking for the two of them, almost recognition, though they clearly hadn't had much to do with Shipley.

Nothing at all to do with Shipley, for over their shoulders spread a crumbling hillside tremulous with laburnum, dark with chestnut trees, and roses showered over the tops of secret garden walls. A little donkey with panniers filled with grasses was being watched on its way by a peasant woman shading her eyes in a dusty, flowery lane. And all beneath a cloudless sky.

And this couple was seated upon an ornamental terrace before a marble balustrade and on the balustrade a slippery fringed shawl and on the shawl a flagon with an inviting lip and beside the flagon a great glass jar with a carved glass stopper. The jar seemed stuffed with spiral layers of orchard fruits, strange, syrupy, glowing things catching the light.

The photograph had already created a stir in Shipley. Often little groups had gathered on the pavement in the cold spring winds and steady northern English rain saying, 'Look at them pears and plums, you could sink your teeth in them, queer aren't they, you can see right through to the gowks. You can just feel the silk in that shawl. He'll be expensive I dare say. It'll be for carriage folk I dare say.'

Florrie Ironside was carriage folk nowadays all right and had been for a long time. Expense meant nothing to her in her jet necklaces and black ruched satin and first-quality Shipley woollen pelisse, her beaded hat from Harrogate, her chunks of ugly jewellery and the vast brass-framed cameo attached to her bosom. The cameo held a tinted representation of her dead husband and a twist of his sandy hair. Florence Ironside sat under a black umbrella in the rain and examined the new shop-front painted coffee-cream with lighter cream blinds each with a golden tassel. It stood between Bogey's Grocers full of cheeses stuck with gluey linen, and Batty's Drapers (founded 1812) stacked up with bales of wool and tweeds and calicos, and fans of cards of button hooks and linen-covered singlet-buttons. Outside the new shop a young man in thin shoes was locking the door behind him as he went off to his lunch. His coat didn't look the cloth for a Shipley spring.

'A newcomer,' she said to the groom, who said he'd heard tell a Hitalian.

A while later Florrie Ironside saw the young man again changing the window, and she stopped the trap to watch. He was lifting away the happy Italian couple and replacing them with a bride alone, startlingly dark, her hair falling in polished ripples, a great Nottingham veil dragging down behind her and swinging round into a pool at her feet. The dress had a straining satin bodice with no shame. The mouth was soft and sulky, swollen with desire; and, good gracious heaven, was the mouth of Hilda Staples' sullen Nellie! Who could have made a beauty of that slow lump? And sitting before that transfer screen with all the moral messages on it and the improving pictures—there was Mr. Gladstone with his rose—the sort of thing decent children used to stick together with flour paste to fill up a winter. If it was Nellie, no wonder the bodice was tight, and just as well that bouquet was the size of a haystack. She looked sultry, though. She'd be admired.

Two sets of fingertips set Nellie gently on the easel and, over the top of her, Signor Settimo's sad eyes met the eyes of Mrs. Ironside in the trap. As the photographer moved sideways and forwards for a moment, to look Nellie over, she saw that he seemed now rather better dressed. He was a delicate-looking young man with a pale face and dark hair pomaded down, the body slight as if it had taken no account of itself since it belonged to a stripling—shoulders birdlike, sloped hips and waist like a dancer's. All this—as he turned and looked at Mrs. Ironside again—with a sense of yearning, of honey for sale. He vanished behind the bead curtain.

'I might get the dog done,' thought Mrs. Ironside, and then aloud, 'I might get the dog done. I've never had the dog done,' and the groom cocked an ear to see if he was to turn and go to the veterinarian's in the High Street. But no command came.

A few days later the trap was again outside the studio and Mrs. Ironside handing the dog down to the groom, who carried it in. Mrs. Ironside sat stately and waiting, and time passed. Mrs. Ironside even had to haul on the reins now and then to keep the pony steady, something she was perfectly able to do even in her black stiff costume, having been a farmer's daughter and well known, before she married Ironside who had made her so rich, for bumping down into Shipley in a shabby old habit on a shabby old cob every Thursday market day.

The groom emerged nervous. There had to be appointments. Yes, he'd said that. Yes, he'd tried—that's why he had been all this time—and, yes, even for dogs. And dogs was altogether dubious anyway. This Settims didn't care for dogs. This Settims stood his distance and got out his handkerchief, sneezing, having some nose trouble. He often drew the line at dogs.

Florrie Ironside then flung the reins away and crashed into the studio with the dog hanging down front and back under her arm. The groom stood waiting, and soon watching the arrival and angry departure of a mother with her swansdowned child. The woman recognised the Ironside conveyance and told the groom that her appointment had been cancelled for a dog, and she might even say for a bitch. The groom, who knew when he was well off (for jobs were scarce), looked steadily ahead and did not reply.

Mrs. Ironside was with Signor Settimo a good three-quarters of an hour and emerged flushed with success, and the dog hanging limp even for a dachshund. Over luncheon with her daughter, Molly, she described the triumphant morning. It had been a struggle to get the better of this Italian even though he was so quiet. He had just stood there at first, watching her and smiling and apologising in a slimy sort of way. He hadn't given an inch until she had told him where she stood in the town, and Mr. Ironside's position there, though dead. And that her address was The Mount. Then he'd been decisive and sensibly got on with the job. Not very talkative, though. Well, he'd certainly learned that foreigners in Shipley have to stand back.

Molly said she'd heard that he was a very *good* photographer and Mrs. Ironside had said, Well, we shall see; and that he was taking a very long time to produce any proofs of his photographs. *Three weeks*, if you please, *three weeks*! 'Pressure of work'—and not able to get away to deliver even in the lunch-hours now, if you please. If you asked her it was all show and lies.

On the day promised for the delivery of the proofs of the portrait of the dog, Mrs. Ironside arranged herself and Molly around the silver tea service in the drawing room at four o'clock as usual and as usual proceeded to eat up all the tea. Signor Settimo was to call at a quarter to five, and an upright chair had been placed for him at an appropriate distance. Mrs. Ironside was for the first time since her widowhood wearing colour—a bunch of cloth violets against the black foulard of her dress above poor old Willy's good-natured face and wisp of dead hair. Molly across on the humpty was also looking neither one thing nor the other, for her mother in a fit of boredom had said Yes, she might bob her hair, and then in a fit of pique, No, she might not shorten her skirts.

So, ridiculous in flounces below her neat modern little head, Molly sat sideways reading a motoring monthly in which lean girls with flying scarves and cigarette holders clasped in their teeth lay back at the wheels of long chassis and sped across the pages like the wind. Their proud, painted, selfish faces stirred Molly. They rattled her. She said, 'I'm glad about the violets, Ma. It's well over the year. Well over. Black, black—it doesn't suit me and Pa wouldn't care.'

Her mother stared as if the fireguard had spoken. She said, 'Your father liked me in black. Black gives authority.'

'Well, I'd like a sea-green now. I'd like one of those motoring duster-coats and actually a car.' (And a man, she thought, to get me away. Any man. I wonder what the Eyetie's like? She's not used to men. She'll shred him. Poor old Pa with his belly and his sandy hair.)

A bell rang faintly far away and Mrs. Ironside instructed Molly to eat the last piece of bread and butter. Molly asked if she should order fresh tea but her mother said no, and a maid came in with a package.

'Where is Mr. Settimo?'

'He said, mum, he couldn't wait, mum.'

'Couldn't?'

'Said he couldn't, mum, pressure of work, mum. Sends his compliments and the bill for the proofs is in the separate envelope.'

Mrs. Ironside thrust up her chin and turned a little blue about the lips and breathed slowly. She slapped down her crumby plate and said, 'Take the tea things. Give me the package. Why isn't it on a salver? What! Account! This isn't an account, it is a ransom. It's more than a doctor!'

But inside the package was a sleek and knowing hound, each hair gleaming, jokey frown-lines wrinkling between the eyes as if he were the most intelligent animal of the ark, as if he were perhaps even trying to understand Italian. His paddle feet hung down showing his beautifully manicured nails and his ears were lifted charmingly and alertly at the root.

'Oh, Ma! It's wonderful! He's the most *wonderful* photographer!'

Mrs. Ironside sat all evening in her chair lifting the proofs of the dog one by one, holding them close to her eyes and then at arm's length. She returned them next day via the groom marked up for enlargement and a note in her wild green ink saying that the account would be settled in full the following week when her considerable order was completed. She gave instructions to the maids that when Mr. Settimo called he was to be shown round to the back door.

But he did not come. Not to either door. Not the next week, nor the one after, nor the one after that. And at last when the groom was sent down to the studio he found a notice in the window saying, *Temporarily closed owing to family bereavement in Cremona*, and Nellie Staples displaced for a swathe of crepe.

'Unprofessional,' said Florrie Ironside. 'Unnecessary. And what has Cremona got to do with it? I thought it was toffee. He'll get nowhere if he can't stick to his last. I'm sure we could never afford to go running about overseas when your father was making his way.'

Molly (eighteen) said, 'But he's young, Ma, you know, and he hasn't any ties. He's only about twenty.'

'Forty-five if a day,' said Florrie, fuming. 'Foreigners are deceptive. All talk and guile. You should remember what your father used to say about them after we'd been to Dusseldorf for our silver wedding. No—he'll go bankrupt.'

But later the next day the photographs of the dog were delivered directly to the back door by Signor Settimo's personal messenger dressed in coffee-coloured uniform and pillbox hat and white gloves under the epaulette. Mind you, May, the maid, said ask her and she'd say it was George Bicker-

staffe's Henry with his face washed and the suit come from that
overgrown page at the Regal cinema.

Mrs. Ironside said only, 'Messenger, my eye,' and sent for
the trap and directed it to Spratpool Street.

In they swept.

'Mr. Settimo,' demanded Florence of the girl at the desk,
who was in coffee-coloured sateen and jewelled bandeau, writing slowly in an order book with her tongue out.

'He's engaged.'

'*Engaged!*'

'He's with a sitter. I can't get at him. Not when he's under
the cloth.'

'Produce him at once. I am Mrs. Ironside.'

The girl knew this. She was Netta Cricklewood of Bogey's
Grocers before being a Shipley solicitor's tea-girl and she had
known Mrs. Ironside from childhood. She sidled off ('Half an
inch of paint and silk stockings') and returned looking sulky
with fear.

'He says to sit down and take a browse through the
albums.'

There was one spindly gold chair, which Florrie regarded
with venom while Mollie, who had been brought along, stood
at the glass door looking out, hoping for motors.

'Come away from there,' said Florrie, 'D'you want all
Shipley to know we're being kept waiting by a tradesman?' and
she glared at Netta Cricklewood and asked if she wasn't missing her earlier professional career.

Netta—could it be her portrait above the desk, a sea nymph
all bare skin and lip-gloss like a concubine?—Netta, recover-
ing, said, 'Thank you very much, I'm not missing anything at
all these days.'

At last came Settimo, clashing through the bead curtain and
bowing out the sitter—an excited shadow—and turning to
Mrs. Ironside his gentle and impervious face.

He bowed.

'I have brought my account.'

'How very prompt. I am greatly obliged.'

'The photographs were very late.'

'I was called away to Cremona.' He let his eyes drift over her black, and old Willy smiling away on her chest. 'In Italy we also pay attention to mourning.'

Molly waited for her mother to embark on the sermon about the necessity for the bereaved to allow hard work to deal with grief and how she herself had *immediately* taken up the reins, winding up a great business with no assistance from any-one, except an only child who knew nothing, not even how to deal with the letters of condolence.

Instead she heard her mother ask if he would photograph her daughter. She, Molly.

Signor Settimo, not wavering by a flicker in Molly's direc-tion, brushed Netta aside and negotiated the appointment himself in the leather-bound book.

Going home, Molly said, 'But I don't want my photograph taken, Ma. Why should I be photographed? I'm not a baby or a bride. They'll think you're trying to get me off.'

'Nonsense. I want a photograph of you for the drawing room. It's always wise to have a likeness. You never know what's going to happen. Look at the Duke of Clarence.'

Molly then wondered if she was going to die and her mother knew something she didn't. She went up and peered in the glass and decided she looked tubercular and became so taken with the idea that she considered making her will until she remembered that she had no money. She sat looking at her mother that evening, trying to see her sitting there soon alone, and maybe weeping. But Molly had a poor imagination.

When the photographs came, Mrs. Ironside put them aside

with scarcely a glance. 'I'm afraid you haven't your mother's presence, Molly.' Molly, flat-chested, taut, anonymous, sat bemused.

For there had been something very queer about Signor Settimo at the sitting, tip-tapping about the studio floor as if he was in church, arranging the folds of the cloth on a trellis behind her—nearer and nearer, circling nearer, touching her cheekbone at last; directing her head to look now at the Pantheon, now at the Bridge of Sighs and now—just here over his head—at the Campanile at Cremona. His neat little shanks made a pair of back legs for the angular dragonfly that fixed its great eye on her.

Molly was unnerved. Again and yet again she waited tensely for him to slide beneath the pall that was the creature's back, to crash the great brass plates together, then to plunge under again and call out his muffled directions. Out would dangle an arm holding in its fingers a soft grey rubber bulb on the end of a tube—there'd been something terrible and exactly like it the nurse used to bring when her father was dying—and the fingers would give a sudden expert squeeze and the flash of deadly lightning would strike.

'These will be very excellent photographs,' said Signor Settimo.

'Will they be as good as the dog's?'

He came dancing across to her then, and lifted dovelike hands on either side of her face as if to cup it. Then he stopped and let the hands and his head tip together first one way then the other as he smiled with the whitest of teeth and the most affectionate lips. He then appeared to recollect himself, and Molly unexpectedly thought of the groom who muttered, 'Jobs is scarce.'

'Miss Ironside,' said Signor Settimo, 'Signorina Ironside—I should very much like to photograph your mother.'

'He said he wanted to photograph you,' said Molly. They were riding lugubriously up and down Shipley leaving cards on people on a dank and sunless afternoon.

'Insolence,' said Florrie, and then, 'Well, I dare say he does. I'm not surprised. The prices he charges he'll need a good bit of advertisement.'

'He's put me in the window.'

'What? He hasn't dared! Without permission? For everyone to see? We have been good enough to give him trade and he hasn't asked permission? How dare he! We're going there at once.' And she gave the groom a prod in the back and they turned about.

In the window of Spratpool Street, there sat straight-eyed Molly with her frozen shoulders awaiting the lightning, and beside her, Lily, daughter of Alderman Bellinger, the late Mr. Ironside's most vulgar and thrusting competitor in the building trade, who had posthumously absorbed him though at an exorbitant price. Lily's portrait was bigger than Molly's.

'This must be stopped. Wait here.' And Florrie was into the shop in three strides. And very quickly out of it again.

Signor Settimo was now on holiday. 'At The Grand at Scarborough,' said Netta with awe. There was only her there, and the messenger. The messenger was sitting looking rather ill on the ornamental chair, picking his teeth. He was without his pill-box and didn't get up.

'I shall complain in writing. Take my daughter from the window.'

'I'd never dare.'

'Then you—' She pointed. She grabbed the messenger by the neck.

'I've not got to touch things,' he said. 'I've got unnatural damp hands.'

'Then I shall.'

And Molly (and Shipley) saw the black arm of Mrs.

Ironside appear like King Arthur's in reverse and pluck her from the window.

Mrs. Ironside was considerably upset and didn't speak all the way home or during tea. She sat in heavy thunder all the evening and the next day when Molly, frightened, at last said, 'There's no need to mind, you know, Ma. He can't hurt you. I mean, you're an old woman and he's only a boy.'

Then Mrs. Ironside leaned across the breakfast table and slapped Molly across the face.

'She did,' said May, who'd been at the sideboard replenishing one of the big steel domes with bacon. 'She did. She slapped her face! And there's Molly runs out and up the stairs crying. That's the front door. Run and get it. I'm hot and cold all over.'

The bell had been rung by Signor Settimo hastening early from the studio in his new motor to apologise for the bish about Molly and Lily Bellinger. The breakfast room door was still open and Mrs. Ironside was shaking at the table, shocked and prior to weeping, but the weeping she set aside. She found her heart was beating fast. She ordered the maid to show the photographer into the morning room. Breathing slowly now, she sat on for a little, wondering at the wonderful sense of lightness in her, the triumph within. She went out to him.

Settimo stood in the window of the morning room beside the metal storks. He stood upon a rich Turkey rug admiring the polish on all the mahogany, the shine on the Dutch tiled grate, the bloom on the escritoire. His fingers stroked a Chinese pot on a plinth of inlaid walnut. Above his head hung the very latest thing—a metal drum with a pink silk frill that contained bulbs of electricity. It was like looking up skirts.

'Cremona,' he was saying, 'Oh, Cremona!'

'Mrs. Ironside,' he said, 'how I should like to make a commemorative album of this house! How nearly it is like my home.'

'Cremona?' Florrie was feeling lighter and lighter; a victor, yet joyously damned. 'Cremona?'

He told her about Northern Italy, the watery flatness of the plains, the reedy River Po (which he pronounced as in pot or tot or clot, in the best possible taste), the dark canyons of the old streets of its cities and how, in Cremona, his own city, the narrow toppling alleys flung black flags of shade. He told how you burst out from under them into the bright sunlight of the piazzas, light that softly bathed the street-long baroque palaces, the gold and pale-pink churches, the tightly bound but generously bulging, beckoning cathedral. He described the boom of the bells, the jingle of the little carriages all ribbons and plumes, the café tables shining with thick linen cloths under the pillars round the cathedral square. There you could sit talking, talking long into the summer night, and nobody to hurry you away.

'Cremona is the essence of dignity and culture and civilisation. Keep Firenze. Keep Roma.'

'I wonder that you could bear to leave it, Mr. Settimo.'

'I wonder, too, but in Cremona there are many photographers. All is weddings—weddings and weddings. Weddings and babies. I was so seldom called upon to photograph a face of experience, of knowledge of the world.'

Florence Ironside was booked in for a sitting at 2:30 P.M. the following Tuesday.

But it was not a success.

Signor Settimo was desolate. It was not a success. Florence (prophetic name) was not herself—hush! He meant it. 'This is not yourself, not your real self sitting there. You pretend to be so bold, so, if you will forgive me, so tight drawn-up. But I cannot see *you*. I cannot feel your essence. All I see and feel are your—certainly magnificent—strength and your ferocity. Hush, yes, your ferocity. Your *enmity*. Oh, relax please, Signora Ironside, you electrify the air.'

'I don't know what you're talking about,' said Florence, lifting her chin, confronting the dragonfly optic and the black hump of Settimo laid along behind. She felt excited. He thought he'd catch her, did he, with all that about sunshine and piazzas? Little Signor Settimo and she, the widow of Willy Ironside of Shipley. She curled her rather pretty, scornful little lips. There came the squeeze and the flash and the crash of thunderbolts and he took the photograph that a long time later went the rounds.

It is always the wrong photograph that goes the rounds.

He came over and stood looking down into her face and said, 'Signora—why are you belligerent?'

'Your English is very good,' she said.

'Of course. I am from Cremona. Do you think I am a Sardinian? Or educated in Shipley?'

He made her sit in the hard spotlight and slid back under the cloth. The silence returned. The bulb was held high, but was not pressed.

Mrs. Ironside's face changed, the small eyes widened, the chin sank down. The lips seemed to soften. He came over and directed the cheekbone towards the Bridge of Sighs. He touched the shoulder of the armoured dress. He lifted one of the hands across the breast, screening poor old Willy.

'I'll take this off,' said Florence, unpinning the brooch, wondering if she had been told to do so or if it was her own idea.

Under the pall he cried, 'Oh—that is so much better. But still—no, I still do not see you. You are unpractised. You cannot give. There is something withheld, something secret about you. Am I looking at a woman or a cold machine? A frightened—forgive me—old maid?'

He squeezed the bulb listlessly and the lightning seemed scarcely to flicker.

'There will be no charge,' he said. 'You have not trusted me. You cannot give. You shall return next week.' He walked with her only as far as the door of the darkroom and dismissed her inattentively.

'He said he wouldn't charge me,' she said to Molly, who had asked no questions and now said nothing. 'And I should think not. He was entirely at fault. He was out of sorts. Very temperamental.' She thought of the horrible slapping of Molly's face. 'Well, who isn't, from time to time. Especially after bereavement. I'm afraid I am sometimes temperamental myself. I do thoughtless things sometimes. I'm sorry, Molly.'

Molly, amazed, said, 'I don't think *I* am temperamental.'

'Oh, but you see all Italians are, and you have your father's colouring, Scottish colouring. I wonder if I have a little drop of Italian blood.'

'They say he's overspending,' said Molly. 'May says there are bills as long as your arm everywhere. And that car isn't paid for, May says. He's in trouble.'

'Oh, but I think he's been used to wealth. He tells me that in Cremona there are streets of nothing but palaces. He only travels for his Art.'

'Are you going back to him then? I know I wouldn't. Ma— I was a bit afraid of him.'

'Oh, of course I'm going back. I'm not a churlish woman, I hope.'

For the next sitting she left off the mourning brooch, laying it down on her dressing table, and turned back into her bedroom at the last minute to change her hat for a great Leghorn straw swooning with flat roses—cream roses—and a veil that tied under the chin, this time with a white velvet ribbon.

'Ah—' said Settimo. 'There! Exactly. Yes. Just like that. Lift the chin a fraction—do not pretend to be *demure*. It hasn't come to that. Smile at me. Mrs. Ironside, I have never seen you openly smile. But that is beautiful. Oh, how beautiful—your lovely smile. You have the lips of a young madonna, Mrs. Ironside. Delicious under the veil.'

His pointed fingers were on her shoulder as she left. 'But, I want more.' He was like a sympathetic doctor. They were alone. Netta and the messenger were nowhere to be seen. She suddenly remembered for some reason that little Henry Bickerstaffe had measles and that Wednesday anyway was Shipley's early-closing day.

He moved his fingers across the back of her neck to the knot of ribbon that held the veil. 'I should like to undo this veil. I should like to see—perhaps unpin—your hair. Had I the money—any money, I am over-spent. I am in deep, deep water owing to circumstances in Cremona—had I any money, I would dress you as a Princess of Piedmont. I would drop your awful English jewels in the river and I would adorn you with moonstones.'

He sent for her again the following Wednesday and she went to him on foot and ('I'm not imagining this, I saw it from the end of Blenheim Terrace and Mrs. Cricklewood saw it, too') she went hatless. Perhaps gloveless. He held back the bead curtain, first drawing down the blind that said 'Half Day Wednesday' over the glass front door. She passed before him into the darkroom.

'All right then. Tek me to Scarborough. I'll say nothing if you'll tek me to Scarborough. Mind you, half Shipley knows. They're all asking me.'

'Netta, I can't take anyone anywhere. This is the reason about the abeyance of the wages. I am in trouble. I am an artist—you know that—not a businessman. I need a business partner of character, if possible with great capital. That is all there is to say. I take you into my confidence. I never have trouble in finding business partners. Never. I have every hope of money—even for Scarborough—quite soon.'

'You mean my Auntie Florrie?'

'Auntie?'

'It's not a real auntie. "Auntie"'s what you call your mother's best friends in England. You may not have it in Cremona. Auntie Florrie was at school with my mam. Auntie Florrie had to walk in to Shipley school five miles. Her Molly and me, we went to different schools, Molly's being private, but *she* was always my Auntie Florrie. She married rich and you see what's become of her, sitting up at that great place and Molly like a cold drink of water and neither of them with a thing to do. Tek me to The Grand. You're on the wrong tack up there, Ferdinando.'

'I don't know what you mean.'

'Half Shipley does then. It's the wonder of the world. And those that knows laughs their heads off and thinks you're a daftie.'

'A—what?'

'I don't know it in Italian. Will you tek me to Scarborough?'

'I can *not*.'

'Then I'll tell yer. I know where you went to the so-called funeral. It was your engagement party—I opened the photos. And I'll tell you you're up the wrong tree with Auntie Florrie. She hasn't a penny after Molly's thirty-five. It's all going to be Molly's. I saw it in the will when I was being a solicitor.'

Signor Settimo looked steadily at Netta with his clever eyes angry and little like those of the Piedmontese bridegroom. He then left her and stepped into his car.

He roared out of Spratpool Street and hurtled out of the town, way past Ilkley and on to the purple moors. Hours went by and in the end the car seemed to drift and sway, to turn back and to take itself home via the dachas on the green slopes surrounding Shipley.

Molly, the girl so mad about cars, Molly, so innocent, so eager for life. Oh, the mistake he had made. He cursed himself. He had an insane desire to proceed at once to The Mount, to sweep up the deep trenched gravel of its drive, to ask to see Molly. But, impossible now.

Yet as he drew near, at the end of The Mount's driveway he let the car dawdle and stop and after a time he heard footsteps crunching in the gravel and he got out of the car and took off his tight little driving helmet and waited.

But it was only the groom in a muffler and an old coat, trailing the dog along behind him; and the groom gave him a look of pity as he passed.

Then the groom called back over his shoulder as he went off down the hill, 'Whichever you're after you're out of luck, Maestro. They're gone, the pair of them. They're gone touring off foreign and both of them miserable, thanks to you. You've ruined them with your magic lanterns.'

III: The Hot Sweets of Cremona

M olly Fielding's daughter Alice and the woman Molly Fielding had liked and had left a ring to were sitting together drinking under the stone canopy and inside the forest of pillars of the great piazza of Cremona. It was a month or so after old Molly's funeral.

They had been a little nervous of going on holiday together. It had been rashly, emotionally arranged, the ghost of the old woman the only bond, for as girls they had not got on, Alice too vehement and self-conscious for the other one.

And their lives and marriages had been very different. The friend was a reticent widow whom Alice had always found rather dull, and Alice was a recent divorcée whom the friend had always thought shallow and too talkative. They were relieved now to find that their conventional upbringing was helping them through the blind spots and the dark pools, that they knew the antique rules for Englishwomen of a certain age on holiday abroad. 'Mustn't forget the postcards. God, so expensive!' 'How about doing our sums? You did these drinks. I paid for the tummy medicine'—and so on. They had looked up assiduously the opening and closing times of the galleries, underlining everything marked with two or three stars.

Alcohol had helped as it does after funerals. They were drinking vermouth now out of little gold-rimmed glasses shaped like convolvus flowers and thinking contentedly that it would soon be lunchtime when there would be wine. After a long siesta they would then set off and wander in the cathedral again, maybe take a little carriage and jingle round the streets of the city. And then—my dear, a *divine* dinner in the dark hotel with the dazzling white cloths thick as blankets, and those great jars of crystallised fruits gleaming on the central table. 'Like Mantegnas,' said the educated friend, and Alice said, 'And we'll try the fegato.'

They sighed and leaned back gazing at the piazza; sixtyish, well-heeled, well-dressed and pleased not to be young.

'I'm pleased not to be young.' The friend examined old Molly's ring on her finger.

'Italy tore me to bits, you know, when I was young,' said Alice. 'All that passion. God—how did we survive? How did we get anything else *done*? Why does time go by so much faster now that we've nothing to do—nothing to obsess us? D'you realise, nobody will ever kiss either of us any more.'

The other one looked across the sunny square crisscrossed by Romeos and Juliets on glittering scooters. The girls tossed their hair and clasped their hands round the boys' waists, rested their beautiful faces sideways against the boys' leather backs. Frighteningly positive, they didn't look as if they dawdled over kissing. The friend knew, and so did Alice, that she had meant to say fuck not kiss, but it had not been possible. They were too old to be able to say aloud the once unthinkable word without seeming outrageous or pathetic, just as they could not wear a skirt halfway up the thigh.

It was not characteristic, rather drunk-sounding, for Alice to say next, 'You can tell when women have stopped being kissed, it's when the lips go indistinct round the edges and the lipstick goes jammy. That was one of Ma's little adages: "Over fifty and lipstick goes jammy."'

'I fell in love with a German in Florence my first time in Italy,' said the friend, 'when I was eighteen. Just after the war. He looked wonderful, like Galahad. I was confused. We'd all just seen the Belsen films. He was so gentle.'

'I came to Italy as an au pair about then,' said Alice, 'to a grand Roman family. Their last au pair had died in a bath at the other end of the palazzo and they hadn't found her for three days. They thought it was *funny*! So poor! They were so poor there was only pasta. I did learn how to eat it though, not to wind it round the fork like the servants do, or so I was told. Some foreign royalty came once and the daughter really did take down curtains to make a dress. Eighteenth-century curtains. All dust in the folds. It was a wonderful dress, too. The Conte made the usual passes. No, he wasn't the one. It was the gardener. Under the olives. On the Campagna. Marvellous. Ma came out to get me back when I wouldn't come home. Thank God, I suppose. Well—I *suppose*. She dragged me off to Parma to buy a ham on the way back! "So cheap, dear." A great purple shank of it. And me weeping.'

'Molly could be pretty ruthless. I saw a photo of her mother once, your grandmother. I suppose that's where it came from.'

'Oh, no,' said Alice. 'No, no, not from her mother. Not from Granny Ironside. Granny put up a good act but she wasn't ruthless in the least.'

'But you never could have met her, Alice. She died before your mother married. How do you know she wasn't ruthless?'

'Mother told me. In a way.'

'But she told me, Molly told me, not long ago, the day she came to lunch last winter and ran about the common, Molly told me that she'd been very frightened of her mother. Said she was a cruel and terrible woman. Well, but you and I talked about it. Awful.'

'Oh, Granny Ironside frightened her all right. Granny Ironside wasn't exactly maternal. But she wasn't ruthless. It was Molly, my ma, who was the ruthless one. Pitiless to herself, too. Ma dealt with her passions like a nun. She seemed—well, she was—affectionate later on, but, you know, amusing, charming Ma was really cold as a fish. She was totally unintuitive and she hadn't a clue about her mother. Her mother needed a mighty rescue.'

'You mean from—where was it—Wigan?'

'Shipley. No. Not a rescue from Shipley. Granny Ironside needed a rescue from her awful fate, her awful, sealed-off, uneducated, empty life. She was a more significant woman than Ma. She went a bit mad, you know. A lot of those women did. That photo of her is a bit mad when you look at it. Dangerously pent-up. She's supposed to have fallen in love with someone absolutely impossible after Grandpa Ironside died. Ma never said who, but she knew. Something to do with a measles epidemic, so maybe it was a doctor. No, I mean it. God knows who he was, it's all garbled. Look, Granny was ugly and sixty and over-rich and the only man she'd ever known was a Shipley builder who left the town only once to go on a builders' spree to Dusseldorf and was out every night of the week in a Shipley pub drinking with his men. She had one child—Ma. Ma, who liked only fast cars, and was cold and bored. Poor Granny—no lover. *Nobody* loved her. Nobody really liked her much. She didn't know how to be likable. And she'd grown far too rich for her country childhood friends.'

'But there was a lover? You said so.'

'I said she fell in love. She was being manipulated in some way, so the story goes. Ma knew it all but she pretended to forget. What she did say was that Granny and nobody else except the solicitor knew that Grandpa had left all the money to her, to Molly, when she was thirty-five. Do you know, it's the cruellest thing a man can do, a will like that? No, maybe it's crueller not to tell the wife and let her find out. Granny did know. All Grandpa Ironside left her was his tinted photograph to wear as a brooch. She wore it, too. And full mourning for a year. D'you think she was hoping for pity when Ma came into the money? The lover I suppose must just have faded out.'

'But wasn't she a dragon? I can see that Settimo photograph now. The first and famous Settimo. My mother had a copy. Settimos are collectors' pieces now.'

'That was the only way she knew how to look. She'd never had a touch of tenderness. D'you know how Granny Ironside died? Do you know what happened?'

'Well—nobody knew. That's what I heard. It was here in Italy. In Cremona. Something not good about it. Didn't Molly somehow miss the funeral? Some scandal?'

'*I* know. I know Ma's version anyway. I got the hang of it through Ma's craziness at the end. I know why she was scared of Grandma's ghost. The ghost that lay in wait.'

'But what had she *done* to Molly?'

'She took her off. Made her leave Shipley. A matter of hours after she realised the lover wanted only Ma's money. She rushed Ma out of England. All Shipley laughing.'

'At Molly?'

'No. At her. At poor old Florrie. She'd been conned by the mysterious lover and they all knew. She, iron Mrs. Ironside of The Mount. She'd been wild for him the last weeks. Hung about outside his house, followed him in the street, showered him with presents. Then she must have found Ma was after him too, or he was after Ma when he somehow found out about the money. She wasn't going to leave Ma behind for him, so she swept her off to Italy. Ma (can you believe it?) caught measles. I haven't found out all about these measles or where they came from but there was *something*. Ma had measles not badly but badly enough and when they'd reached Milan and she was getting better she used to sit forlorn in the hotel while Granny went violently about seeing the sights. There's a Last Supper or something. Well, in the hotel there was a middle-aged Englishman in a nice checked suit. He had sandy hair like Ma's father. He was the only man Ma had ever been in a room alone with and he was as bored as she was with Italy and they talked about cars. He drove a Lagonda and lived near Epsom. Perfect for her, my old Pa. They were engaged in five days.

'She never said a word of course. Granny hurtled her off to Florence and Siena, and bashed her round galleries, churches, the lot, beating down her own humiliation, wild as a fury till Ma was tired out and said, "No more. I want to go home."

'They had reached here, Cremona. Granny had got stranger than ever. She was tramping the city alone at night. She would come back at midnight and fling herself across a bed. Whaleboned, stout Victorian matron, taught that you never go out unchaperoned and never show your love.

'The evening Ma broke down and said she was going to get married to the man in the checked suit they were in the hotel dining room. It might even have been this one. It probably was. It's still the only good one. Granny took a great bottle of those fruit things and flung it to the ground and smashed it. And she took hold of Ma round the neck and shook and shook her. Yes. The management had to separate them and put Granny Ironside to bed. Can you imagine! "*Inglese! Non possibile!*" etc. And off goes Ma on the train the same night, all alone, to Milan and the founder member of the Lagonda Club. My father-to-be.'

'But whatever—?'

'Whatever happened to Florence Ironside? She caught the measles and died. She "had them on her", as they say. She caught them badly and her heart gave way. She's buried here—well, you know that, I told you. My poor old grandmamma. Daddy came from Milan and saw to it all. Consul, telegrams, funeral. Ma told me that he thought she should have come back here with him, but she sat it out in Milan. That's why she wasn't at her mother's funeral.

'I didn't know till Ma's end, her terrible end when her mother's presence was eating away under the surface of the memory—the awful last bit, when Florrie stood about the streets and lanes of Rickmansworth watching for her daughter, in the corners of rooms or peeping from windows or just inside the front door of her little house at the Final Resting Place. But it was then, when Ma had begun to plead with me to buy her dead mother sponge cakes for tea, that I began to think about Grandma.'

'Not to start *liking* her?'

'Understanding her. A little. I know now that what she was saying to Ma in the Last Battle of Cremona, throwing the fruit about, was that Ma should marry only for love. It wouldn't matter if the man did not love her. Forget that. If she never out-and-out loved someone (and you know Ma never did; not out-and-out; certainly not me; certainly not Pa, she didn't bother with him much even when he was dying, she was at a car rally), if her daughter was never going to love someone, love till it aches, said Granny Ironside, she'd be dead for ever. To marry for escape, to marry for money, to marry from boredom, or for protection or security were immoral motives. Granny Ironside was ahead of her time. She had come to see— God knows how—that Victorian, middle-class marriage was most terribly sad.

'"And *disgusting*," apparently she roared at Ma, at Molly her taut little daughter. (And think: sex was never mentioned then between mother and daughter except in a creepy whispering way.) "You'll lie there in the bed every night putting up with it, going through with it, maybe in the end not altogether disliking it, even in a vague way looking forward to it, at last treating it like a ridiculous duty. Immoral! Pathetic! Oh, you antiseptic, grasping girls." "For God's sake, *love*," she was crying, and all the Piedmontese as shocked as an English boarding house as they dragged her up the stairs. All so sorry for Molly sitting there clutching her dinner napkin. Such a bleak little face.

'So Ma left Cremona an hour later. Left her mother the bill, and it was vast because of the broken fruits, and sent Daddy to clear up.'

'But Molly did love people, Alice. She loved lots of people. Look at the huge funeral.'

'She was *affectionate*—as affectionate and nice as pie. But I don't think Daddy had much of a time. It was separate rooms from the start, you know, and you never saw a cooler widow. I'm very much an only child. After Pa, it was always women friends. No more men. And she was always bringing them to Italy. No reverberations. Just charming, leisurely little motoring tours. God—how could she? Lipstick, permed hair, good clothes and everything treated lightly. She kept clear of thinking. No religion, no politics (except you couldn't even *know* a socialist), no failures, no pain. Not a weed in her garden. Her table silver always shining, and a garage like an operating theatre, not a spot of oil on the floor. Love? Not a breath of it, ever.'

'She did mock, rather.'

'Oh, she mocked me about loving Italy. She came here, it always seemed to me, to cock a snook at it. "You never caught me, see!" But she used to say to me, "You're being Italian again, Alice, with your big black eyes. I wonder where you came from? If you'd been Granny's daughter not mine we wouldn't have been surprised."'

'It sounds as if Florrie's lover was *Italian*.'

'The only Italians in Shipley were ice-cream sellers and organ grinders. Unless of course it was Mr. Settimo, the photographer. The mind boggles. Maybe Ma had had a Settimo fling. No, I was born *years* later. My black eyes must be telegony.'

'What's telegony?'

'Well I never!' Alice looked just like Molly for a moment. Molly's glint. 'And all your brains! You ought to do crosswords. Telegony is when sexual intercourse produces offspring who look like a previous impregnator.'

'That's not possible.'

'Of course not. Yet farmers believe it. It happens to sheep and cattle. And Crufts won't look at a bitch that's been out with a mongrel, even if there's been no issue. Royalty feels the same, come to that. Telegony is the belief that the female can be changed metabolically by a particular lover.'

'That's rubbish. Ridiculous. Necromancy.'

'I know. Yet why are we in Cremona? It's not on the tourist beat for a tiny ten-day Italian holiday.'

'We're here partly, I thought, to visit your Grandmother Ironside's grave with your granddaughter who's arriving any minute. And it's a month after your own mother's funeral. And Cremona must have been a refrain in your family for years. Almost in your genes.'

'Exactly. Metaphorical telegony.'

'Oh, Alice, what cock! Everyone looks up family graves. It's ancient custom. A taste people have.'

'I wonder if it will be Avril's? She's probably furious with me for dragging her here when we could have met her in Venice.'

'I don't think so, Alice. New Zealanders never mind going places. They're like Scottish people. They mostly *are* Scottish people. What does she look like, your granddaughter? I hope she's not like Florrie Ironside.'

'I've not seen her in years. Her father, my ewe lamb, was dark, of course. Very. The mother—oh, I don't know. She comes from Dunedin. Anyway, Avril will be here any minute, dear thing. I left a note in the hotel to say where we would be.'

But Avril from Dunedin didn't show up as they sat in the piazza, and it was late evening before a lanky, delicate emu of a girl in long khaki shorts and a cowboy hat and bearing an enormous pack appeared before them in the restaurant of the hotel. Gently mannered, hesitant, she greeted the wrong woman as her grandmother before being redirected.

And she was certainly not telegonic Italian. Even metaphorically. She was yellow-haired, quiet and mild, and her thoughts were far away.

Yes, she'd come from Venice. She had been there for a week. Yes, she was travelling alone—well, sort of alone. There was someone she had come back to Italy to meet.

Well, had expected to meet; but just at present he had not got in touch. She'd left messages behind in Venice. Yes, an Italian (the freckly Scottish skin blazed). She had met him when she was in Italy two years ago. 'But look, it doesn't matter. Grandma, could I have some of those bright fruit things in the jars?'

'Of course,' the waiter said and smiled, fishing down into the vast glass bell with tongs, breaking the spiral pattern within, holding out a tiny pear the size of her thumb, so transparent you could see through to its spine and brown-gold pips. Then a grape like a water drop, then an amethyst plum, a ruby currant. An apricot dipped in sunset.

She asked for more.

'Signorina, five is enough.'

She watched them glowing on the shiny white plate. 'So lovely. I'd like a photograph.

'Oh, help!' she cried. 'But they're *hot*! They are killing me. They are burning my throat. They are burning right down to my *heart.*'

'They are mustards, signorina. Beautiful mustards. They look so sweet but they are mustards. Very ancient. "The mustards of Cremona." And see—you will find them only here.'

They laughed together, she and the waiter, as her blue eyes ran with tears. And then someone came to the table to say that there was a telephone call for the signorina, and she fled from the restaurant.

And her cup runneth over.

The next day was Sunday. The grave-seeking had been postponed. The granddaughter was not with the two elderly women. She had gone to the station to meet his train.

The two English women walked about in the spring sunshine and sat again in the Piazza Cathedrale. They listened to the great bells. They watched a priest freewheeling out of the cathedral doors on a bicycle, feet in the air, grinning for Easter.

It was a fashionable, traditional day for weddings and at about eleven o'clock they began. Brides stood in the piazza at the centre of their attendant family groups, and each group was sucked, eddy by eddy, into the cathedral and each group emerged again with a foamy wedded bride.

Then each group stood for a moment uneasy in the sunlight after the darkness of the church, and from the crowd before them stepped out the photographers. They stood for an instant in charge of time, each one the conductor of an orchestra, a judge at tribunal, a general before battle. They cried out. They moved people to different positions. They demanded the buttoning of coats, the arrangement of hands, the carriage of heads.

'Look at her. Look at each other,' they cried. 'Now at me. Look at me. Look into each other's eyes. Now—kiss her hand. Exactly so.' Then back within the crowd they stepped, or paced impatiently in the square, awaiting their next victims.

Wedding after wedding after wedding, bride after bride, like puffs of foam, surrounded by bouquets of bridesmaids. Stiff egg-white dresses swung in the breeze, a veil suddenly flew up in the air like a pillar of salt. Wedding after wedding after wedding floated and chattered its way down the steps. Each bridal party floated and chattered, floated and chattered its way into the side streets of the city.

THE BOY WHO TURNED INTO A BIKE

N ancy and Clancy were two little babies who were born on the same day in the same hospital and lived next door to each other for years and years.

Nancy loved Clancy and Clancy loved Nancy, but Clancy loved Nancy more.

Nancy was a rose-and-gold round girl, rather big and sleepy. Clancy was a little rat of a boy, rather small and sharp. When they played doctors and nurses Clancy was always the patient and Nancy the kind, kind nurse. Oh, how he loved his Nancy as she patted and soothed and caressed him.

So they grew up and went to school together, hand in hand, and waited for each other at the end of each school day. At first they were taken and fetched by a parent, usually Nancy's mother because Clancy's mother was always at the Bowlerama or the Bingo or down the pub. Nancy's mother was a great one for being at the Hospice shop or working for Save the Trees or Keeping Britain Tidy, and was never late at the school gate although she worked. She was a curtain-maker, sewing at home.

Well, childhood passed and Nancy changed. Boys began to hang around. Nancy draped herself about the front doorstep, against the doorpost, discussing homework and pop. She was always keen to go dancing. Clancy hadn't grown that much. He spent a lot of time out the front with bits of bikes, oiling and welding and easing and squeezing. He never looked up when Nancy went off to the dancing and she never looked at him. But both of them knew exactly what the other one was up to.

Sometimes even now if there was a crisis on, or around Christmas, Nancy and Clancy met up together alone. They lolled over the telly like husband and wife in Clancy's front room, never needing to speak. Just sometimes, 'How's the bike, then, Clancy?' 'What's your exams like, Nancy?' When Nancy was ill once and couldn't get up—it was about a boy, her mother told Clancy's mother: love pains—Clancy went round pretending he wanted a drop of oil and sat in Nancy's kitchen. He never asked for her or how she was, just sat in the kitchen eating Nancy's mother's fairy cakes while she went on about Nancy, and how disappointing she was and what bad company she kept.

But soon there was someone else coming to Nancy's door, not a schoolboy but a man, all flash jeans and earrings. A student. Older than Nancy, with a guitar, and he helped her with her A levels and was besotted. And Nancy, shrugging and yawning, went off with him down the path as Clancy sat at his desk in his front room, studying cycling form. He never needed to do much school work, exams never being anything to him.

Oh Nancy and Clancy—the trouble to come!

Soon there was a serpent calling for rosy-posy Nancy in a car. He would roar up and sit in the road with the radio blasting down the street as he lit up a joint. He didn't trouble to get out of the car, a roofless sports car, bright yellow. Nancy would come running down the path in her mini-frill, black boob-tube and heavy leggings, with her hair done up in barley-sugar bundles and her voice gone silly. And Clancy in his black shell-suit next door, looking polished like a black beetle, lean as a ferret, was all the time on the phone in his front room organising the local cycling club, the Gleaming Wheelers, of which he was founder, member, treasurer, secretary and president. The rounder and lovelier and noisier Nancy became, the skinnier, twitchier and less articulate grew Clancy.

Clancy's house began to fill up with trophies from the cycling. First they covered the spaces on the walls of his small bedroom where his bike posters and a few wheels hung. Next they spread over the walls of the front room. Then they lined both sides of the passage and began to climb the stairs. Photographs of Clancy appeared in *Cycling News* and the local papers; and after the night of Nancy's engagement party to the snake in the MG, Clancy won a remarkable hundred in Northants that brought him to the notice of the national press. He couldn't go to Nancy's celebration because of the hundred, the hundred being on a Sunday and Nancy's betrothal the Saturday night before, when Clancy had to have his sleep. Whether he got it or not in his narrow bed next door, with the noise of the pre-nuptial heavy-metal thudding through walls and piercing almost to shattering the closed windows, we shall never know. It was silent enough when Clancy left for his race at 5:00 A.M., picked up by some other ferret-like beings in a minibus with bike racks. Exhaustion oozed from the interior of Nancy's house in that dawn. There were a dozen cars parked all anywhere in the road, some with their doors open, and vomit in the tulips. A cold brisk spring day for Clancy and colder still in Northamptonshire. Up and down the flat, windswept roads, around the great curves of the silver River Nene, went Clancy, in and out of the icy spires of all the famous churches.

Not that Clancy saw any of it. Head down, bottom up, hands steady, legs like pistons up near his ears—all sinew, eyes narrowed—away he went, never looking for an instant at the gauge upon his wrist that checked the heart rate, never deigning to suck from the vitaminised bottle on the tight and glittering oxbow handlebars. He broke a national record that morning (3.31.52) and there was champagne and shouting and it was Clancy-talk at the Northants clubhouse the best part of the night. Some old spindle-shanked veteran, seventy if a day and still doing a good 4.31.00—a man made of ropework and leather with the fanatical gleaming eye of one who has given his life to the road—this old vet. said he saw the Arc de Triomphe in the tea leaves.

Clancy spoke little, as always. The habit had given him status. Some thought Clancy rather a comic little turn. So silent. No friends. Girls didn't exist. Hardly drank a drop. By trade he was a computer guy, and you can be that without speaking much, but he was a puzzle to his work mates, with whom he never conversed at all. They saw him arriving every day on a different bike, working-out in the Gents and jogging in the lunch break, and after the hundred one or two of them saw his face in the tabloids and were impressed. 'He's nuts,' they said. 'Cycling mad. Nothing else to him. But he's a consistent guy.'

Then something happened. Clancy's mum packed up and went to live with the manager of the Bowlerama. (His dad had packed up long ago.) She said she was sick of nothing but bikes all over the place and no conversation. 'Clancy's gone funny,' she said. 'See how he gets on without me.' Clancy's mum said she didn't know where Clancy came from and if she hadn't seen for herself the minute he was born she'd have said there'd been a mix-up. That Nancy next door now, there's a smashing girl with a bit of fun about her and her parents nothing but stuffed pudding.

So Clancy's house grew very dirty. From the outside you'd say it was taken over by squatters. Inside it looked like a bike shop, overrun at weekends by little streamlined people, crowds of them, with an eye for nothing but a bike.

Then Nancy's engagement was broken off, though she kept the ring, having paid for it herself, and she slammed the doors a lot and laughed over-loudly and wore don't-care clothes and went off with her parents to the Costa del Sol to get over it, Clancy saying he'd see to the cat and the rubbish and the pipes, it being wintertime. He took custody of the keys from Nancy's father, who slapped him on what passed for his shoulder as he left and said, 'Good lad, Clancy. Why can't she marry you?'

Not that he really meant it, Clancy now being dead eccentric with glittering eyes and twitching hands and an inward-turning heart. But he was much improved in appearance, fit and healthy and weather-beaten and self-confident in his way, people coming to his door for autographs and articles appearing about him in the Sundays entitled *Tour de France 2000?* and *Pride of the Midlands: Cert.* and *Wellingborough Wheels Olympic Hope.* All true—but you wouldn't want him in the family. Like a foreigner, he was. Inhuman. Dehumanised.

So Clancy took the keys of Nancy's house that fortnight; and every evening, be it ever so late, he'd let himself in and lock the door behind him, and when he'd fed the cat and picked up the junk mail and put it in the box marked Junk Mail he went up to Nancy's bedroom and touched her bed and opened her wardrobe and her chest of drawers and rubbed his little wedge of face into her knickers and bras and her all-over-lace shortie nighties. Once or twice he took off his shoes, turned back the bed cover and got into her brown satin sheets and lay still. He looked at the posters on her walls. Elvis types, rubber-necks, prize-fighters. There was nobody who looked the least like him.

Yet he knew she loved him.

Even when she came back from Spain with a great hairy thing with a paunch at twenty-five and all tattoos and boots, even when she paraded this dream-boy up and down the path next door, even when she introduced him, 'This is Darien, Clancy; we're engaged,' he knew she loved him. Him. Clancy. She flounced about when he just said, 'Hi, Darien,' and went on mending a back sprocket, garage doors behind him open to reveal a laboratory of cyclomatory science. 'Good luck,' he said. The Adonis smirked.

Nancy came round that night, a bit later, on her own. It was the first time she had come round and flopped down on the old sofa since they were kids.

'Can I come in? Heck—you want a few windows open in here. Is this the kitchen? I can't see space for a knife and fork.'

He cleared a stool of cycling magazines and moved the long drape of socks and sweat shirts on the string between the sink and the back door. He went to the sink and started cleaning oil off his hands. 'D'you want a Coke, Nancy?'

They were easygoing as two pensioners, yet they'd not talked for years.

'OK, if you can find one. It's for real this time, Clance. I'm going to do it this time.'

'Why?'

'He's strong. He's nice. He loves me.'

'If that's it, you could have me.'

'Don't be daft.' She looked terrified. She looked appalled. 'Be like marrying your brother.'

'You never had one. I never had a sister. It'd be good.'

'I'm not in your world, Clancy.'

'I don't care about my world, Nance.'

When he said this, standing amid all the paraphernalia—the holy icons on the wall, his lifeblood, his empire—she felt the power of him and ran off back home.

Her mother asked her what was wrong and was she crying and she said no, she'd been over to Clancy and he was pathetic. Just pathetic. And she wasn't having him to the wedding.

'She won't have you to the wedding, Clancy,' said her mother one day when he was disappearing off in his fast car with the bikes in a trailer, sleek like for racehorses. 'I'm ever so sorry, Clancy.'

'I couldn't come anyway,' he said. 'I've got the Nantwich Spa to Scroxton Fifty that day.'

He won it of course. It was his biggest win yet. They wanted to give him a ball. But he came home. Drove himself all the way home that night, got in at three in the morning. Not a sign of a wedding about Nancy's house. It had all been done down the Rotary with red carpets and a toastmaster and white ribbons and everything, a big confetti do. Clancy never looked towards the place as he let himself into his garage, thin, metallic little ferret Clancy, the hero of the world.

And the world never saw him again. Nobody ever saw him again.

Nancy's mother came looking for him in a day or two. She'd heard his telephones ringing and ringing. The place was empty. The cycling people came next. Then the gas man and the electricity and the Council. Then little clutches of people together. Then the press. Then the police. All the world came knocking, but Nancy's mother had seen no sign of him. Had she the keys? No, she had not.

It seemed, though, that Nancy had a key. She'd had one for some time. He'd given it to her when they were both eight and he had been provided with one of his own. Sometimes, between lovers, when Clancy was well away and after his mother's departure, Nancy would let herself into Clancy's house round the back and wander about in it and clear up a bit where once they used to sit hugging mugs of cocoa or bubbling down their straws into pop, or blowing sprays of biscuit crumbs in each other's face, laughing. She would clean round the bath and basin upstairs and even make his bed and look at all the posters on the wall, all the makes of bike. Examine all the trophies.

She would relive the one occasion when he had come in unexpectedly and found her there, a day when he'd not done very well in a Huntingdon–Lincoln Seventy-five and he was dejected. And sweaty. He had stood numb and she had taken him in her arms and they had lain together on the bed wrapped and lapped, soft and kind, warm and true, as if for ever. They never knew which one of them it was who had pulled away.

Clancy's mother came back after Clancy disappeared. She had been off with a pop group half her age and was into holistic medicine and E-tabs and seemed uncertain who Clancy had been. The police were stumped, the Sally Army too, and there was a lot of publicity and talk of murder by jealous competitors, though this is scarcely the way of the cycling world.

The house was sold, Clancy's mother needing money, and in the garage into which Clancy had last stepped was found, standing among his other bicycles, one of the most exquisite crafting: under twenty-five ounces, light enough to lift by a finger, equipped with every known and unknown development of bicycle wizardry.

Nancy, when she saw it, knew that it was Clancy. 'Can I have it?' she asked.

'What do you want with a bike?' asked his mother. 'I'm the one that should have it. It's all I'll have to remember him by. I'll take a thousand pounds.'

'Done,' said Nancy, and wheeled it away.

It lived at home with her, at first in the *en-suite* garage of the detached house in Park Drive, and after that, in its Jamaican-style extension; then, in the built-on cedar-wood conservatory. But this she found too cold for it in winter, even with rugs and blankets, so it came into the kitchen and stood by the Aga and every time she passed it she stroked it. When she took it up into their bedroom, however, her husband threatened to leave her. Once, when, during the menopause, she took it into her bed, he did leave her.

He came back, though. He had seen doctors about her and had counsellors come round to talk to her. These people spoke of mania and she threw a chair at them and climbed passionately on top of Clancy and rode away.

Away and away she rode on the long firm saddle, up and

down, up and down the hills. The hills flew from her as she rode. She rode like Juliet fleeing towards her tomb, and 'Clancy, Clancy, Clancy' yearned her heart.

MISSING THE MIDNIGHT

One Christmas Eve long ago, when I was twenty, I was sitting in the London train at York station, waiting for it to start. I was in a first-class carriage. I had been pushed into it. The rest of the train was packed. This compartment must have been unlocked at the last minute, like they sometimes do. Maybe it was because I had so much luggage. I was very glad to be alone. The compartment was sumptuous, with grey and pink velour seats and armrests and white cloths to rest your head against. I'd never travelled first class.

Just as the last doors were slamming, three people came into the compartment who looked as if they were there by right. They sat down two and one, the young man and the young woman side by side across from me, near the corridor, the old man on my side with the spare seat between us. I kept my face turned away from them but I could see them reflected in the window against the cold, black night. I had my hand up against my face.

I had my hand up against my face because I was weeping. The tears welled and welled. There had been no sign of tears when I was saying my bright goodbyes to the friend who was seeing me on to the train. I had waited to be alone. Now they rolled down my face and the front of my dismal mackintosh, and they would not stop.

I was leaving college a year early, having failed my exams and because the man I loved had told me the week before that he had found someone else. I was going home to my family, whom I despised and who had never liked me and were about to like me less. I had told them everything. Got it over in a letter. I hadn't yet told my mother, though, something which would cause her deeper distress—she was always in shallow distress—that I had also lately lost my faith. Anthropology had been my subject. I had just come to terms with the fact that it had destroyed my Christianity totally.

My Christianity had always been on a fragile footing on account of my mother's obsession with it. All she had seemed to be thinking about the previous night when I rang her was that if I was catching this late train I would miss the Midnight.

'But that means you'll be missing the Midnight,' she said. 'I'd have thought that the least you could do is come with me to the Midnight.' Then she said something nauseous and unforgivable to a daughter lost: '*All* the mothers will be there with their college daughters.' Oh my God.

All my mother ever thought about was what the neighbours might say, just as all my father ever thought about was how my achievements might improve his image at the bank, where he had been a desk clerk for most of his life. My father drank. He drank in the greenhouse at the end of our long, narrow garden in Watford. The greenhouse was packed with splendid tomato plants in summer and with heavy-headed old-English-sheepdog chrysanthemums in winter. Under its benches, all the year round, stood several pairs of wellingtons, and in every wellington stood a bottle. The bottles were never mentioned. They changed from full to empty to full again, invisibly. When my father came out of the greenhouse he would go upstairs to bed and cry. Then my mother would rest her head against the sitting room mantelpiece and cry too. Then, as she also did after she and I had quarrelled, she would fling on her coat and dash to the church for comfort.

And she always came back much better. I would hear her feet tap-tapping briskly home along the pavement as I sat in my bedroom doing my homework. I used always to be doing my homework because I so wanted to get to college.

After the church visits my mother would sing to herself in the kitchen and start preparing a huge meal for my brother. She always felt forgiven after her prayers but she never came up to see me. Her life was my brother. He was my father's life too. He was supposed to be delicate and he had been long-awaited. When I was born, eight years before him, there had been a telegram from my father's family saying, 'Pity it isn't a boy.' My brother was in fact far from delicate. He was surly and uncommunicative and had the muscles of a carthorse. He detested me.

The only time I had been happy since my brother was born was the summer before, when I was in love. It was amazing how much happier my family had been then, too. Much more cheerful, and nicer to me. My mother had gone round saying, 'Esther's engaged to a graduate.' I put my hand to my face and the tears rolled.

I could not ignore my fellow passengers. The smell of them was so arresting—the smell of beautiful tweed clothes, shoe leather, pipe-smokers' best tobacco and some wonderful scent. There was a glow now in the compartment. Even in the glass there was a blur like a rosy sunset.

It was the young woman. She had stood up—we were on the move now—to go down the corridor. She drew back the glass door and slid it shut again outside, turning back and looking down through it at the young man. I felt for a handkerchief and took a quick glance.

She was the most lovely looking girl, in a glorious red coat. Her expensive hair was dark and silky, with shadows in it. Long pearls swung. Big pearl earrings. Huge, soft Italian bag. The hand that rested on the door latch outside wore a huge square diamond. Shiny red lipstick. She smiled down. He smiled up. They were enchanted with each other and enchanted because they felt their families were enchanted too.

I was astonished. There she stood. My mother always said that you should not be seen either entering or leaving a lavatory, yet here was this goddess, unhurried, waving her fingers at a man when she was on the way there.

The fiancé leaned comfortably back and smiled across at the man opposite, who could not be anybody but his father. He had the same lanky ease, though he was thinner and greyer and was wearing a dog-collar. This old priest now looked across at me, and smiled.

The trio seemed to me to be the most enviable human beings I had ever seen. It seemed impossible that anything could harm them: easy, worldly, confident, rich, blooming with health; failure, rejection, guilt, all unknown to them. And how they loved each other at this wonderful point in their lives! When the girl came back they all smiled at one another all over again.

I could see that the girl did not belong quite to the same world as the priest. I knew she thought him just rather an old duck and that she had no notion of his job. I don't know how I knew this, but I did. And I saw that the son had moved some way into the girl's world, and would go farther into it. He'd got clear of all the church stuff. But nobody was worrying.

Was there a mother? Dead? What had she been? Cardigans and untidy hair and no time for anything? Or well-heeled, high-heeled bishop's daughter? Was there a sister? No, there was no sister. I knew the old man would have liked a daughter. You could tell that by the loving look he was giving the girl who was to become one to him.

Soon the fiancé fell asleep. Maybe we all fell asleep, for suddenly we were going through Peterborough and I was listening to a conversation taking shape between the girl and the priest, who, now virtually alone with her, was sounding rather shy.

'We shan't be in until after ten o'clock, I'm afraid,' he said. 'Of course, it's much quicker than it used to be.'

'Oh, *much* quicker.'

'I suppose we'll be able to find a taxi. Christmas Eve. It may be rather difficult.'

'Oh yes, it may be *frightfully* difficult.'

'Andrew is very resourceful.'

'Oh, he's absolutely *marvellously* resourceful.'

'I'm afraid we shall miss the Midnight.'

'The Midnight?'

'The service. The midnight Christmas Eve service. Perhaps you don't go?'

'I'm afraid I don't usually—'

'D'you know, I don't blame you. I don't greatly enjoy it either, unless it's in the country. In London, people come crashing in from parties. The smell of alcohol at the altar rail can be quite overpowering.'

She looked bewildered.

'I should leave it till the morning if I were you,' he said. 'It's quieter. More serious people.'

Her red lips smiled. She said she would ask Andrew.

'I don't really care for Christmas Eve at all,' he said. He had removed his glasses to polish them. His eyes looked weak, but were clear bright blue. 'Now, I don't know what you think, but I believe it must have been a very dark day for Our Lady.'

She wriggled inside the fuchsia coat and slowly began to blush. She lifted the diamond-hung hand to her hair.

'Think of it. Fully nine months pregnant on that road. Nazareth to Bethlehem. Winter weather. Well, we're now told it was in the spring. March. But it can be diabolical in the Mediterranean in March. I don't know if you've ever been to Galilee?'

The shiny lips said that they had never been to Galilee.

'Can be dreadful, I believe. And the birth beginning. Far from her mother. And the first child's always slow. Contractions probably started on the road. On foot or on a

mule of some kind. One hopes there were some women about.
And the birth itself in the stable. We're told it was an "annexe"
now, but I prefer stable. Just think about it: blood in the
straw ... the afterbirth ... '

He was unaware of her embarrassment.

She had no notion what to say. She was the colour of her
coat. At last—'We always have a family party actually on
Christmas Eve. Absolutely lots of us. Terrific fun. I'm afraid
we're not exactly churchgoers, any of us.'

'You will be having a church wedding, though?'

'Oh, golly, yes.'

'I'd very much like to marry you,' he said, lovingly, 'if that
were possible.'

She looked startled. Then slowly it dawned. 'Oh—yes! Of
course. Actually, I think Mummy has some sort of tame bishop,
but I'm sure ... '

'Perhaps I could assist?'

'Assist? Oh, yes—assist. Of course.'

He hadn't got there yet. The chasm was still just under the
snow. He noticed me looking across at him and, at once and
unselfconsciously, he smiled. I turned quickly away to the
night, trying not to hear my mother's voice: 'I don't care what
you say, Esther, there *is* a difference. Being a Christian does
show.'

'You might just be interested in this,' I heard the priest say
to the girl. He had brought out of his pocket a leather pouch,
squarish, like a double spectacle case, and he leaned towards
her, elbows on knees, and opened it.

She made a little movement forwards. Her hair brushed the
fiancé's shoulder. 'How pretty. What is it?'

Had she expected jewels? A family necklace?

'What dear little bottles! Sweet little silver thing.'

'It's a pyx. A "viaticum", the whole thing's called. And
something called an "oil stock". It's for taking the Sacrament

to the sick in an emergency. I like to have it with me. It's an old-fashioned thing to do nowadays. It was a present from my parishioners. Very generous.'

She touched a little flask. 'Is it all right to touch?'

'Of course.'

'What are these?'

'Those are the oils. For Holy Unction. We anoint the dying.'

She jumped back. 'You mean—like the Egyptians? Embalming fluid?'

'No, just oils. Very ancient idea. Long pre-Christian, I dare say.' He knew that I was looking across again and he turned towards me and said, 'Wouldn't you, my dear?'

'Yes.'

How did he know me?

'It's for people on their last legs,' he said. 'Last gasp. *In extremis.*'

'Can it bring them back to life?' she asked. 'Is it sort of *magic*?'

'Well, yes. It has been known to restore life. We don't call it magic, but, yes—it has been known.'

He was looking at me.

When we reached King's Cross they were quick at gathering up their luggage. I took much longer to assemble mine, which was mostly in parcels spread about the overhead racks. My two great suitcases stood outside in the corridor. I had no money for a taxi and I wasn't at all sure how I was going to get all this to the Watford train. There might just possibly be a porter, but I had no money for the tip.

I let them go ahead of me, the girl first, still smiling, Andrew behind, touching her elbow, then the priest winding a long, soft woollen scarf round his neck. A present? From someone he loved? Someone who loved him?

I had no presents for anyone this year. Why should I? They wouldn't care. There'd be none for me, or maybe just a token.

I didn't care, either. Home in shame. A grim time coming. 'God help me,' I said automatically, in my heart.

The priest turned before he stepped out of the train. He smiled at me again. He still held the leather pouch. He lifted it in his hand in blessing.

They had all three disappeared by the time I got myself together and started to shamble after them down the platform. There was a tremendous queue for taxis, so Andrew must have been at his most resourceful.

I didn't need a taxi, though, or a train, or anything else. Both my parents and my brother were gathered at the platform gate.

THE ZOO AT CHRISTMAS

Christmas Eve, and twelve of the clock.
  'Now they are all on their knees,'
An elder said as we sat in a flock
  By the embers in hearthside ease.

We pictured the meek mild creatures where
  They dwelt in their strawy pen,
Nor did it occur to one of us there
  To doubt they were kneeling then.

So fair a fancy few would weave
  In these years! Yet, I feel,
If someone said on Christmas Eve,
  'Come; see the oxen kneel,

'In the lonely barton by yonder coomb
  Our childhood used to know,'
I should go with him in the gloom,
  Hoping it might be so.

'The Oxen', Thomas Hardy

A pale, still day, the sky hanging white and low. It is the morning of Christmas Eve. The girl on the gate locks up at noon and waits around for the cleaner over in Refreshments. They go off together through the main gates, chatting down the lane to the pub. Over the other side of the Zoo, near Birds and Reptiles, the two resident keepers finish checking things and go off towards mince pies and a glass, the telly and the tree.

No human life stirs now within the Zoo. The toilets are locked; the kitchen of the cafeteria is washed down. Metallic, cold and colourless. The tigers look across. At it. Through it. Past it. Into the hoofstock enclosure. The tigers are fed on Tuesdays. Their weekly meal. This is Thursday. Not an urgent day. A flake or two of snow falls.

Word goes round. Electricity passes between cages without visible device. Ears can be switched on and off from within, out of boredom or pique or from the need for higher ruminations, particularly if we are talking tigers.

Tigers listen to other voices.

The feebler animals, the almost-humanoids, are always fussing to get through to the tigers. The tigers don't notice them. They pace. They pace and pace, turning on their own tails, on their own dilemmas. Pace and pace.

Suddenly they speak. The Zoo listens. It is like Jove talking in the heavens. Whoever Jove is. The tigers stop pacing and listen to their own echo, flick the tongue. Yawn. Great sabres glisten. Then they flow lightly up the walkways kindly provided by the management, liquefy themselves along them, turn on to their long, striped, brush-stroked backs, raise their great paws, expose the loose material that hangs below the abdomen, silk and fluff, close their eyes. They ponder in their hearts the problem of the hoofstock.

The domestic hoofstock is recent. It consists of cattle, givers of milk and meat. Oxen and asses and silly great cows; farm-yard creatures who have been introduced to the outskirts of the Zoo to familiarise children with the idea that all creatures are one. Ha!

The tigers drowse.

The less domestic hoofstock, the great bison, have been

penned nearby, their mountainous necks like deformed oak trees. They look puzzled. Born in captivity, they have never roamed a plain, yet somehow they cannot feel that they are cows. 'They'll be giving kids rides on them next,' say the tigers. 'Look what happened to the elephants.'

Over in the sand paddock an elephant trumpets. Two Canadian wolves suddenly come trotting out of their den and stand listening. They run together up to the scrubby roof of the den and lift their noses. They start to howl, first one and then the other, like whales calling under the sea. Long, cold music. Something's afoot. Here and there throughout the Zoo, other messages pass. Lemurs, little black faces wrapped in granny swan's-down, let out bellows from unlikely lips. The great gibbons whoop. The strange snow leopard runs up and down its high platform on its big fur-soled bedroom slippers. It flings its wonderful misty tail around its neck like Marlene Dietrich.

'Who brought in hoofstock to unsettle us?' muse the tigers. 'Farmyard domestics. Thomas Hardy!'

For it is the new hoofstock who have put about this legend of Thomas Hardy's, that animals—particularly oxen, who are the elect—are wont to kneel before their Creator on Christmas Eve. They worship the Christ child. And sing.

'We do it, too,' says a Jacob's sheep. 'Several kinds of farm animals were present at the Nativity. We *should* worship.'

'I wasn't present at the Nativity,' says Ackroyd, the Siberian tiger. 'And Thomas Hardy was an agnostic.'

'Sing?' the other tigers say. '*Sing?*'

'We sing. We worship,' say the hoofstock.

'You don't catch me copying anything human,' says Ackroyd. Ackroyd is bitter. Ackroyd is not himself. He has not been himself for three months, since he ate his keeper.

The golden-lion tamarins, their black leather faces tiny as a baby's fist, scream and chatter at the idea of kneeling and singing, and worshipping their Creator, but they have been persuaded—oh, weeks ago—by the languid, pleasant cattle to give it a try. In fact, it is they who have organised the whole outing tonight, to the nearby church. They have done all the publicity. They have liaised with visiting squirrels and rabbits who know the neighbourhood. The venue is the farmer's field outside the Zoo; the time, 23:00 hours. A local sheep will lead them.

Escape from the Zoo will of course be no problem, for there is an excellent P.O.W. network of tunnels, always has been. The serval cats and bush-dogs make use of it regularly for night-time forages down the M2. The panther is scarcely ever at home. He went off as far as Canterbury the other day (Hallowe'en, the fool) and walked round the Cathedral during evensong. It was in the papers. He was compared to some tom-cat on Exmoor. Washed his face in the sacristy.

'But that's panthers for you,' trembled the Zoo's one old lion (Theodore). 'They like humans. They feel affection.'

'Well, so does he,' said an elk, nodding at murderous Ackroyd. '*He* feels affection.'

Ackroyd looked baffled, but unrepentant. Tigers and penitence do not mingle.

'It's true,' called an elephant. 'Affection was what started it with that tiger. Up with his dinner-plate paws on the feller's shoulders. Lick, lick ... Next thing, the keeper's in bits and Ackroyd's getting bashed with an iron spade, and then put in Solitary. I've seen cats do it with kittens.'

'Hit them with spades?'

'Don't be foolish. Licking. Love breeds violence; it's better avoided.'

'Only certain kinds of love,' said the yearning, ugly tapir with his anal-looking snout. 'Not worship.'

'*Worship!*' said the elephants among themselves. 'What do any of us know about worship? We're not lapdogs.'

'Just what *we* say,' fussed the Low-Church wallabies, the

Quakerish giraffes, the pacifist bongos. 'What do any of us really know about love? But Thomas Hardy says that once a year, on Christmas Eve, we catch a glimmer. We are enabled to express our love to God and the Christ child. The experience is said to be agreeable.'

'God?' thinks Wallace, the gorilla, in the distance. He is the oldest inhabitant. He sits all day in the corner of his empire, the Great Gorillarium. He takes a straw from between his toes and holds it for an hour or two in his fist, pondering. His hand is the hand of an old farmer, purple, square-knuckled, with round grey nails. His domed, grizzled head is the shape of the helmet of the Black Prince. It is set between huge humped shoulders. Carefully he inserts the straw into the syrup bottle attached to the side of his cage, and sucks. He draws it out and re-examines it. Around him silly spider monkeys swing and spring. Two fluffy black baby gorillas, born last year, roll about covered in straw, the cage their world.

But Wallace can remember the rainforest. It returns to him in dreams; horizons beyond the diamond-shaped wire, vistas clear of hairless humans patched about with cloth. Winds and great rains. Scents of a river. Here, the snow is grey. Wallace in his thirty years has seen snow before. It does not excite him. Not as it does the snow leopard, who will now be up on his tree-shelf, purring. Bad luck for the public that it's not an open afternoon. They stand around for hours waiting to hear the snow leopard purr. Purring is his only sound.

Gorillas don't purr.

Pleasure? Happiness? Wallace's ancient eyes, the eyes that humans cannot face, the eyes that say, 'I am before The Fall. I am the one that knows'—Wallace's eyes ask: 'God? Christ?' Then, hours later, 'Worship?'

Yet he goes off with the rest. He accompanies them this night.

Nobody has expected him at all, but he turns up first. Timid antelopes, afraid of being late, come second. They are astounded to see his looming shape. They flicker off into the lane and stand between the farmer's hedge and the Canadian wolves, who, it being Christmas Eve, are uninterested in them. Next, the poor mangy lion, Theodore, comes creeping out of the escape tunnel and lies down with some local lambs. Red Kent cattle are standing about and the panther passes the time of night with them. The tamarins run about everywhere, flexing their tiny black hands, like tour guides with clipboards, and enigmatic langurs, like oriental restaurateurs on their night off, assist them. Where are the elephants?

'The tunnel's too small for them,' says a gibbon. 'They'll be kneeling at home.'

The giraffes?

'Yes. A giraffe has promised to be here. Vera, a nice creature. If her structure permits it.'

And, yes, here she is. Her delicate, knobbly, anxious little head emerges from the tunnel like a birth.

Monkeys galore follow her. It is 23:45. A quarter of an hour to go. '*Christmas Eve, and twelve of the clock,*' quotes an old ibex. '*Now they are all on their knees.*'

All is silent. Not a cold night. Snow settles lightly on the ground, on fur and hide. The snow leopard moves to a little distance on account of his rarity and distinction. He purrs. He sounds like a distant motorbike.

'This looks like the lot of us,' says the most human, the most mistrusted animal, the pied ruffed lemur, a donnish, dangly fellow once thought to be a form of Madagascan man who climbed trees in his pyjamas. 'Orl aboard, lads.'

But then there paced from the tunnel three tigers: Hilda, Enid—and Ackroyd himself.

Now St Francis, Easingbourne, is very close to the Zoo.

Like many other old English churches built on pagan sites, it stands on a knoll. It is near the turn-off for the Channel Tunnel, down a wooded lane. Well before the Danes, things of a nasty nature went on here, and although a Christian presence was established in the sixth century the atmosphere is still not altogether settled. There is a sacrificial aroma. Two strange animal heads are carved on either side of the church porch. They're in Pevsner. Tall dark trees stand close.

For many years this church has been closed, but recent guidebooks have drawn attention to the beauty of the setting, especially in the spring when the knoll is covered with blossoming cherries, so that tonight, for the first time in ages, a celebration of the Midnight Mass is to take place, by candlelight. The approaching animals, who had banked on privacy, see the glow from coloured windows, hear the deep chords of an organ within.

'But it's *always* been empty,' fusses a sheep. '*Always* quite left to ourselves. Except for the angels. They arrive on the half-hour in the sky above. That's when we go into Latin.'

The three tigers stand apart, looking across the graveyard at the church with their terrible eyes. They lie down among the tombs.

One or two people are arriving—not many. They are walking up the path to the porch, passing under a bunch of mistletoe reminiscent of other times.

A woman with a small, muffled-up boy pauses beneath the mistletoe as she straightens him out; Terry Hogbin, thought to be retarded. He looks out over the graveyard and waves at a lynx. His mother pulls him into church.

'So we just wait here, then, do we?' asks a nervous bongo, most beautiful, most fleet of all antelopes, most aristocratic of hoofstock.

'I don't know. This isn't in the poem,' says a common sort of nilgai. 'Ask the bloody tamarins.'

The tamarins confer manically together. They can't say, they can't say. Stay or go?

The gorilla, Wallace, decides it. He sighs, raises his vast grey bottom and lopes on fingers and toes into church, where he sits in one of the empty pews at the back, a space before him and an aisle to his side. The rest, except for the tigers, follow without demur. The old lion Theodore snuffs about and settles by the shelves at the door, flat out, his chin in the hymn books.

The tigers sit out in the graveyard. Their sleek, ringed tails twitch once. Twice. Then first Hilda, followed by Enid, and at last Ackroyd get up and slide seamlessly in.

Melting snow from the pelts of the animals forms pools on the medieval flagstones. A smell arises, like fierce incense.

A parishioner sneezes.

The organ strikes up the first and most glorious Christmas hymn.

'Mum,' says Terry Hogbin, 'look at all them animals.' She says shut up and turn round.

But neither she nor Terry, nor any of them there, ever forgot the music of that night.

The parishioners said it was like a tape. There was a new vicar, a woman. They hadn't got to know her yet and she must have set something up. It was as good as the Bach Choir, they said, or the Nine Lessons and Carols at King's College Chapel. It was like angels.

And they talked of how the candlelight had shone in a most peculiar way. The crib with its holy family, surrounded by cardboard animals, had been bathed in a midnight sunshine. The baby in the hay had stretched out His arms towards a glorious world nobody there had ever suspected. It was a pity that Terry Hogbin had upset his mother by tugging at her sleeve and talking about giraffes.

And there was that stranger, an old hunchback, who came up after the Blessing to look in the crib. And made off. And the doll they had used for the Christ child had disappeared with him.

And, come to that, so had the woman priest. She'd stood out at the church door in the snow after the service saying happy Christmas to everyone, and good night, and nobody ever saw her again. Margaret Bean, her name was. A name with a ring to it, like it might be a martyr's.

And Ackroyd had gone missing, too, the tiger who had eaten his keeper. His tracks had not been among the others making their way home; tracks that were to amaze many people the next morning. Ackroyd wasn't caught until the day after Boxing Day, and in a very confused state. He remained confused, even desolate, ever afterwards. All his life. But tigers are funny.

As for old Wallace, he took the doll from the crib up to his private lodging in the cage top, and would sit staring at it, quite still, for hours. When the silly spider monkeys tried to get hold of it and snatch it about, he would show his might. He would rise up in his terrible strength and beat upon his black, rock-hard breast, though (it has to be said) he hadn't much of a notion why.

O ld Filth had been a delightful man. The occasional kink, but a delightful man. A self-mocking man. The name had been his own invention, a joke against himself: a well-worn joke now but he had been the one to think of it first. 'Failed In London Try Hong Kong.' Good old legal joke.

He was Old Filth, QC, useful and dependable advocate, who would never have made judge in England. Never have made judge anywhere, come to that, for it was not what he had ever wanted. 'Failed' was his joke, for he had had exactly the career he had planned, to practise at the English Bar yet live as close to the Orient as possible.

He'd been born in Malaya more than eighty years ago, into a diplomatic British family, his muse a girl with loving, rounded arms. He had played in the village with the village children. They had filled him with love and superstitions and the tangled forests of the fiery folktales he had loved. Old Filth still spoke Malay and when he did you heard an unsuspected voice. All his life he had kept a regard for eastern values, the courtesy, the hospitality, the respect for money, the decorum, the importance of food, the discretion, the cleverness. He had married a Scotswoman born in Peking. She was dumpy and tweedy, with broad shoulders, but she too spoke some Mandarin and liked oriental ways. She had a Chinese passion for jewellery. Her strong, Scottish fingers rattled the trays of jade in the market, stirring the stones about like pebbles on a beach. 'When you do that,' Old Filth would say, 'your eyes are almond-shaped.' 'Poor old Betty,' he often thought now. She had died after their retirement to Dorset.

And why ever Dorset? Nobody knew. Some tradition, perhaps. But if any pair of human beings had been born to be Hong Kong expats, members of the Cricket Club, the Jockey Club, stalwarts of the English lending library, props of St Andrew's Church, they were Filth and Betty. People, you'd say, who'd always be able to keep some servants, ever be happy hosts to any friend of a friend who was visiting the Colony. When you thought of Betty, you saw her at her round rosewood dining-table, looking about her to see if plates were empty, tinkling her little bell to summon the smiling girls in their household livery of identical cheongsams. Such perfectly international people, Old Filth and Betty. Ornaments to every one of the memorial services in St John's Cathedral that in the last years had been falling on them thick and fast.

Was it the thought of having to survive in Hong Kong on a pension, then? But the part of Dorset they had chosen was far from cheap, and surely Old Filth must have stashed away a packet? (Another of the reasons, he had always said so jollily, for not becoming a judge.) And they had no children. No responsibilities. No one to come home for.

Or was it—the most likely thing—1997? Was it the unbearableness of being left behind to bow to the barbarians? The unknown Chinese who would not be feeding them sweets and telling them fairy tales? Neither of them was keen on the unknown. Already, some years before they left, English was not being spoken in shops and hotels so often or so well. Many faces had disappeared to London and Seattle and Toronto and rich people's children had vanished to English boarding schools. Big houses on The Peak were in darkness behind steel grilles. At Betty's favourite jeweller, the little girls threading beads, who still appeared to be sixteen though she had known them twenty years, looked up more slowly now when she walked in. They still kept their fixed smiles, but found fewer good stones for her. Chinese women she knew had not the same difficulty.

So, suddenly, Old Filth and Betty were gone, gone for ever from the sky-high curtain-drops of glittering lights, gold and soft green and rose, from the busy waters of the harbour and the perpetual drama of every sort of boat—the junks and oil tankers and private yachts, and the ancient and comforting dark-green Star-ferries that chugged back and forth to Kowloon all day and most of the night. 'This deck accommodates 319 passengers.' Filth had loved the certainty of the '19'.

They were gone, moved far from any friend, to a house deep in the Donheads on the Wiltshire–Dorset border, an old low stone house that could not be seen from its gate. A rough drive climbed past it and out of sight. The house sat on a small plateau looking down over forests of every sort and colour of English tree. Far away, the horizon was a long scalpel line of milky chalk down, dappled with shadows drawn across it by the clouds above.

No place in the world could be less like Hong Kong. Yet it was not so remote that a doctor might start suggesting in a few years' time that it would be kind to the Social Services if they were to move nearer civilisation. There was a village half a mile up the main road that passed their gate; and half a mile in the other direction, also up a hill, for their drive ran down into a dip, was a church and a shop. There were other more modern, if invisible, houses in the trees. There was even a house next door, its outer gate alongside theirs, its drive curving upwards in the same way and disappearing, as did their own, out of sight. So they were secluded but not cut off.

And it worked. They made it work. Well, they were people who would see to it that the end of their lives worked. They changed. They discarded much. They went out and about very little. But they put their hearts into becoming content, safe behind the lock on their old-fashioned farmhouse door that could never be left accidentally on the latch. Old Filth gardened and read thrillers and biographies and worked now and then in his tool shed. He kept his QC's wig in its black-and-gold oval box on the hearth like a grey cat in a basket; then, as nobody but Betty was there to be amused, he moved it after a time to his wardrobe to lie with his black silk stockings and buckled shoes. Betty spent time sewing and looking out of the window at the trees. They went to the supermarket most weeks in their modest car and a woman came in four times a week to clean and cook and do the laundry. Betty said the legacy Hong Kong had left them was the inability to do their own washing. After Betty died, Old Filth took everything from her jewel box and distributed it. He was leaving all his money to the Barristers' Benevolent Association, he said, because nobody felt much benevolence towards barristers. It was sad, really, that there was no one to appreciate the little joke. Nice man. Always had been.

It was the cleaning lady who destroyed it all.

One morning, letting herself in with her door key, talking even before she was over the threshold, 'Well,' she said, 'what about this, then? You never hear anything in this place. Next door must have moved. There's removal vans all up and down the drive and loads of new stuff getting carried in. They say it's another lawyer from Singapore, like you.'

'Hong Kong,' said Old Filth, automatically and as usual.

'Hong Kong, then. They'll be wanting help but they're out of luck. I'm well-suited here, you're not to worry. I'll find them someone. I've enough to do.'

A few days later Old Filth enquired if she'd heard anything more and was told, courtesy of the village shop, the new neighbour's name. It was indeed the name of another Hong Kong lawyer and it was the name of the only man in either his professional or private life that Old Filth had ever detested. The extraordinary effect this man had had upon him over thirty years ago and for many years after—and it had been much noticed and the usually cautious Filth had not cared—was like the venom that sprayed out from the mouths of the dragons in his old nanny's stories.

And the same had gone for Terry Veneering's opinion of Old Filth.

Nobody knew why. It was almost a chemical, a physical thing. In Hong Kong, Old Filth, kind Old Filth, and swashbuckling Veneering did not 'have words', they spat poisons. They did not cross swords, they set about each other with scimitars. Old Filth believed that jumped-up Terry Veneering was all that was wrong with the English masters of the Colony—arrogant, blustering, loud, cynical, narrow and far too athletic. Without such as him, who knows? Veneering treated the Chinese as if they were invisible, flung himself into pompous rites of Empire, strutted at ceremonies, cringed before the Governor, drank too much. In court he was known for treating his opponent to spates of personal abuse. Once, in an interminable case against Old Filth, about a housing estate in the New Territories that had been built over a Chinese graveyard and had mysteriously refused to prosper, Veneering spent days sneering at primitive beliefs. Or so Old Filth said. What Veneering said about Old Filth he never enquired but there was a mutual, cold and seething dislike.

And somehow or other Veneering got away with everything. He bestrode the Colony like a colossus, booming on at parties about his excellence. During a state visit of royalty he was rumoured to have boasted about his boy at Eton. Later it was 'my boy at Cambridge', then 'my lad in the Guards'.

Betty loathed him, and Old Filth's first thought when he heard that Veneering had become his new neighbour was:

'Thank God Betty's gone.' His second thought was: 'I shall have to move.'

However, the next-door house was as invisible as Old Filth's; and its garden quite secret, behind a long stand of firs that grew broader and taller all the time. Even when leaves of other trees fell, there was no sight or sound of him. 'He's a widower living alone,' said the cleaning lady. 'His wife was a Chinese.' Old Filth remembered then that Veneering had married a Chinese woman. Strange to have forgotten. Why did the idea stir up such hatred again? He remembered the wife now, her downcast eyes and the curious chandelier earrings she wore. He remembered her at a racecourse in a bright-yellow silk dress, Veneering alongside—great, coarse, golden fellow, six foot two, with his strangled voice trying to sound public school.

Old Filth dozed off then with this picture before him, wondering at the clarity of an image thirty years old when what happened yesterday had receded into utter darkness. He was eighty-three now. Veneering must be almost eighty. Well, they could each keep their own corner. They need never meet.

Nor did they. The year went by, and the next one. A friend from Hong Kong called on Old Filth and said, 'I believe Terry Veneering lives somewhere down here, too. Do you ever come across him?'

'He's next door. No. Never.'

'Next door? My dear fellow—!'

'I'd like to have moved away.'

'But you mean you've never—?'

'No.'

'And he's made no ... gesture?'

'Christopher, your memory is short.'

'Well, I knew you were— You were both irrational in that direction, but—'

Old Filth walked his friend to the gate. Beside it stood Veneering's gate, overhung with ragged yews. A short length of drainpipe, to take a morning newspaper, was attached to Veneering's gate. It was identical to the one that had been attached to Old Filth's gate for many years. 'He copied my drainpipe,' said Old Filth. 'He never had an original notion.'

'I have half a mind to call.'

'Well, you needn't come and see me again if you do,' said courteous Old Filth.

Seated in his car the friend considered the mystery of the fixations that survive dotage and how wise he had been to stay in Hong Kong.

'You don't feel like a visit?' he asked out of the window. 'Why not come back for Christmas? It's not so much changed that there'll ever be anywhere else like it.'

But Old Filth said that he didn't stir at Christmas. Just a taxi to the White Hart at Salisbury for luncheon. Good place. Not too many paper hats and streamers.

'Hong Kong is still all streamers,' said the friend. 'I remember Betty with streamers tangled up in her gold chains.'

But Old Filth just thanked him and waved him off.

He thought of him again on Christmas morning, waiting for the taxi to the White Hart, watching from a window whose panes were almost blocked with snow, snow that had been falling when he'd opened his bedroom curtains five hours ago at seven o'clock. Big, fast, determined flakes. They fell and fell. They danced. They mesmerised. After a few minutes you couldn't tell if they were going up or down. Thinking of the road at the end of the drive, the deep hollow there, he wondered if the taxi would make it. At twelve-fifteen he thought he might ring and ask, but waited until twelve-thirty as it seemed tetchy to fuss. He discovered that the telephone was not working.

'Ah,' he said, 'ha.'

There were mince pies and a ham shank. A good bottle some-where. He'd be all right. A pity, though. Break with tradition.

He stood staring at the Christmas cards. Fewer again this year. As for presents, nothing except one from his cousin at Hainault. Always two handkerchiefs. Well, more than he ever sent her. He must remember to send some flowers or some-thing. He picked up a large, glossy card and read: 'A Merry Christmas from The Ideal Tailor, Century Arcade, Star Building, to our esteemed client.' Every year. Never failed. Still had his suits. Twenty years old. Snowflakes danced around a Chinese house on stilts. Red Chinese characters and a rosy Father Christmas in the corner.

Suddenly he missed Betty. Longed for Betty. Felt that if he turned round quickly, there she would be.

But she was not.

Outside there was a strange sound, a long sliding noise and a thump. A heavy thump. It might well be the taxi skidding on the drive and hitting the house. Filth opened the front door and saw nothing but snow. He stepped quickly out on to his doorstep for a moment, to look down the drive, and the front door swung to behind him, fastening with a solid, pre-war click.

He was in bedroom slippers. Otherwise he was wearing trousers, a singlet—which he always wore, being a gentleman, thank God—shirt and tie and a thin cashmere cardigan Betty had bought him years ago. It was already sopped through.

Filth walked delicately round the outside of the house, bent forward, screwing up his eyes against the snow, to see if by any chance . . . but he knew that the back door was locked and all the windows. He turned off towards the toolshed, over the invisible slippery grass. Locked. He thought of the car in the garage. He hadn't driven it for some time. Mrs. Thing did the shopping now. It was scarcely used. But maybe the garage?

The garage was locked.

Nothing for it but to get down the drive somehow and wait for the taxi under Veneering's yews.

On his tiptoe way he passed the heap of snow that had fallen off the roof and sounded like a slithering car. 'I'm a bloody old fool,' said Filth.

At the gate he looked out upon the road. It was a beautiful gleaming sheet of snow in both directions. Nothing had disturbed it for many hours. All was silent as death. Filth turned and looked up Veneering's drive.

That, too, was untouched; unmarked by birds, un-pocked by falling berries. Snow and snow. Falling and falling. Thick, wet, ice-cold. His bald head, ice-cold. Snow had gathered inside his collar, his cardigan, his slippers. Ice-cold. His hands were freezing as he grasped first at one yew branch and then another and, hand over hand, made his way up Veneering's drive.

'He'll have gone to the son,' said Old Filth. 'That, or there'll be some house party going on. Golfers. Smart solicitors.'

But the house was dark and seemed empty, as if it had been abandoned for years.

Old Filth rang the bell and stood in the porch and heard the bell tinkle far away, like Betty's at the rosewood dining-table in the Mid Levels.

'And what the hell do I do next?' he thought. 'He's probably gone to visit that fellow Christopher and they're carousing in the Peninsular. It'll be—what? Late night now. They'll have reached the brandy and cigars and all that vulgarity. Probably kill them.'

'Hello?'

A light had been switched on and a face looked out from a side window. Then the front door opened and a bent old man with a strand or two of still-blond hair peered round it.

'Filth? Come in.'

'Thank you.'

'No coat?'

'I just stepped across. I was looking out for a taxi. For the White Hart. Christmas luncheon. Just hanging about. I thought I'd call and ...'

'Merry Christmas. Good of you.'

They stood in the drear, un-hollied hall.

'I'll get you a towel. Better take off your cardigan—I'll get you another. Whisky?'

In the brown and freezing sitting room a huge jigsaw puzzle only one-eighth completed was laid out across a table. Table and jigsaw were thick with dust. The venture had a hopeless look. 'Too much damn sky,' said Veneering as they stood looking down at it. 'I'll put another bar on. You must be cold. Maybe we'll hear your cab from here, but I doubt it. I'd guess it won't get through.'

'I wonder if I could use your phone? Mine seems to be defunct.'

'Mine, too, I'd guess, if yours is,' said Veneering. 'Try, by all means. I scarcely use it.'

The phone was dead.

They sat down before two small red wire-worms of the electric fire. 'Some sort of antique,' thought Filth. 'Haven't seen one of those in sixty years.' In a display case by the chimney-piece he saw a pair of old exotic earrings. The fire, the earrings, the whisky, the jigsaw, the silence and the eerily falling snow made him all at once want to weep.

'I was sorry to hear about Betty,' said Veneering.

'I was sorry about Elsie,' said Filth, remembering her name and her still and beautiful Chinese face. 'Is your son—?'

'Dead,' said Veneering. 'Killed. Army.'

'I am so very sorry. So dreadfully sorry. I hadn't heard.'

'We don't hear much these days, do we? Maybe we did too much hearing. Too many Hearings.'

Filth watched the arthritic, stooped figure shamble across the room to the decanter.

'Not good for the bones, this climate,' said Veneering.

'Did you never think of staying on?'

'Good God, no.'

'It suited you so well.' Then Filth said something very odd. 'Better than us, I always thought. Betty was very Scottish, you know.'

'Plenty of Scots in Hong Kong,' said Veneering. 'You two seemed absolutely welded there. Betty and her Chinese jewellery.'

'Oh, she tried,' said Filth, sadly.

'Another?'

'I should be getting home.'

It dawned on Old Filth that he would have to ask a favour of Veneering. He'd already lost a good point by coming round for help. Veneering was no fool. He'd spotted the dead-telephone business. It would be difficult to turn this round—make something of being the first to break the silence. Maturity. Magnanimity. Christmas. Hint of a larger spirit.

He wouldn't mention being locked out.

But how was he going to get home? The cleaning lady's key was three miles away and she wasn't coming in until the New Year. He could hardly stay here—good God, with Veneering!

'I've thought of coming to see you,' said Veneering. 'Several times, as a matter of fact, this past year. Getting on, both of us. Lot of water under the bridge and so on.'

Old Filth was silent. He himself had not thought of doing anything of the sort, and could not pretend. Never had known how to pretend. But he wished now . . .

'Couldn't think of a good excuse,' said Veneering. 'Bit afraid of the reception. Bloody hot-tempered type, I used to be. We weren't exactly similar.'

'I've nearly forgotten what type I was,' said Old Filth, again surprising himself. 'Not much of anything, I expect.'

'Bloody good advocate,' said Veneering.

'I'm told you made a damn good judge,' said Filth, remembering this was true.

'Only excuse I could think of was a feeble one. We've got a key of yours here, hanging in the pantry. Front-door key. Your address on the label. Must have been there for years. Some neighbours being neighbourly long ago, I expect. Maybe you have one of mine?'

'No,' said Filth. 'No. I've not seen one.'

'Could have let myself in, any time,' said Veneering. 'Murdered you in your bed.' There was a flash of the old black mischief. 'Must you go? I don't think there's going to be a taxi. It'll never make the hill. I'll get that key unless you want me to hold on to it for an emergency?'

'No,' said Filth. 'I'll take it and see if it works.'

On Veneering's porch, wearing Veneering's (frightful) overcoat, Filth paused. The snow was easing. He heard himself say, 'Boxing Day tomorrow. If you're on your own, I've a ham shank and some decent claret.'

'Pleasure,' said Veneering.

On his own doorstep Old Filth thought, Will it turn?

It did.

His house was beautifully warm but he made up the fire. He started thinking, of all things, about shark's-fin soup. There was a tin of it somewhere. And they could have prawns out of the freezer, and rice. Nothing easier. Tin of crab-meat, with the avocado, and parmesan on top. Spot of soy sauce.

Extraordinary Christmas.

THE GREEN MAN

An Eternity
The Green Man is no enemy of Christ.

Ronald Blythe

1 THE GREEN MAN

The Green Man stood in the fields. In the darkness of winter he was only a shadow.

People going to the tip to throw away their Christmas trees noticed the shadow as their cars sped down the lanes. 'That shadow,' they said. 'Over there.'

Later, in January, the shadow looked like a stump or a post. 'Tree struck by lightning over there,' they said as they rushed along to work at the power-station across the fields. 'Unsightly-looking thing.' If they were local people who had lived here some time they said, 'Look, there's that stump thing again. Strange how you never seem to notice until it's back.'

When blowy March came and the days seemed to lighten over the dunes, and you could hear the sea tossing and see it spouting up, people on their way to early holidays across the water and beyond the Alps would say, 'Well, someone's been planting seeds. There's a scarecrow. Spring will likely come.'

For the Green Man would now be standing with arms astretch and head askew and all his tatters flying, blustering grey and black and dun against the dun fields and the grey sky and the black thorn-bushes. There was beginning to be something rakish and reckless now about the Green Man.

Then in April the Green Man stood forth in cold sunshine, his hands folded over the top of his hoe and his chin on his hands, and in the dawn light of Eastertime people talking or jogging or riding by, eating things and laughing, quarrelling, shouting and singing, saw him there clearly, and bright green.

His old black clothes looked green and his winter skin looked bronze-green like a Malay's. His eyes were amber-green and one minute you saw him, and the next minute you didn't.

'Did you see that Man!?'

'What man?'

'That Man over there in that field. No—too late. It's gone now. Like a statue. Gold. No, green.'

'It must be advertising something.'

'Did you see that *man*?' the children cried, looking backwards from car windows, and the grown-ups went on talking or didn't bother to answer.

The old country people would say, 'Maybe it's the Green Man.'

'What's the Green Man?'

'Nobody knows. He's some man that's always been around here. I used to see him when I was little. I'd have thought he'd be dead by now.'

'The Green Man?' the granny would say. Then: 'Never! It couldn't be. I used to see the Green Man when I was a child and, even then, there was talk of him being as old as Time. He had other names, too. He lived hereabouts somewhere.'

Then a leery, queery old voice from somebody wrapped up in the back of the car among the babies—it would be something after the nature of a great-grandfather—would say, 'I seed the Green Man wunst when I were in me bassinette in petticoats. We called him Green Man or mebbe wildman. And my old pa, he said his old pa seed the Wild Green Man one day. It was the day my old greaty-greaty-grandpop went marching long this lane in his cherry-coloured coat, to the field of Waterloo.'

'The only Green Man I know,' the Dad would say as he drove the car, far too fast, round corners of the lane that, after all, were once the right-angled bends round the fields, 'is a pub,' and he'd rush them along towards the motorway that joined up with the Channel Tunnel or the ferry.

'If it was the Green Man,' the children would sometimes say as they stood on the deck of the ferry and looked back at the sparkling white cliffs with their grass-green icing, 'however *old* can he be? He could be a hundred.'

Nobody knew.

And nobody knows.

Under different names the Green Man may be a thousand years old. Or ten thousand. But his eyes are young and bright and by the time it's midsummer he is looking dangerously attractive and permanent. He has never had a grey hair in his head. In his sea-green eyes of July is a far-away magical gaze, if you can get near enough to see it. But it is hard to get near. Now you see him, now you don't. The field is empty and you'll be lucky to catch a glimmer of a face between branches, down the coppice. Did you see a figure at work with a bill-hook by the blackthorn in white bloom? Maybe you didn't.

Or he may pass you silently on the dyke above, when you're fishing the field drains. In the warm dusk at the top of summer he is like the nightingale and gone for deep woodland places. At dawn he is like the skylark, a speck on the blue sky.

Do not imagine that the Green Man is soft and gentle on his

land. For all his stillness he is given to rages. He likes to observe and see things right.

'Get off your backsides,' he has been known to roar. 'Keep to your element.' He shouts this at seed-time and harvest, yells at those—there aren't many—who know him well.

Sadie and Patsy and Billy, the next-farm children, know him well, and they hang around him and huggle his legs and ankles. They tickle the bare place between his boots and his trouser bottoms, they tease him with teazles.

'Get off your backsides and out of this drill,' yells the Green Man at these babies. 'This drill!' he yells.

A drill is a long straight furrow in the earth into which the seeds are trickled and then covered up. The Green Man makes thousands of drills across the earth until it looks like corduroy cloth. The seeds grow and turn into one thing or another. They whiten with tendrilly peas, they turn green-gold with barley. Barley whiskers are the colour of a princess's hair.

'Get off my *land*,' bellows the Green Man as he sees the cat coming, on tiptoe, paddling and playing, chewing at the barley stalks in the heat. 'Get off my *back*,' he thunders next, as the cat comes lapping and weaving and purring and winding around him, growling like a motor, springing up, all claws, to land like needles on the Green Man's shoulders and even his head. Very bad language follows then. 'Get off, you filthy scat-scumfish cat. Each to his *element*.'

The cat drops off the Green Man and lies on its back and shows the Green Man its fluffy white stomach and grins up at him. All animals are interested in the Green Man, but he by no means treats them like pets. And he doesn't treat people like pets.

As the year passes, the Green Man keeps away from people more and more. In high summer, deep in the trees he watches, very stiff and silent.

He will watch in secret. You can see carvings of him in churches like this. Watching you. It has always been so. He has always been there. Sometimes he is a leaf-mask on a frieze. Sometimes he looks like leaves only.

2 THE GREEN MAN MOUNTS A MOUSE HUNT

The Green Man keeps a house for comfort, but he's seldom inside it. He has had wives in his time, maybe hundreds, and they have tried to care for it. One wife cannot have been long-since, for he has twelve sons and four daughters living, very sturdy. Of course they may be much older than they look.

The twelve sons are scattered about the world, as sons tend to be, but the four daughters visit regularly, as daughters are more likely to do. The house is like a lark's nest lying low in the fields. The doors and the windows of the house are always open until the daughters close them. They visit, bringing bread and milk and lamb chops and shortbread, cleaning fluids, dishcloths and porridge. They flick about with feather dusters and say, 'This place gets no better. Lord, how it smells of mice!' They go looking for their father in the flicker of the poplars and down the marsh and across the fields near the sea.

The mice are not in the house at all on these occasions. Mice can smell daughters as daughters can smell mice. When they hear the daughters' cars arriving, their noses twitch and they're off into the bushes.

But when the daughters have gone away again, the mice creep greedily back.

The mice are fieldmice, but this is a misnomer. They should be called pantrymice or cupboardmice or pocketmice. They run in the Green Man's chests of drawers and armoires, in his bags of meal and flour. They run among the dishcloths and in the Green Man's little-used blanket. They lie, fat and lazy, in the fold of his folded deck-chair. They nestle in his boots and nest in his woollen cardigan and in the pocket of the mackintosh that hangs on the back of the kitchen door.

Do not imagine that the Green Man is a saint to these mice.

The weather one spring was cruelly sharp and perhaps the Green Man was feeling the weight of his two or three thousand years. He was using his house for sleeping every night. He was even occasionally lighting his dangerous paraffin stove which lit with a pop and a blob.

One day he lay down on his couch in the daytime, sneezing, with his cushion and his rug. He felt heavy with years and he coughed as he slept. And awoke to the mice running across his face like rain. He felt them running about in his blanket and snuffling at his toes. There was activity in his green-gold hair. With a roar he lit the lamp and found a mouse making off with a green curl to her nest in his boot.

'This must end!' cried the Green Man. 'The time has come. Each to his *element*.' And the next day he set off down the lane with his cheque-book and confronted the corn chandler's in the High Street of the nearest market town. The corn chandler's stands between the supermarket and the popso-bar, but it does a good trade.

How very strange the Green Man looked, holding out his cheque-book, demanding a writing implement. 'Mouse poison,' cried the Green Man: 'a quantity.'

Someone ran out into the yard and called in others. 'There's a right one here.'

'Who is it? What is it? Where's it from? Is it human? Why's it green?'

The old pale-faced corn chandler sat by the fire in the back of the office. 'It'll be the Green Man,' he said.

'Is it the Council? Is it political? Is it trouble?'
'It's the Green Man.'

'He's for killing mice. He's no Green Man. Is he out of a fairground?'

'Don't thwart him,' said the corn chandler. 'Don't thwart the Green Man,' he said, poking the fire.

The Green Man walked back along the ice-rutted lanes and the cold air puffed from his mouth like a dragon. 'Mice,' he muttered, 'mice. Each to his element.'

When he reached home he called, 'This is to fettle you. Back to your fields,' and he lifted the lid of the flour kist and saw fat, snoring, distended mice from weeks back lying like drunken skiers in the snow. They looked comfortable and in bliss.

These were the ones who were still sleeping and hadn't realised yet that the more flour they ate, the less likely they would be to get out. There were a number of dead ones. The Green Man tipped the whole brigade out into the grass. The ones who could still snore woke up and made off, looking foolish.

The foolish look of the released mice amused the Green Man, and he liked them after all as they ran away. Then he looked with shame at the mouse poison in the great drum he had bought from the corn chandler. Where to put it for safety until he could take it back and swap it for seed?

He put the drum inside the flour crock for the moment and went off to the fields, where he stood planning the year in the March weather.

The Green Man can make mistakes, for he is a man.

3 THE GREEN MAN GOES TO THE SEASIDE

Usually the Green Man keeps away from the ocean. He likes the drains and dykes and goits and runnels that water his land and the green rushes that spike them. He watches the arrows of the water voles, the mirror the water makes for sailing swans or flying geese. The eyes of these creatures watch the Green Man as he passes. None of them comments.

But beyond the dykes and the marsh is the sea, which is not the natural element of the Green Man. Sometimes when a sheep strays to the strand he has to go down there looking for it, but the sea feels hostile and full of anachronisms.

Most of all the Green Man detests mermaids. Whenever he is forced to go anywhere near the sea he keeps his eyes off the rocks.

'Yoo-hoo, coo-eee,' call the mermaids, giggling and twiddling their golden ringlets through their fingers. 'Who can't swim, then, Lover-boy?' Two of the mermaids are called Ermentrude and Cayley.

'Coo-eee, Green Man, you don't dare touch us.'

'Half-and-halves,' mutters the Green Man. 'No sense of their element.' He watches his dog, and only his dog. His dog is flurrying the sheep home. 'Neither wet nor dry,' snarls the Green Man. 'Beyond my understanding.'

But one day the mermaids are so provocative and insolent that the Green Man turns and walks right into the sea.

Ermentrude and Cayley are so surprised they forget to slither away, and sit with their pouty little mouths each in an oh! They throw up their hands, ooh la! Ermentrude's golden comb decorated with limpets falls into the sea.

The Green Man seizes the two mermaids, one under each arm. Abandoning the sheep and his dog, he marches back over the dry land, leaving marsh and dykes and drains behind him. Two gliding swans behold him from the water and raise their eyebrows.

'Help, help,' squeak the percussive mermaids and wave their little white arms out front, their tails wagging, slap, slap, behind.

The Green Man goes into his house and tucks both mermaids under one arm for a moment while he fills up the bathtub from the keg. Then he slings the pair of them in.

'Sit there,' he says, 'till I think what to do with you. Each to his element. Find what it is.'

He goes off to dig his potatoes.

'He's coming back again,' say the water voles. They had caught sight of his retreating figure and thought he had been very successfully fishing.

'He's coming back again,' says the next-door farmer (Jackson), who is the grandson of Sadie-long-ago. He has seen the Green Man pass, but only from the front. 'He's abducting women now,' he says. 'This might be nasty.'

Jackson goes into the Green Man's house and sees two girls' heads looking over the edge of the bath-tub. When they see the next-door farmer they begin to giggle and sing, so that he says, 'Well! So you were willing, were you? I'm disgusted,' and slams off.

The water voles tell it all to some seagulls. Seagulls think they are nobody's fool. They take nothing on trust. They fly to the bathroom window and look in. Twirling fishtails whirlpool the water. 'Couple of fish,' they report. 'No worries.'

The four daughters of the Green Man happen to be visiting that day and they are surprised to see the mermaids in the bath-tub. By this time the mermaids are growing tetchy and needing salt.

'There'll be big damages for this,' screeches Ermentrude.

'It's a scandal,' squawks Cayley. 'It's a threat to the environment. Haphazard. Erratic. He's a danger to the community. *Green* Man, my tail!'

The daughters found a small tin hip-bath, filled it with tank water and took the mermaids, one at a time, back to the sea. The tide had gone out and they had a long walk. Each mermaid delivered a separate scolding all the way, protesting that it was dangerous for them to be separated, and similar rubbish.

'Shut up,' said the daughters, 'or we'll drop you in the shallows and you'll have to wriggle off like eels in an ungainly way.'

'Stuff you all,' said the mermaids as they each glided quickly into the deep.

The daughters noticed the Green Man digging his potatoes as, carrying the empty hip-bath, they returned from the sea for the second time and they were so cross with him that they passed him by without speaking. When they were back in the house, though, they made tea and caught each other's glance and couldn't stop laughing.

'You should have sliced them in half,' said the Green Man coming in; 'I was thinking of it. Mermaid-tail fillet is a little-known delicacy, too sensible a concept for fairy tale.'

'It *is* a fairy tail,' said the most amusing of the daughters, but all the others—and the Green Man—groaned.

'And *you* thought to be a conservationist!' said the eldest daughter.

'I don't know why,' said the Green Man. 'Most of it's guess-work. Folklorists. Folk-laureates.' (Now the amusing daughter groaned.) 'Each to his element,' said the Green Man. 'No messing.'

The mermaids were no bother to the Green Man after this. Ermentrude's golden comb with the limpets was washed up at Ramsgate and sold at a boot fair.

4 THE GREEN MAN GOES WITH THE DEVIL TO THE MOON

It was one evening in early summer when the Green Man met the Devil under an apple tree in the orchard.

'I'd heard you favoured fruit,' said the Green Man, offering him a Worcester Pearmain.

'Good evening,' said the Devil, with a charming, quizzical look; 'I'd been hoping we'd meet.'

The Green Man looked hard at the Devil and thought, 'But this must be a looking-glass. He is just like me.'

The Green Man walked all round the apple tree and examined the Devil from every side. It could not be a looking-glass, because the Green Man could see the back of the Devil's neck, which was creased with lines as deep as the bark of an old tree. He felt the back of his own neck and found them there too.

Coming round in front again he watched the Devil picking his pointed teeth with a twig, and saw that the Devil's eyes were his own eyes at certain times or phases of the moon. They were watchful and knowing and on the hypnotic side.

'We have not been introduced,' said the Green Man defensively.

'Oh, yes, we have,' said the Devil. 'We're reintroduced every day of our lives.'

'Your place is in hell,' said the Green Man. 'Each to his element.'

'My place is with you,' said the Devil. 'I'm in my element with you. Every minute of the day. You can't get away from me. Look at those mice and those mermaids.'

'I spared the mice and the mermaids,' said the Green Man.

'Only just,' said the Devil. 'And your daughters did the clearing-up. And what about your twelve sons?'

The Green Man fell silent. 'They are grown and flown,' he said. 'We are part of one another, therefore I have no guilt. I cannot go searching for them specifically. It isn't my destiny.'

'I have things to show you,' said the Devil. 'Perhaps you will accompany me to the moon and find your destiny?'

On the moon the two twins sat side by side upon a rock and looked down upon the beautiful blue planet, so small in the sky.

'Yours,' said the Devil.

'It's been said before,' said the Green Man. 'Are the conditions the same?'

'Yours,' said the Devil again. 'Here's a zap. Zap it.'

'No,' said the Green Man.

'Why not? The earth has never been good to you. Look how you've worked for it and loved it. Do you imagine that *places* love you back? A landscape doesn't hesitate to destroy you. Your fate has been predicted since humanity could predict. You are touched with death. You are strangled by the living green. Look at the old carvings of you in all those churches and ancient palaces. In the end you will vanish from the earth.'

'I keep away from carvings.'

'The Greeks and Romans made stone effigies of you and the Christians made copies. Over half the world there are images of you with vines growing like moustaches out of your nostrils. Then from your ears, and even your tongue. Sometimes they even grow from your eyeballs. Your beautiful face is the face of grief. You are born to die. It is eternal sorrow that stares through the leaves. Sad and bound is the Green Man.'

'There is Christ,' said the Green Man.

'Is there?' asked the Devil.

'Go on, zap them,' said the Devil. 'Zap them all, down there. You could.'

'They are my sons and daughters.'

'They don't care for you. You are nothing but a nuisance to them. You embarrass your sons. Your death would be welcome. You are a burden and a reproach.'

'They are part of me, my twelve sons. And my four daughters.'

'I'm part of you, too,' said the Devil. 'Let 'em go.'

The Green Man sat silent.

'The moon is clean and free,' said the Devil, 'untainted as yet by human wickedness. You with your green fingers could bring here the first new shoot, which would break into grasses and flowers, crops and forests. You could create a new world, perfect in God's sight. You yourself could be God. The wilderness would flower like no earthly paradise. Let the old world go.'

'I'd need the earth for back-up,' said the Green Man, weakening; and as he said it, some moss that had become caught in his hair—from a low branch of the apple tree—slid out of his leafy curls. A spider that had been living in the moss began a hasty thread from the curls to the moondust.

The Green Man watched the spider, which went tearing about here and there and bouncing up and down like a yo-yo. The Green Man held out his finger and tweaked the spider back, and for want of anywhere better flicked him up into his hair again. 'I cannot leave the greenwood,' he said.

'Almost everything else has,' said the Devil. 'And what do you mean "greenwood"? D'you think you're Shakespeare or something?'

'I'm something,' said the Green Man.

'You're nothing at all,' said the Devil. 'You don't know who you are or what you are. All this about elements, you don't know your own. Nobody believes in you. You're kids'-book stuff. They don't even call pubs after you any more. They change them to something from Walt Disney. The only ones who go on about you now are black-magic freaks who think you're something to do with me.'

'Not quite the only ones,' said the Green Man.

'Well—who else? The has-beens, the *hoi polloi*, the folk historians?'

'Sadie and Billy believed in me,' said the Green Man, 'and Patsy. And the corn chandler.'

'Who he?' asked the Devil, commonly.

'The water voles, the geese, the mice and the mermaids believe in me.'

'Oh, Christ!' said the Devil.

'Oh, *what*?' said the Green Man.

The Devil stirred up the moondust with his finger, gently, so that the pressure didn't bounce him away. He seemed unenthusiastic about answering.

'D'you really think Christ cares about you?' he said at last. 'Think what a world you live in. Think what a wonder it could be and what he's allowed you to do with it. I tell you—forget him. Zap it. And him. Create the moon.'

'The moon is created.'

'Re-create it. Clothe it. Beautify it above the earth. Look at the potential, man. Look around you. A pure new architecture, rivers of silver, mountains of gold. After you've moved the space-trash of course.'

'I would spawn more.'

'Technology, man, technology. Enlightened clearances create a world of light. Get the straw from your hair. You spend whole days, whole years, scything the grass of an orchard nobody needs. You can get bags of apples half the price in the supermarket. And think of the space on the moon. You could do it. With my help. All you have to do is believe in me.'

The Green Man tried now, seriously, to consider the Devil's rational good sense and to analyse what the earth and the moon really meant for him. He thought of the moon's calm light as it sailed above the branches of the orchard.

'It's not for me to change it,' he said.

'I'm disappointed in you,' said the Devil.

'I'm disappointed in *you*,' said the Green Man.

'But *why*?' asked the Devil with his sweet and loving smile.

'You're nothing but my shabby self,' said the Green Man. 'You're the dark side of my soul. You're *déjà vu*.'

The Devil then threw a rock at him and vanished and the Green Man in an instant was back in the orchard, under a Ribston Pippin. It was cold and raining and the fruits above his head looked ungrateful and sour. He found himself weeping and weak.

'I must sleep,' he said, 'here in the grass and the rain. When I wake perhaps I won't feel that it's been a defeat,' and he fell asleep in the grass that would be cut for hay on Saturday.

The spider walked out of his hair and spun a beautiful web across his tired eyes.

5 THE GREEN MAN ATTENDS A PLACE OF WORSHIP

At harvest festival, like many farmers since its ancient institution and maybe only out of pagan habit, the Green Man sometimes goes to church. He goes to the early morning service, where there are few people. The church has always been lovingly decorated for harvest with flowers and vines and bines and trails of hops. There is bread, plaited or covered in cobnuts or marked into gold squares. There are no sheaves of corn these days, but tins of baked beans that are later taken to patients in hospital. Patients in hospital would be bewildered by sheaves. They are rather bewildered by baked beans and usually hand them over to their visitors. The visitors take them home and give them to their children when there has to be a contribution to the next school fête. The baked beans bought at the fête will be half-price and often come back to church for the next harvest festival. This is country life.

The Green Man is hard to discern among the hop bines and the baked beans in the church at harvest, but he is there if you look hard enough. He doesn't sit in the body of the church but tends to be up in the chancel, leaning against a pillar, peering through the decorations of harvest green and gold. Up above him on a corbel (*c.* 1220) his own effigy looks down. It is his own head, wrapped in vine leaves like a Greek dinner.

The Green Man's head, so beautiful, passionate, tormented,

ardent, is being eaten up by oak leaves. He stares down at the living Green Man—who is listening gratefully to the Collect—and around the church which is his prison.

'I see myself everywhere,' says the living Green Man. 'First in the orchard,' he says, 'then on the moon. Good likenesses, though by no means exact. And I'm supposedly defunct. I am seldom noticed and when I am noticed everyone sees someone different: a tree, a scarecrow, a saint, a devil, or "That old guy on the farm; bit out of his element these days. Belongs to the past." They do not *peruse* my face. Sometimes they see me, sometimes they don't.'

'The fruits in their season,' intones the parson.

At the Gospel the Green Man turns to face the east end of the church, as has been his medieval way. This brings him to face his companions along the pew. It is the choir-stall pew of Transept Manor. Lord Transept and Lady Serena Transept, their cheerful cousin and the dog, stand in a row. All remain face forward in the aristocratic low-church way except the dog, who decides to face west and wag its tail at the Green Man. The cheerful cousin waves her handkerchief.

After the service Lady Serena Transept—tall, flat and slender as her ancestor who lies on top of a nearby tomb in wimple, camisole and long stone robe and who looks much like her except that Lady Serena has a long hooky nose. The ancestor had one too, but it was snipped off into a Cromwellian pocket—Lady Serena Transept turns to the Green Man and lays a long-fingered paw upon his Sunday-best green tweed arm. 'Come to breakfast,' she says.

So they all set forth to Transept Manor, Lady Serena driving fast, through the swishing puddles of the mile-long avenue of dead elms. Lord Transept broods alongside and the cousin sits in the back humming hymns with the dog, who looks delighted. In the manor kitchen they drink tea and eat toast and the cousin selects the numbers for her lottery ticket and the dog lies ecstatic in the Green Man's lap. His lordship hangs in looming thought and Lady Serena strokes the back of the Green Man's hand.

'I never thought to meet you,' she said. 'I've looked up at you for years on the corbel.'

'Corbels and capitals, tympana and misericords,' says the Green Man: 'I'm all over the place yet nobody knows who I am. I am not all stone. I come to church for all the great festivals.'

'I know. I have seen you. So has my dog, but we never dared speak. I *feel* that I know you. I *know* that I know you. One knows a lot about the person one prays next to.'

'Marmalade,' says his lordship.

'Tootle-oo,' sings the daft cousin.

The dog sighs.

Outside, the rain has stopped and the drops on the bumpy diamonds of the window-panes turn the day to wet gold. Sunshine breaks across the cauliflower fields and lights a lanternyard of fruit trees, ten miles of hop-gardens, three needle spires and a stretch of Roman road on the horizon, where big lorries and tractor-vans roll along like toys.

The beams in the manor-house kitchen are made from oaks that may have dropped acorns on legionaries. Whoever decided to make a kitchen of them didn't bother to take off all the bark. There are bumps and sawn circles where branches have been trimmed off to be slung on to fires to roast oxen. The Green Man, surveying these timbers, reflects that there is nothing like them on the moon.

'Soon we shall *all* go to the moon,' says the jolly cousin.

His lordship says, 'These days I'm only able to put one foot in front of another.'

'Sometimes,' says his sister, 'you can't even do that.'

This scene in the manor kitchen the Green Man finds very comforting.

Lady Serena Transept walks with the Green Man part of the way home. He pushes his bicycle beside her along the avenue and she jumps the puddles like a giraffe (and she all of ninety), her spindle legs in thick, lace-patterned stockings.

'We are both old things,' she says: 'antiques. I and His Lordship and the Manor will soon be gone, and all our kind.'

'And, no doubt, I,' says the Green Man.

'Oh, I don't think so,' she says. 'I'd doubt that very seriously.'

6 THE GREEN MAN AND THE LOSS-ADJUSTER'S WOMAN

The Green Man is in the coppice, lean as a sapling, pausing with his axe, peering from his deep-set eyes through the silver branches. Who is this walking over the meadow towards his house? She disappears in a fold of the field where the house lies, and after some time she re-emerges and walks towards him. She has passed through his house, front door to back, for both stand open. Here she comes on her high heels, a snake, very thin, smoking a cigarette, which she throws away into the coppice. The Green Man is invisible in the bouquets of the ash clumps, his face dappled so that leaves seem to flicker and caress his cheeks, to sweep out of his eyebrows. *Who's this then?*

He watches carefully to make sure that the cigarette lies dead in the wood-chippings and the wood anemones. There is no glow.

She passes. She has a mean look. She wears town clothes, not warm enough, but quite respectable. She places her feet with care and they take her out of sight down to the great May trees and beyond; beyond the struggling elms and the whispering poplars, over the marsh. There she goes. Only a dot now. Over the marsh to the seaside.

Now, she is returning, and she passes through the coppice again and he sees her little watchful face. It is a closed face.

This time she side-steps his hidden house and soon he hears a motor starting up and driving away. The silence flows over the land again to be broken before long by the Green Man as he flings his axe against the sapling stalks in rhythmic chopping.

He works until nightfall and the wind has changed and comes off the sea and he feels cold. He walks home thinking, I shall sleep indoors tonight. He has his axe over his shoulder and he whistles for the dog, but the dog doesn't come. He thinks of hot porridge and hot tea and maybe whisky before bed.

But there is no bed. There is no couch. There is no table. There is no chair. Gone is the small wooden-handled herb-chopper of ancient design, the barometer given him by the peripatetic academic folklorist, the hat that once belonged to Oliver Cromwell, willed him by a former Lord Transept. Gone are the books from the shelf, the lustre jug from the dresser, the gold comb with the seashells he bought at the door and has never liked. Gone is the black iron kettle on the chain and the iron griddle that hung from the rafters, the great court-cupboard mysteriously carved in Bremen and the jerry-pot of Meissen. Gone is the dog.

The Green Man walks in the east wind, calling for the dog. When at last he returns, he makes porridge, but not in the black pot, which needs both hands to be lifted to the fire and is lined with heavy silver; for that is gone.

There is a very old hearth-mat made of coloured scraps of cloth from God knows which countries and the Green Man wraps himself in this and sleeps upon the floor.

In the morning, or perhaps several mornings later, come some daughters lovely as lilies, early, and see upon the floor this long roly-poly with head and feet stuck out at either end and all the tufted patches of old garment-scraps in between. There is the scrap of an eighteenth-century smock, a nineteenth-century bloomer, a snicket of liberty bodice with a very small pearl button, the edge of a milkmaid's petticoat and a glimpse of lavender silk from the wedding dress worn by who knows who in the Green Man's history, and all the women in it. His green feet are sockless for his socks are gone. His green hair floats about, for gone is his limpet-covered comb. The Green Man in his bedding roll is like a multi-coloured almond-slice in the window of an eccentric pastry cook.

The dog, all burrs and sorrow, lies close beside him on the floor.

Mugged! Dead! Police! Robbers!

Certainly robbers.

Retribution! Revenge!

But the Green Man sits up on an apple box and takes a mug of tea and picks burrs off the dog. The dog cannot stop shivering.

'Oh, we'll catch them all right,' says the policeman—a fishy, flashy fellow who has a past and doubtful friends. The Green Man has often heard him, sniffing about. 'We'll soon get the Loss-Adjuster in.' The Green Man is unaware of loss-adjusters and presumes them to be philosophers.

'You might also like a counsellor,' says the young policegirl, overweight and gorgeous. *I could counsel you*, her eyes say to the exotic animal-eyes of the Green Man, *after hours*.

'I have suffered no loss,' says the Green Man. 'I shall miss the little herb-chopper. And my socks, for they were knitted by someone close to me.'

'He enjoys frugality,' say the daughters, putting up a new

bed and couch, setting stainless steel on the shelf. 'He's in his element away from plenty.'

The Green Man strokes his dog.

'Do you bring a charge then?' asks the policeman.

'Yes,' say the daughters.

'No,' says the Green Man. 'No charge, free for all.' Then, looking at the policeman, he says, 'I shall lose nothing.'

'I'd not count on that, Grandad. There was a big antiques fair at Newark last week and all will be gone to Holland in containers by now. You'll be insured of course? The Loss-Adjuster will see to you.'

The Green Man is not conversant with details of insurance policies.

Each to his element.

The policegirl can't keep away. She calls early and late, but after a time she does not find the Green Man at home. She shouts to him across the marshes, but there is no reply. He sleeps out in the coppices among the wood anemones and relies on Indian Take-Aways from the next-door farmers, old and young Mr. Jackson. 'Hello?' she calls. 'Are you there? It's me, Pearly.' She thinks of him all the time. She will never forget him. She is never to meet such another. She wanders, dreaming through the coppice, in her black police shoes, over the dykes. The long wet grasses brush her strapping legs. She leaves a daring note one day on the new plastic table in the kitchen, with a box of chocolates and a dozen pairs of socks marked 'Nylon Rich'.

The Green Man doesn't understand the note and feeds the chocolates to the dog. The socks revolt him.

One day, comes the first woman again on her high heels over the meadow. She looks to left and right and smokes her cigarette and when she gets to the coppice this time her eyes have become accustomed to the light and she sees the Green Man standing there. She makes to throw away the cigarette but then rubs it out on the sole of her shoe and puts it in her pocket. 'Hi,' she says. She seems uneasy. He does not speak.

'My partner is the Loss-Adjuster and he's down in the car, waiting.'

'I have not suffered loss.'

'You have been victimised. By someone who knew everything about you.'

'*Everything* about me?'

She blushes, and pretends to be bored. 'He's come to make an assessment.'

'An assessment of me?'

'He's the policeman's twin brother.'

'Ah.'

There falls a silence until the Green Man walks across to her in the whispering wood-chips that scent the air among the wood anemones. There are bluebells now, too. Such bluebells! Smoke on summer eves. The scent of bluebells lasts for one week only.

The Green Man carries his glistening axe over his shoulder and comes close to the woman and looks down, down into her troubled eyes. He takes the axe from his shoulder with both his hands and holds it high.

She cannot move.

Then he places it in the woman's stained hands with their chipped red nails and says, 'Take this, too.'

She throws it to the ground and runs away, stumbling back across the meadow.

As she passes the house the dog shoots out and goes for her heels, snap, snap. He remembers her. He remembers, too, the Loss-Adjuster who is sitting in the car.

The Loss-Adjuster is not keen to get out of the car.

'He won't take money,' says the woman, falling into the seat beside him, the dog raising merry hell.

'Why you all over 'im? Let 'im be,' says the Loss-Adjuster. He smells of guilt and sweating fear that glistens on his cheeks.

'He could get us caught,' squeals his woman.

'Get on, 'e's a lunatic.'

'I don't know what he is,' she says, crying.

The Green Man stands now on a rise behind the invisible house, watching them. The evening sun flames on his wood-land limbs, his axe gleams, his hair blows green in the wind.

''e's from the sixties. 'e was a drug-addict,' says the Loss-Adjuster. 'There's stories about 'im. Forget it, can't you?'

'We've got to get it all back to him. He's bad news.'

''e doesn't want it,' says the Loss-Adjuster. 'Pearl said. She's gone soft on 'im.'

Then the Loss-Adjuster's woman is filled with a raving jeal-ousy and she tries to get out of the car. 'I must go back and be with the Green Man,' she cries, and the sweaty Loss-Adjuster socks her and starts the car and tries to drive it away down the lanes where sometimes farm machinery passes along, each machine the length and height of a street of houses. One of these in a moment meets the Loss-Adjuster and his Moll on the corner of a flax field, oh, such a colour, more gentle, more shadowy blue even than bluebells, blue as a tender morning sky and now splattered all over with scarlet.

The policegirl is back soon to try to counsel the Green Man all over again in his double tragedy, but he looks over her head, far, far away.

'Don't you care about *anything*?' she weeps then. '*Why* can't you need comfort?'

So he takes her home for a time, then makes her some tea in a tin mug and sends her away with the multi-coloured rug of paduasoy and glazed linen and sprig-muslin snips, of velveteen and taffeta and tussore, a shred or two of hair shirt but much *point d'ésprit* and threadwork and black work and bead work and hedebo, and rich lazy-daisy and faggoting and Venetian *toile cirée*. The old rug is backed with flour bags, and she keeps it all her life.

7 THE GREEN MAN MEETS HIS MAKER

The gold-and-rose-coloured autumn is gone and in November come the wind and the rain and the Green Man's twelve sons in a minibus. He sees it from his kitchen window, and closes his eyes. In they all stream. 'What a disgrace! You look ill! You look haggard! Who looks after you? Where are our sisters?'

'They are on a short holiday in the south of France.'

'Lucky for some. *They* don't work like we do. *We* can't afford holidays in the south of France. And how stupid, too, the south of France at this time of the year. You are living so poor. You need paint and wallpaper. Your roof is full of holes. You will shame us in the neighbourhood. What's for dinner?'

'I'm afraid I no longer eat dinner. I no longer need it.'

'You are undernourished. You have leaves in your hair. Let me get on the blower for supplies, carpenters, painters. Amenities.'

'Amenities?'

'The electricity board, the telephone centre, the television and video shop.'

'And to the Authorities,' says the eldest son. 'There are excellent homes for the elderly.'

'I am not elderly,' says the Green Man, 'I am the Green Man.'

'Hello? Hello? Yes, he needs help. He is alone. Practically *unfurnished*. We think it has affected his mind.'

'Out!' shouts the Green Man. 'The lot of you. Back to your element,' and he picks up a flail that leans by the back door and begins to strike out about him, clubbing some of them on the head.

They scatter in their sharp suits, clutching their mobile phones. All except the youngest, who turns back and says, 'Sorry it's been so long, Dad. It's easy to forget the passage of time.'

'I've stood so long in the passage of time,' says the Green Man; 'it is my home sweet home.'

'Can you manage?' asks the youngest son (and another one, possibly Number Six, who's not as bad as most of the rest, peeps round the door and fingers his club tie). 'Have you enough money?'

'Money has never been a trouble to me.'

'Have you enough food?' and he lifts the lid of the flour crock and sees the drum marked MOUSE POISON.

'Mouse poison in the flour crock!' cries the eldest awful son with his blow-dried hair, coming back into the kitchen. '*That* does it. Not fit to live alone.' He picks up the drum and makes off with it to the minibus, where the rest of the brothers are glaring through the windows.

'We'll take it back to the corn chandler and get him to send you some bread,' says the kindly, though feeble, youngest son.

'He doesn't deliver.'

'I'm sure that he would.'

'Goodbye,' says the Green Man, stern as Ulysses.

He watches the minibus depart, driven erratically and bad-temperedly by the eldest son. The youngest son waves from the window.

'Thank God,' says the Green Man and lies down on his old couch and listens to the silence. After a time, edging into the silence, a wind begins to blow across his fields, a soft wind but whispering of winter. The Green Man sleeps.

Then the Green Man has a dream. He dreams that the wind

has strengthened and is tearing at his house in the fold of the fields and that he hears branches and sheds come crashing down. He dreams that he goes to fasten the clattery window in the kitchen, and there outside, beneath a leafless tree in the apple orchard, stands a figure who looks as if he owns the place. Before shutting the window the Green Man shouts, 'Get off my land.'

Then he wraps himself in an extra sack and goes outdoors. 'What do you think you're doing in my orchard?' he cries.

'I'm standing on next year's daffodils,' says the man.

The man's clothes do not blow in the mighty wind. Otherwise his figure is similar to that of the Green Man. He is tall and lean and wears something much like a sack. This time it is certainly not the Devil.

The Green Man thinks again, 'I must be seeing through a looking-glass,' and he walks right round the man. The man's hair is longer than the Devil's so that the Green Man cannot examine the lines in his neck. Nevertheless he thinks, 'This is myself.' But when he has come full circle and looks into the man's eyes, he sees that the man is Christ.

The Green Man falls to his knees, but Christ raises him up.

'Your troubles are over,' says Christ.

'You mean I am about to die?'

'I mean that there is no Death,' says Christ. 'Today you will be with me in paradise.'

'But I'm the Green Man. The earth is my element. This is my tragedy. You know this. I am bound and tied. The very meaning of me is not known. You do not include me.'

Christ said, 'The Green Man is no enemy of Christ.'

The Green Man woke from his dreams and the wind was not the soft wind to which he had fallen asleep: it was shrieking and howling as it had done in the dream orchard.

It was daylight, and he went to fasten the clattering window, outside which nobody stood under the trees.

'I shall eat some bread,' said the Green Man. He felt very tired. 'And I shall drink some water.' Then he remembered that the flour crock was empty. The water down in the field dyke felt far away.

So he thought, 'I'll rest a bit longer,' and lay down again on the couch. Soon he began to feel peaceful. 'I shall wait here for Death,' he said. 'Here it comes.'

Soon, far away down the lanes, he heard the sound of Death approaching. It was a great black Yamaha. Its rider sat astride it, a black figure in black visor and black armour. Black gauntlets grasped the black handlebars. The noise of the great bike seemed to silence the wind.

'It is here,' said the Green Man as the motorbike shuddered, surged and stopped at his gate. He walked to his front door and opened it on the black day.

Death pushed his steed right to the Green Man's threshold. Fastened to its flank was a box with a lid and a strap.

'Too small for a coffin,' thought the Green Man. 'Maybe it's for my ashes.'

'Can I bring it round the back,' asked Death, 'in case it gets nicked at all?'

'*Nicked*?' said the Green Man. 'I don't think Nick's here any more. He's gone. You needn't fear him. This is a good place now, and I am ready to die.'

'To *die*?' said Death. 'Oh, come on now!' And Death removed the black helmet and unzipped the black leathers.

Out stepped a girl like a spring flower, and all of sixteen. 'I am the corn chandler's daughter,' she said, 'and I've brought you some bread.'

They looked, and they loved.

'It is a miracle!' said the corn chandler's daughter in the Green Man's arms.

'It is heaven!' she said on the Green Man's couch.

'And it is impossible,' she said in the Green Man's bed, 'for I am to be married on Saturday to Jackson, your next-door farmer.'

And she was. The bells of the steeple rang out for her (a quiet bride) on the Saturday afternoon.

Earlier that week, one bright and frosty day, they had begun to toll for many hours, a peal for each year of the Green Man's life. The mice heard the knell in the pockets of the old mackintosh on the back of his kitchen door. The water voles and the swans heard it in the dykes. The geese heard it, flying south. The seagulls heard it. (They think they are nobody's fool and guessed what it was.) Sadie and Billy and Patsy and their grandchildren heard it on the farms around and said, 'How endlessly it tolls. It must be for the Green Man.'

Deep in the winter sea the mermaids heard it, and didn't much care. The twelve sons didn't hear it because they were all at foreign conferences, but the four daughters on a cold beach in France heard it in their hearts. A shiver passed among them and they looked at one another sadly. Lady Serena Transept and her cousin and the dog heard it and went specially to sit in the Manor pew to listen; and occasionally the dog howled. Above them the head on the stone corbel peered through its leaves to watch the ringers and Lord Transept, who had asked particularly to toll the final knell.

In the high street of the market town the corn chandler heard it and he smiled. He knew the future, being a reading man.

And was unsurprised, therefore, some years later, a green-eyed grandson on his knee, to hear that somebody going through the lanes towards the tip to dump his Christmas tree had seen a shadow standing in the fields.

SOUL MATES

When Francis Phipps retired, he and his wife, Patricia, took a week's holiday on the Isles of Scilly. They were a prudent pair and had booked the best room in the hotel the previous summer. It had always been summer when they holidayed on the Scillies long ago, with their young children, all now successfully scattered about the world.

Patricia Phipps had been uncertain about this return visit (and the long motorway journey *à deux*). She thought it might be sad. But Francis said, 'What nonsense! How delightful to be going back again with enough money for a luxurious hotel instead of the sandy-floored pub with its one bathroom.'

'We shall take plenty of books,' he said. 'The daffodils will be at their best. We shall walk. The food should be marvellous and with luck there'll be very few people.'

But it was cold. Their room was glorious, but stood at the end of several blustery corridors and three of its walls were windows on to the sea. The sea sucked and roared and ground and slapped against the very foundations of the single-storey hotel and seemed, in some way, to tower over them in their beds. Beyond the spraying breakers they could see the shine and dazzle of it to the far horizon. The Phippses seemed to swing with the sea when they closed their eyes.

Each day they walked in the salty wind, along lanes lined with chill, flattened daffodils that ran in trickles and eddies and torrents. Their shouting yellow was round every red boulder, every stiff, black escallonia hedge.

After luncheon they slept. After dinner they read their books. It was a hotel of great discretion and, although always full, seemed empty. There were a few couples of the Phippses' age, a tense little writer person with frizzy, iron-grey hair, a desolate-looking woman in a wonderful beaded dress of bright-blue wool, and a Yorkshire couple, she fat and amiable, he gaunt and glum. The wife smiled eagerly across the restaurant at the Phippses.

'Bit ominous, the wife,' said Francis. 'She looks as if she might *divulge*.'

'We can keep her at bay,' said Patricia.

Patricia was tired. The past few months of small, decorous but nevertheless emotional retirement parties for Francis had drained them both. Since the university, where they had met forty years ago, Francis had served his country and his Department and Pat had served him. Her achievement had been to create his setting, which was a tranquil house in Dulwich and dignified hospitality. In its long green garden there hung a pink hammock between a walnut tree and a pear.

Two nights before the end of their holiday, Pat felt a great longing to be back in this garden, and Francis, at the same moment, holding the door for her to pass into the long corridors *en route* for dinner, said, 'I'd say that a week was about long enough here, Patricia. Wouldn't you?'

There was a slight easing-up, though, tonight in the dining room. Somebody was laughing softly as they went in, and the grizzled novelist, wearing a black velvet suit, was drinking her coffee at the table of the wronged woman in the couture dress. The Yorkshire wife, rosy from the weather, was now looking hungrier than ever for conversation, and at last called shamelessly across from her table to the Phippses that her holiday was nearly over, and was theirs? She had to be back in Boroughbridge on Saturday, for her results.

'Oh,' said Pat. 'Examination results?'

'Yes, I'm afraid so. I've had a medical examination. We're rather wondering What They Will Have Found.'

Francis picked up his napkin and Pat picked up the menu. As she looked up from it, she met the glance of one of the other couples, sitting across from them, rather in the shadow of the staircase. The woman smiled at her like a sister. Pat thought for a second that she was looking in a glass.

When the pair left their table, the man came over and smiled at Francis. 'Good evening.'

'Good evening.'

The woman said to Patricia, 'I'm afraid things tend to get rather chatty by Thursday. Beware of people with operations!'

Later the four found themselves together in the television room, waiting for the News, and the other man ('Phillips—Jocelyn Phillips. My wife—Evelyn') said that nowadays he hated the News.

'We sit in horror,' said Francis. 'We fear for our young.'

'You sound exactly like Jocelyn,' said the wife. 'Now—let me guess. You are at the Bar? A judge?'

'A civil servant. I have just retired.'

'Me, too,' said Phillips. 'Foreign Office. I went last year.'

The men bought brandy for each other and the women drank liqueurs. Conversation flowered. They were like old friends.

The next day they all walked together to the tropical gardens and Evelyn and Pat found a mutual interest in lilies. Automatically the four met up again after dinner, and at bedtime Jocelyn Phillips said how much they had enjoyed the day. Francis, for years considered to be the coldest of fish, said, 'It has been *delightful* to meet you.'

Coming over to the Phippses' table at breakfast next day, Evelyn said, 'Now—look. I do hope you don't think us *quite* extraordinary, but we wondered if you'd come and stay with us tonight, on your way home? We're hardly off your route and it would break up the awful motorway journey a bit.'

Francis, standing, clutching his napkin, said, 'But how *very* kind.'

'Excellent idea,' Jocelyn called across.

At the reception desk, as they paid their bills, all four turned to one another.

'D'you know—' said Francis. 'If you really mean it—?'

'Of *course* we do. Give us an hour's start to make things ready.'

'Well, this is *most* friendly ... Pat—?'

'But I should love to.'

Address and directions given, everybody climbed into the helicopter for the mainland and their parked cars. Pat was surprised to see the woman in the couture dress and the writer saying affectionate goodbyes to the Yorkshire couple. She and Francis waved off the Phillipses and went to the nearby village for coffee and to look for a potted plant to take as a present.

'What an extraordinary thing we're doing,' she said. 'Whatever would the children say? They may be *anyone*. Serial killers. Somehow—did you think they looked rather ... cold, when they went off? Remote?'

'Nonsense,' he said. 'They're exactly like us. It's great luck. You hardly ever meet your own sort these days.'

Pat thought of the novelist and the rich woman and the Yorkshire pair. None of them had said goodbye to her. She felt suddenly miserable. Cut off.

Miles further on, deep into Devonshire, Francis said at last, 'Oh, well ... It *is* a slight risk, I suppose. "Never take up with people you meet on holiday", and so on. But we've not met people we've felt so at home with for years. We must be almost at their turning, are we not?'

The motorway exit was just ahead and he swung towards it much too fast. As always she said, 'I hate the way you do that. You should let me drive.' Usually he didn't answer, but today he said, 'Wrist a bit wonky. Traffic's much worse these days. I must say I don't enjoy driving any more. Train next time.'

They reached the A-road, then the roundabout for the byroad, and then—yes, here it was—the turning for the house (no signpost) and the little lane.

The lane was long. It turned at sharp angles, like the corridors at the hotel. It narrowed and became unkempt. Grass grew down a central ridge. Hedges gave way to a long, metal field-fence and through it could be seen a red-brick house with lattice windows, standing well back from the road and surrounded by grass. Its front and back doors were standing wide open so that you could see down a flagstoned passage to more green fields behind.

'Is it genuine?' asked Pat. 'Or pseudo-Tudo?'

'Can't tell,' he said. 'Very cunning if it's pseudo.'

They stepped from the car into total silence. Crocuses along the front of the house looked like flowers painted on a calendar.

'It's empty,' she said. 'They can't have arrived.'

'It can't be,' said Francis: 'the doors are open.' He knocked. 'Hello there? Hello?'

Not liking to walk in, they went round the side of the house to the back. A barn. A double garage. A shed or stable far across the field. No life.

'Maybe it's the wrong house,' said Francis. '*Hello?*'

Suddenly, there were the Phillipses far away beside the shed, standing quite still. And then, as if a pause-button had been released, they began to move forward over the grass. They looked graver sort of people than those in the hotel.

But this passed at once. The Phippses were welcomed warmly and the men went off to get the luggage from the car.

Evelyn took Pat into the house and the green spring day went in with them. There were books everywhere, an open log fire, photographs of exemplary children on a grand piano, a nice old overhead clothes-airer on the ceiling of the red-and-yellow tiled kitchen.

'I feel I've known this house all my life,' said Pat. 'It's like my old home.'

'The four of us are so alike,' said Evelyn. 'Have you noticed that we all have androgynous names?'

Pat looked away and said she hoped that Evelyn didn't think that she and Francis were androgynous.

Evelyn laughed brightly and said she had really meant *genderless*. 'All our names are *genderless*. It's so good to be genderless now.'

'What did you do as a young woman, Pat?' she asked later, washing salad in cold water.

'Well, nothing, I suppose. After I left Oxford.'

Evelyn, amazed, cried, 'But neither did I! I married straight from Cambridge. I thought there was nobody left like us.'

Dinner was perfect. Duck and green peas and a crème brûlée.

'But however did you spirit it all up in an hour?' asked Francis.

Jocelyn produced a second bottle of superb wine.

Their bedroom was old-rose chintz and a four-poster. There were flowers, and hot-water bottles.

'It is *heaven*!' said Pat. She wondered whether to kiss Evelyn's cheek, or even Jocelyn's. She let it go.

Francis, flushed with duck and claret, said, 'Yes. Heaven.' He paused. 'The hotel was good,' he said, 'but we were restless there. It was the sea.'

'Ah, the sea,' said Jocelyn Phillips.

'We shall sleep tonight,' said Pat. '*Utterly*.'

And they did sleep. They slept until nearly ten o'clock the following morning, and could not believe it.

They awoke to silence.

'My God,' said Francis, 'we'd better get on if we're to be home before we hit the rush hour. Better miss a bath.'

'Hello?' Pat called on the stairs. In the hall. 'We're thoroughly ashamed of ourselves. Hello?'

No sound.

They looked in kitchen, dining room, drawing room, study. There was no trace of last night's dinner or sign of today's breakfast. Front and back doors stood open.

'D'you think we could look in the bedrooms?'

There was nobody there.

In the Phillipses' bedroom not a thing was out of place. No clothes over chairs, no holiday unpacking, not a hair in a comb. The beds were carefully made up.

The Phippses went outside. Barn, garage and shed watched them, but there was nobody. Pat pointed. 'Was that there last night?' Across the garden a large, lazy pink hammock was slung between trees.

'Well, look here,' Francis said, 'we have to go. This is ridiculous. I'll leave a note. It's very upsetting.'

He wrote the note and propped it against the kitchen telephone, where the red message-light flashed.

'D'you think we should press it?' he said.

'No,' she said. 'No. Don't,' and grabbed his arm.

'Why not?'

'*No!*'

They closed the back door and the front door. It was some sort of a gesture. It had to be done. They drove away down the drive.

'I don't like doing this,' he said. 'I don't like it at all. I should have pressed that button. Well ... we'll ring them up tonight. Naturally—'

'I'm not sure,' she said. 'I'm not sure I want to. I'm not sure we shall be able to. Oh, Francis, I'm not sure we'll get home.'

He took her hand and held it as he drove. Steering one-handed along the lane beside the wire fence, they both looked together at the house as they passed it by.

The front door and the back stood wide open again. They could see clearly to the green fields beyond.

The People on Privilege Hill

Drenching, soaking, relentless rain. Black cold rain for black cold winter Dorsetshire. Edward Feathers loved rain but warm rain, falling through oriental air, steam rising from sweating earth, dripping, glistening drops that rolled across banana leaves, rain that wetted the pelts of monkeys. Bloody Dorset, his retirement home. He was cold and old. He was cold and old and going out to lunch with a woman called Dulcie he'd never much liked. His wife Betty had been dead some years.

'I am rich,' announced Feathers—Sir Edward Feathers QC—to his affluent surroundings. On the walls of the vestibule of his house hung watercolours of Bengal and Malaya painted a hundred years ago by English memsahibs under parasols, sitting at their easels out of doors in long petticoats and cotton skirts with tulle and ribbons and painting aprons made of something called 'crash'.

'Very good, too, those paintings,' he thought. 'Worth a lot of money now.'

Under his button-booted feet was a rug from Tashkent. Nearby stood a throne of rose-coloured silk, very tattered. Betty had fallen in love with it once, in Dacca. Nearby was a brass and ironwood umbrella stand with many spikes sticking out of it. Feathers turned to the umbrella stand, chose an umbrella, shook it loose: a fine black silk with a malacca handle and initialled gold band. He did not open it in the house on account of the bad luck this would unleash. A fresh wave of rain lashed at the windows. 'I could order a cab,' he said aloud. He had been a famous barrister and the sound of his voice had been part of his fortune. The old 'Oxford accent', now very rare, comforted him sometimes. 'I am rich. It's only a few minutes away. The fare is not the issue. It is a matter of legs. If I lose the use of my legs,' he said, for he was far into his eighties, 'I'm finished. I shall walk.'

Rain beat against the fanlight above the front door. There was a long ring on the bell and a battering at the knocker. His neighbour stood there in a dreadful anorak and without an umbrella.

'Oh yes, Veneering,' said Feathers, unenthusiastic. 'You'd better come in. But I'm just going out.'

'May I share your car?' asked Veneering. 'To Dulcie's?'

'I'm not taking the car.' (Veneering was the meanest man ever to make a fortune at the Bar except for old what's-his-name, Fiscal-Smith, in the north.) 'By the time I've got it out of the garage and turned it round I could be there. I didn't know you were going to Dulcie's.'

'Oh yes. Big do,' said Veneering. 'Party for some cousin. We'll walk together, then. Are you ready?'

Feathers was wearing a magnificent twenty-year-old double-breasted three-piece suit. All his working life he had been called Filth not only because of the old joke (Failed In London Try Hong Kong) but because nobody had ever seen him other than immaculate: scrubbed, polished, barbered, manicured, brushed, combed, perfect. At any moment of his life Feathers could have been presented to the Queen.

'Are *you* ready?' he asked.

'I'll take the anorak off,' said Veneering, his scruffy old rival who now lived next door, 'when we get there. Don't *you* need a coat?'

'I have my umbrella,' said Feathers.

'Oh yes, I could borrow one of your umbrellas. Thanks.'

And Veneering stepped in from the downpour bringing some of it with him. He squelched over to the Benares pillar and started poking about, coming up with a delicate pink parasol with a black tassel.

Both men regarded it.

'No,' said Feathers. 'That's a lady's parasol. Betty's.'

Veneering ran his arthritic fingers down the silk. Outside the rain had hushed. 'Just for down the road,' he said. 'I'd enjoy carrying it. I remember it.'

'It's not on offer,' said Feathers. 'Sorry.'

But Veneering, like some evil gnome, was over the doorstep again, introducing the parasol to the outer air. It flew up at once, giving a glow to his face as he looked up into its lacquered struts. He twirled it about. 'Aha,' he said.

Down came the rain again and Feathers, with a leonine roar of disgust, turned back to the umbrella-stand. Somewhere in the bottom of it were stubby common umbrellas that snapped open when you pressed a button. Right for Veneering.

'We'll be late,' said Veneering from the drive, considering Feathers's old man's backside bent over the umbrella-stand, floppy down the backs of his thighs. (Losing his flanks. Bad sign. Senile.) Veneering still had the bright blue eyes of a young man. Cunning eyes. And strong flanks. 'In fact we're late already. It's after one.' He knew that to be late was for Feathers a mortal sin.

So Feathers abandoned the search, checked his pockets for house keys, slammed the front door behind him and sprang off down the drive on his emu legs under an impeccable black dome, overtaking Veneering's short but sturdy legs, that thirty years ago had bestridden the colony of Hong Kong and the international legal world—and quite a few of its women.

Veneering trotted, under the apricot satin, way behind.

One behind the other they advanced up the village hill

beneath overhanging trees, turned to the right by the church, splashed on. It was rather further to walk than Feathers had remembered. On they went in silence except for the now only murmuring rain, towards Privilege Road.

Dulcie's address was Privilege House, seat at one time, she said, of the famous house of the Privé-Lièges who had arrived with the Conqueror. Those who had lived in the village all their lives—few enough now—were doubtful about the Privé-Lièges and thought that as children they had been told of some village privies once constructed up there. Dulcie's husband, now dead, had said, 'Well, as long as nobody tells Dulcie. Unless of course the privies were Roman.' He had been a lawyer too and had retired early to the south-west to read Thomas Hardy. He'd had private means, and needed them with Dulcie.

There had been some Hardy-esque dwellings around Privilege House with thatch and rats, but now these were glorified as second homes with gloss paint and lined curtains and polished door knockers. The owners came thundering down now and then on Friday nights in cars like Iraqi tanks stuffed with food from suburban farmers' markets. They thundered back to London on the Monday morning. Gravel and laurel had appeared around the cottages and in front of Dulcie's Norman demesne. A metal post said 'Privilege Road'. The post had distressed her. But she was an unbeatable woman.

Feathers paused at the top of the hill outside a cot (four bed, two bath) and called over his shoulder, 'Who the hell is this?' For a squat sort of fellow was approaching from a lateral direction, on their port bow. He presented himself into the rain as a pair of feet and an umbrella spread over the body at waist level. Head down, most of him was invisible. The umbrella had spikes sticking out here and there, and the cloth was tattered and rusty. A weapon that had known campaigns.

When it came up close, the feet stopped and the umbrella was raised to reveal a face as hard as wood.

'Good God!' said Veneering. 'It's Fiscal-Smith,' and the rain began to bucket down again upon the three of them.

'Oh, good morning,' said Fiscal-Smith. 'Haven't seen you, Feathers, since just after Betty died. Haven't seen you, Veneering, since that embarrassing little matter in the New Territories. Nice little case. Nice little milch cow for me. Pity the way they went after you in the Law Reports. Are you going to Dulcie's?'

'I suppose you're the cousin,' said Veneering.

'What cousin? I was a friend of poor old Bill till he dropped me for Thomas Hardy. Come on, let's keep going. I'm getting wet.'

In single file the three old judges pressed ahead: black silk, apricot toile and bundle of prongs.

Fiscal-Smith made uncouth noises that in another man might have indicated mirth, and they reached Dulcie's tall main gate, firmly closed. Through the wrought iron there was very much on view a lawn and terrace of simulated stone and along the side of the house a conservatory that was filled with coloured moons. They were umbrellas all open and all wet.

'Whoever can be coming?' said Feathers, who originally had thought he was the only guest. 'Must be dozens.'

'Yes, there *was* some point to the cousin,' said Veneering, 'but I can't remember what. She talks too fast.'

'It's a monk,' said Fiscal-Smith. 'Not a cousin but a monk. Though of course a monk *could* be a cousin. Look at John the Baptist.'

'A monk? At Dulcie's?'

'Yes. A Jesuit. He's off to the islands to prepare for his final vows. This is his last blow-out. She's taking him to the airport afterwards, as soon as we've left.'

Feathers winced at 'blow-out'. He was not a Catholic, or anything, really, except when reading the Book of Common Prayer or during the Sunday C of E service if it was 1666, but he didn't like to hear of a 'blow-out' before vows.

'*What* airport?' asked Veneering. 'Our airport? The airport at the end of the universe?' for he sometimes read modern books.

Feathers, who did not, suspected nastiness.

'Dulcie's a kind woman,' he said, suppressing the slight thrill of excitement at the thought of her puffy raspberry lips. 'Very kind. And the wine will be good. But she's obviously asked a horde,' he added with a breath of regret. 'There are dozens of umbrellas.'

In the conservatory trench six or so of them seemed to stir, rubbing shoulders like impounded cattle.

Feathers, the one who saw Dulcie most often, knew that the wrought-iron gate was never unlocked and was only a viewing station, so he led the way round the house and they were about to left-wheel into a gravel patch when a car—ample but not urban—pounced up behind them, swerved in front of them, swung round at the side door and blocked their path. Doors were flung open and a lean girl with a cigarette in her mouth jumped out. She ground the cigarette stub under her heel, like the serpent in Eden, and began to decant two disabled elderly women. They were supplied with umbrellas and directed, limping, to the door. One of them had a fruity cough. The three widowed judges might have been spectres.

'God!' said Fiscal-Smith. 'Who are they?'

'It's the heavenly twins,' said Feathers with one of his roaring cries. 'Sing in the church choir. Splendidly.' He found himself again defensive about the unloved territory of his old age and surprised himself. When had Fiscal-Smith last been near a church? Or bloody Veneering? Never.

'Who's the third?' asked Fiscal-Smith. 'Is she local?'

'She'll be the carer,' said Feathers. 'Probably from Lithuania.'

'This is going to be a rave,' said Veneering, and Feathers felt displeased again and almost said, 'We're all going to get old *one* day,' but remembered that he'd soon be ninety.

A blaze of yellow light washed suddenly across the rainy sky, ripping the clouds and silhouetting the tree clumps on Privilege Hill. He thought: 'I should have brought something for Dulcie, some flowers. Betty would have brought flowers. Or jam or something.' And was mortified to see some sort of offering emerging from Veneering's disgusting anorak and— great heaven!—something appearing in Fiscal-Smith's mean paw. Feathers belonged to an age when you didn't take presents or write thank-you letters for luncheon but he wasn't sure, all at once, that Dulcie did. He glared at Fiscal-Smith's rather old-looking package.

'It's a box of tea,' said Fiscal-Smith. 'Christmas-pudding flavour from Fortnum and Mason. I've had it for years. I'm not sure if you can get it now. Given it by a client before I took Silk. In the sixties.'

'I wonder what the monk will bring,' said Veneering. He seemed to be cheering up, having seen the carer's legs.

And here was Dulcie coming to welcome them, shrieking prettily in grey mohair and pearls; leading them to the pool of drying umbrellas. 'Just drop them down. In the conservatory trough. It's near the hot pipes. It's where I dry my dahlias. They love it. Don't they look pretty? Sometimes I think they'll all *rise* into the air.'

('She's insane,' thought Feathers.)

'And I must run to my soufflé,' she called. 'Do go in. Get a drink. Awful rain. So good of you to come out. Introduce yourselves.'

In the sitting room there was no sign of the guest of honour. The carer was pouring herself an enormous drink. The cleaning lady of the village, Kate, was handing round titbits. She knew the guests intimately. 'I told you not to wear that shirt until I'd turned the collar,' she hissed at Veneering.

They all drank and the rain rattled down on the glass roof of the umbrella house. The clocks ticked.

'What's that over there?' asked Veneering.

A boy was regarding them from a doorway.

'A boy, I think,' said Feathers, a childless man.

'Maybe this is the cousin. Hello there! Who're you? Are you Dulcie's young cousin?'

The boy said nothing but padded after them as they carried their drinks into another room, where he continued to stare. 'Hand the nuts round,' said Kate the cleaner. 'Be polite,' but the boy took no notice. He approached Veneering and inspected him further.

'Why ever should I be Granny's cousin?'

Veneering, unused for many years to being cross-questioned, said, 'We understood we were to meet a cousin.'

'No. It's a monk. Do you play music?'

'Me?' said Veneering. 'Why?'

'I just wondered. I play cello and drums.'

'Oh. Good!'

'In America, I'm an American citizen. I don't come over often.'

'That explains everything.' (God, I'm hungry!)

'What do you mean?'

'Don't you say "sir" in America? I thought all American children were polite now.'

'Actually, not all. Sir. I know one who goes straight over to the fridge in people's houses and looks in to see what they've got.'

(Fiendishly hungry.)

'Would you have guessed I was American? I don't do the voice. I *can* do the voice but only at school. My parents are British. I won't salute the flag either.'

'You have a lot of confidence. How old are you?'

'I'm eight. But I'm not confident. I don't do anything wrong. I believe in God. I say my prayers.'

'I think we're all getting into deep water here,' said Fiscal-Smith, carrying away his gin-and-mixed. 'Off you go, boy. Help in the kitchen.'

The boy took no notice. He was concentrating on Veneering. 'Sir,' he said, 'do you, by any chance, play the drums?'

'*Off* you go now!' cried Dulcie, sweeping in and pushing the child under her grandmotherly arm out of the path of the three great men. 'This is Herman. My grandson. He's eight. I'm giving my daughter a break. Herman, pass the nuts.'

'My *wretched* monk,' Dulcie said. 'I don't think we'll wait. Oh, well, if you're sure you don't mind. The soufflé will be ready in about ten minutes and then we can't wait a moment more.' (Feathers's tummy rumbled.)

'But *do* you play the drums?' insisted Herman, circling Veneering before whose face hardened criminals had crumbled. Herman's face held up.

'I do, as a matter of fact,' Veneering said, turning away to take a canapé.

'They've given me some. Granny did. For my birthday. Come and see.'

And like Mary's lamb, Judge Veneering followed the child to a chaotic playroom where drums in all their glory were set up near a piano.

'I didn't know there was a piano here,' said Veneering to himself, but aloud. 'And a Bechstein.' He sat down and played a little.

Herman hove up alongside and said, 'You're good. I knew you'd be good.'

'Are you good?'

'No. Not at piano. I do a bit of cello. It's mostly the drums.'

Veneering, feet among toys, began to tap his toes and the Bechstein sang. Then it began to sing more noisily and Veneering closed his eyes, put his chin in the air and howled like a dog.

'Hey. Great!' said Herman, thumping him.

'Honky-tonk.' Veneering began to bob up and down.

'What's honky-tonk? D'you want to hear some drumming? Sir?'

'*Herman,*' called his grandmother.

'Better go,' said Veneering. Then he let his voice become a black man's voice and began singing the Blues.

'Better not,' said Herman. 'Well, not before lunch.'

The child sat close against Veneering at the table, gazing up at his yellow old face.

'Herman, pass the bread,' said Dulcie, but all Herman did was ask, 'Did you ever have a boy like me that played drums?'

'I did,' said Veneering, surprising people.

'After lunch can we have a go at them?'

'Eat your soufflé,' said Dulcie, and Herman obediently polished it off, wondering why something so deflated and leathery should be considered better than doughnuts or cake.

There was a pause after the plates were taken away and, unthinkably, Veneering, his eyes askew with gin and wine, excused himself and made again for the piano, Herman trotting behind.

'Oh no, I won't have this,' said Dulcie.

'America, I suppose,' said Feathers.

A torrent of honky-tonk flowed out of the playroom and some loud cries. The drums began.

Bass drums, floor-tom, normal-tom, cymbals. High-hat, crash-ride, thin *crash*! And now, now, the metallic stroking, the brush, the whispering ghost—listen, listen—and now the big bass drum. Hammers on the pedals, cross arms, cross legs, tap tap, paradiddle, paradiddle, let go! Hammer on pedal now then—HIGH HAT! CRASH RIDE! THIN CRASH!

The glass doors of the conservatory, now filming up, shook as if they'd received the tremors of a not-too-distant earthquake, and a new sound joined the drums as Veneering began to sing and almost outstrip the tremors. Not a word could be heard round the dining table and Dulcie rushed out of the room. As she left, came the crescendo and the music ceased, to reverberations and cackling laughter.

'*Herman!* Please return to the table. Don't dare to monopolise Judge Veneering.'

And Herman, staggering dazed from the mountain tops, let his small jaw drop and fell off his perch, scattering instruments.

Veneering sat on at the piano, hands on knees, chin on chest, enwrapped in pleasure. Then quietly, he began to play again.

'No—I'm sorry, Terry'—she had remembered his nasty little name—'I'm sorry but I think the latecomer has just arrived. Come at once.'

There was a commotion going on in the hall.

'Dear Terry—*please*. It's boeuf bourguignon.'

Veneering jumped up and embraced her, grinning. 'Honky-tonk!' he said. 'He's good, that boy. Tremendous on the normal-tom. Could hear that bass a quarter-mile away. Beautiful brush on the snare.' He went back to the dining room rubbing his hands. 'Been playing the Blues,' he said to one and all.

'You haven't,' said Herman.

'Well, the Pale-Rose Pinks,' said Veneering. 'Near enough.'

'Veneering, more wine,' said Feathers warningly.

'Much better not,' said Fiscal-Smith.

The two damaged sisters sat, making patterns on the damask with their fingers.

'Hey! Could he play as well as me, your son?' asked Herman in an American accent.

There was a pause.

'Probably,' said Veneering.

'Did he make it? Was he a star? In music?'

'No. He died.'

'What did he die of?'

'Be quiet, boy!' Feathers roared.

'Now,' said Dulcie. 'Now, I do believe—here is our monk. Father Ambrose. On his way to St Umbrage's on the island of Skelt.'

'Bullet,' said Veneering. 'Soldier.'

'It's stupid to be a soldier if you can play music.'

'As you say. Quite so. Now, get on with your lunch, boy. We've plainsong ahead of us.'

But the plainsong was not to be. Nor did the monk join them for lunch. Kate the cleaner put her head round the dining room door and asked to speak to Dulcie for a moment—outside.

And Dulcie returned with stony face and sat down, and Kate, unsmiling, carried in the stew. 'Take Father Ambrose's place away,' said Dulcie. 'Thank you, Kate. It will give us more room.'

Cautious silence emanated from the guests. There was electricity in the air. In the very curtains. Time passed. The carer thought that she would kill for a cigarette.

'If he's not coming in, Granny,' asked Herman, loud and clear, 'can I have some more stew? It's great.'

Dulcie looked at him and loved him, and there was a chorus about the excellence of the stew, and Fiscal-Smith said it was not a stew but a veritable *daube* as in the famous lunch in *To the Lighthouse*.

'I've no idea,' said Dulcie grandly. 'I bought it for freezing.

From the farmers' market, months ago. I don't think I've ever been to a lighthouse.'

'Virginia Woolf couldn't have given us a stew like this. Or a *daube*,' said one of the sisters (Olga), who had once been up at Oxford.

'She wasn't much of a cook,' said the other one (Fairy). 'But you don't expect it, when people have inner lives.'

'As we must suppose,' Feathers put in quickly, before Dulcie realised what Fairy had said, 'this monk has. He is certainly without inner manners.'

Everyone waited for Dulcie to say something but she didn't. Then, 'Granny, why are you crying?' and Herman ran to her and stroked her arm. 'Hey, Granny, we don't care about the monk.'

'He—he suddenly felt—indisposed and—he vanished.' Her lunch party—her reputation as the hostess on Privilege Hill—gone. They would all laugh about it for ever.

Dulcie couldn't stop imagining. She could hear the very words. '*That* brought her down a peg. Asked this VIP bishop, or archbishop, or [in time] the Prince of Wales, and he took one step inside the house and went right out again. And she'd offered to drive him to the airport. What a snob! Of course, Kate knows more than she'll say. There must be something scandalous. Drunken singing and drums. African drumming. Yes—at Dulcie's. But Kate is very loyal. They'll all be leaving her a nice fat legacy.'

'A funny business. He probably caught sight of the other guests.'

'Or the dreadful grandson.'

Etc.

Then someone would be sure to say, 'D'you think there *was* a monk? Dulcie's getting . . . well, I'll say nothing.'

'Yes, there *was* someone. Standing looking in at them over

that trough of umbrellas. Some of them saw him. Dripping wet.'

'Didn't he have an umbrella himself?'

'No. I don't think they carry them. He was wearing see-through plastic. It shone. Round his head was a halo.'

'On Privilege Hill?'

'Yes. It was like *Star Wars*.'

'Well, it makes a change.'

The story died away. The Iraq war and the condition of the Health Service and global warming took over. The weather continued rainy. The old twins continued to drowse. The carer had home thoughts from abroad and considered how English country life is more like Chekhov than *The Archers* or Thomas Hardy or even the Updike ethic with which it is sometimes compared. She would write a paper on the subject on her return to Poland.

But the startling image of the dripping monk remained with her. She felt like posting him an umbrella.

Kate, the ubiquitous cleaner, told her friend the gardener, 'Oh yes, he was real all right. And young. And sort of holy-looking.'

The gardener said, 'Watch it! You'll get like them. They're all bats around here.'

'I feel like giving him an umbrella,' Kate said, 'Wonderful smile.'

And one day Dulcie, in the kitchen alone with the gardener, Herman visiting Judge Veneering for a jam session, said, 'Don't tell anyone this, but that day, Father Ambrose in the rain, I kept thinking of Easter morning. The love that flowed from the tomb. Then the disappearance. I want to *give* him something.' She splashed gin into her tonic.

'Don't have another of those,' said the gardener to his employer.

Later, to old Feathers, who had called to present her with his dead wife's pink umbrella, having wrested it the day before with difficulty from Veneering, she said: 'I want to give him something.'

'Come, Dulcie. He behaved like a churl.'

'Oh, no. He must suddenly have been taken ill. I *did* know him, you know. We met at a day of silence in the cathedral.'

'Silence?'

'Yes. But our eyes met.'

'And he wangled a lunch and a lift?'

'Oh, didn't *wangle*. He wouldn't *wangle*. We talked for a few minutes.'

'A fast worker.'

'Well, so was Christ,' said Dulcie smugly.

Feathers, wishing he could tell all this rubbish to his dear dead wife, said, 'You're in love with the perisher, Dulcie.'

'Certainly not. And we're all perishers. I just need to fill the blank. To know why he melted away.'

'He probably caught sight of Herman.'

'How dare you!'

'No—I mean it. Monks have to keep their distance from small boys.'

And Dulcie yearned for her dear dead husband to kick Feathers out of the house.

'I have a notion to send that . . . person in the garden—an umbrella,' said one twin to the other. 'I shall send it to Farm Street. In London. The Jesuit HQ. "To Father Ambrose, from a friend, kindly forward to St Umbrage on Skelt."' The other twin nodded.

Fiscal-Smith, who never wasted time, had already laid his plans. On his train home to the north on his second-class return ticket bought months ago (like the stew) to get the benefit of a cheaper fare, he thought he would do something memorable. Send the monk a light-hearted present. An umbrella would be amusing. He would send him his own. It was, after all, time for a new one. And he had had a delightful day.

'Staunch fellow,' he thought. 'Standing out there in the rain.'

Veneering phoned Feathers to see if Feathers would go in with him on an umbrella for that fellow at Dulcie's on the way to the Scottish islands, the fellow who didn't turn up. Feathers said no and put the phone down. Feathers, a travelled man and good at general knowledge, had never heard of an island called Skelt or a saint called Umbrage. No flies on Judge Feathers. Hence Veneering because the pleasure of the lunch party would not leave him—the boy who liked him, the Bechstein, the drumming, the jam sessions to come—amazed himself by ordering an umbrella from Harrods and having it sent.

Five parcels were delivered soon afterwards to Farm Street Church. One parcel had wires and rags sticking out of it. And because it was a sensitive time just then in Irish politics, and because the parcels were all rather in the shape of rifles, the Farm Street divines called the police.

Old Filth was right. The Jesuits had never heard of Father Ambrose. So they kept the umbrellas (for a rainy day, ho-ho) except for Fiscal-Smith's. And that they chucked in the bin.

The stories in this collection first appeared in the following publications:

'Hetty Sleeping'—*Woman*, 1977

'Lunch with Ruth Sykes'—*Family Circle*, 1977

'The Great, Grand Soap-Water Kick'—*The Sidmouth Letters*, Hamish Hamilton, 1980

'The Sidmouth Letters'—*The Sidmouth Letters*, Hamish Hamilton, 1980

'A Spot of Gothic'—*The Sidmouth Letters*, Hamish Hamilton, 1980

'The Tribute'—*The Sidmouth Letters*, Hamish Hamilton, 1980

'The Pig Boy'—*Good Housekeeping*, 1982

'Rode by all with Pride'—*London Tales*, Hamish Hamilton, 1983

'The Easter Lilies'—*The Pangs of Love*, Hamish Hamilton, 1983

'The First Adam'—*The Pangs of Love*, Hamish Hamilton, 1983

'The Pangs of Love'—*The Pangs of Love*, Hamish Hamilton, 1983

'Stone Trees'—*The Pangs of Love*, Hamish Hamilton, 1983

'An Unknown Child'—*The Pangs of Love*, Hamish Hamilton, 1983

'Showing the Flag'—*Winter's Tales*, Constable, 1987

'Swan'—*Swan*, Julia MacRae, 1987

'Damage'—*Showing the Flag*, Hamish Hamilton, 1989

'The Dixie Girls'—*Showing the Flag*, Hamish Hamilton, 1989

'Groundlings'—*Showing the Flag*, Hamish Hamilton, 1989

'Grace'—*Daily Telegraph*, 1994

'Miss Mistletoe'—*The Oldie*, 1994

'Telegony'—*Going into a Dark House*, Sinclair-Stevenson, 1994

'The Boy who Turned into a Bike'—*You*, 1995

'Missing the Midnight'—*The Oldie*, 1995

'The Zoo at Christmas'—*The Spectator*, 1995

'Old Filth'—*The Oldie*, 1996

'The Green Man'—*Missing the Midnight*, Sinclair-Stevenson, 1997

'Soul Mates'—*Missing the Midnight*, Sinclair-Stevenson, 1997

'The People on Privilege Hill'—*The People on Privilege Hill*, Chatto & Windus, 2007

ABOUT THE AUTHOR

Jane Gardam is the only writer to have been twice awarded the Whitbread Prize for Best Novel of the Year. She has published four volumes of acclaimed stories, including *Black Faces, White Faces* (winner of the David Higham Prize and the Royal Society for Literature's Winifred Holtby Prize). Her novels include *God on the Rocks* (shortlisted for the Booker Prize), *A Long Way from Verona, Crusoe's Daughter,* and the Old Filth trilogy: *Old Filth* (finalist for the Orange Prize), *The Man in the Wooden Hat* (finalist for the Los Angeles Book Prize), and *Last Friends.* She lives in the south of England near the sea.